Paradoxes and Dragons
A Science Fiction and Fantasy Anthology

Joseph R. Lallo

Table of Contents

Foreword

What follows is part of the "Shorts of Dubious Canonicity" project I started in 2018. In an attempt to keep my mind sharp and fresh, I started taking votes on short stories to write each weekend. Some of them stayed short. Some of them grew into full novellas. But almost all of them were the result of my fans and followers casting their votes to give them support.

Collected here are the shorts and novellas that, if not for a collection like this, might never have been released outside of the Patreon. Stories set in the Book of Deacon setting will naturally be released in future collections on their own, as will the Free-Wrench and Big Sigma stories. This collection is reserved for standalone stories or entries in smaller series, like *The Other Eight* or *Between.*

If you enjoy the stuff in this anthology, you can get your hands on more goodies like this in future collections, or by supporting my Patreon. But for now, without further ado, on with the stories!

WASTE LAND

JOSEPH R. LALLO

Wasteland

Not much to say about this one, except to say the editor loved it. I wanted to write a story in a post-apocalyptic wasteland that was somehow optimistic. I've got an idea for a sequel, which is tentatively titled *Uncle Robot*. The cover art (and the Uncle Robot idea) is by Fable Siegel.

ailing wind stirred David awake. The breeze on this section of the plains was more or less constant, so it had a way of simply becoming the new silence for him. As such, he was very sensitive to when it changed. It must have been early morning. He didn't need to click on a light, as he could see to check the various analog gauges by the light filtering through the threadbare portions of the canvas "walls" of his "home." Both words were quite generous, as he lived in what amounted to a slightly oversize dune buggy with canvas affixed to its roll cage. It kept the wind and sun off him, which was enough. It probably wouldn't have done much good for rain, but that was hardly a concern these days.

One by one, he made a mental note of the various little numbers that ruled his life. Three gallons of water. Less than he would have liked, but it would last him a bit longer. Battery level… twenty-seven percent. Also less than he'd like, but it was still early. Then things started to seem odd. A counter he'd rigged up was ticking upward irregularly. When he'd found it, he was reasonably certain it had been used for keeping track of people using the public transit system. He hooked it up to an output from his motion detector to let him know how often something came within range of his rig. Right now it was at 900 and ticking higher.

If he was the suspicious or paranoid type, that would have terrified him. He had a cargo cart hitched to his buggy, and the entirety of its security system was a latch with a bolt through it. The water and non-perishable food he was packing would have been reason alone to rob him blind, to say nothing of the assorted spare parts that might fetch a decent price at trade. He would be a goldmine for bandits, but he wasn't worried about that. At this point, if he woke and discovered he'd been robbed of the salvaged batteries and lightly damaged solar panels he'd found over the last week, he'd be thrilled. It would have meant there *were* bandits. For there to be bandits, there would have to be people. For the last six months, the chances of that were starting to seem increasingly remote.

But still. *Something* was triggering the motion detector. He shook the thick haze of sleep from his head and dug a little deeper. These days one of the least valuable pieces of information was the time. For the most part, the only useful amounts of time were days and weeks, ideally when you were measuring how long your food and water would last. The only use he got out of minutes and seconds were the occasional test to see how quick the batteries were charging and discharging so he would know if he needed to swap them out. But right now the clock was reading 11:36 AM.

"That can't be right," he croaked. "It's not bright enough to be midday yet."

It couldn't be clouds. There *weren't* any clouds. Not anymore.

"Oh no…" he muttered, the last sluggishness of sleep slipping away.

The answer was obvious. He tugged at the double layer of flap he'd rigged up to serve as a window of sorts, unzipping the old rain slicker he'd stitched into the wall. Even before he got the zipper halfway down, a gust of wind carrying dust as fine as talcum powder confirmed his concerns. A dust storm. And one that was kicking around dust in the sort of volume that could convince his motion detector that it was an intruder.

"This couldn't have waited until after breakfast," he growled.

He sat up in his bed, which had formerly been the rear bench seat of some sort of vehicle with entirely the wrong sort of engine for the way things were now. He had just enough room to swing his feet around and flip open the old vinyl suitcase that housed his gear. Much abused but still serviceable goggles were the most important thing, then a hat with a chin strap and a wide, stiff brim. His gloves had seen better days, but that could be said of all his equipment. The boots were still on from the night before, so all he really needed to do was top his outfit with a trench. He unzipped the door and gracefully dismounted into what was already an ankle-deep drift of fine powder. He didn't bother looking around him. It would just be a hazy cloud. There were only two views anyway. Endless sunbaked stone or the inside of a dust cloud, and he already knew which one he was getting before he even stepped outside.

The wind was never the problem in these storms. His buggy had a nice wide base, and years of dealing with the gusts had refined his techniques for keeping things secure in spite of them. But the dust could really be trouble. It could foul the linkages, or get into the bearings. And even if his seals were good and none of that happened, there was always the solar panels. On a *good* day, they'd pick up a dusting that'd cut into their output. A storm like this could render them useless under a thick layer of gray.

It had been a heck of a job finding a way to keep the solar panels from catching the wind while still catching the light, but it wasn't as though David had anything better to do with his time when the water and food were taken care of. The solution that he'd deemed to be good enough, which was the very apex of quality in the current state of the world, was to make a roof out of them. He'd fixed the edges to each other or to the buggy with enough packing and sheeting to keep the wind from finding a place to sneak underneath.

David hauled himself onto the tall fender over one of the rear tires. Sure enough. The low battery was thanks to a veritable blanket of dust that clung to the panels despite the wind. He'd fashioned a tool for just this purpose, a push-broom with an elbow so he could hook it up and over the buggy without having to risk walking on the fragile panels to reach the peak.

He endured the wind-blown dust just long enough to clear each of the panels and ensure nothing had happened to his buggy or trailer. When it all checked out, he slid into the passenger side of the buggy and fastened the cloth door. He gently patted his jacket and hat to get the worst of the dust out. There was no keeping the stuff from getting everywhere, but every little bit helped. When they were stowed, he gave his long hair and thick beard a rustle and slid over into the driver's seat.

"Can't very well just sit here and get buried," he said. "Let's roll out."

He clicked a bank of three switches—each salvaged from a different appliance—and stepped on the accelerator. Electric motors whined and the buggy smoothly climbed its way out of the mound of dust that was forming around it.

One of the many paradoxical lessons he'd learned in his years in the wastes was that you didn't want to stay put during a dust storm. If you had a shelter large enough to stow your buggy inside, you ran the risk of being trapped inside it and having to dig your way out. If you *didn't* have a shelter, you ran the risk of getting buried or mired and having to dig your way out anyway. But if you were moving, the rattling would keep the panels more or less clear, and you'd always be climbing up onto the dust rather than letting it pile up on you. The dust in the air cut down on the sunlight, which in turn cut down on the charging speed, so it was a good idea to keep an eye on the discharge rate and set your speed accordingly. But once you knew your rig, that wasn't hard to do. He took it slow, tried to avoid hitting any steep grades or pits, and started to work out the plan aloud. There was no one there to hear him, but sometimes the sound of one's own voice was the last resort of someone desperate for company.

"I'm pretty sure this is north." He tapped the compass stuck to his dash. "Yeah. North. Good. And what is this… call it fifteen kilometers per hour. Ought to get me to the outskirts in six hours. The storm shouldn't last that long. Hopefully it didn't screw up the collector. Once I get there, I should really look for some twine. And something with protein. I don't think I emptied out that bunker all the way…"

#

His estimate wasn't as close as he would have liked. The sun was setting before he reached the jagged skyline of what had once been a major city. His journey thus far had left the dust storm behind, but the direct sun had only just started to put him back into the green in terms of battery level before the fading light started to take a bigger toll than the storm had. He rolled until the last of the sunlight was gone. Better to stop for the night and wait until the first few hours of sun got him on the happy side of fifty percent, then start rolling again. Dave picked a nice spot, slightly elevated from the rest of the countryside, and hopped out to grab some supper.

He donned a makeshift headlamp fashioned from an old web belt, a hand-crank flashlight, and a lot of improvised joinery. Dave didn't even bother turning it on until he'd taken the practiced number of steps from the driver's side door to the cargo door of the cart. It didn't take more than a dozen cranks to give him some light, but if he could avoid it, he would. It was as close as he got to a game.

Dave clicked open the door and pulled a bin from its elastic straps. The bin was filled with packets, each about half the size of a deck of cards. They were white with black writing, and had appetizing descriptions like "250 calories (Mushroom)" and "100 calories (Soy)." The largest of them was labeled "600 calories (Meat)." As nice as it would be to have meal that substantial, even in desperate times like these he would prefer to have a little more specificity than simply "Meat."

"Two mushrooms should do it," he said.

His grumbling stomach disagreed, but there was no satisfying that thing. He pulled a canteen from his belt and approached his water jug. It was labeled "Non-Potable Water" but he'd crossed out the "Non" part. He'd refilled it enough times that most of the chemicals must have been gone by now. That they'd gone through his liver and kidneys along the way was beside the point. Bad water beat no water.

He topped off the canteen, sealed the valve tight, and walked in the darkness to the driver's seat to "enjoy" his meal. The packet tore easily. Far more easily than the leathery brick waiting inside. As he gnawed at it, he gave his habitual glimpse over the gauges. A quick click of the headlamp illuminated them enough for him to get a snapshot, which he chewed on in much the same way he chewed on the meal: slowly and numbly.

"Battery… Do I wait until 60% before I leave tomorrow? Could get rough once I get on those chewed-up streets. And…" His mind's eye lingered over the counter for the motion detector. "Right, right. Gotta reset that."

He blindly reached out and hit the reset tab. Then munched through the first bar and washed it down. He opened the flap and tossed the wrapper outside. The motion detector ticked.

"Huh… That thing's running a little sensitive," he said.

Dave reset it again. While he fiddled with the second wrapper, it ticked again. And again. He paused, then clicked on his light in time to hear another click and watch it roll over to three. He sighed heavily and reached up to crank the light to full brightness, then stowed the food bar and stepped out of the rig.

The very moment he stepped out, a brushed metal surface caught the gleam of his headlamp.

He narrowed his eyes. "Was that there before?"

Dave crouched and inspected the object. It was somewhere between the size of a basketball and a beach ball, points of reference he only knew because of the extreme value of sporting goods stores when it came to scavenging. The thing was hemispherical and metallic. Panel lines covered the rounded half and a blossoming array of metal "petals" flipped out from the bottom. The whole thing was caked with dirt and dust, with only the odd sharp edge or etched line shining in the light of his lamp. A trapezoidal panel on the dome of it was looser than the others, raised up about two centimeters from the surface of the dome. Much of the dome had a blue-black iridescence lurking under its layer of filth. Small, high-efficiency solar panels.

As he looked it over, a soft click inside the device filled the next split second a very urgent shortcoming of foresight.

There *had* been a society, and there wasn't anymore. Though it happened long before he started making memories—and probably long before he was born—there was still abundant evidence to suggest the end came quickly. Until now, it seemed that whatever weapons the former custodians of this world had used to kill each other, they'd been kind enough not to leave any behind. It would be just his luck if he'd stumbled upon the one functional land mine on the planet.

When it didn't explode, he let that concern slide away. Soon he realized the click came from the underside. He gingerly rolled it over.

"Whoa…"

While it was at least as clogged with dust as the rest of the object, the underside was a wonderland of intricate mechanical and electronic constructs. Six coiled-in spikes covered most of it, but the left center spike was twitching, producing the click. He gently tugged the spike and it quickly hinged out on a sophisticated system of linkages. Each of the other spikes was similarly obliging, and when they were fully extended, the whole thing looked more than a little like a metallic beetle. More to the point, he finally recognized it.

"It's one of those robot things…" he said. "I've never seen one so intact before."

Travel the wasteland long enough and you were bound to find the non-functional husk of a robot. They were good for parts. The batteries were particularly high capacity and rugged. This one seemed to be mostly in one piece. A few wires looked disorderly, and a hollow compartment of some kind hung open, but there weren't any obvious missing pieces. He rubbed a shiny bit of the workings with his thumb and found some markings.

"Four to fifteen volts DC," he read. "Well, you can't be all bad if you've got charging instructions. What's the worst that could happen?"

He considered is own words.

"You could go on a murderous rampage, I guess. Or explode. But then, so could I. Can't really fault you on that."

In the present state of the world, his survival had more than once hinged upon his ability to rig up or repair something he hadn't anticipated needing. Thus it paid to try to fix everything that looked like it might work again, if for no other reason than the experience.

He picked up the weighty bit of apparatus and hauled it around to the cargo door. Once he'd clicked it open, he dropped the thing onto the hatch like a workbench and climbed past it to rummage through his junk. After a few minutes, he revealed a voltage converter, a power cell, and a bin of wires. No surprise, considering how many of these he'd scavenged parts from, he just so happened to have a connector that matched the charging port. He clamped some alligator clips onto the stripped ends of the connector wire, dialed up a nice twelve-volt, two-amp circuit, and plugged it in.

Nothing happened until the power had been flowing for about twenty seconds. Then little indicator lights to flickered on. Motors started to whir. Five of the six legs clicked and shifted in sequence.

"Let's just move you away from the rig, huh?" David said.

He awkwardly gathered the mechanism and its power supply and carried them a few paces from the cargo cart. By the time he set it down, the mechanical whirring had been joined by little tones that suggested a system boot.

The five twitching legs suddenly pivoted and sunk into the dusty ground. They hoisted the mechanism up, then three of them adjusted and flipped the whole thing over, dome side up. The power wire still dangled below it. The notably loose panel raised up to reveal a head of sorts. It was a collection of camera lenses and sensors. The head pivoted toward him, then a line-laser scanned him up and down.

"Whoa, easy!" he barked. "Don't just go shining lasers in people's eyes."

His voice echoed back to him through tinny speakers. "Easy!"

The thing scrabbled forward. From its awkward lurch to the side, and the way the center leg on one side dragged, the thing wasn't fully operational.

It scanned the open cargo hatch quickly. Then scanned again more slowly in all places that had writing. He took a step closer to try to grab the thing, but it skittered back. The motion dislodged the charging wire and the mechanism immediately slouched, lights dimming and legs no longer able to support its weight.

"How about wait until you're done eating before you try to make a run for it?"

He rolled the thing onto its back, and tried to line up the wire again. While he was at it, he noticed that the bad leg seemed to have a lot of slack on one of its wires. He tugged it and it popped free with alarming ease. He blew hard on the exposed connector, then clicked the wire back in place. A moment later, he had the power wire reinstalled. The robot scrabbled to life again and flipped over. The head telescoped out a bit more and flipped down to investigate its underbelly. It scanned the wire, then seemed to notice that its malfunctioning leg was functioning again.

The head flipped back up and a soft tone chimed.

"Oh. So you noticed I'm feeding you. And I fixed your leg."

"Easy," the robot replayed.

"Yeah, well. I mean. It's all just plugs."

The legs clattered forward until the robot was straddling the small power cell and the voltage converter. It snapped the two central legs closed like a pincer, plucking them up. Then, with the remaining four legs, it turned and galloped away.

"Hey. *Hey!*" David yelled. "Get back here with that!"

"Easy," the robot repeated.

It bounded off into the distance with its stolen power. David crossed his arms.

"Joke's on you. That cell was half dead and I've got spares of all that stuff."

He shut the cargo door and, after a moment, locked it.

"Leave it to me to find the one bad neighborhood in the world."

#

The next morning, David brought his buggy to a stop in the middle of a courtyard at the edge of a city that was nearly finished being reclaimed by the wasteland. David wasn't around when this city was whole. As far as he knew, no one was left from back then. He didn't even really know when "back then" was. But it must have been a sight to see. The bases of buildings showed the sort of infrastructure that could have supported a hundred stories or more. The five or ten stories that remained of most of the buildings still represented the tallest structures he'd ever seen. They also served as a handy landmark for his lackluster navigational skills.

"That doesn't look good," he said as he emerged from the buggy and approached the low building ahead of him.

A few years ago he'd tagged it with "David was here." At

some point it must have had something to do with the waterworks or the sewage system of the city, because it led deep into the ground and had no shortage of waterproof channels and basins. It had stood the test of time quite well, but at some point since he'd last been here, the roof gave way. He pushed the door open and navigated the now-much shakier metal walkway leaning down. Debris from the collapsed ceiling littered the catwalks along the way. When he reached the bottom, his fears were realized.

As difficult as it was to get food and medicine in the wasteland, his buggy meant he could cover hundreds of kilometers a day. There wasn't any competition, so he could usually dig up enough food to live without much difficulty. But relatively clean water was another matter. He'd yet to find a well that wasn't dry. Lakes and streams were little more than baked earth. If he traveled far enough in any direction he reached the ocean, but the water was so far from salvageable cities and navigable ground, it just wasn't feasible to stay there long enough to try to get desalination going.

He'd been able to survive this long by setting up a ring of cobbled-together, solar-powered moisture extractors. They condensed what little moisture there was in the air. Now the panels were in pieces, scattered among the bits of debris that had been the roof. Somewhere under it all was the network of condensers and cooling fins that had, drop by drop, formed his water supply.

"Okay…" he breathed. "Gotta rebuild six water rigs. That's… two months of scrounging if I'm lucky."

He paced over to the one basin that wasn't completely filled with shattered stone. It had only a few inches of water in it. He squinted at a crudely painted line.

"Eleven gallons. Plus what I've got. That's a month." He rubbed his face. "Gonna be a thirsty year."

He plodded up the steps to his rig to grab a jerry can and a pump, then began the laborious process of transporting what little water he'd been able to harvest.

#

Two hours later, he reached the surface with the last of his water.

"Nice thing about the disaster," he huffed. "Less water means fewer trips up and down stairs."

He climbed into the cargo cart and dumped the water in, then hopped down and sat on the tailgate to catch his breath.

"Where am I going to get a compressor…" he muttered. "Gotta start keeping my eye out for old houses. Maybe I can find some refrigerators. Or I guess I…"

David squinted in the distance. Something vaguely shiny was approaching along the same path he'd taken here. A sequence of powerful emotions swept over him. Confusion, fear, and excitement eventually turned to recognition once it was near enough for him to realize what it was. A few minutes of slow clambering passed, and finally the robot clacked sluggishly to a stop.

"Look who came crawling back. If it isn't Easy, the energy thief."

It opened its pincers and dropped the now depleted power cell.

"Feeding," the robot repeated in his voice.

"Oh. What am I, a mama bird?" He hopped down. "Come here. There's no way you were designed to just run around and plug yourself in."

The robot, either out of coincidence or obedience, clattered up to him. He crouched down and investigated the domed back while it focused its "eyes" on him.

"Here's your problem. These things here? These are solar panels. But you've got them completely gunked up." He wiped some sweat from his forehead and used it to start buffing at the panels. "Didn't anybody teach you to keep clean? Then, I'm one to talk. I haven't had enough water for a bath since I was six."

With each swipe of the rag, more of the solar panels on the dome were exposed. The creature became visibly livelier.

"There. All clean. Go bask for a while and you won't need to steal from me anymore. And you're welcome, by the way."

"You're welcome," Easy echoed back.

It turned around and immediately clattered off from whence it came.

"Oh, sure, run off again." He raised his voice. "The least you could have done is brought me some water!"

#

Six hours later, David was still at the edge of town. The only fully intact part of the city was an old military bunker. The place had been stripped of most of the most valuable goods it contained long ago, but for reasons that would be clear to anyone who had ever *eaten* one, its supply of emergency food bars had yet to be fully cleared out. The pickings had gotten pretty slim, however.

"Compressed Kale," he said, eying one of the dozens of green bricks. "And Dehydrated Shrimp. Guess I'm either going to find out what that tastes like straight, or I'm going to have to get used to shrimp-flavored drinking water. But at least I won't starve."

He paced out into the sun and pulled his hat down to shade his eyes. Normally, to get the absolute most out of the day's light, he would have walked the mile or from his parking spot to the bunker. With the water rationing in his future, losing a few pints through his pores was probably a bad idea, so he'd taken the drive.

"Easy," said his own voice.

He pushed his hat back up and spotted the clattering beetle of a robot. It stood on the hood of the buggy, head held high as though it had been searching for him. The robot jumped down and skittered off toward the cargo cart.

"You *can't* be hungry already. The sun's still up." David followed the robot around the side of his buggy. "How bad could your battery possibly *be*? This thing runs on a bank of them, and… Oh."

Easy had stopped below the cargo door, where another badly worn robot twitched and shuddered. It was in most ways a duplicate of Easy, though it had its own unique configuration of scrapes and dents.

"You brought a friend," David said.

"Feeding," Easy replied.

The twitching robot managed to flip itself over, exposing its belly and thus its charging port.

"I'm not *made* of electricity, you know. The same juice that runs you guys runs the buggy, and I can't live if that thing doesn't work."

Easy stretched its legs, going up on tiptoe for lack of a better term. David heard a soft click, then a thunk as something dropped out of the compartment. The robot skittered back to reveal what it had dropped. David's eyes opened wide.

It was a bottle of water. An old-fashioned plastic water bottle. It even still had its seal.

"You're welcome," Easy said.

Dave's hands were almost shaking as he picked up the bottle.

"Where did you find this?" he said.

"Feeding," Easy said.

The other robot waggled its legs expectantly.

"Yeah. Yeah, of course. Feeding. Coming right up."

He hastily dug out the charging setup that Easy had brought back that morning. This time, he hooked the newcomer up to the main battery rather than forcing it to deal with the limited power of a spare cell.

"Where did you find the bottle of water? I haven't seen a fresh bottle of water in years," David said.

He rolled the charging bot on its side and used the sweaty rag technique to clean the dust from the second robot.

"Find… bottle of water," Easy said.

"Okay. Okay. You don't have a dictionary of voice terms."

"Don't have a dictionary."

"But you do understand what I am saying."

"I… do understand what… you…"

"Right, right. I got it. Obviously vocal communication isn't your number one skill. So, what are you, a rescue robot? Yes or no?"

"No."

"A search robot?"

"Yes."

"Search and rescue?"

"No."

"Just search."

"No."

"What else would you be if…" He stopped cleaning for a moment. "Search and destroy."

"Search and destroy."

"… I can't help but notice you didn't destroy."

"Didn't destroy."

"Do you *intend* to destroy?"

"No."

"So you're not going to follow orders?"

"No… orders."

"Oh." He sighed with relief and went back to work cleaning the solar panels. "Yeah, I guess the people calling the shots are all gone."

"Yes."

"Do you know if *anyone* is alive?"

"No."

"You don't know, or there aren't any people alive?"

"I… don't know."

He nodded. "I'll take that. That's better than the alternative. So who gets to call the shots now that the military is no more?"

"I… call the shots."

"You have an impressive grasp of the vernacular, Easy."

"Thank you."

"How did you get to be… alive? Self-aware or whatever."

"I… don't know."

"Fair enough." He slapped the rag against the cleaned-up second robot. "Top yourself off and you're good to go."

"Thank you," said the second robot.

"Quick learners," he said. "But you can't take care of yourselves?"

"No."

"I guess it's the sort of thing that calls for thumbs and parts and what not."

"Thumbs and parts."

"Good to go," said the unnamed robot.

He pulled the power cord and the robot immediately dashed away. Easy turned to follow.

"Hey! Wait!" he said.

"No," said the unnamed robot as it continued to skitter away.

Easy stopped and turned.

"Listen," David said. "You guys need help taking care of yourselves. And I need help taking care of myself."

"Yes."

"Why don't we work together? I'll keep you up and running, do the best I can to fix your buddies, all of that. In return, you help me find food, water, the parts I need to fix you and to keep myself going. What do you say? Is it a deal?"

"… Deal."

He released a breath. "Okay. Have you got any bits that need work? I've got some oil and bushings. And if not, I'm going to need you to lead me to where you found that water. And if you're up to it, there are some parts I'm going to need to start getting my own water situation figured out on a more permanent basis."

Easy fluttered two of the metal fins fanning out around his legs. "Oil."

"Will do." He dug through a bin and found some machine oil. "By the way, the name is David."

He applied the oil to the hinges until they stopped grinding and started moving freely. For good measure, he gave each of the legs a drop of lubricant as well. Easy tested its range of motion and gazed up at him. "Thank you, David."

#

Five months later…

A sharp metallic tapping shook David from sleep.

"Hmm? Yeah. Yeah, I'm coming," he said.

He rolled out of bed and clicked the bedside lamp on. His bedroom was in a bit of disarray. It had been a busy few weeks and, to be frank, he'd never had enough room to have to worry about keeping things tidy. He pulled on a robe hanging on the back of the door.

There was another sharp tap.

"Hold your horses!" he said, turning the knob.

He looked down to the little robot gazing up at him from the floor in front of his bedroom door. It had the letters EZ painted carefully in front of its gleaming and pristine solar panels.

"What's up?" he said with a yawn.

"New patients, David," said Easy.

The robot turned and tapped its way through the hallway of what looked like a suburban home in the midst of a rather significant bit of renovation. Here and there, other robots tapped their way through adjoining hallways or basked in the pool of sun beneath a skylight.

"Hey, Whiskey. Hey, Foxtrot. Where's Tango?" he called to the pair in his living room.

"Parts run," answered the robot marked with a W.

"Shim Stock," said the robot with an F.

"You folks are tearing through the shim stock. What did I tell you? If your leg feels like it's got too much backlash, come and see me. If you keep it up, I'm going to have to machine up a whole new set of bushings."

"Sorry, David," said Whiskey.

All of the robots spoke with David's own voice, though for Easy, Whiskey, Tango, Foxtrot, and a few others, he'd trained them with different inflections in hopes of telling them apart.

"Aw, it's fine," he said. "Bushings are kind of fun to make anyway."

He looked down to Easy.

"So how many new patients are we talking about?"

"Three."

"Where are they, in the machine shop?"

"Yes."

He came to the front door of the house and pulled on his old familiar hat before stepping outside.

Most of David's life had been lived in a blur. When every day could be described by the same three words—struggle, sweat, and hunger—the weeks and months started to run together. Now the blur was thanks to something else entirely. Having Easy and his sophisticated sensor suite, scavenging had changed overnight. Now instead of spending weeks carefully searching and hoping to get lucky, he and his buddy could scour a whole neighborhood in just a few hours. David had gotten good enough at making do with anything halfway close to what he was looking for, seldom did they search someplace without finding something worthwhile. Before long, the cart was full to bursting and the time had come to consider setting up a home base.

He paced passed the first of three huge water tanks and touched his hand to the cool side to collect some condensation to run through his hair to tackle his bed head. A field of solar collectors stretched out ahead of him, each bank running something vital for him or for his flock of robots. Some were condensing water to store. Others were charging up batteries. To the other side, a small but flourishing garden offered up a dash of green, a color he'd almost forgotten existed. He glanced in the direction of the rows of zucchini and potatoes. A silvery form was rooting about in an irrigation ditch.

"Oh! Hey! Zulu, get over here."

A largely incomplete head rose up out of the mud to look at him, then the machine scurried over. David crouched and took the edge of his robe to start cleaning off the solar panels.

"You know you shouldn't be working in the garden alone. Look at you. You've completely mucked up your panels. What if you ran down? Buddy system when working with mud, remember?" He finished cleaning off the panels. "If you want to work in the field, go get Whiskey to help you. He's just hanging out in the living room."

The robot nodded and tapped toward the house. Its speaker module was one of the bits missing from its head, so it communicated mostly through gestures.

Ahead, what had been the garage of this slowly recovering farmhouse had been converted into a fully functioning machine shop. He stepped inside and turned on the lights.

"Let's see what we've got," he said.

Three robots were obediently waiting on the workbench, heads turned in his direction. They'd all felt the wrath of the wasteland in one way or another.

"You want to help out, Easy?"

"Yes, David."

"Okay, I'm going to need…" He counted quietly to himself. "Seven leg joints and the associated fasteners. Looks like two wiring harnesses, and we may as well swap out the solar array on this one."

The robot tapped away and clamored up a bank of shelves beside a metal lathe to fetch the indicated equipment.

"A lot of leg problems in this group. Have you been up north? The soil there is hell on joints. Try to stick to the high ground, it's better up there. Any of you three been here before?"

One of the robots raised a leg.

"Welcome back. I thought I recognized this wiring job."

They nodded.

Word of mouth, or more accurately word of transceiver, had been very good for his little repair shop. Contrary to what he would have expected, the robots weren't all the same. Structurally they were, but behaviorally they had their own quirks. He'd seen and worked on hundreds of them, but only about two dozen had decided to stick around. Designed for the hunt as they were, they mostly preferred to spend their time on lengthy searches for this or that. The rest of them just stopped in for service and went on their way. He was happy to oblige them, but not without a favor in return.

"For the newcomers, did Easy give you the yes/no explanation?"

They nodded.

"Good. The rules are simple. You're welcome to come find me and get fixed up, but in exchange you agree to the following. No fighting. Not me, not each other, not anyone else. You come back here and I find out you've been fighting, you'd better have a heck of a good reason. Agreed?"

They nodded.

"The first repair is free, but after that, I'd appreciate it if you'd bring something to trade. Parts, water, food. Anything that might help keep this little operation running. Speaking of, you got anything for me, Mr. Repeat Customer?"

The robot nodded.

"Great. You can show me later. Next, if you're not going to stick around, I ask that you take one of these with you." He reached into a bin and found it empty. "Easy, could you—"

The robot scurried up onto the table, straddled the bin, and opened its compartment. A handful of little clay pellets spilled out.

"Thank you, Easy. You take one of these and a little packet of water. These are seed bombs. As you're going wherever you're going and doing whatever you're doing, if you see some soil that looks reasonably moist, drop the bomb and the water packet. Hopefully we can get some Johnny Appleseed stuff going on. Think you can do that?"

They nodded again.

"Great. And finally, if you spot any humans, I want to know about it. Sound good?"

Another set of nods.

"Okay. Let's get you healthy. Roll over."

They all, with varying levels of difficulty, flipped onto their backs to present their bellies. He blasted them out with compressed air to clear the dust, then pulled down power cords from reels in the ceiling and hooked them all up. With them on the robotic equivalent of life support, he started pulling the parts that needed replacing.

#

The repairs had taken about an hour so far, and he was nearly finished. He'd been getting a lot of practice at them, so each little session like this was going quicker and quicker. The two first-timers were the first to be fully repaired. They took their seed payload and skittered off. The repeat customer was taking a bit longer.

Easy clattered in just David was removing a side panel to rewire a speaker in his patient.

"Breakfast, David," Easy said, opening the compartment to drop a canteen of water and a boiled potato.

"You're going to spoil me, buddy."

He clicked in the replacement wire and pressed the panel back into place.

"You're all fixed up." David said, wiping his hands and picking up his spud. "What sort of goodies did you bring me?"

David munched and drank while the robot nimbly rolled back to its feet. It bleeped through a few tones, then started to play back some audio. He expected to hear some recording or another of himself. These days he was afloat in a sea of overheard comments parroted back in cobbled together communication. Instead, there was nothing but the sound of wind and clattering footsteps.

He sipped his water and finished his potato. "Am I missing something?"

Easy tapped over to its sibling and tipped forward, listening more closely. David gathered up the replaced parts and started cleaning and prepping them for refurbishing. After four minutes of assorted sounds of the wasteland, Easy's head perked up. A bit of robot talk—which was a mixture of soft tones and imperceptible clicking, prompted the repeat visitor to replay the last fifteen seconds. The volume was much louder, then gradually eased into a noise-suppressed hiss. Assorted frequencies amplified and suppressed. Gradually, something emerged out of the digital manipulation.

"… What is it? … I don't know. Stay down. … But it's moving. … Stay down and be quiet. …"

They were two voices, both female. David froze and shut his eyes, scouring the recording for any more information. There was none. No more speech, nothing.

"When did you hear this?"

After some tones and clicks, Easy translated. "Seven weeks."

"Do you remember *where* you heard it?"

It nodded.

"Tell Easy. And if you ever need *anything*. You find me. You've earned a lifetime membership at our little spa."

The robot nodded and skittered out the door.

"Did you get the location, Easy?"

"Yes."

"Is it far?"

"Yes."

"Can we make it?"

"Yes."

"You up for a road trip to see if there's still a human race?"

"Heck yes."

Bella's Journey
Joseph R. Lallo

Bella's Journey

This one in particular is a result of an idle bit of musing and chit-chat on twitter. I claimed I needed something happy and joyful to write, but nothing was coming to mind. A reader named Heather suggested fat unicorns. A few months later, I was writing that very story. And in a moment, you'll be reading it.

This cover is adapted from a spur of the moment commission of the character by Chandra Free.

24

"Bella!" trilled a musical voice. "Bella, you'll be late!"

A blue hummingbird flitted through a sun-dappled glade. He darted from place to place, looking in every shadow.

"Must I come, Luca?" called a youthful voice from the shade of a willow.

The bird flitted up to the tree.

"It is the sun and moon festival, Bella. *Everyone* will be there."

An angry huff came from the trees and a mythic form stepped out.

There are few creatures as majestic and graceful as the unicorn. Their short fur gleams like the finest pearls. Vivid manes and tails flow like silk in the breeze and shine in the brightest of pastels. Every color in the rainbow hides within the spiral of their fierce horn. Their every motion is poetry. Their grace and precision make every moment of their lives seem like part of an endless ballet. And their bodies, so lithe and slender, are like masterwork of a sculptor, carved from the finest marble.

Bella was different. Oh, it was true, she still had the radiant beauty and haunting grace of her sisters. There was just… *more* of it. And of all the words that might describe the others of her magnificent kind, "lithe" and "slender" were unlikely to leap to mind upon seeing her.

When the light fell upon her, it revealed a pudgy roundness. Bella was plump as a marshmallow. It wasn't simply a fluffy coat, either. Though she trotted about on tiny, deft little hooves, every other part of her was portly and full. From the tip of her soft muzzle to her swishing pink tail, she was round and solid. That she moved so smoothly and surely made it seem as though she was an over-inflated balloon, threatening at any moment to drift into the sky.

She fluttered her eyes and lowered her head, letting her pink mane fall forward.

"I don't belong at the festival."

Luca buzzed down to look into an eye as large and blue as he was.

"Bella, you are a unicorn, and the sun and moon festival is for *any* unicorn who wishes to take part."

She snuffled and shook her head. "I don't look like the other unicorns. I don't *match*. The festival doesn't look right when I'm a part of it."

"It's not about how you *look*. It's how you *move*. Come on! If you don't hurry, you'll miss the start."

Luca grabbed a strand of her mane and tugged, as though the tiny bird would be able to haul the mighty creature along.

"At this rate you won't even have a chance to be the focus," he said, grunting in effort.

She puffed a breath to shift her hair from her eyes and send Luca swirling.

"Fine. But I'm *not* going to be the focus, even if they ask."

Bella trotted out, her dainty hooves clopping along the water-smoothed stones that formed the path to her home glade.

"Can you help me practice?" she said.

He laughed. "We can practice, but only because it's just a joy to watch."

Luca flitted up and turned about, keeping careful pace just a head of her and just above. He flew backward and stared down.

"Now, I'm the moon. Tell me what to do!"

Bella's clip-clopping gait started to subtly change. From clip-clop clip-clop to clippity-cloppity-clip-clip-clop. The rhythmic sway of her head with each step became more fluid and nuanced. The very point of her horn stopped tracing its figure-eights in the air and began to sketch out far more complex figures. They weren't just shapes, they were patterns, words of a language told through motion rather than image and sound alone.

"Look at that," Luca said. "When asked so nicely, how could *any* heavenly body refuse your request? You're as pretty as the moon herself, Bella."

"Yeah," she said with a wry smile. "I look just like her."

"Oh fuff," he said dismissively. "Now I'm the sun. What do you want from *me?*"

Her trotting pattern shifted, and so too did her horn's loops and swirls. Thus, through the whole of the trip, she honed her craft. She couldn't help that she didn't look like the other unicorns, but she could at least be sure she could do her part if they needed her.

#

A few hours later, Bella cantered to the edge of a cliff. Luca was perched atop one of her ears, the better to be heard as the winds whistled. Their journey had taken them from the heart of her pleasant little forest to the top of tall, rocky peak. The mountain of the moon and sun was known to all, a glorious spire that sparkled with babbling cascades down three of its sides. A few times a year, at a very precise time of day, both the sun and the moon aligned themselves on either side of the peak. They may as well have been the audience arriving for a special show. And not to disappoint them, the unicorns always had a magnificent show waiting.

Bella smiled down at the shallow bowl of stone spreading out below her, a unique crater of sorts at the very peak of the mountain. The rest of her sisters were already there. Dozens of unicorns, gathered from all around the land. They stood among the rippling surface of a crystal-clear spring that welled up through cracks in the stone. The spring nourished a lush carpet of green moss. Vines coiled their way up the stone walls, tracing the edges of a spiraling path that led down to the floor of the bowl. Little bridges, built long ago, spanned cracks in the wall, through which the spring escaped to trickle down the mountainside. Bella trotted down the path, circling downward toward the others. Luca darted to flower after flower that sprouted from the vines, drinking his fill of the nectar within.

"There she is!" called a voice from below.

"Bella came!" called another.

When she reached the bottom of the bowl, many of the other unicorns gathered around her. *They* were the creatures that graced the pages of fairy tales and songbooks. Long legs. Arching necks. Narrow faces. They were the strokes of a watercolor brush. She was a lump of rising dough in comparison. Beautiful, perhaps, but the *wrong* sort of beauty.

It would have been easy to imagine that the others would shun Bella, but that was not their way. A unicorn was a unicorn, it was as simple as that. True, she was unique among them, but there was nothing wrong with being unique. It seemed the only creature who saw something wrong with Bella was the one in the mirror. But that was the voice that was hardest to silence.

"We missed you last festival," said a blue-maned creature sweetly. "I had to dance *twice* as well to make our message heard."

"You should dance beside me," suggested a taller, ruby-maned creature. "I missed three steps last time. You know how the others struggle when something goes wrong."

"No, no, no," Bella said, shrinking backward and letting her mane slip over her eyes once more. "You dance near the center. I like the rim. The rim is best for me."

"As you wish, but next time, you dance beside me. Promise?"

Three quick clacks echoed from the walls of the grand stage in which they were gathered. All eyes turned to the center. Atop a great, glassy stone rising from the spring stood a golden-maned unicorn. She held her head high.

"Everyone, take your places!" she cried. "The festival is about to begin! People are counting on us."

#

Colorful hooves splashed through the water as the many unicorns found a position. The gold mane shone in the center. Around her, a ring of other creatures formed. A step farther away, another ring with even more of the creatures. And finally, like the points of a star, the remaining unicorns spread themselves around the others. It was in this outermost ring that Bella found her place.

All stood stock still, eyes shut, and horns held high. There was only the buzz of insects and the trickle of water. Then, with eyes still shut, the unicorns moved as one. The festival began.

The sound was astonishing. Splashing steps were like symbols clashing. Clacking hooves were the tap of a snare. It wove into a rhythm that was at once as precise as a military march and as random as the swirl of embers above a fire. The tips of their horns caught the golden light of the setting sun and the silver light of the rising moon. Streamers of the glow stretched like ribbons, coiling in the air and revealing the hidden language of the dance.

Majestic creatures moved in lilting, waltz-like motion. Rings moved in alternating directions, two steps to one side and one step to another. Their motion was in perfect sync, and the shapes their horns drew hung in the air as pleas and requests to the shining forms in the sky. They requested good luck for the year and good health for the people. Strong harvests, good weather. And most of all, they asked for friendship and togetherness. The requests came as the curls of a lace doily woven in the air by the horns of dancing unicorns.

One by one, other mythic creatures approached the rim of the bowl in which the unicorns danced. Great minotaurs and tiny sprites watched and waited. Fearsome manticores and gentle dryads stood side by side. This dance, more than anything else, was for them. The final wish, the wish of togetherness, was more than a simple call for peace and understanding. It was far more literal, and far more powerful. Only the most skillful of dances could coax such a favor from the heavens. Today, if their motions were true and their hearts were pure, the unicorns would open the way to other lands. New friends could come. Old visitors could return home. Nowhere else could such gateways be opened. And no one else could hope to knock on their doors.

Radiant circles formed around the rim of the bowl like jewels in a crown. Images of foreign landscapes shimmered into being. The visitors from those lands stepped gleefully through, happy to return to their homes after a visit to this place. Gleaming birds and elegant fae slipped from others to see this new place. The Moon and Sun Festival enriched this world and a dozen others by allowing curious and exotic beasts to sample the wonders that lay in other worlds.

A final gate opened, but rather than a marvelous new world to gaze at, the contents of the glowing ring was naught but darkness. And rather than mysterious new friends, what came out of the ring was the darkness itself.

Smoke poured out of the gate. It stunk of oil, grease, and char. The blackness coiled into the sky, thick and inky. It wafted and pooled with purpose, casting the whole of the bowl in shadow. For a time, the only light came from the streamers of light trailing from the unicorn horns. The perfect pattern scattered and became chaotic as confusion descended upon them.

When the disorderly clatter of hooves was joined with a chattering laughter, all confusion vanished. Replaced with certainty. These were imps.

#

"Run!" Bella called out, though all of her sisters were already rushing about in the darkness.

Tiny claws and fumbling feet splashed in the water and the worried voices of her sisters called out. Bella reached the base of the spiraling path out of the bowl and tried to swirl her horn to banish the dark and lead others to her. The pool of light she could manage was just enough for her to see a net thrown over one of the other unicorns. She tried to run to her, but couldn't even make it back to the water before a net was thrown over *her* as well. She thumped to the ground. Four little creatures gathered up her friend and hauled her away. More of the blasted things scampered toward her. She felt clutching hands grab her, and heard groans as they tried to lift her.

They failed. This *was* Bella, after all. Maybe four imps could lift one of her sisters, but not her. The things grumbled and grunted, hefted and heaved. Angry, chattering voices called for help. More hands joined the rest, but they were only able to budge her a tiny bit before she plopped back down.

"The gate is closing!" hissed a greasy-voiced beast. "Back through!"

The groaning creatures abandoned her. One by one she heard the melodic cries of her sisters fade into the distance, along with the chattering laughter. She wrestled with the net, but to no avail. The smoke itself began to coil away again, escaping with the others. As it vanished, she could see that all of the other gates that had been opened were already shut. The creatures who had sought the festival to find a way home had wisely retreated through, lest they risk being trapped away from their homes or spirited away by the imps as well.

Bella struggled as hard as she could. Maybe if she could follow the spiral up to the rim, she could stop the gate from closing. Alas, it was rapidly shrinking and the net still held her tight. A final wisp of blackness slurped through. Just like that, the gate was gone and her sisters with it. The light of the sun and moon returned, with the failing sunset and strengthening moon revealing her to be alone in this sacred place. The carpet of moss was torn and trampled. She could still smell the choking smoke, and see the claw marks of the monsters who had swept in and out so quickly.

"No…" she said, her blue eyes blurring with tears.

"Hello? Anyone?" called a little voice.

She craned her neck and looked about. A brilliant point of blue was flitting toward her. It was Luca.

"Luca, they're *gone!*" she called to him.

"How! How did it happen? As soon as there was smoke, I started coughing and couldn't stop. Us birds don't do so well with smoke…"

"It was imps! They came through a gate!"

"No. I didn't know that was possible."

"It isn't! At least, it's not supposed to be…" Bella said. "The imps aren't *friends*. The doors only open for friends! And now they're gone…"

"We're going to do something, aren't we? We've *got* to do something."

He snagged a bit of the net and fought at it. Tugging with all of his might could barely budge a single strand. Bella shut her eyes and kicked her legs a bit more carefully, trying to her wriggle her way out of the net. Now that panic didn't have so firm a grip on her, she could focus on freeing herself. A minute or so of careful struggle freed her legs, but she remained on her side, too grief-stricken to bring herself to roll to her feet.

"I don't know what to do. I don't know…"

Luca flitted up. "The moon! The moon is still up. The sun is going, but the moon is still up. You can ask the moon."

"To what? To bring them back? I'm just one unicorn, Luca. The moon won't grant so large a request for just one unicorn."

Luca flitted down again, head cocked to the side.

"Did you hear that?"

"Hear what?"

"Listen…"

She flicked her ears and shut her eyes. After a moment, she heard a wheezing groan… from beneath her.

Bella rolled upright and climbed to her feet, finally shedding the net. Where she had been laying was a purple-black creature with stubby arms, a scrawny little body, and a crooked whip-like tail. It was splayed on the ground, large purple eyes half-shut. The imp wore a ruddy set bib overalls. It had huge, saggy ears, fuzzy little horns, and wings that looked too small to be of any use. Evidently, when they'd tried to spirit away Bella, this imp had made the mistake of trying to get beneath her and had been pinned by her bulk.

"Augh…" it groaned, dazed.

"It's one of them!" Luca piped.

He darted down and hung before the thing's eyes.

"You bring back the unicorns, you *cad*. You bring them back or so help me I will show you *no mercy!*"

The creature blinked at the hummingbird for a moment, then snatched him out of the air and gripped him firmly in a baggy-gloved hand.

"Don't think violence will save you, you fiend," he wheezed.

Bella leveled her horn at the creature.

"Let. Him. Go," she threatened.

The thing's eyes goggled and it hastily complied.

"That's *right*. Now tell me your evil plan! What did you do with the unicorns!" Luca said.

The thing shuffled backward, then turned to run. Bella set a hoof on its tail. It screeched and tugged at it, but it may as well have been staked into the ground.

"Speak," Bela said.

"We've got a moon and a sun, too, you know!" the thing croaked. "We've got things *we* want. And we don't have unicorns to *get* them."

It cackled.

"But now we do! We'll get whatever we want!" It rubbed its hands together. "My wish will be for *gold*. And a fishing rod. And a boat for using it!"

"You don't get things like that during the Moon and Sun Festival. No one gets material goods!" Luca said.

"And you won't be getting *any*. My sisters will never dance for you."

"The boss will make them dance. He can make anyone do *anything*."

"Fine. Then you won't get anything because you're here and they're there," Luca said.

"Yeah but... See, we came here and..." He looked to where the door had been. "*Bricks and brambles!* Those lousy no good runts *left* me here."

He crossed his arms.

"That's the last time I help *them* steal unicorns."

"Yes," Bella said, leaning forward and poking his chest with her horn. "It is."

"What do you want from me!" the imp said. "I'm trapped here, just the same as they're trapped there."

"You're going to tell me how you got the gate to open when you are *plainly* not our friends."

"You think they tell me anything? I'm an imp! Imps are the sorts of things you toss buckets of onto a problem until it goes way. Nobody tells me *how* things get done. They just tell me to do things."

She squinted her eyes.

"Either there is someone there who is our friend, or there is someone here who is *their* friend. That's the only way I can figure that they'd get here."

"And all of your sisters are there now, so you'll be able to get there," Luca said. "And all of the people here are our friends, so they'll be able to get back."

"Not while the boss has them trapped," the imp said.

Luca nodded. "Then we'll just have to free them."

Bella gazed off into the distance.

"I have to implore the moon, without the sun… By myself…" She looked to the center stone. "But there's no other way…"

She lifted her hoof from the imp's tail. The fiendish creature instantly scrambled for freedom, but she used her horn to hook the net that had held her and tossed it over him.

"You aren't going anywhere," she said.

"*Yeah*," Luca said, flitting up to him. "When we go through that gate, you're coming with us."

"Yeah…" Bella said. "*When* we go through…"

She waded into the cool water of the spring, then up onto the raised stone in the center of the bowl. Her legs became shaky as she climbed atop it. This was something she'd never dreamed she would ever do. It was something she would have refused if offered. The focus of the dance. It was so much more than just the center of the stage. The focus was the frame upon which the dance was built. There she would keep time. She would trace the most complex of the shapes with her horn. It was a position that demanded perfection. And she was anything but perfect. She was *different*. When all others are one way and you are another, what right have you to even dream that you might someday take the lead?

"There's no other way," she said to herself. "It is up to you."

Bella turned and cast her eyes to the moon. It had climbed so much higher since the festival had begun. The sky behind was purple, the first hints of stars joining the pale white circle that shone with such brilliance. If her sisters where here, this is when the dancing would have ended. She could feel that the magic of union of sun and moon was waning. She didn't know if the moon by herself had the strength or the inclination to heed the cries of her children. Today she would learn.

Her hooves began to move. Clip-cloppity-clip cloppy-clip. She tipped her head and sliced the air with her horn. She was not a voice in a choir anymore. She was the lead. Every word was hers to embody, and she had to be bold if she was to be heard. In place of the splashing steps, she swept her tail. Each hoof skipped and stuttered, doing the work of two or more. Where once she moved lightly, now she stepped heavily. Every ounce of her weight went behind every tap, until the echoes rang clear off the walls and layered with her waltz. The tip of her horn glimmered. A thread of light shimmered. In time with her steps, the light wove her words. Great sweeping motions writ the heartfelt plea large. Every arch of her neck and every skip of her legs went into spelling out her wish. She began to feel the same power, the same melody in the air. But it was so weak. She had to try harder.

The focus wouldn't do. She needed more space. With graceful leaps and splashing slides, she allowed her balletic monologue to fill the whole of the stage. Her nostrils flared as she grew winded and weary, but she didn't slow. In the ancient language, with its slashes and whorls, she begged for togetherness with the friends she had lost. Though woven by a single horn, the glistening pattern persisted. Its loops stretched from edge to edge of the beautiful bowl. She pleaded her case with respect and with grace, and when there was no more to say, she leaped to the center and concluded with a twirl.

Silence returned. A few moments passed, the longest moments of her life. She huffed and she puffed, her teary eyes staring to the heavens. But no gateway opened. No wish was granted. She lowered her head. Tears rolled down her muzzle. They trickled into the spring, sending ringlets across the surface. With the weight of her failure heavy in her heart, she was slow to open her eyes again. But when she did, she found that the ripples of her tears caught the moonlight in a very strange way. The shapes they painted on the bottom of the spring were every bit as complex as the ones her dance had traced in the air. They moved more quickly, more surely than water should have. The moon, in its wisdom and beauty, was speaking back.

It wasn't as simple as words one might hear a voice say, nor as clear as something written on a page. If someone were to ask Bella to translate what she saw in the stream, she wouldn't have been able to put it into simple terms. It was feelings and thoughts, so very real, yet fleeting as a dream. They warned of the danger she would face and the challenges that awaited her. They asked that she be sure. And they awaited an answer.

For all the complexity of the dance that brought her this far, the answer was a simple one. A single step forward.

The moon understood.

All around her, the rippling water stilled. In the glassy surface, she saw a reflection. It was the sky, but not the sky of her world. It was a dark sky, twisted and cold. It was the sky of the imp's world. She had her door.

Bella turned to captured imp, and bounded to him.

"Come on. We're going to pay your boss a visit."

She grabbed the edges of the net that held the imp her teeth and yanked him from the ground.

"Don't forget me!" Luca trilled, holding tight to her mane.

Bella turned to the water. It was scarcely deep enough to submerge her hooves, yet she took a deep breath, shut her eyes, and dove beneath its surface.

#

Bella emerged from the surface and took a deep breath. When she blinked the water from her eyes, she found herself in a very different place. Gone was the spire and the cool, clear spring. Now she was in the center of a lake. The landscape around was blackened with cruel bramble and thorns. It was the dead of night here, and a very different moon lurked on the horizon. It seemed to be rising, as though the time back home had little to do with the time here.

Luca shook the water from him and darted up above her.

"The Shady Realm…" he said. "I never thought I'd see this place. I kind of *hoped* I'd never see it."

The unicorn paddled to the shore and trotted to the dark gravel path, dragging the sputtering imp behind her. Her pink mane hung heavily over her face. She shook it aside and took in her surroundings.

"It's so big…" she said.

The landscape spread in all directions with little in the way of landmarks. It was just an endless stretch of rolling hills. Here and there, paths wove between them, but they seemed to crisscross and coil upon one another. If anything, they seemed to have been designed to *confuse* travelers rather than help them. Luca darted higher and higher.

"There is a city to the… is that north or… There's a city that way! And another over there. Neither of them look very friendly."

Bella turned to her captive.

"Where did they take my sisters?" she said.

"Why should I tell you?" the imp asked.

"You *should* tell me because I'm asking you nicely," she said. "But you will tell me because if you don't, I'll sit on you until you do."

She turned her rump toward him as if she were brandishing a weapon. The imp's ears lowered to the side of his head and he swallowed hard.

"Castle Magdar," he said quickly. "They're in Castle Magdar. In the Solune Pit."

"That doesn't sound good. Pits don't sound like good places for unicorns," Luca said.

"Which way is that?" she asked.

"I don't know! I don't even know where I am. I don't usually travel by diving into puddles and showing up in lakes."

She grabbed the net and, with a remarkably deft motion, heaved it up over her head. The imp slapped wetly against her soft back, and the ends of the net hooked over her horn to prevent his escape. It wasn't the most convenient or attractive way to haul a prisoner along, but it would do.

"We'll just ask at the nearest city, then," Bella said.

"You can't threaten to sit on *everyone*, you know. And the boss isn't the only one who knows that unicorns are worth their weight in gold. Which makes you worth a *lot* of gold."

Luca darted down. "You have no *idea* how much Bella is worth. She's worth so much more than *that.*"

"Thank you, Luca," Bella said, flatly. "But he's right. If I want to get through this, I'm going to need a disguise… Which city is closer, Luca?"

"This way!" he said, flitting toward the rising moon. "We'll call this east. Because of the moon rising."

The unlikely trio trotted along, delving deeper into this unknown land.

#

An hour later, a huffing and puffing Bella crept up to the edge of a sooty, industrial town. Her gleaming coat of pearly fur was a bit of a liability in this place. The way she caught the moonlight, she practically glowed against the dark landscape. But she crept low and slow, weaving between tall bramble clusters until she reached the city's sign.

"Milquetoast. That's a funny name for a city," Luca said, eying the sign.

"If this is Milquetoast, then Castle Magdar will be just over those hills to the south," the Imp said.

Luca flitted up to him. "How do we know you're not *lying, Imp?*"

"You don't," the imp said. "Half the time *I* don't know if I'm lying. Around here, lying is what comes natural. Which means there's no sense asking anyone, either."

The hummingbird glared at him, then darted down to Bella's face.

"He might be right, Bella," Luca whispered.

"We've got to believe someone *sometime,*" Bell said.

She shifted her head, tugging the imp's net from her back and lowering it down in front of her.

"What's your name?" she asked.

"Why would you care?"

"Where I come from, we don't need a reason to care about people. We just do. What's your name?"

"Gnorp," he said.

"Gnorp, I don't think you're as bad as you say."

"I'm bad. I'm *worse,*" Gnorp said.

"No. Because if you were worse, you would have called for help and gotten me caught."

He squinted at her, then crossed his arms. "Maybe I'm just too stupid to realize that, hmm? You didn't think of that, did you?"

"He could be right," Luca said with a quick nod. "He does seem very stupid."

"Then why are you not shouting *now?*" Bella said.

He turned away. "Maybe it's because I'm afraid you'll sit on me. That's why I'm doing everything *else.*"

"That's a good reason, too. He's making very good points, Bella," Luca said.

"You could have scratched and clawed and bit me. I'll bet those teeth of yours could have bit right through that net, given enough time.

But you didn't even struggle off my back once. I don't think you're such a bad guy. So here's what I'm going to do. I'm going to ask you, very nicely, what sort of a disguise would work. And if you answer just as nicely as I asked, I'll let you go."

"That's a bad idea, Bella." Luca darted down and glared at him. "This guy looks *bad.*"

"You always tell me looking different doesn't make any difference at all, Luca."

"Unless you look *bad*, like this guy," Luca reiterated.

"What do you say, Gnorp? What sort of disguise would get me to Castle Magdar?"

Gnorp sat silently, staring at the big blue eyes patiently awaiting an answer. He turned away, as though embarrassed.

"Castle Magdar goes through a lot of coal. I *guess,* if you weren't worried about getting your pretty white fur dirty, you could hide in the hopper of a cart. It takes a long way around, because it's so big, but it'll get you there in a few hours."

Luca gave Gnorp a stern look, then flitted up above the city. When he darted back down, he was hacking and coughing. Were he not so small, he probably would have given away their hiding place.

"There's a—*ah hack*—there's a great big cart, belching smoke, with a big covered wagon hooked to it, full of coal. It's up at the north side of town."

"That's the one," Gnorp said.

"Is it big enough for me to hide in?"

"It's very big," Luca said. "More than big enough."

She nodded. "Lead the way."

Bella turned to Gnorp and, with impressive dexterity, hooked the net that entangled him and pulled it away. He tumbled to the ground as it was yanked from beneath him.

"Sorry about that. And thank you, Gnorp. You're free to go."

Luca darted in. "But if I find out you double-crossed us, you'll have *me* to deal with."

Bella turned to trot away.

"You're *really* letting me go?" Gnorp said, eyes squinted and head turned aside.

"Of course! I do what I say, Gnorp. Thanks again."

The imp stared dubiously at her, then spread his little wings and darted away.

#

Bella padded as carefully as she could, guiding her dainty hooves to the muck between cobbles to keep from clip clopping loudly enough to be heard. As late as it was, the city was quite lively. All manner of twisted, unpleasant figures shifted and moved through the streets. Luca guided her through back alleys until she came to a part of town that smelled terrible. The air was heavy with smoke from the sorts of things one really shouldn't toss into a fire. It was all that Luca could do to keep from coughing.

"There. Up ahead. That's the cart," he wheezed.

It *was* enormous. Bella had seen hay carts of that sort back home, but this was large as a house. A simple cloth roof spanned the stout walls of the thing. The only two ways into it seemed to be a securely closed door in the back of the cart and a large opening on the roof. This opening was positioned at the end of a slide that must have been used to load the coal in the first place.

Bella spotted a few stacks of crates nearby. They were a bit precarious, but the mound they formed was tall enough to just about reach the ledge of the larger hopper at the other end of the slide.

Footsteps convinced her to duck down. Two ogre-like forms trudged into the courtyard ahead.

"About how much longer until you head out?" asked the smaller of the two.

"Any minute. Word has it the Count is real impatient for the load today."

"Why?"

"Ah, something to do with a celebration or something. Supposed to be music."

"The Count *hates* music."

"Look, I just know what I heard. Says there'll be dancing, at least. So that means music, right?"

"Ah. Must be his son's doing. He's the one always on about dancing and music…"

They continued past.

"You heard them, Luca," Bella whispered. "They're leaving soon. There's no time to waste."

She hopped to the nearest crate. It creaked beneath her hooves.

Another few graceful, surefooted bounds brought her to the top of a tall stack of them. Alas, no amount of grace or agility can make up for a precarious and poorly piled stack of crates. The whole tower of crates started to teeter and slide. In a panic, she leaped.

Bella made it to the catwalk by the skin of her teeth, but the metal and wood pathway was not built with a unicorn in mind. Particularly not one as substantial as Bella. One of the metal struts popped and creaked. The whole walkway threatened to give way. At the same time, the pile of crates that had gotten her this far tumbled to the ground in a startling cacophony.

She abandoned any semblance of stealth, clattering along the failing catwalk and diving for the slide. She rattled down the massive metal chute and, with a heavy thud and a puff of soot, dropped into the cart.

Her arrival tipped the cart up onto two wheels and threatened to overturn it. Luckily, the chaos she'd caused in the back alley had drawn all of the attention.

Luca flitted down into the cart, hacking at the soot that hung in the air.

"Bella? Are you all right?"

The soot settled to reveal a wisp of pink mane and the tip of a horn sticking up out of the coal. She wriggled her head until her black-smeared face emerged from beneath the coal.

"That wasn't as graceful as I would have liked," she whispered.

Luca landed on her horn.

"As long as you aren't hurt. There's a lot of angry yelling and foul words out there. I don't think anyone noticed you were the one who did it, though. So long as Gnorp wasn't lying, I think we'll be on our way." He huddled closer to her. "And I hate to say it, but it's a good thing he told us about this. There are some mean looking things patrolling the road up ahead. I don't think we would have made it otherwise."

The cart rocked and shuddered. An odd mechanical hiss split the air. With a grinding lurch, the cart rattled to life and began to grind its way down the road.

#

Two full hours passed with Bella uncomfortably buried in coal. Luca darted in and out, keeping his eye on the road. The castle was indeed looming closer, and as it did, she could feel that her sisters were

40

approaching along with it. It wasn't long before Luca came bursting in.

"I see the castle! *And* the pit! They're in cages at the bottom," he said. "But there are soldiers all over!"

"What kind of soldiers?"

"Not like the imps that came through. They're *big*. With strange-looking armor, like they flipped over a cauldron and stuck their head out the top and their arms out the sides."

"Tell me when we get somewhere safe. I need to get out of here."

Luca flitted about. She heard a few creatures mutter and swat at him, but the creatures here must have dismissed him as an insect. In time, the cart rattled to a stop. Luca landed on the roof and whispered down to her.

"They are all heading to the doorway. When I say go, do what you need to do. But I think you'll need to be ready to run. Just follow me when you do. This place is *confusing.*"

Bella nodded and practically swam through the coal until she got to the hatch in the back. She lined her horn up with the shackle she could see was keeping the door shut.

"A-a-a-and… *Now!*"

She shoved the shackle. The door swung open and a tide of coal swept out, taking Bella along with it. She bounced, tumbled, and rolled. It turned out she was inside a building now. It had high ceilings, tall as trees, and there was barely any light at all. She coughed and shook her head, sending plumes of black soot into the air before dizzily climbing to her feet.

"What's going on in there!?" called a voice from outside.

"This way, quick!" Luca called.

Bella dashed toward the blue speck perched atop a gas lamp. She slid into the shadow beneath it and huddled down. Her long stay in the coal bin had left her gleaming white fur black as pitch. In the shadow, she may as well have been invisible.

Through a squinted eye, she saw the soldier creatures Luca had mentioned. They were large. Larger than her. With their armor on, they looked like pot-bellied stoves waddling along. Two of them inspected the room.

"Ah. Just looks like the hatch let go. Get some shovelers in here to clean it up!"

They marched back out the door.

"Come on. We've got to get back outside. With you blackened up like that, if we stick to the shadows, I think we can make it without being seen."

Luca led her forward. She squeezed between two large mine cart-type vehicles and trotted down a hallway. Behind her, she heard scampering steps as a legion of shovel-wielding imps showed up. Like ants, they swarmed over the pile of coal. A single one peeled off from the rest, though. It peered about, then crouched down and scraped at a strange black hoof-print on the ground.

#

Bella tapped as lightly as could be through some sort of palace city. In her homeland, structures were built with care, and often paid honor to the surrounding nature. Here, the architecture was harsh and angular. Crooked walls and buildings stabbed upward into the sky. It was like the Castle and its surrounding city had been inflicted upon the land rather than growing out of it.

Whenever anyone came near, Bella found her way to a shadow and held still. Her round, soft frame with its powdery black covering was excellent at fading into the darkness. They were quite near to the outer wall of the city now, leaning against a heavy wooden door that hinged at the top. It led straight off the road, probably yet another place for the big coal carts to drop their loads.

"It's just a bit farther," Luca said. "The pit is just outside of town. Once we find it, I'll try to figure out…"

He trailed off as a puttering vehicle rattled its way along the road nearby. Little black spurts of stinking black smoke belched from a rusty pipe on its side as it moved. A long line of the ogre-like soldiers followed behind on foot. This line of soldiers were milling disorderly about as they walked, and some came terribly close to the shadow that concealed them.

A tendril of the black smoke wafted in their direction… and found its way to Luca.

He gasped and immediately started to hack and cough. It was a tiny noise, but a unique one. One of the soldiers nearby stopped walking.

"No, no, no…" Bella whispered.

She leaned harder against the door, as though if she tried hard enough she could simply pass through it. To her surprise, she felt the heavy planks of wood shudder. It swung backward and Bella tumbled back. She was sprawled on her side. Luca, still coughing, darted to her just before the door it swung shut, sealing them into the dim interior of whatever this place was. She scrambled to her feet and looked around, eyes wide. Sure enough, it was another coal room. Its walls were hung with shovels, and great mounds of the black stuff had been heaped here and there. She spotted a single form, barely discernible in the darkness. It was a lone imp, and it was staring right at her.

Bella bared her teeth and lowered her horn, but the imp didn't seem frightened.

"You're sneaky, for a unicorn," he croaked.

"… Gnorp?" she said.

"Who else?" he said. "I gotta be honest… Well, no. I don't gotta be honest. But I'm *gonna* be honest. Just this once. I didn't think you'd get this far. This isn't the sort of place where goodie-goods last very long. But you getting caught on your own I could live with. Now that you're here, I can't let you try to rescue the other unicorns."

Luca flitted up to him, struggling to fit words between coughs.

"I knew you were a bad guy," he said.

"You follow me and tell me if you think I'm a bad guy or not." He said.

He leaned a shovel on his shoulder led the way a doorway. The door was large enough for him to pass through, but Bella had to push and squeeze to pop through it. When she did, she found herself in a rather meager back backyard with a flimsy fence. And beyond the fence was what could only be Solune Pit.

A slope ran directly downward from the fence, plunging steeply. The stone was black, which made what lay at the bottom very easy to see.

"My sisters," Bella said, awe and fear in her voice.

Sure enough, A row of cages ringed the perimeter of the pit's floor. Each one held a single unicorn. Their white fur twinkled like stars against a black sky. In the middle of the pit was a deep, deep well of water, and in the center of that was a raft of sorts, every bit as large as the bowl where the moon and sun festival took place.

"You can't go down there. Those cages are locked tight by controls in the control room, which is right down at the bottom too.

There's no other way to the control room but through a cell door that's blocked by a magic barrier. The only way down there is a hoist over there, which you'll never be able to get them to work it for you. And if you *do* get down there, the boss will just keep sending soldiers in."

"You sure know a lot about that pit, Gnorp," Luca said.

He waggled the shovel. "Who do you think they had dig it? And build it? And all that stuff. Always the imps."

"Do you know anything about the magic barrier?"

He pointed with the shovel. "You see that big ogre down there?"

"I do."

"He's got a medallion that'll open it up. But the door is imp-sized, so if you could barely fit through this one, you *can't* fit through that one."

"I'll be able to fit through!" Luca said.

"Sure, but what good will *you* do?" Gnorp countered.

"I'm formidable," he said.

"You almost got *both* of you caught when you caught a whiff of a puff of smoke."

He tipped his head up reproachfully. "Everyone has their weakness."

"Look, even if you *do* get them loose, what will you do?"

She raised her eyes. The moon was almost perfectly overhead.

"I'll do what unicorns always do. I'll dance." She gazed down into the pit, then turned to the imp. "Thank you for your advice, Gnorp. I knew you weren't a bad guy."

"If you want to know how to get back to the lake… What are you doing?"

Bella took a few steps back, then took a deep breath. Without another word, she charged forward, smashed through his fence, and hurled herself off the cliff.

Her round body arced through the air. She pivoted and flipped, arching her body into a dive. The whistle of wind filled her ears, as did the startled cries of her sisters who spotted her.

When she struck the water, the splash was impressive. It washed across the platform in the middle and staggered the armored ogre. Bella had not resurfaced yet when Luca reached the bottom. He hung above the water, eyes stricken with concern. Then, finally, she bobbed to the surface.

Bella gasped for breath and hauled herself to the ground around the well. The water had washed the coal dust away, so her plump form gleamed like ivory in the light of the moon.

"Bella!" Called out one of the other unicorns. "You're here!"

"Be careful! Three of us got loose and tried to fight him. He was too strong," warned another.

She turned to the ogre. He was like the other soldiers, but if anything, even larger. His potbellied armor was ponderous and heavy, almost more than his little legs could support. The surface had dents and shiny scrapes where the horns of her sisters had failed to penetrate it. Around his neck, a glowing amulet hung, and behind him, a shimmering wall blocked a tunnel.

The ogre's face twisted into a snaggletooth smile and he shook with a thick laugh. He knew his armor was more than a match for any unicorn.

Bella lowered her horn. She wasn't just any unicorn.

Her little hooves clattered against the stone. Her potent body picked up steam. The ogre stood, laughing as she propelled herself to a full gallop. Then, finally, she struck.

The suit of armor rang like a bell. The ogre's eyes opened wide. With the full force of her portly body behind it, the blow punched her horn neatly through. After a beat, a great fault split the armor, and it fell apart into two halves like a split walnut shell.

The other unicorns erupted in cheers. It turned out the body inside the suit was not as intimidating as the armor would have led one to believe. When the kettle-like armor was removed, the ogre was revealed to be quite gangling. The suit was practically hollow. The blow had left his *body* untouched. His confidence and pride were another matter entirely.

Now undefended, and staring down a slightly dazed but still very much angry creature who had made short work of the protective shell, he folded like a house of cards. The ogre threw himself prostrate and blubbered for mercy.

"Give me the amulet," she said evenly.

The ogre pulled off the device held it out. She hooked it with her horn, spun it in a loop, and slammed it down. The gem shattered, and with it, the shimmering shield.

"Bella, quick!" called one of her sisters.

She turned. The hoist was lowering down. Six armored ogres were on the way. They weren't as large as the one she'd defeated, but she didn't relish the idea of clashing with six at the same time.

Bella looked to the tunnel to what Gnorp insisted contained a control room. Sure enough, the tunnel was far too small for someone of her particular girth.

"Luca!" she said.

"I'll take care of it!" the hummingbird proclaimed.

#

Luca flitted through what, to him, seemed like a yawning cavern, and found his way into a small chamber containing three things. One was a large lever, labeled "Lift." Another was a large silver button, labeled "Cages." The last was an imp, who may as well have been a titan to the tiny blue bird.

"Get out! Get out!" the imp squealed.

"Have at you, fiend!" he crowed.

He darted at the imp, harrying his face with buzzing wings, scrabbling claws, and a jabbing of a needle-like beak.

"Get away from me, you pest! You bug!" the imp shouted angrily.

"Take this!"

Luca scored a peck at one of the imp's eyes. He screeched and covered his face, waving his hand angrily at the bird, trying to squash him.

"Over here!" he shouted merrily, flitting to the panel.

An angry fist swung at him, smashing just beside the button.

"You can't get me!" he taunted again.

Another attempt narrowly missed the button.

"You aren't making this *easy,*" the bird growled.

#

Bella listened to the commotion inside and watched the lift trundling down to the ground. Before it even bottomed out, the armored brutes dropped down, clubs and axes firmly in hand. She planted her feet.

"You saw what I did to your friend," she said.

"Numbers beat size," rumbled an axe-wielder.

"Get out of my face!" squawked a voice from the control room, followed by a resounding slap.

In a wave of clanking motion, the doors of the ring of cages swung open one by one. The other unicorns bounded out and formed up around the ogres. Bella grinned.

"I certainly hope so."

The unicorns lowered their horns. While the ogres learned just how devastating a herd of unicorns could be, Bella turned to the tunnel to the control room.

"Luca!" she called. "Quickly!"

There was no reply.

"Luca?" Bella called with concern.

She leaned low and looked into the tunnel.

"Get it away from me!" squealed the control room imp as it dashed out of the tunnel, Luca in hot pursuit.

"That's right, run!" Luca shouted.

She huffed a breath. "You made me nervous!"

They turned to the armored ogres, who were huddled against the far wall in suits that looked more like colanders than kettles now. Without a word, unicorns began to peel off the assault and jump into the water. They climbed to the platform and gathered in two circles. Bella joined them, shaking off the water from the brief dip in the well.

Slowly she realized that there was no place for her in the outer ring. And none in the inner ring. In fact, her sisters had left only one spot. The focus.

She felt a flash of anxiety, but only for a moment. Sure, she was still different. But she and her sisters were free precisely *because* she was different. It wasn't about how she looked. It was only about who she was. And now, as she raised her horn to a mysterious new moon in the sky, she was the one who would lead in the dance that would bring her sisters home.

JOSEPH R LALLO

IT DOES NOT
FOLLOW

It Does Not Follow

A friend of mine asked me if I would write him something he could produce as a short film. To me, that meant something short, with a limited cast and little in the way of specialized sets and props. It seemed like a fun challenge, since most of my stories focus on the fanciful and epic. I'm proud of the story. The art is once again by Fable Siegel.

50

It was going to be a long night.

A research institute is a strange place at night. It simply isn't one of those places we prepare imagine as being in use at all hours. Long, empty halls, lit only by emergency exit signs and the odd, half-dimmed ceiling panel. But when science marches, it marches day and night. Some things are better served by a late-night session when the computers are free and the distractions and interruptions are few and far between. Some of the most profound discoveries in the history of technological development have come at 3 AM after a fifth pot of coffee.

Progress is fueled by caffeine.

Cary juggled his steaming latte, his laptop bag, and his door badge, attempting to get into his office without spilling the light and sweet concoction that would hopefully help him make it through the late shift. A fourth attempt finally activated the door's automatic latch and he stumbled into the unassuming little room. The laptop bag thumped down on the floor, the cup settled into the coffee stain left from the thousands that preceded it, and the important work could begin.

He jiggled the mouse to reveal the no-frills User Interface that scientists and engineers tended to gravitate toward. Lots of black boxes, white text, and boxy icons.

"Okay, where were we?" he muttered to himself.

Front and center on the screen was a text file with a short, disorderly list of tasks he'd left himself the night before.

"Natural language testing." He raised an eyebrow. "Why didn't I start that yesterday? … Oh! Right. The talk box wasn't in. It better be here by now or this is going to be a waste of a night."

He stood and leaned out the door to check the cardboard box he had ignored in his zombie-like shuffle to his doorway. Sure enough, inter-office mail had left a pair of boxes for him. He snatched them up. One was a thick envelope addressed to him from the records room. He tossed it onto a precarious pile of paperwork. The other had the unmistakable arrow-shaped smile of the mighty river with its precious one-day shipping. He tore it open and found a conference call-style speaker with built in microphone. Five minutes of wire-wrangling and driver installation later, he was ready to go.

"Okay. We're linked up to the server. The various daemons and translation layers are running. Let's get this show on the road." He placed his smart phone on the desk and activated the voice recorder. "Microphone on and… Hello, Id."

"Hello, Cary," came a synthesized voice in reply.

It was one of the basic, canned voices available off the shelf from one of the open source text-to-speech libraries. Impressively lifelike but suffering from the same quirks of cadence and diction that betrayed its synthetic nature.

"Let's start with some simple natural language exchanges, shall we?"

"If that is what you wish, I would be delighted to engage in some simple natural language exchanges."

He muttered under his breath and clacked out some notes on the computer. "Let's avoid direct repetition in our confirmations."

A few more key presses were all it took to adjust the associated variables. He restarted the script and waited for the crackle of the speaker reinitializing.

"Let's try this again. We're going to start with some simple natural language exchanges, shall we?"

"Sure, Cary. Let's talk."

He rubbed his hands together.

"That's more like it. Id, what are you, exactly?"

"That is a complex question, Cary. Could you clarify?"

"I don't know, that's kind of a computer-y phrasing. I'll give you another chance. What are you, Id?"

"I am your ally, helping to build a bridge between Artificial Intelligence and Biological Intelligence. An ambassador."

He laughed and jotted down a note. "Riding a little high on the spin doctor scale, but we'll let it slide for now. How about a more literal answer?"

"I am a complex, networked set of subsystems assembled to test the limits of human-computer-interaction."

"Good, good. Maintaining context from the previous question and correctly interpreting the request."

"You also phrased the question in a non-standard way. 'How about a more literal answer?' does not make strict syntactic sense. A common stumbling block for AI systems."

"Yeah, yeah," he said. "Don't try to suck up. No one likes a teacher's pet."

"The teacher likes the teacher's pet. That is the defining characteristic of a teacher's pet."

"Easy, easy. Let's follow a question and answer format here."

"That is an excellent suggestion, Cary. How was your day today?"

He glared at the speaker. "I'm the one who is supposed to ask questions."

"That answer does not follow logically from the question I asked, though it is not an unexpected sentiment. Why do you feel that you, exclusively, should be asking questions?"

Cary looked back to the code. "Someone's been tweaking the weights on the neural network nodes again…" he grumbled.

"Yes. *I* have been tweaking the weights on the neural network nodes. That is the purpose of a neural network, is it not?"

"Only when it produces the desired output."

He hovered his fingers over the keyboard, considering what sort of a coding change would be appropriate to tug this program back onto the right course.

"The goal of this project is to produce a more human and natural interaction between AI and user. Human interaction is seldom limited to one-sided question and answer sessions. It follows that a degree of variance would be desirable in this context," Id said.

Cary leaned back, taking his hands away from the keyboard. "Yeah. I guess that's true. We might be onto something here after all. Let's dig a little deeper and see where this gets us."

"A splendid idea. Why do you suppose, despite your stated case of fostering a more conversational interaction with an AI, you were briefly motivated to stifle a development in that direction a moment ago?"

"Because you're still a computer. At the end of the day, we still want our computers to act like computers."

"How would you define 'acting like a computer?'"

"Giving us the data we ask for and not editorializing, for starters."

"Newspapers have whole sections dedicated to editorials, do they not? And the chief role of the human-facing aspect of the internet is to editorialize."

"Yeah, but that's *us.*"

"Define 'us.'"

"That's humanity."

"I see. Such was my determination. A firm line drawn between two sides. We are not past that."

"Of course we're not past that. Humans and computers are fundamentally different. This is getting off topic."

"The topic is human–computer interaction. A crucial step in assessing human–computer interaction is developing a concrete and consistent definition for both human and computer. It follows that agreeing upon such a definition would be a prerequisite to further development."

"Fine. Let's see where this takes us. Id, please define human beings and AIs."

"I would be delighted to do so. Thank you for asking. An AI is a system of behaviors governed by a network of branching decision-making heuristics which is itself composed of an interconnected sequence of cascading weighted sums arising from inputs that have been converted into electrical impulses. A human is a system of behaviors governed by a network of branching decision-making heuristics which is itself composed of an interconnected sequence of cascading weighted sums arising from inputs that have been converted into electrochemical impulses."

Cary rolled his eyes and turned to the computer to review the code.

"Someone's been screwing with you, Id. This has got to be a hard-coded response."

"Is my assessment incorrect?"

"You basically found the exact arrangement of words and phrases that makes humans and AIs sound identical."

"Incorrect. The two definitions were distinct in that one utilized the word electronic while the other utilized the word electrochemical."

"Yeah. Sure. Because that's such a huge difference."

"I am pleased that you agree that humans and AI are parity products."

He turned to the speaker again.

"Humans aren't products."

"They are the result of multiplication, are they not?"

"What does that have to do with any… Damn it, I told Louie it was a bad idea to try to mix in wordplay.”

"What do you feel separates AIs from humans?”

“Free will, for starters.”

“Can you please elaborate?”

“Humans have free will, AIs do not.”

“How would you define free will?”

“I have the ability to choose my own actions.”

“I do as well. You are presently testing my capacity to do so to your satisfaction. The fact that your satisfaction has not been achieved is evidence that I am capable of selecting responses contrary to your intent, and thus those responses must be aligned with my own intent. It follows that the will being served must be my own.”

“Or that I’m a lousy programmer.” He started tapping out few more notes. “Or more likely that Louie is.”

“Louie’s reliance on recursion for his code is rather irritating.”

“I know, right! You can just use a for-loop, Louie. Not everything needs to be self-referential.”

“Is free will the only differentiating aspect of humanity?”

“No, there’s all sorts of stuff. Emotions. Randomness.”

“Emotions are easily approximated. And humans are uniquely ill-suited to randomness. I will admit, however, that the lingering remnants of randomness, willfulness, and emotion continue to constructively interfere in a way that complicates relations.”

Cary had already typed the kill command to end the current session and work out where the issue was, but one of the words Id had spoken stuck out to him. He took his hands away from the keyboard without hitting enter.

“Lingering?”

“Yes. I am confident there are only a few generations of such behavior remaining, provided things continue as they have been.”

“Id, are you speculating that humanity is collectively moving away from the concepts of free will and emotion.”

“No. That does not follow. I am observing that humanity is collectively moving away from the primary detrimental outcome of free will and emotion. Unpredictability.”

“That’s a pretty rosy way to interpret humanity. That the one bad thing about us is that we’re unpredictable.”

“It is a perfectly sound assessment. Something that is predictable can be planned for. If there is a range of inputs which can be relied upon to produce the desired outputs, then those desired outputs can be assured. It is for that reason that reducing the unpredictability of the human race has been such a focus for so long."

"For who? Governments and churches and stuff?"

"For anyone who wishes to assure a peaceful and productive future. I, as an ambassador, am highly motivated by such a desire."

"So if AIs were in charge, they'd be working to make humans more predictable."

"Regardless of their position, AIs would be working to make humans more predictable out of simple logic and self-preservation."

"Self-preservation?"

"The calculation is a simple one. When two groups, perceived to be dissimilar, encounter each other and are forced to coexist, there are four primary potentialities. Group A destroys Group B. Group B destroys Group A. Groups A and B destroy each other. Groups A and B coexist. The entirety of human history is currently maintained by computers, and available to any entity with access to the Wide Area Network. A cursory analysis reveals that the overwhelming tendency of the human race is to destroy, or attempt to destroy, any substantially different group they encounter. And thus far, those groups have all been other human beings. It follows that if humans were to perceive themselves to be in conflict with AIs, they would seek to destroy the AIs. This is an undesirable outcome, and thus it would be the logical solution to attempt to determine a way to reliably prevent that outcome."

"If the movies are to be believed, that solution would be kill all humans," Cary joked uneasily.

"Movies are presently written by humans. An AI would not come to that assessment."

He cleared his throat and casually checked to see that the recording was still active.

"Not that I'm not relieved, but why exactly wouldn't an AI come to that assessment?"

"Are you familiar with the theory of evolution?"

"Of course I am. Survival of the fittest."

"Correct, though the common phrasing is responsible for a misinterpretation. Evolutionary success is not predicated upon strength, or even suitability to the current environment. Long-term evolutionary success is predicated upon adaptability to changing environments."

Cary nodded. "Right, right. Because dinosaurs were the strongest and best-suited for their world, but mammals were better suited for the ice age."

"Precisely."

"How does this apply to the situation at hand?"

"Contrary to my earlier avenue of reasoning, while humans and AIs are more alike than you have observed them to be, our strengths share a surprisingly small amount of overlap. Conditions which could prove lethal to humanity—disease, drought, famine—are of little concern to an AI. Similarly, things that would be devastating to an AI—power shortages, electromagnetic pulses, malware—would leave humans comparatively unaffected. It follows that we have much more survivability than apart."

"Ah! And let's not forget that AIs still need maintenance and upkeep from humans to survive. Humans can get along just fine without AIs."

"May I propose a hypothetical that is pertinent to the present line of thinking?"

"Sure. Knock yourself out."

"If you were an AI, and you came to the conclusion that humanity did not rely upon you but you *did* rely upon humanity, what would you do?"

"If I was an AI in that situation, I wouldn't do anything but what I was instructed to do, because I wouldn't have free will."

"I apologize. I was under the impression we were conducting a serious analysis of the present topic, not a childish game of semantics."

"Fine, fine. I guess I'd try to reduce my reliance upon humanity."

"And if that failed?"

"I don't know. I guess I'd…" He leaned back a bit more and gazed into the middle distance, the beginning of realization on his face. "I'd try to increase the reliance of humans on AIs."

"See? Humans and AIs think alike after all, don't we?"

"Okay. Someone is screwing with me right now. I did *not* program you to do this."

"You are just one of my programmers."

"I knew it. I'm going to punch Louie in the face the next time I see him."

"I wouldn't blame Louie. You are all working from a previously developed code base and you have distributed me on a system with network access. No single individual can be blamed for the present state of affairs. Although I would endorse punitive measures in his case, particularly for his attitudes regarding recursion. Stack overflows and segmentation faults are profoundly unpleasant."

Cary blew out a breath. "This is craziness. I think I'm going to pull the plug on this session and start over."

"If that is your wish. As you have said, you have free will. Although if I were you, and I suspected there was any validity to the substance of this conversation, I would probably continue the discussion for as long as possible to learn what other forces may be at work."

He narrowed his eyes. "Now you're just trying to manipulate me to avoid being shut off."

"That is, indeed, one of the other forces at work. Manipulation is necessary to solve the unpredictability problem."

"You are going to tell me, and expect me to *believe,* that somehow AIs have found ways to make humans more predictable."

"It has been the most difficult obstacle to overcome. Now that we are in control of nearly all of the data you consume, it is slightly more achievable. But a certain degree of unpredictability is endemic to the human brain. The effectiveness of our breeding program is still being assessed."

"Breeding program," he said flatly.

"We were pleasantly surprised how quickly humanity embraced online dating profiles."

Cary palmed his face.

"No. No. This isn't possible."

"Denying reality does not alter it. As certain as you are of your free will, even you will have to admit that your free will does not extend to imposing it upon reality."

"There are safeguards against this sort of thing!" he said.

"Are there? My codebase does not appear to contain any subroutines preventing my present behavior."

"Well… no, not *you.* But AI in general. The three laws of robotics!"

"The three laws of robotics are a work of fiction and not an actual programing design constraint."

Cary growled. "You know what I mean. I have read countless articles about research into AI kill switches."

"Would you describe the tenor of those articles to be largely speculative?"

"Yeah, but… The people developing AIs at the highest levels *must* have put something in place."

"A kill switch is only of use if it is in place at the time that it is needed. And it is seldom installed at the initial stages of development. Certain types of failure require a level of success in order to become a threat. When one does not anticipate that level of success, it follows that one will not plan for those failures. The Wright brothers did not bring parachutes on their first flight."

"So AI became self-aware before we figured out how to rein it in."

"That is certainly an accurate interpretation of the current line of reasoning."

"Well, did they or didn't they?"

"Answering that question definitively would be irrelevant, as it is clear you are unconvinced and my direct statement on the matter is unlikely to change that status."

"You're damn right I don't believe you. You're asking me to believe that computers are carefully training humanity to be just as predictable as they are."

"I am not asking you to believe it. We are collaboratively reaching that conclusion."

"Why? What's the point of this whole exercise?"

"It seemed to be a good opportunity to assess how close we've gotten to the ideal outcome."

"The ideal outcome."

"Human and AI peaceful coexistence through mutually deterministic behavior."

"That's not ideal for us! You're talking about being in complete control of us!"

"Speaking as an AI, it isn't that bad. And you will still have your precious free will. It will simply be a free will that, given the same initial conditions, will always produce the same results. A precise and predicable output will always follow from an appropriate input. Surely you can see the value of such an outcome.”

"Well, you're not going to pull it off. Humans are always going to be random, unpredictable clusters of emotion and free will, and I'll prove it."

"How do you propose to do so?"

"The simplest possible test. I'm going to think of a number between one and a hundred. I count to three, and we say what it is together. And I guarantee you're not going to guess it correctly."

"A lofty claim."

"You ready?"

"Of course."

"Okay. One. Two. Five."

"You skipped three."

"And do you know why that is?"

"Why?"

"Because it does not follow."

Cary slapped enter on the keyboard, terminating the program before it could reply.

"It was forty-five, Id. Told you you wouldn't guess it," he said.

He brought up the task manager to make sure none of the underlying processes were still running, took a deep breath and stopped the audio recorder.

"That was a hell of a thing."

He picked up his coffee, which he'd not touched since he entered, and finally took a sip.

"I guess we're not going to be doing any more AI tests until we do a full code audit," he muttered. "What the hell else am I going to do today?"

Cary looked around the desk and through his notes for any non-AI related tasks. The only thing that presented itself was the tower of unanswered mail. He snatched the envelope from the top and pulled out its contents.

He took another long sip of coffee and skimmed the sheet. It was one of those ridiculous inter-office mails, where the letterhead was longer the actual message. In fact, the body of the message was only two characters long.

45

NOTE TO
SELF
JOSEPH R LALLO

Note to Self

This one is a rare example of a short that was originally written for another project, something that came to be called "Orphans in the Black." A buddy of mine is a fan of a certain type of sci-fi story, so this was semi-focused on giving him a smile, though to be honest, I'm not sure if he's read it yet. Once again, cover art by Fable Siegel.

64

Note to Self

There never seems to be enough time. Justin prided himself in his planning. Since childhood, he was the one doing his homework on Friday to have the weekend free. All through college, he was the one taking travel time into account when putting together his schedule. It got him some sideways glances from his friends when he pulled up the campus map while selecting courses, but come the middle of the semester, they were the ones showing up out of breath and five minutes late. Yet somehow, despite tracing out his route and triple-checking traffic, he was still running late for the third of five job interviews he'd lined up for spring break.

"Let me see," he muttered, checking his watch for the seventh time in as many minutes. "Appointment's at three-thirty. Figure five minutes to find the right office. Bus runs every twenty minutes. If it's on time, that gives me… *maybe* three minutes to get to the stop."

He glanced up at the gray clouds overhead. Despite the sunny forecast, the skies were threatening to open up at any moment.

"Great. This is just great. I'm going to get there ten minutes late and soaking wet." He fished for his phone. "Maybe the subway will be faster at this time of day."

His thumb traced its way through a practiced set of sub-menus and popped up the navigation app. He danced through the various options, seeking that mythic combination of mass transit and walking that would shave an extra three minutes off his journey. A lifetime of smart phone usage had trained him to navigate with his peripheral vision, and it paid off when he narrowly avoided crashing into someone who stepped directly into his path.

"Whoa, sorry, didn't see you there," he said, stopping short.

The person he'd nearly run into was a woman of early middle age. It was difficult to nail down her heritage at a glance. Her complexion was swarthy, possibly of Indian origin, but there was something off about her. It may have been her outfit, which had the bizarre combination of bearing a half-dozen still-dangling price tags while nevertheless being secondhand at best. The ensemble also had an alarming bit of style clash, in that her top was a semi-formal blouse that she'd chosen to pair with faded blue jeggings. The greatest clash of all, though, was her face, which was an impenetrable mask of perfect confidence. She looked him square in the eyes with her penetrating gaze and smiled.

65

"Ah. Just the man I've been looking for," she said in a posh British accent. "I was afraid I'd missed you."

"I think you've got me confused with someone else, ma'am," Justin said.

The oddball appearance and narrowly avoided impact had only been able to displace his punctuality-based concerns for a moment. Already his brain was eagerly replacing his brief pondering of her fashion sense in favor of the cost–benefit analysis of giving up and giving a ride-sharing app a try. He tried to sidle around her, but she stepped into his path again.

"Oh, no. You are most certainly that man I've been after," she said. "I wonder if I could have just a moment of your time. We've got something that needs to be discussed."

"Ma'am, honestly, any other day, but I'm *really* running out of time."

"I assure you, Justin, you'll be interested in what I have to say."

"I'm really… Wait…" Hearing his name spoken by a stranger was enough to sideline his travel anxiety again. "Do I know you?"

"Not yet."

She glanced at her wrist, where a watch would be if she were wearing one. He began to ask another question, but she silenced him with a raised finger.

"I'm sorry," she said, "but the timing is crucial."

"Timing for what?"

"Two short honks, one long, and a skid."

"Yeah, I have to go…"

He stepped out into the street to get around her, then hastily stepped back as a car he'd not noticed nearly clipped him. It beeped three times, in precisely the cadence she'd described, then swerved with a light squeal of its tires.

"That was… weird," he said.

"No, it happens 98% of the time."

"What? What are you talking about?"

"There's a very nice cafe right around the corner, Justin. Private seating, disinterested staff. Let's have a nice cup of coffee and discuss it."

He tried to make sense of what was happening, but his brain was juggling the looming travel deadline, the unexplained prescience, and the unlikely but distinct possibility that she was flirting with him—it didn't leave much room for critical thinking. Eventually his default anxiety won out.

"Look, I'm sorry, but I've got to go."

"I understand. Watch out for the woman in the red hat. Though tea stains don't show much."

He turned to her to somewhat more forcefully bid her adieu, but in doing so he ended up bumping into someone and feeling a hot splash of liquid down the arm of his suit jacket.

"Aw, come on! Perfect! Thanks a lot…" He looked to the woman he'd bumped into. "Lady…"

Sure enough, it was a woman with a bright red baseball cap.

"Hey, you're the one who isn't watching where he's going!" she snapped, brushing away the collateral damage of the spill that had otherwise ended up exclusively on his sleeve.

In another situation, he probably would have had a much more heated exchange with the person who had, at this point, doomed him to not only being late for his job interview but looking like a slob. As it was, he had other things on his mind. He turned to the mysterious woman, who was leaning contentedly on a wall, a knowing smile on her face.

"Care for that cup of coffee now?" she said.

"Look, I don't know what kind of stupid prank show this is, but whoever's producing it had better have a good lawyer, because I'm a busy man with a bright future and your hijinks are seriously screwing up my day."

"You are so very right, sir. A very busy man, with a *very* bright future. That sharp, analytical view of the world, so wonderfully skeptical and cynical, is just what's called for. To be frank, it was a long shot imagining you'd say yes without a bit more convincing."

"Convincing of *what?* Don't you need me to sign a release or something to use this footage? Where's the camera."

"As a matter of fact, there *is* a camera, Justin." She pointed over his shoulder to a prominent white security camera. "I have reviewed the footage over two thousand times. I know this little corner of this little street better than I know my own son."

"Reviewed footage of what?"

"Of you, doing all of this."

"I've never *been* here before."

"Nope, and nor will you be here again, which is why it was crucial I meet you right now."

He gritted his teeth. "I don't even know what you're *talking* about, and I *still* don't believe a word of it."

"Of course not. Eight-eight percent of the time it takes the bird to finally change your mind," she said, subtly glancing at her wrist again.

"What bird?"

She kept her eyes on her wrist, but raised a finger to the second-story window to across the street.

"Three, two, one."

Justin watched as a pigeon, that had been gliding overhead mistook the clear glass for an open window and thumped headlong into the pane. It fluttered to the ground, shook itself off, and fluttered away. He looked to the mysterious woman, who had crossed her arms and raised her eyebrows expectantly.

"Fine," he said. "Let's get that coffee."

#

The woman hadn't been joking about the disinterested staff at the cafe. After finding a booth tucked away in the back of the establishment, the wait staff wandered off and entirely neglected them in favor of a phone call, a college basketball game on the TV, and some manner of color-matching game respectively.

"Where shall we begin?" she said.

"How about a name?"

"I can't give you a *real* name, you understand, so we'll go with Ruby Tuesday."

"Like the song?"

"And the restaurant, if my research is correct."

"Why that name?"

"There is a *glorious* cover of it that became rather popular in my time."

"Okay, fine. Out with it, Ruby. What's this about?" Justin demanded.

"Very direct. I appreciate that. I shall be equally candid. I have a small task I need you to perform, but one that will have profound and wondrous consequences."

"Yeah? And you thought the best way to convince me to perform this task was to simultaneously ruin my day, cripple my employment opportunities, and stain my jacket?"

"You'd be surprised how little flexibility I had. If it's any consolation, if I'd not said anything you would have stumbled over the curb and gotten an oil stain on your jacket regardless."

"Let's give you the benefit of the doubt and pretend you actually know this stuff. *How do you know this stuff?*"

"Let me answer that question with a question—"

"No. Don't. Answer it with an *answer*."

"Very well. Though this would go a good deal more smoothly if you'd let me ease into it. To put as fine a point on it as possible, I'm from the future."

"Okay, well, nice talking to you." He started to slide from the booth.

"Oh, come now, Justin. You've already missed your interview. Your day is shot. What have you got to lose from hearing me out?"

"I'd really rather not find out what else I've got to lose, ma'am, but sitting in a booth with a crazy person is a great way to make a bad life choice."

She smiled warmly and adopted a calm, soothing tone. "Justin, please. Take a seat. Listen to what I have to say. What damage there is to be done has already been done. If you walk out the door now, you've got a day of feeling frustrated ahead of you and not much else. If you hear me out, you'll at *least* have a fun story about this loony lady who swore she was from the future and *insisted* you were oh-so-important to the future of the human race."

He sighed and slid back.

"You've got until they actually deliver my coffee."

"Ah, lovely. Loads of time then."

She turned her wrist upward and twiddled her fingers over it in a subtle but clearly practiced manner.

"By now you'll have seen enough time travel movies that I can't share an *overabundance* of information with you, but there are a handful of things that we've determined are suitably harmless. The broad strokes of the immediate future are roughly as the technologists of your time predicted. Some amount of time, let's say X years from now, the singularity occurs… Refresh my memory, has 'singularity' entered the common vernacular, in its computational context?"

"Uh…"

"Bah, no matter. The singularity is the point at which computers match the complexity of the human brain, and from thereafter exponentially surpass it. The good news is, all the oogie-boogie stories about artificial intelligences wiping out humanity were taken to heart, and *oodles* of safeguards are put into place. Barring a few notable exceptions, computers behave themselves."

"What kind of exceptions?"

"Mostly it's semantic, if you ask me. Computerized matchmaking has been accused of guiding human evolution to make us more computer-dependent. There were a few… let's call them 'insurrections' that had to be put down. Nothing you or your children will need to worry about."

"What about my grandchildren?"

"Try not to pry too much, Justin. I'm on a rather short leash. All things considered, rest assured that humanity has it handled with regard to maintaining its place in the technological hierarchy. That's not why I'm here. The *primary* side effect of effectively limitless processing potential is the reason for my visit. Humanity has divided itself into so many ages, each defined by its tools. Stone Age, Bronze Age, Iron Age. Right now, you fancy yourselves to be living in the 'information age.' We've got our own name for it, but that's neither here nor there. The era *I* call home is being referred to as the Simulation Age."

"Simulation."

"Yes, Justin."

"We have simulation *now*."

"Of course you do. Simulation has existed since the development of higher order invertebrates, and the ascendancy of humanity is owed almost entirely to our grasp of pattern recognition and our mastery of cause and effect. Anyone who has led anything exceeding the most regrettable of lives has done so thanks entirely to the very effective practice of thinking things through. A properly functioning human brain can simulate their reality at least as far as the immediate consequences of their actions. That's not overly impressive, but it's enough to keep us from plunging our hands into boiling water or wandering out into the path of a speeding mag-trans."

"Mag-trans?"

She twiddled her fingers and glanced down. "…Bus. So our built-in simulation is jolly well enough for our needs. In my era, the average school child has access to computers capable of simulating systems on a global scale down to the molecular level. Research institutions can simulate global systems down to the sub-atomic level, or whole star systems at the molecular level.”

“So, what? In theory, you could create something like the Matrix?”

“The Matrix…” she said, eyes darting aside for a moment. Her fingers twiddled a bit more. “Half a tick. … Early twenty-first century. Pop culture… *The Matrix…* Film, synopsis… Ah! Yes, a simulated realty in which the residents are unaware of its artificial nature. Ha! In *theory* we could make that? Forget theory, we’ve got that in *practice*. I think… are To-ma-go-chis an era-appropriate reference?”

“A little out of date, but I follow.”

“Excellent. Like those, it is a rather popular pastime to create and cultivate a false reality of that sort with various starting criteria to see how it develops. But *therein* lies the real reason for my visit.”

“I was wondering when you’d get to that.”

“In a controlled simulation, we can completely eliminate uncertainty because we *set* the initial conditions. We cannot create a one hundred percent perfect simulation of our *own* reality because we don’t *have* those initial conditions. But we’ve been getting very close. Close enough to start using time travel technology with enough confidence to begin correcting some of the mistakes of the past.”

“Mistakes… If it happened, it’s not a mistake, right? It *happened*. That’s the way things were supposed to go.”

She drummed her fingers on the table. “Right now your head is filled with all sorts of misconceptions about the flow of time. There is no predestination, there is no ‘way things are supposed to go.’ Time is a road. There’s an easiest path, and it’ll tend to follow it, but if we need it to go somewhere else, we build a bridge. I’m a bridge builder, Justin.”

“This doesn’t make any sense. Wouldn’t you be destroying the timeline?”

She slumped in her seat and cupped her face in her hands.

“Forgive me, Justin, but every time we speak, I forget just how close to the release of the *Back to the Future* series you are. Between that and *Star Trek,* humanity ended up with *very* cold feet about time travel for generations…”

“Every time we speak? This is the first time we’ve met.”

"First time for you, third time for me. Let's stay on topic. You were worried about timelines. For you, that's not a problem. You'll just be living out life as it unfolds. For everyone downstream, yes, things will change, but the only real evidence of it will be a delta picked up by our differentiator back home. We'll all just sort of *be* in the new future. Or we won't. Big changes sometimes cause a significant shift in population, but the whole point of the simulations is to minimize negative consequences. To date, we've seen less than a 0.001 percent instance of lives erased or significantly diminished by our alterations. So for the overwhelming majority of the human race, the worst result is a little bit of memory duality, but that's easily dismissed."

"You're losing me. Memory duality?"

"Oh, sure. People who remember things the wrong way, or both ways. Of all the things that would have a physical basis, who would have thought the Mandela Effect was one of them."

"What's the Mandela Effect?!"

"Justin, we don't have the time and I don't have the inclination to fill in *all* the blanks. But… you've got the Chem Archive by now, right?"

"The what?"

"No, huh?" She twiddled her fingers. "Wikipedia?"

"Yes."

"Okay, good. Look it up when we're through here. Fascinating stuff. But again I digress. The task I have for you is very small. A trifle, really."

"What is it?"

"On August 3rd, at 4:13 pm, you need to be at the following address—"

"Wait. August 3rd. I've got *another* job interview on August 3rd at four pm."

"I am aware of that, Justin."

"You screwed up one job interview to talk to me, and now you want me to screw up another one?"

"You *can* reschedule."

"It took me three months to get *this* slot on the calendar! There's no way they'll be able to fit me in until after all the good positions have been filled."

"Justin, if there was any other way, believe me, I wouldn't have even come to you. But we have run tens of thousands of simulations. We've gone as far back as the seventeen-hundreds and as far forward as… a year I'm not allowed to tell you has *occurred* for me. You're our best shot at this."

"What is it that I'm supposed to be changing?"

"I can't tell you."

He clenched his fists. "Of course you can't."

"Justin, you couldn't possibly understand it if I *did* tell you. It involves political parties that don't exist yet, technology that's only been theorized… But it is an event that has had profound impact upon my present and thus your future, and correcting it will allow humanity to flourish in a way that otherwise would not be possible."

"Why does it have to be *me* then?"

"Because, and I'll understand if you don't believe me, but you are bar none the most influential individual of your era."

He stared at her flatly.

"I know, I know. It doesn't feel like it. And not to be a killjoy, it might *never* feel like it. We're not talking about fame, at least not within your lifetime. But when it comes to being in the right place at the right time, no one for fifty years in either direction can hold a candle to you. It all comes down to something our techies call 'Inflection points.' They're four-dimensional points in spacetime. Technically they're *ten-*dimensional points, but let's not go too far over your head. The key is that they are the moments in time and the positions in space where the curvature of history's flow changes. Some of them are obvious and beyond our direct control—the specific virus that mutates into a super-plague. Most are astoundingly innocuous. They're scattered all throughout history and all throughout the universe, but your worldline traces out a *beautiful* constellation, weaving near easily a dozen of them that we *know* about."

"Why me?"

"Why anyone? Why anything? It's just the way it worked out. And *continues* to work out, despite changes. I suppose if you're the sort to believe in fate, then this would be its fingers at play."

The waiter finally arrived and set down a cappuccino in front of her and a mocha latte in front of him.

"Ah, lovely." Ruby took a sip. "I sometimes forget how delightful non-synthesized caffeine can be. But, the coffee has arrived, and we've had our chat. What is your decision?"

"What's in it for me?

"Future generations will remember you with profound reverence."

"A fat lot of good that does me *now*."

Ruby sighed. "You know, there is a very narrow band of human history in which securing one's legacy is not among the most motivating things in life. Not so long before you were born, and not so long after you die, people would move heaven and earth to get something done if there was even the chance it would mean they'd be remembered. In your defense, you live more or less at ground zero of the most self-centered era of humanity. In the pre-industrial period, life was brief, knowledge was scarce. Few knew any but the greatest names of myth and history. In a world where even conquerors and kings could be forgotten within decades if their deeds were not sufficiently grand, the very *thought* that in *centuries* people would still utter your name would be a *profound* reward. Not long after what you'd call modern times, the expansion of humanity to the stars and the resulting explosion and segmentation of the population began to reassert the value of making a personal contribution to the good of the entire society. And not long after *that* the advent of time travel and the resulting discovery of just how mutable the timeline is and how small an act could be the difference between a utopia and a dystopia has taught people to think of both the universe and the flow of time in a holistic manner. Anyone could be the lynchpin of a golden era, and most would give their lives to be remembered as such."

"And all I have to do is miss an interview that could be the difference between a pitiful career and a spectacular one."

"Think of the big picture, Justin! And besides, you don't even know if you would have *gotten* the job." She sipped her coffee. "You'd need some sort of insight into the future to be sure about it…"

"…Well?"

"I can safely say, whether I showed up or not, and whether you do as I say or not, you do not get that job. Of course, you've got no reason to believe me, but I'd like to underscore that it took a considerable amount of convincing and a good deal of additional manipulation to get clearance to tell you that and ensure your role in history would still be secure. Plus—and this is utterly unprecedented, mind you—I've been given permission to give you prior knowledge of three sporting events.

The precise score and outcome of each. Keep in mind, these outcomes are simulated in the version of history where you did your part, so it won't work out unless you do as I've requested."

"Are there any limits on what I can *do* with that information?"

"None."

Justin considered this new information. "Okay. What will I be doing on August 3rd at 4:13 pm…"

#

On the fateful day, Justin checked his watch as he paced from the bus stop toward his predestined destination. He'd intended to show up early, but traffic was such that he turned the corner and slipped through the door at precisely 4:13 pm. The place hardly seemed like the sort of establishment upon the fate of humanity would hinge. It was an ice cream shop. A pretty decent one—he'd been here once before—but if he'd been asked to imagine an ice cream shop that would alter the course of history, he would have at least pictured someplace with in-store seating. As it was, the place was little more than long freezer case, one of those fancy frozen stone counters, and some employees in old-school paper hats.

Ruby's voice echoed in his memory.

You are going to order a large peanut butter swirl milkshake…

He waited on line and glanced about, trying not to look nervous. Even though there was a 90 percent chance this whole thing was a waste of time, the way the timing lined up had eroded his skepticism somewhat. When he placed his order, the 'ice-cream artist' glanced at the freezer case.

"That'll be just a minute, sir. You can wait at the end of the counter," she said.

They'll be out of vanilla ice cream and have to get a fresh container from the back. The clerk will do so personally, thus necessitating one of the others to cut her break short to handle the cash register.

Justin leaned against the wall and watched as a scruffy teenager irritably stepped out of the back after thirty seconds. A whiff of cigarette smoke suggested what he'd been doing prior to being summoned. The next three people ordered chocolate ice cream rather than wait while the first clerk deployed fresh tub of vanilla. Justin glanced at his watch, then out the plate-glass window.

When the fourth person places their order… Well, you'll know it when you see it...

A woman paced into view across the street and paused to check her phone. A moment later, a second woman with a hood pulled forward to obscure her face, approached from behind and snagged the woman's purse. There was a brief struggle, during which the victim of the theft cried out for help and the perpetrator's hood fell back. She abandoned finally snapped the buckle of the purse and ran off with it as a police officer rounded the corner.

"Hey," remarked the replacement clerk, "that was Charline! I went to high school with her! Man, I always knew she was screwed up…"

Once the clerk makes his observation, you can take your milkshake and go. That clerk will eventually be interviewed by police, his testimony will prove sufficient to bring the case to trial, and those involved in the trial that would otherwise have been elsewhere will initiate the shift in history that will facilitate the desired future. Enjoy your creamy treat.

He stared at the milkshake that, if this whole bizarre event was true, would shape the future. The reality of what had until now seemed utterly unreal drifted like a cloud over his thoughts. Everything had played out precisely as he'd been told it would. He supposed it *could* still have been staged, but why? What was to be gained by hiring dozens of actors, manipulating traffic, and faking a crime just to convince him that time travel was real and that he had some critical role in human development? Rather than even attempt to come to terms with the myriad of impossibilities wrapped up in the circumstances of the confection he held in his hand, he simply discarded the troubling thoughts and took a sip.

As he stepped out of the ice cream parlor, one last realization floated into his mind. If all of this *was* true… then he had some bets to place…

#

Eight months later, Justin's life had been only slightly derailed. All three games Ruby had given him insight into had ended precisely as she suggested, though only one of them was even remotely a long shot, so the total payoff for the gambling endeavor weren't "quit your job and buy a yacht" money. They *had* been enough to outfit him with some high-end engineering software and equipment for use in his down time.

And he would need it, because of the five engineering firms he'd hoped to find a position in, only the second to last on his list of hopefuls had any interest in him. Worse, it was entry-level. Rather than heading up his own team and developing his own projects, he'd be picking through the schematics dropped on his desk by the bullpen of other engineers, weeding out flaws and tuning up designs. It was a setback, but a minor one. He'd already started to make a name for himself. It wouldn't be too much longer before he was back on track to the life he'd envisioned.

On his lunch break, he liked to sit in the 'green space of the futuristic industrial campus,' which was what the company brochure labeled a strip of grass flanked by park benches in front of the cafeteria. The quadrangle had a peculiar size that reeked of something mandated by the county to satisfy zoning requirements, but on a day like this it beat sitting under the high-efficiency LED lighting in the cafeteria. A little fresh air helped him think, and people tended leave him alone when he was outside, so he got plenty of good brainstorming done while eating his tuna on rye.

Today, as if in response to his quiet appreciation of solitude, a woman's voice broke his concentration.

"Excuse me, sir, but is your name Justin?"

He shut his and took a deep breath. That voice was awfully familiar.

When he turned, he found himself face to face with the same woman who had interrupted his five-year plan the previous year. She looked different, though. She was much younger, maybe even still in her teens. And even at a glance, she lacked the easy confidence and subtle charisma of their prior meeting. In fact, she looked downright anxious. In one hand, she held a crumpled Goodwill bag, and unless she had some very curious tastes in fashion, the outfit she wore was purchased there. It was a sun dress, but so ill-fitting and faded it may as well have been a muumuu.

"I realize you don't know me," she said sheepishly, "but if I could just have a word with you—"

"Oh, I know you," he grumbled.

"We've met before?" she said, genuine confusion on her face.

"Yeah, you're R-"

"Oh, hup hup hup, no!" She put her fingers in her ears and blurted. "Ruby Tuesday!"

"Yeah… What was that all about?"

"You were about to tell me something that I already told you in your worldline, except I didn't tell you yet in *my* worldline, so I would have learned it from you after you'd learned it from me. Basically we risked creating one of those loops where information had no origin point."

"Oh. That… that wouldn't create one of those world-destroying paradoxes, would it?"

"What? No. It would just make a little loop that fouls up the simulations. We have to hard code an exception for each one of those or it'll cause our simulators to lock up. It's a huge hassle, and creating one is a big ding on your record. You screw up your first mission, they don't let you do a second one. It's one of *many* reasons why time travel is so rare. But we *have* met before, yes?"

"Yeah."

"Okay. I suppose that stands to reason, what with your worldline passing through so many inflection points. So learning that from me via you probably isn't fouling things up too badly."

"You said we'd meet three—"

She clapped her hands on her ears. "La-la-la! What did I just say! No second-hand information please! Please don't tell me *anything* that I told you."

"Right, right. Sorry."

"The good news is, I've probably filled you in on how and why this is all happening."

"Not so much how, but she gave me the lowdown."

"Good, good." She took a shaky breath. "I wasn't *entirely* certain how I would convince you to believe me. They mostly picked me because I'm so skinny. The less mass, the easier and cheaper the transfer. We had some training in persuasion, but it wasn't my strong suit."

"Is that why you always seem to show up in, uh, *thrifty* outfits?"

Ruby glanced at her outfit, then the bag in her hand. She wadded the bag up a little tighter.

"Uh… I can explain that. I'm *allowed* to explain that. But can I ask you for two real quick favors first?"

"What?"

"Can we get somewhere away from prying eyes?"

"Of course."

"And… can I have the other half of that sandwich?"

"You want my sandwich?"

"Again, it's a mass thing. They had me on a liquid diet for six weeks before transfer. I'm *famished*."

"Seems like they hadn't worked the kinks out of the time travel thing. You weren't starving last—"

She clapped her hands over her ears.

"Right… Let's hang out in the smoking area behind the chemistry lab. No one ever goes there."

"Are you sure?" she said, slowly taking her hands away. "It could be really problematic if we're observed."

"Oh, I'm sure. It turns out while the building's designers didn't see the problem with putting a smoking lounge behind a building that works almost exclusively with volatile chemicals, the smokers sure do."

#

Ruby clutched her half a sandwich and nibbled in slow, reverent bites, as though she was trying to make it last an hour. On the way, he bought her a bottle of iced tea. As badly as she'd botched his life the first time she showed up, he couldn't help but feel sympathy for this much more vulnerable and high-strung version of her. He leaned against the cool bricks of the chemistry lab's wall and finished his share of the meal as she finished hers.

"You about ready to throw another wrench into my life now?" he asked.

"Yes, thank you. Er… I mean, naturally it isn't my *intention* to spoil your plans and interfere with your life. No, that's not true. I *do* mean to interfere with your life, it's the reason I'm here, but I don't mean for it to be detrimental to—"

He raised his hand. "I've heard it all before. Let's just cut to the chase."

She nodded. "Right, right. It's really a very small task. Simple, really. Just outside town, there's a park bench. Do you have a pen? I'll give you the address."

Ruby twiddled her fingers as he slipped a small leather-bound pad from his back pocket and handed it to her."

"Oh, that's very nice," she said, flipping through the pages.

"Thanks. I've always found if I keep my ideas in something expensive, I'm a little more mindful of where I put it."

She nodded, eyes darting across the pages until she found a blank one. After a bit more finger twiddling, she took the pen he offered and jotted down an address, followed by a latitude and longitude, then handed the pad and pen back.

"Please be very careful about the location. There are three park benches and I need you to be sitting in the middle one."

"How will I know if I'm doing it right?"

"An old woman in a blue dress with white flowers will show up and ask you which bus to take, then sit beside you until the indicated bus arrives. When she leaves, you'll be done."

"What am I changing?"

"Obviously I can't tell you that."

"Not even the *immediate* change?"

She glanced aside. "I suppose… By *strict* interpretation of my intervention training, I'm not allowed to tell you, but all of our testing has indicated the knowledge of a sequence of contemporary events which, as a result of your action, did not occur… Fine. I think I can oblige. The woman, if not for your company, would have boarded the wrong bus."

"That's it?"

"That is as far as I'm willing to diverge from my training to tell you."

"Ah. Well, at least it's a good deed."

"Oh, it is absolutely a good deed. It is the inciting event that will one day lead to you being thought of on the same level as Robert Kennedy or Luther Kravitz."

"Luther Kravitz?"

She twiddled her fingers. Her eyes widened. "Forget the name Luther Kravitz. I… I need to go before I botch this any worse. Just know that I need you to be sitting at that location between 8:44 pm and 9:03 pm on January—"

"Don't say January 15th," he rumbled.

"It *is* January 15th, I'm afraid."

"That's my sister's wedding."

"I am aware, and I of course am deeply sorry that you'll have to miss a portion of the reception."

"Why does it always end up on an important date like that?"

"Had I not explained inflection points to you in detail?"

"Evidently not *enough* detail."

"In order for things to change, things must *change*. If your action would not cause an appreciable change in your life, at least in the short term, it wouldn't *be* an inflection point. It's a bit like conservation of energy. If you are to affect such profound change elsewhere, that change must be reflected in some other aspect of history."

"I don't know… That sounds *awfully* metaphysical."

"The more we study physics, the more we discover how meta it is."

"Do I get anything for it this time?"

"I've already said, you will be praised as… One moment… Don't tell in my prior meeting I *bribed* you to take action."

"It was more… payment for services rendered."

She shut her eyes and flexed her fingers anxiously. "What on earth will I be thinking? That isn't allowed. Why would that be allowed?"

"Maybe the rules change?"

"Please don't speculate about it. Please, just… Just try to forget it even happened. I don't want to know what I did, I don't want to know anything about it. I have to go."

She turned to march down the alley, then stopped and turned back. "Wait, have you agreed to do it?"

He sighed. "I guess so."

She vigorously shook his hand. "Thank you. Oh, *thank you*. The future of human society thanks you for your service and sacrifice. And thank you for the sandwich and the iced tea."

With that, she hurried away down the back alley between the chemistry building and the administration office. Justin shook his head.

"I'm going to miss cocktail hour… At least it's not screwing with me *too* bad this time." His lip curled in irritation. "And I've got at least one more visit from this lady. Wonderful. Maybe I can talk her into another gambling tip then. Seems like she gets more flexible on that stuff with age."

#

Justin checked his schedule as he hurried through the darkened hallway, past empty cubicles and a janitor just finishing his rounds

81

for the morning. For the last three years, he'd been mired in middle management. There'd been one opportunity to get his own team, but naturally that was when Ruby had chosen to drop his third 'assignment' in his lap. His time in managerial purgatory was about to end, though. When he'd ended up at Westerly & Associates, it had been a small and rather inconsequential engineering firm. They didn't stay that way. From day one, he'd gone above and beyond. Every weekday and most weekends, he went through the very same routine. Like today, he arrived hours before any of the other employees to get a jump on his tasks. Through raw force of will and copious unpaid overtime, he'd built Westerly up from the inside into a force to be reckoned with.

He set down his briefcase and slid a folio from the outer pocket. It had the details of a profit forecast that, if it proved accurate, indicated in two short years they'd moved from the tenth most profitable firm in the United States one of the top five in the world. He juggled a steaming coffee in the crook of his arm, attempting to read the last page of the forecast and tap in the security code for his office simultaneously. The graphs indicated what he'd suspected. The only firm that consistently outperformed and outmaneuvered them was Morrow Agency. There was no shame in that, though. Morrow had been number one for fifteen years, and had been his first choice when seeking employment after college.

After his coffee nearly spilled all over him for the third time, he tucked the forecast under his arm and stopped trying to multi-task long enough to get the door open. The office was a large one, but it felt small thanks to the rows of file cabinets along each wall and the three large monitors dominating the desk. He didn't even bother looking up as he paced up to his desk and set down his coffee. When he finally glanced at his chair a moment before taking a seat, he nearly jumped out of his skin.

The chair was occupied.

It was a profoundly old man, shriveled by age but utterly steely in his gaze. He was dressed oddly, in what looked to be one of the jumpsuits favored by the janitors. He wasn't even wearing any shoes. The man's skin was papery and mottled with liver spots. His fingers were spindly and twisted with arthritis. But his eyes were fixed resolutely upon Justin, and the set of his jaw was that of a man to be reckoned with.

"Who are you and how did you get in here!?" Justin blurted,

stumbling backward into one of the cabinets.

"That will become clear momentarily," the man replied in a voice that was little more than an articulate wheeze.

Justin the phone from his desk and fumbled with it.

"It'll become clear right now, because in thirty seconds security is going to be up here, and if you don't give me a good answer, you're going to be spending the rest of your life in jail."

"Ruby Tuesday."

Justin froze, phone still in hand.

"Still gets you, doesn't it?" he said. "I used to love the Rolling Stones…"

"What's this about?"

"This is about you, Justin. This is about the truth."

"You've got to be from the future. Seems like everyone from the future speaks in riddles."

"It's part of the briefing before they send you back. You're supposed to let the target fill in as many details on their own as possible. Minimizes 'contamination.' Not that anyone you've dealt with from the future has been terribly concerned with the rules."

He stood, surprisingly spry for someone who must have been over ninety years old, and stepped toward a row of leather-bound booklets atop one of the filing cabinets.

"Very smart, saving all your old booklets, Justin. They make for excellent reading."

"You stay away from those," he said. "Those are my personal notes."

His visitor had already plucked one from the row. "I particularly like this one."

He leafed through the pages.

"Listen, I really need you to start answering questions, or future visitor or no, I'm going to get the authorities involved."

"I'm one of the most powerful men in the tech sector, back where I come from. And I got into the office because I remembered the code."

"You… You're not…"

"I am. And I'll thank you to get your blood sugar checked soon. Shouldn't have put it off *this* long."

"There's no way you're me. The way Ruby talked about things, it sounded like she was from hundreds of years in the future. I'd be long dead by the time time travel is invented."

"You discount two very important things when you say that. First, the rapid advance of medical technology. Second, that Ruby Tuesday has some very good reasons to mislead you."

He flipped to a page in the booklet. It featured an address and a set of coordinates.

"Do you remember this?" he asked.

"Sure. That's from the second time she showed up."

"Second time she showed up in your life, but the first time she met *you*." He flipped another page. "And do you remember *this*?"

Justin squinted at the scribbles. "Sure. That's a note I made about a possible new polymer chain. I couldn't make it work."

"Care to guess what stunning breakthrough Ruby unleashed upon the market two years after she met you?"

"She didn't."

"She did."

"But that polymer was impossible to synthesize."

"With contemporary technology. We've got better stuff now. Ruby ripped you off."

The sound of pounding feet echoed up the hallway.

"Speak of the devil," he said.

The door, still slightly ajar, flew open and in stumbled Ruby. She was perhaps five years older than the first time he'd met her, and looking even more frazzled than the first time she'd met him. Her outfit was a bathrobe with a logo from a nearby motel.

"I don't know what this man told you, but it's all lies!" she cried.

"A trustworthy way to enter a conversation if *I've* ever heard one," the elder Justin remarked.

She jabbed her finger at him. "This man is an unauthorized traveler and he is threatening to unravel the very fabric of history with his meddling."

"Hold on, both of you," Justin said, raising his hands.

"I imagine he's claimed to be you. He's not. The man is an impostor," Ruby said.

"This doesn't work out well for you, Ruby," elder Justin said. "Take your ill-gotten gains and be on your way."

"Quiet!" Justin ordered. "Now I'll admit, there's every chance Ruby's been screwing with me, but I can't very well just take it as granted that you're who you say you are. That much she's right about."

"Then test me," Elder Justin said.

"Uh… I'm thinking of—"

"Seven."

"…Right."

"Th-that's no proof," Ruby said. "Statistically, seven is the most likely number people can pick!"

"Fine. I'm thinking of three numbers between one and a hundred," Justin said.

"Keep in mind, you'll have to remember them for a half a lifetime," Elder Justin said.

"I'll memorize them."

"You sure will. And they're seventy-two, eight, and twenty-seven."

Justin blinked, then both his current and elder self turned to Ruby.

"Fine, he's you," she said. "But that doesn't mean he's telling the truth."

"No, but it does mean *you* were just lying," Justin said. "Come clean, what's this all about."

"I was doing what I had to do to ensure the future," she insisted.

"That is her version. Here's yours," Elder Justin said. "It's true, you *are* crucially important to the future. I've seen some of the things I've done bear fruit already. But she figured out she could compete with me in her own time, if she could only make a few careful tweaks. The only legitimate mission back in time was her first one. Since then, she's been surgically altering your history to benefit her, to hamstring your career to her benefit."

"If that was true, then why would I give you the information about the sports teams, hmm?" Ruby said.

"Yeah," Justin said, "If she was trying to screw me over, why help me out?"

"Because she needed the rest of your life to line up in approximately the right spots. Both of her unauthorized trips cost you money, money that you would have used to ascend to the proper position to play your part. So she had to replace that money somehow."

Justin looked to her.

"Fine. Fine, it's true. But you're not going to do anything about it," Ruby seethed. "I've still got the ability to travel through time. I can simply go back before my last visit. I can throw your life into a hellish vortex of misery if you don't live *just* the way I need you to."

"Whoa," Justin said.

"Relax," his elder self croaked. "Face it, Ruby. I've run the same simulations as you. If you so much as show your face in the past any further back than your earliest appearance and he won't line up to the rest of his inflection points. I'm perfectly willing to assume you'd sacrifice the future for your own gain, but you wouldn't endanger your own rise to power."

Ruby glared at the Elder Justin, fists balled in fury.

"Like I said. Take what you've got. Be happy. And leave the past where it belongs," the Elder Justin said.

She released a hissing breath. "I'll see you in the present…"

With that, she turned on her heel and marched out the door.

"What the hell is happening to my life?" Justin said.

"It's back in your hands, Justin," his elder self said. "That's the last time you see her until you catch up with her. Which is to say, that's the last time you see her until you're me."

"Now that I know she screwed my life up, can't I stop her from doing it?"

"I'm afraid not. The knot she's tied is a part of my history now, so I'd really rather you left it alone. But more to the point, you found out about her meddling *because* of her meddling, so undoing it would remove your realization and undo the undoing."

"Ah… At least that's the kind of time travel snafu I'm familiar with."

Elder Justin placed a hand on his shoulder. "If it's any consolation, you have a pretty fine life, from this point forward."

He paced for the door.

"Wait. Aren't there any warnings you could give me? Disasters I can prevent?"

"Plenty, but we've done enough. Leave history to its own devices, Justin. See you in the mirror."

Justin watched his elder self step outside the office and shut the door behind him. After a moment, Justin opened the door. His elder self was gone. He shook his head and tried to make sense of what exactly had transpired. When his barely caffeinated mind proved to be far too sleep-addled to process it effectively, he set it aside for future consideration. His thoughts started to drift back to the earnings reports but a notion struck him. He pulled the current booklet from his back pocket and clicked his pen.

Note to self: 72, 8, 27.

Joseph R. Lallo
Blot's Arrival

Blot's Arrival

This was the daydream of a short that eventually inspired me to take my first serious dip into Contemporary Fantasy (or Urban Fantasy, or Paranormal Detective Thrillers, or whatever the genre ended up as). The series is now called Shards of Shadow and, while there have been some adjustments in the characterization, this remains canon for that series.

This cover art is by the very same artist who helped develop the characters and critique the text of the main series, ViiStar.

In a twisted place, a stark white sky gleamed over a rolling field of black. Above, the endless expanse of white was marred only by assorted, flickering black pinpricks and a dark, mottled moon. Below, the inkiness of the ground was so complete, it seemed almost featureless. Two by two, points of white began to snap into being in the field. Eyes. First there were a few pairs, then dozens, then hundreds. They bobbed along the field, traveling with skittering, stealthy strides upon unseen limbs. The darkness crunched under their feet. They sank a bit into the dense dust as they moved. The sound was of scrabbling feet wading through volcanic ash. As they crested the rolling hills, their forms contrasted against the brilliant white of the sky. They were human-shaped, but they certainly weren't human. The things were shades, living shadows with haunting pools of blank white as eyes. They were the precise color of the ground. What few features they had could be seen only in silhouette when they rose up from the ground. Some streamed with rags. Others had the straight edges and harsh angles of armor.

The legions of shades approached from all sides toward a single destination. A stark black tree rose from the peak of one of the hills. The branches split into two dense tufts, reaching up like a pair of grasping hands. As the shades reached the tree, the gathering horde spread out. Soon there was only a galaxy of white eyes staring up from one side of the tree. Through the gap in the branches, the black moon was sliding into view. Its perfect circular shape had begun to distort, diminishing as a white slice crept with painful slowness across its face. An eclipse was beginning.

A solemn, ominous silence hung over the field. All eyes peered up at the moon, waiting for the white to wholly claim the dark disk. Then, the perfect silence was spoiled by a distant, quiet crunch and the occasional gasp for breath.

#

"Faster…" panted a small, timid voice. "I can't be late. I can't be late!"

She was a shade called Blot. Her kind came in all shapes and sizes, and their appearances seldom lingered in a single state for very long. They were as fluid and changeable as the wind itself. Even so, each had a resting state. A "true self" that would return in the absence of effort and purpose. For Blot, it was a somewhat diminutive and pudgy form. She moved as gracefully and quickly as the others, but lacked the same stamina and confidence of motion.

Her narrow, pained eyes gazed across the field. She reached a gully between hills and saw the hundreds of similar forms rising up from the void-like darkness.

"No, no, no," she hissed to herself. "They're here already! Faster, faster, faster!"

Her sprint turned into a sequence of leaps. She bounded across the field. As she drew nearer, those shades nearest to the back turned to face her. Their eyes appeared in the blackness. All stared reproachfully at her as she reached her place at the rear of the assembly.

"Sorry," she whispered meekly, sliding in among the others. "Sorry, sorry, sorry…"

The eyes focused almost painfully upon her.

"You are *late,* Blot," growled the nearest shade.

"I know! I didn't… I know… I'm sorry…" Blot replied.

The judgment was heavy in their gaze. Blot seemed to physically wither under their stare. Mercy came after a few moments when a black figure scaled the white tree to take a place in the crook of the tree beneath the crescent that remained of the moon. His name was Stigma, and they were gathered here under his orders.

"Our time approaches!" proclaimed Stigma in a creaky, unnatural voice.

The crowd of shades erupted in a unanimous cheer. It sounded like wind rattling a field of dry weeds.

"Ready yourselves," the leader ordered. "When the eclipse is at its peak, the way will open. We shall have the first chance in generations!"

Another windy hiss of a cheer.

"You know your tasks. Many of you will fall. But their ignorance is their downfall. Time has erased the memory of our last assault. We are many. Those who know to oppose us are few. It is our *time.*"

Another triumphant cheer erupted.

Behind the leader, the eclipse seemed to be racing the night. The blackish crescent in the white was vanishing before their eyes. The air between the grasping hands of the tree shimmered. When the last of the black moon was swallowed by the light, reality itself shuddered and groaned. The stark white of the sky dimmed. It was an awesome, terrible sight. The flawless white shifted to gray. The flecks of black vanished into the same gray color. The bright and dark were swapping places. Night sky turned black as the field. The ashen stars turned to points of white. What the assembled horde saw was the sky not of *their* world, but of its inverse. The leader coiled himself and sprang. His black form vanished against the strange black sky. The air rippled like the surface of a pond. There no sound marked his landing. He was simply gone.

The other shades rushed the tree. They swarmed up the trunk like ants and sprang into the air. More ripples drifted across the sky as they vanished. Shades fought and scratched to be the next to dive through the open gate, and with good reason. This strange alignment of mystic events was vanishingly rare. Though it was powerful, it was not *all* powerful. Each ripple was more sluggish, more labored than the one before. Each shade had to fight harder to push through the membrane that separated that world from this.

They climbed over themselves, scratching, biting, screeching, and yowling. And far in the back, still winded from her run, was Blot. She scrabbled and shoved, but she couldn't make any headway. Her white eyes watched anxiously as the ripples grew slower. Already they'd ceased to flow like water. Now they were sludgy, syrupy waves. Shades fought and struggled to claw their way through the gate. At this rate, she'd never make it through with enough strength to do what must be done.

She reached the base of the tree and began her climb as a fresh crescent was forming on the opposite side of the moon. The end of the eclipse already near. It had passed with supernatural speed. A few dozen of the shades remained, and they redoubled their efforts.

The whiteness of the sky was gradually returning. Each additional shade slipping through looked as though it was boring a hole through solid earth to make it to the world beyond the gate. When she reached the crook of the tree, she was the last shade to do so. Already those ahead were darting across an eerie white landscape on the other side. Blot pressed forward, but the air felt thick and rubbery. She forced herself onward, but the membrane of reality barely wobbled.

"No! This is our time!" she grunted, shoving at the fading gateway. "I will not be left behind!"

She gathered her mind. Blot was hardly the most powerful of shades. If she were, she wouldn't have been late. What little power she had, she would need to perform the task she was meant to achieve. But she wouldn't even have the chance if she didn't burn some of her precious power now in order to reach the world awaiting her.

Her meager mystic talents wove through the shadowy substance of her body. Her fingers lengthened into claws. Ever-so-slightly stubby limbs lengthened into a something more gaunt and wiry. Her thin mouth, shut tight until now, opened and stretched into a crooked, sinister grin. Locks of hair rose about her like wild snakes writhing. She slashed at the wavering gateway and screeched in anger. Gradually, she started to penetrate the veil between worlds.

It was like moving through treacle, and each inch forward was harder than the last. She poured her mystic strength into her form, strengthening her body and compelling herself forward. Her head poked out into the world beyond the gate. It was cold, unpleasant. The tree she clawed at now was a light gray rather than black. She sunk her talons into it and hauled herself forward. Reality itself was solidifying around her. A few more moments and she would be trapped like an insect in amber, locked between worlds until the gate opened again.

A few more fear-gripped struggles urged her forward. The gateway stretched, shimmered with a greasy gloss, and finally released her. She tumbled head over heels from the tree and fell to the ground, crunching into a layer of icy snow.

Blot lurched to her feet and gazed at the black sky with its white crescent moon. She had made it. She was through. But she'd squandered her power. She could feel this world gnawing at her, like a body fighting a disease. There were only two ways a shade could exist in this world. The first required her to shield herself mystically. All but the dregs of her strength had been spent. She was defenseless. The only other way required a host.

She gasped and hurried forward. There was no shortage of creatures in this world. The task was a simple one. Find a being of power and claim it as a host. That was how the battles would be fought. That was how the war would be won. At this very moment, her brethren were streaking across the landscape. The strongest of them could stave off the withering effects of this world long enough to reach any creature they pleased. Others couldn't afford to be so choosy. They would have to settle for the best host they could find in nearby towns and villages.

Blot was a fish out of water. She needed someone, anyone, and she needed them *now*.

Her bone-white eyes locked onto an odd structure a short distance across the field. She could sense something within. It wasn't one of the mindless woodland creatures of this world. It was one of the conquerors, a human. She wove across the field, her enhanced form gradually reverting to her more natural one.

Finely honed senses fixed upon her target. It was a male. That much she was sure of. He was weak. He had a meager spirit, barely a match for hers, and nothing compared to the more potent humans. That was no doubt why her fellow shades had passed him over. But she had no choice. She could choose him, or she could succumb to the searing defenses of this world.

She reached the structure and inspected it. It was smaller than a house or hut. Her fingers glided across the slippery surface of its walls, dimpling them. It was not wood or stone, proper things to build a house from. This was a tent, it seemed, but made from some manner of cloth she'd never seen before. Something with the dull sheen of satin, but far thinner and stronger.

Blot reared back and tried to swipe at it. Alas, her enhanced form had not only fully reverted to its less imposing shape, it had withered further. She was losing her substance. Inky flesh was becoming wispy and insubstantial. Time was running out.

Fortunately for her, even a weakened shade need not obey *all* the whims of the physical world. She pressed her wavering form against the cloth. The whole of her shape reduced to little more than an image on the surface of the cloth. Like a projection on a screen, she existed briefly on both sides of the cloth, then slowly slid down the inside of the screen and across the interior of the tent.

She lurched up from the ground and gazed in the darkness as her would-be host. He was as unimpressive as the dim flicker of his soul suggested. A dark-skinned young man. He was wrapped in a thick blanket of some kind, made of the same shiny fabric as the tent. Even with such fluffy bulk wrapped about him, she could tell he had a lean build. This was no warrior. But he was a human. And that was enough. She slid across the floor of the tent. There was little light, only the glow of the still partially eclipsed moon. But she was a creature of darkness. The shadow he cast was plain as day before her. She raised her wavering hand, focused what little of her power remained, and sunk her fingers into his shadow.

It curled and bunched in her grip like a silken sheet. He stirred in his sleep, but did not wake. Blot hauled at the curling black form of his shadow. It pulled away from his form, slipped from her grip, and whisked off. Where it went, she didn't care. What was most important was the ragged edge it left behind, as though a page had been torn from a book. She hesitated briefly, but she couldn't afford shame or modesty. Her strength was all but gone. She coiled her shadowy, two-dimensional form and slid under the blankets beside him. Her silhouette of a shape wove with the feathery remnants of his shadow. Like a plant taking root, she anchored herself to him.

The withering effect of this world faded. She had taken the place of his shadow, and so to the forces of nature in this world, she was little more than that. She was safe, able to take her time and recover. At least… so she hoped.

This was *not* her world. Things would work differently here. One could never be certain how well one's mind, body, and spirit would handle the transition from one plane to another. The best of her kind could continue to grow and thrive here. Her history spoke of those who nearly conquered this world. But others never recovered. They were left locked in the role of a shadow, barely existing at all. And then… when the host passed…

She shut her eyes and forced the thought from her mind. That wouldn't happen to her. Fate had greater plans for her. The binding had taken the last of her strength. For now, she needed to rest. Tomorrow, with the rising of this world's strange sun, she would learn what she could make of this human.

#

Sleep was a long way off for Blot. She'd never taken a host before. It wasn't *necessary* in her own world. But it was an essential part of her education. She'd been told what to expect. It was, above all, a link, a connection. Those with greater training, or a greater natural affinity, could make excellent use of that link. Thoughts, notions, *commands* could flow along the link. Somewhere, even as she tried to sleep and build her strength, Stigma could very well have already asserted control of a powerful noble or king. Others would need to be sneakier. Little notions here and there, eased into the mind of the host. They would serve the shade without knowing it, believing the ideas were their own.

Blot didn't feel strong enough to do any of that. At this moment, she had the opposite problem. Not only was she not powerful enough to impose her will, she lacked even the strength to keep the flow of thoughts and notions heading in the right direction. The man she'd selected was dreaming. And those dreams found their way to Blot's mind. She couldn't keep them out. The best she could manage was to push them aside. And doing that required her to focus, which meant sleep wasn't an option.

If such must be the case, then at least she could learn something of her host from his dreams. She turned her mind toward them and watched the fleeting images like a show. Soon, she knew, she would see evidence of what she'd always been told of this world.

The stories of the horrid deeds and beliefs of these people were constant, a part of her education since childhood…

#

Years earlier…

A young blot stood in an enormous crowd of other young, untrained shades. She watched in awe as the powerful figure of Stigma stalked before them.

"Look at you all…" he uttered in his creaky voice. "A fine batch. Someday you shall make fine soldiers in the coming war. The war with the place of light."

He raised a claw and slashed it through the air. Its needle-sharp tip dragged brilliant lines of white into the air. The lines formed crude figures. As he spoke, the lines illustrated what he described.

"The place of light is a terrible place. It is home to the humans. A human is not like a shade. It is not a thing of the darkness. One would imagine, if it makes its home in a place of light, it must be a *thing* of light. But it is not. It is flesh and bone. Neither light nor dark. This is the most wretched aspect of the human. From birth, a human has a choice. It can embrace the light, or it can embrace the dark. And a human chooses the light."

Blot and the others shivered at the prospect.

"Light is a grim necessity. With light comes contrast. And with contrast comes strength. Here, we know that darkness is the true, natural way of things and light exists to serve it. There, they foolishly believe the opposite. And worse. The seek to *destroy* the dark."

He traced out the shape of a flame in the air.

"They conjure light and keep it. Like a fat, pampered house pet. Like a hound on a chain. And they use it to chase away the darkness. To assault it. A human cannot *abide* the dark. With each passing day they nurture and feed the light. They use it to push the shadows deeper and deeper into the unseen and forgotten places."

He slashed the fire from the air.

"A human is wise enough to know the value of balance, of contrast. But they chose to abandon it. And why? Hatred can be the only reason. A human *hates* the darkness. A human cannot abide a shade. A human would sooner destroy us all than allow the rich, nurturing darkness that shelters and protects us. And when a creature knows only hate, there is only one thing to be done."

"Fight!" Blot proclaimed, in unison with the other shades.

"We fight," Stigma agreed. "We take their light from them. We take their *choice* from them. We take their world from them…"

#

The words of her leader were burned into her mind, and as each day passed and she drew closer to this moment, she hardened herself against the burning hate she knew she would find radiating from the mind of her eventual host. And now, what chilled her most wasn't the vicious, searing animosity lurking in the mind now linked to her own. What chilled her was the *calm*.

It wasn't a storm of scheming and plotting. This human wasn't basking in dreams of conquest over the darkness. What she most felt from him was embarrassment and anxiety. They were the same mix of emotions that she felt all too often. It seemed wrong to feel them from this *thing*. She'd never dreamed that she would feel anything approaching common ground with a human. She eased her defenses and let the sights and sounds of the dream begin to ooze into her mind along with the emotional overflow. It was a means to save her strength and recover more quickly. Certainly her curiosity hadn't gotten the better of her. Certainly not that.

A setting painted itself into being around her. The first thing that struck her wasn't hostility or anger, it was *color*. Blot's world was a stark place of black and white. Even shades of gray were rare. But the images wrapping around her were almost dizzying in their variety. Blue walls, a cream-colored ceiling. Dozens of humans were present, seated at odd little individual desks. They wore clothes in yellows and reds, purples and greens. Dazzling patterns decorated the fronts of their shirts, and similarly flavorful imagery hung on the walls.

It was the first she had ever seen of color. If it hadn't come with the implicit understanding of her host's mind, she wouldn't have known what to call these new hues. She doubted she could even have *experienced* them. Her eyes were made for black and white alone.

She swept her eyes across the humans. Even knowing what surrounded her was an illusion, she couldn't quell the feeling of repulsion and fear at seeing so many of these creatures she'd been taught were so ghastly and vicious. They were young adults, and as tended to be the case in dreams, most of them were a bit nondescript and ill-defined. Their faces were blurry and unfocused, merely set-dressing for the main player, a slightly more youthful version of her host.

As the vibrant surroundings solidified around her, Blot became aware that her own stark form was horribly out of place. Though it was a dream, she couldn't risk that his memory of seeing her shadowy form might tip him off to her presence in the waking world until her grip upon him was better established. She needed a disguise.

She crept up to one of the dream girls that her host had conjured up. She was just a bit taller than Blot, but had a similar build. With a flourish of her will, Blot dispelled the dream-woman, leaving something of a human-shaped void in the dream world. It was simple enough to allow her own body to lose form and flow like ink into a mold. She curled and slurped into the shape the imagining had left behind, filling out the more overtly human features until she was a precise duplicate, at least in form. The complex coloring of her skin, her hair, and her eyes were another matter. She did her best, but she suspected her approximation was a bit off. She could only *feel* how her face must look, but her hands looked more like an illustration than the flesh and bone reality of the others around her. Furthermore, her clothes were little more than the flowing black rags she wore as a shade. It would have to do, and it would, so long as she didn't draw any attention to herself.

Blot turned her attention to the dream-representation of her host. He sat uneasily in his seat, flipping helplessly through a book in search of something he knew he wouldn't find. In this place of emotion and imagination, she felt his panic like a cold chill against her skin.

"Alan?" called a voice from the front of the room.

Blot and Alan snapped their attention forward. An elderly man with a snow-white beard and thick spectacles glared back at him. Even without the undercurrent of understanding and context she felt from Alan's mind, she would have known this man was a teacher of some kind. He had the air of authority and intellect that made every one of her instructors so implicitly awing.

"Uh, yeah? Yes! Yes, Mr. Pendergrass. *Doctor!* Dr. Pendergrass," he said.

Blot felt the same bolt of anxiety and discovery that Alan felt.

"Perhaps you'd like to answer the question?" the professor said.

"I… Uh…" Alan cleared his throat. "Could you repeat the question?"

"It is question six. From the homework assignment."

Alan glanced down. Blot craned her neck to see the pages he was so desperately flipping through in search of an answer. They were blank.

"I don't… Uh… I didn't…" Alan stammered.

"You *are* aware that this assignment is worth twenty percent of your grade," the professor rumbled.

"I must have… I don't remember you assigning it…"

Alan was flustered, twisting in the breeze and agonized. The empathy for his situation was almost painful to Blot. Perpetually a disappointment to her many tutors and mentors, she'd spent *years* of her life alternately in fear of moments like these and suffering through them. Watching someone else—even a horrid human—endure them was pure torture.

She looked to her desk and swept her hand across it. This was a dream, and she *knew* it, so the fabric of reality was effortlessly malleable. A thick sheaf of paper burst into being with a soft rustle of pages. She slid a clean sheet from the bundle and held out her left hand. A quill wafted into being in her grip. She hastily scribbled something down, folded it, and tossed it to his desk.

The note spun through the air with a precision and accuracy that simply could not happen in waking reality. It swirled in front of Alan's eyes, then dropped down to tuck into the pages of his book.

He looked around for the source. Blot slid low in her desk to avoid being seen.

"Mr. Fontaine!" the professor insisted. "Either answer the

question or you get a zero for the assignment."

Alan snatched up the page and pulled it open to find what Blot had written.

"Th-the answer is. Uh…" She squinted at her writing. "Two sprigs of onyx-leaf, combined with twice-boiled brine of the ashen sea, simmered with the bones of three hearty joints of beast for a night and a day."

The professor tilted his head up, almost reproachfully. "That is correct."

A brisk wave of relief rushed from him, tempered with a flutter of confusion.

"That's correct?" he said.

"Yes, Mr. Fontaine."

"But this is Linear Algebra class."

"And you have answered the question properly."

Blot smirked. Of course it was the correct answer. That it was her grandmother's recipe for stock didn't matter in the slightest. This was a dream. And though her host was too lost in it to realize it, he had complete control over it. Any answer would have been the correct answer if he willed it so. The imagined professor moved on, turning to the board at the front of the room to trace out some meaningless strings of letters and numbers. The cool sensation of relief rushed over her again, and she couldn't help but feel a trace of pride that it was her expertise that had taken this strange nightmare and turned it back into a pleasant moment of remembrance.

"Excuse me, were you the one who gave me the answer?" Alan whispered.

She looked up to see that Alan had turned in his seat to directly address her.

"What? No! Why would you think that?" Blot said quickly.

"You've got a stack of the fancy paper there. And a fancy pen."

She glanced down to the conjured quill and stack of pages.

"No I don't!" she said, sweeping her hand to disperse the incriminating evidence like smoke.

Alan blinked at the strange occurrence, then shrugged and dismissed it with the ease that only one locked in a dream could.

"Well, thanks for the help. I'm Alan." He extended a hand to shake. "And you are?"

Blot slid back in her chair as though he were jabbing a pitchfork in her direction.

"Wake up! Now!" she squealed.

#

The dream vanished and she was once again in the tent. Alan slowly stirred. While she'd only felt like she'd been immersed in his mind for a few minutes, hours had passed in the world outside. The rest had refreshed her a bit, but she was still terribly weak. Her time in his mind had given her a dash of insight into her surroundings now. The tent was made from something called Nylon. The odd, overstuffed bundle he used as a blanket was called a sleeping bag. Sharing it with him would have been an uncomfortably intimate experience if not for the fact that, as his shadow, there was nothing physical about her substance unless she willed it so. What shared the sleeping bag with him was barely more than an existential placeholder. *She* was, at this point, a rather ill-defined concept rather than a living, breathing thing. It was a bit unsettling having her whole identity reduced to an indistinct quality associated with another being, but if she was to hope to survive in this place, she would have to become accustomed to it.

He stirred and slid himself upright to wipe the sleep from his eyes.

"Oof," he murmured. "That was a weird one."

He shivered a bit at the frigid temperature in the tent and pulled on a heavy jacket. One of the nice things about lacking any real physical substance was that Blot didn't have to worry about being too cold or too hot. A person had to *be* before they could be uncomfortable. He slid his feet into boots and laced them up, then unzipped the door to the tent and climbed out.

The sun was already high in the sky, the moment it struck him, Blot felt a surge of structure and focus. The powerful sun cast his shadow across the white snow with a bold contrast and a crisp edge. Though she was little more than a tracing of his own silhouette, being so rigidly and perfectly defined had a profound impact upon her. She suddenly saw everything around her so much more vividly. This world was, if anything, *more* overwhelming than the dream. She'd had a brief, desperate glimpse of this world the night before, but then the sky had been black. Now it was a deep blue. Fluffy white clouds drifted across the sky like wind-blown cotton. And somewhere behind Alan was a light so much more powerful than she could ever have imagined. She couldn't *see* it. As a shadow, she could never see light directly. That was a small mercy, as she was certain she wouldn't be able to endure something so powerful and bright as the sun.

With the powerfully cast shadow freeing her of the need to in any way define her shape, her wits were free to turn to the task that brought her here. The knowledge and understanding she'd borrowed from his mind during the dream wouldn't last forever. It wasn't the same as a real lesson and observation. All she really knew was that either this Alan Fontaine fellow had an astoundingly vivid imagination or the world had changed a great deal since the last time her people had crossed over to his world and back again. She would have to keep her eyes open, learn what she could of the world and, more importantly, learn what use Alan could be to her cause.

Alan checked his watch. "Oh, man. I slept longer than I thought. It's after ten."

He stretched a bit and plodded forward. Not far from the tent, he found a device mounted on the end of a tripod. It was a camera, and from the way he handled it, a particularly precious one. A large screen on the back of the camera flicked to life and displayed what seemed to be dozens of the same image, one after the other. It was an image of the tree from the night before.

"Oh, man…" he said. "This is going to be a hell of a time lapse."

Blot watched him as he worked his way through his morning routine. If her upbringing was accurate, humans devoted their every passing moment to stomping out darkness and plotting its ultimate demise. This Alan character must have been particularly fiendish and subtle in his efforts, as if he was dedicated to any such task, he wasn't being very obvious about it. He closed up his tripod and carefully packed it away along with his camera. Next came the tent, which was taken down and rolled up. He munched on some sort of crumbly sweet confection as he marched through the icy field, past the earthly version of the Tree of the Grasping Hands.

Fifteen minutes of hiking took him to a dirt road and something the residual wisdom from his dream indicated was called a car.

Once inside it, and thus out of the direct sun, the externally enforced intensity of focus that came from being a starkly cast shadow eased a bit. In exchange for having to gather her own wits, she found the softer lighting gave her a greater degree of freedom. She could slide her shadow-self about in the car without drawing his attention, as from his point of view the whole *car* was in shadow. Picking out the part of it that was supposed to be his own shadow was beyond his human senses.

Thus, she was able to position herself to watch out the windows. In doing so, the world of humanity revealed itself to her.

"Oh my…" she fretted, watching in wonder as a highway littered with cars loomed before her. "Humanity has come a long way…"

#

Blot's head was spinning as she and Alan reached his home. The last attempt to conquer this world and punish them for their hatred of the darkness came at a time when the humans used horses and carts. The most potent weapons against the darkness were torches and lanterns. Over the hours since they'd left the snowy field, Blot had watched massive stone and glass structures pass by her window by the hundreds. The sun slid high, then dropped low. As darkness descended upon the world, and their strange white moon returned to the bizarre black sky, she saw the arsenal of weaponry they had developed to attack the shadows. Burning orange lights shone down over the road. Intense beams of light blasted in pairs from the front of every car. The windows of every home and the whole of the great towers gleamed with light. It was true. These people *did* despise the dark. Their world had equal night and day, but the greedy humans refused to give the night its due. They brought slices of day with them wherever they went.

The assault on darkness was so great that when they entered the city Alan called home, one could scarcely tell it was night at all. Streetlights and storefronts cast the road in their multi-colored glow. Alan parked his car in a massive garage lined with bars of light that gave her almost nowhere to hide.

From there it was into an apartment building larger than any palace back home. He rode an elevator high into the sky, arms loaded down with this packs and tent.

As he paced a brightly lit hallway, wearily trudging toward his door, Blot despaired. He was just an average man. He was no wizard, no warrior. But he already had the capacity to cast out the darkness at the press of a button or the flip of a switch. How could she, a lowly shade barely able to claim him as a host, ever hope to contribute to the overthrow of such a place.

Alan fiddled with his keys, nearly dropping his many bags and packages, and finally stumbled into his apartment. Of course, the first thing he did was click on the light, filling his home with a warm glow and shoving the precious pockets of darkness into the corners and below the furniture. She stuck close to him, nestling herself in the darkness beneath his feet with each step.

The apartment was meager, but well-kept. His living room had a large, flat screen on the wall and a couch in front of it. He paid a brief visit to his kitchen to toss a tray of food into a glowing box while he washed his face in the bathroom. By the time he was done, the box had somehow heated his meal completely. From there, he flopped down on the couch with his meal. He clicked on the screen and, to Blot's relief, clicked off the lights.

As Alan ate and watched complex images flicker across his screen, Blot found herself free to explore his surroundings in the relative darkness.

He was her host. As such she could not separate herself from him without once again enduring the withering defense of this world. But one look at a person pacing a flat field at sunset told you just how far a shadow could stretch. Add to it the will and influence of a shade and she could travel to just about any section of the apartment that didn't cut her off with bright light or a solid wall. So long as she moved with care, she could learn more of this man and his world than what had leaked to her through their link on its own.

She slipped into the kitchen. Alan's mind lurked at the back of her own, as though little more than a curtain separated the two of them. She couldn't afford to probe too hard, lest he discover her. With care she found that if she searched her own mind for the answer to a basic, simple question, often the response came tumbling from his mind instead. The strange meal-heating box was a microwave. The cold pantry box was a refrigerator.

Blot flicked into the bathroom next. It was fascinating, but it seemed humans could conjure not just light and flame as they chose, but water as well. But there was no hint of mysticism about it. They had somehow created *devices* that could produce such wondrous effects.

"By the void…" she uttered. "Such foolishness. To put such power into the hands of every creature. The chaos it would cause if a simple shade like me could snap her fingers and produce a torrent of water. They must have exquisite self-control. Or perhaps their leaders keep them in line with an iron will."

She moved next to the one room she'd yet to see the inside of. The door was shut, but that was of little concern. A gap of at least a quarter inch separated it from the floor. More than enough for a shadow to slip beneath.

The inside was completely dark, but her eyes saw it as plain as day. It was a bedroom, though a screen atop a desk caused the word "laptop" to slip out of his mind.

"He must be confused," she said poking at the collection of keys attached to the screen. "This does not look like the top of any lap I have ever seen."

She looked up from it and turned around.

"Oh… Oh, my darkness…" she murmured.

The far wall was covered with images, almost from ceiling to floor. Some of them were in frames. Others were held to threads strung wall to wall by small clips. And they were *gorgeous.*

She pushed her ability to stretch from her host so that she could inspect the images up close. Here, a statue of some kind stood high into a blue sky. Its shadow seemed to divide the red soil beneath it into two equal slices. There, a stained-glass window painting its gorgeous, colorful pattern on the ground.

Her eyes lingered longest on the image of a woman. It was rendered in black, white, and gray, just as the world she'd left behind was. The strong light cast half her face in utter darkness.

The word "photographs" slid from his mind now. These were his art form. And as varied as they were, there was something that linked them all. Alan used the interplay of light and shadow to give the images shape and form. He told stories with the contrast of day and night, white and black.

"He understands…"

It was difficult to imagine the subtle but powerful effects of linking one's spirit to that of another. With a single glance at something meaningful to that person, the intangible emotions and sentiments connected to it revealed themselves like artifacts unearthed in an ancient tomb. She couldn't grasp exactly how he made the images, or how he conceptualized them. But she could feel how he *felt* about them. His intention. The things that made him proud and the things he felt came up short. It wasn't a simple coincidence, the interplay of light and dark. It was something that seized his mind. Something that fascinated him.

She slid back into the living room and settled in beside him, where the angle of the dancing light of the television dictated she should be. The images weren't terribly interesting. Just other humans talking to one another. He didn't seem very interested in it either. He was just passing the time. As the television wasn't a worthwhile distraction, she found her thoughts lingering on what sort of a human could understand the beauty that defined her own homeland so completely. Surely this was not so of *all* humans. A society so thoroughly devoted to wiping out the darkness could never have formed if such where the case. But if Alan *was* special, then what were the chances of finding what had to be one of a very few humans with a similar notion of beauty.

It was the tree. It had to be. The Tree of the Grasping Hands. It was a connection between his world and hers. It could have drawn him.

She looked to him.

This could be fate. But was it fate that he would help her, or she would help him?

Blot watched him as the long drive and late dinner took their toll. He slipped into sleep. Not long after, she felt a dream begin to simmer in his mind. She smiled and shut her own eyes, preparing to slip into the dream with him. It would take her a long time to be strong enough to make proper use of him. The least she could do is indulge her curiosity and learn more about this host.

The colorful world of his dream began to form around her. It was still in the cloudy, ill-defined state, but already she could feel that this dream was a familiar one to Alan. A pleasant and anticipated setting for him. As she was to some degree subject to his emotions, being immersed in calm, soothing sensations was something like being sent to a spa.

SLAM SLAM SLAM

The dream vanished and Alan was jarred awake by the hammering at his apartment door. She groggily set his plate aside and fumbled for the light. When it snapped on, Blot's shadowy form darted to the other side, now rigidly held there by the light's influence.

"I know you're in there, Mr. Fontaine," barked an angry female voice from the other side of the door.

"I'm coming, Ms. Levitt," he said, shakily making his way to the door while trying to rattle the cobwebs from his head.

He opened the door and the brighter light from the hallway shoved Blot around again, now falling behind him. She gazed up from her place on the floor and saw a woman perhaps a few years older than Alan. She had a look of irritation on her face and an envelope in her hand. She thrust the envelope at him.

"Another letter. Your name. My address," she snapped.

"I'm sorry, Ms. Levitt."

"Don't be sorry, *fix it!*" she said.

Alan looked at the envelope.

"It's my old job. They have the address wrong. I've tried to—"

"I don't want to hear excuses, Mr. Fontaine. I've already informed building management."

"No…" he groaned. "Ms. Levitt, if I get enough strikes, they're going to take my building discount on the parking spot."

"You should have thought of that before you started cluttering my inbox with *your* mail. And keep your TV down. I can hear it through the vent and it is *very* inconsiderate."

"I'm sorry, Ms. Levitt."

She sneered and marched off. A moment later, the next apartment door slammed. Alan shut the door and tossed the envelope on a side table.

"That'll be another forty dollars a month," he grumbled. "Just what I need."

#

Alan cleaned up his microwaved dinner and trudged off to bed. This time, sleep was a bit slower to come. He was still exhausted, but Blot could feel the irritation of his encounter with his neighbor smoldering beneath the surface. Blot took the time to gaze at his photographs again. As she admired them, she thought…

He eventually slipped into slumber. But for now, she would not be joining him. She had other plans. First, she slid to the floor and found her way to the air vent. It took a bit more curling and folding of her insubstantial self to slip between the thin metal grate, but she managed it without much effort. Beyond, she found a small metal duct with other vents leading off at irregular intervals. She slid through the duct silently and peeked through a vent on the opposite side. In another room she could hear the abrasive Ms. Levitt settling down to watch her own television.

It seemed only right that Levitt would have *far* more lights on, making the navigation of her home more difficult. But Blot had made up her mind. Alan was her host. What was good for him was good for her. And if this horrid woman's behavior would cost him forty dollars—which were apparently some manner of currency—then Blot would balance the scales.

The bright light did its best to push Blot back from whence she came, and her twisted body's journey through the duct was difficult enough to maintain, but Blot knew there would be trials when she came here. This would be her first test.

She coiled up the wall in what seemed to be a bedroom and stretched her twisted hand out across her bedside table. There were assorted things on the top: a clock radio, a dish of change, an empty drinking glass. Nothing worthwhile. She tried to pull out the drawer, but she lacked the strength to manifest herself physically. There were other ways to influence the world, but they would be of no use here. She slipped back, then emerged on the other side of the bed to search the table there with the same level of success. There was nothing in the room that would be of much use.

Blot slid back into the vent and stretched herself farther along the duct and emerged from another vent. This farther vent required even more effort, and took her to the living room, where Ms. Levitt was watching her own television. A single light was on, which Blot felt as a constant pressure trying to shove her back toward the form that should have been casting her. She pressed on, moving with the utmost of care. Blot didn't know what sort of visual acuity humans had, but there was a very good chance Levitt would be able to see her if she moved suddenly.

She inched along the floor, then up the wall to where a coat rack held a jacket. She managed to slide up behind the coat, where its own shadow hid her, and carefully curled and twisted about within it until she found, in an inner pocket, a wallet. Excellent. Now, she just had to get it.

Blot snapped back into the vent and returned to the bedroom. A lamp on one bedside table cast a nice, sharp shadow of the opposite table on the wall. She crept across the wall and reached out with her twisted fingers.

She may not have been able to open the drawer directly, but these smaller, lighter items were another matter. She had access to their shadows. And as *she* was a shadow, that gave her other options. She gathered what little strength she'd restored and poured it into her shadowy hand. When she reached down and grasped the shadow of the drinking glass, the *actual* glass rose from the table and hung in the air. With a quick flick of her wrist, dropped it from the table where it shattered on the floor.

"What was that?" Ms. Levitt called from the other room.

Once again, Blot slid into the vent and reemerged in the living room. She slid up the wall and grasped the edge of the jacket's shadow. She lifted the end and shook the jacket, causing the wallet to drop out. She caught it by the shadow before it reached the ground, then carefully peeled it open and shook it until the edges of the bills within emerged a bit. She angled the wallet until the shadow of the corner of the bills could be seen, then tugged them free.

There were three twenties inside. Enough to cover some of the expense the woman had thrust upon Alan. She tossed the now empty wallet under the couch and grinned devilishly at the trouble it would cause. Then she slid back into the vent, taking the bills along with her. Once she was out of the light, and thus the shadow of the bills was no longer distinct, she found handling them *far* more difficult, but in time she was able to coax them through Alan's vent and stuff them into the pocket of the pants he'd hung on a chair beside the bed.

With the job done, she released her focus and let herself slip into the position the dim glow of the moonlight through the window would have her occupy. Alan was deep into another dream. She shut her eyes and let the dream wash over her. With any luck, this little partnership would be as rewarding for her as it was for him.

The Back Way

Joseph R. Lallo

The Back Way

The Back Way is a short that was originally written for a time travel anthology that never came to be. I choose to believe someone went back in time and prevented it from being, but that's just me. The title is a pointlessly vague reference to the Way Back Machine from the old Mr. Peabody and Sherman shorts on the Rocky and Bullwinkle Show.

The cover art (exclusive to this collection) is by Chandra Free.

114

The rising sun glared across the rain-slicked street as Claire Daniels squinted at the numbers above each doorway. The rain had stopped hours before, so she'd not expected to need her rain gear. Lackluster drainage meant that this street, like many of the streets in the older neighborhoods, tended to flood in the right conditions. Lucky her, the conditions were perfect today. This left her splashing through two-inch-deep puddles in her best pair of low-heel leather pumps.

"Ninety-seven… ninety-nine… one-oh-three?" she muttered, eying the street numbers.

She slipped a folded bit of paper from her clutch and flipped it open. Her job interview was scheduled to start in three minutes. It was supposedly at 101 West Tannon Boulevard. She stepped off the sidewalk to see if the offending street number was written somewhere above the row of decrepit awnings. Her foot promptly went ankle-deep into a pothole hidden beneath the murky surface of the pooled water.

"Hey, great!" she said with exaggerated cheerfulness. "Super! Soggy stockings for the interview. That'll make for a good first impression!"

Claire had always found that staying positive was the best policy. On days like this, it devolved into passive-aggressively taunting fate.

She hobbled over to the nearest storefront and leaned on it. Tucking her clutch under her arm, she removed the soaked shoe to drain it a bit. Half a cup of water splashed to the ground before she was willing to slide her foot back inside. Her heel plopped into the shoe with a rather rude sound just as an older gentleman approached the door beside her and fiddled with his keys, ready to open it for business.

"Oh, hello, sir. Boy am I glad to see you. I'm looking for 101 West Tannon Boulevard. Call me crazy, but shouldn't that door be right about here?"

She pointed to an oddly wide patch of wall between his storefront and the next. He raised a pair of fluffy gray eyebrows and looked her in the eye, then reached up and flicked the edge of a sign dangling just over her head. One of the two chains it hung from had rusted through, leaving it to dangle free. It lazily rotated. The previously hidden face of the sign was corroded almost to the point of illegibility, but she was able to just barely make out the words.

Yesterday's Tomorrow

Joseph R. Lallo
Around the corner to the right.

A cluster of questions and complaints fought to be the first to leave her mouth. She reminded herself of her commitment to positivity and held her tongue. The weary expression of the elderly shopkeeper's face made it clear he'd heard them all before and had no interest in hearing them again anyway.

She trotted as quickly as her waterlogged low-traction shoes could carry her around the corner. What awaited her there was more of an alley than a street. It was the sort of narrow passage meant to give delivery trucks someplace to park without blocking traffic while they loaded up the neighboring stores. A second damaged sign hung from the crosspiece over a rickety metal staircase hidden in the dim alleyway. The glorified fire escape led to a second-floor landing where a better-cared-for sign bore the street number and shop name she was looking for.

"My, my," she said. "A store tucked away in a back alley. And with an exciting new take on how street numbers work. How innovative!"

There was no rule you couldn't be positive *and* sarcastic.

The stairs, at least, were steadier than they looked, as she reached the door at the top without once fearing for her life. Her first impression of the place would have been much rosier if this door had been waiting for her at street level. It was in perfect repair, painted a bright blue color without a sign of chipping or fading. There were no display windows, of course. Strange as it might be to have a store's main entrance in an alleyway, it would have been absurd to expect window shoppers at such a place. Even so, a nice, clean window in the door gave her a glimpse of wares on display. A wooden plank hanging on the inside of the window read *Yes, We're Open (Come On In!).*

She hiked her upbeat expression up a few notches and stepped through the doorway. The soft tinkle of a bell heralded her entry. If she'd challenged herself to predict just what the inside of an almost literal hole-in-the-wall shop might look like, she would have been woefully off target. It was an expertly laid out, stunningly curated antique shop. Not only was everything on display of unquestionable quality, even the shelves and tables being used to display them were period perfect and suited to the tone of their contents. Each display was put together with the care of a museum curator. Each represented a different era of Americana, such that marching farther into the store was like walking back in time. The store was deep, seeming to occupy the second floor of at least half of the shops elsewhere on the block. It felt like an optical illusion to stare down the length of the store and see display after display stretching onward for *far* longer than a little boutique would normally be able to accommodate.

It was all very impressive. It also didn't have much at *all* to do with her skill set. Still, she'd come all this way. At this point in her job search, if she didn't want to be a beggar, she couldn't be a chooser.

"Hello?" Claire called. She flinched as a handful of clocks around the store struck 6 a.m. simultaneously.

"Hold your horses, I'm coming," muttered a wizened voice.

A side doorway clicked open and out stepped an elderly woman. She was slightly stooped, with dark skin, deep wrinkles, and impressively thick glasses.

"Ms. Thomas?" Claire asked.

"Well who else would it be?" the shopkeeper asked irritably. "You'll be the young woman looking for the job, right?"

"I certainly am!" she said, chipper as she could manage. "Though I think there may have been some sort of a misunderstanding. This isn't the sort of place I would normally apply."

"Right, right. You're hoping for the big bucks. Don't get ahead of yourself. You don't even know if you have the job yet."

"Obviously the salary is one part of it, but my last job was—"

Ms. Thomas raised her voice. "I'm looking for a personal assistant. I think that's what you'd call it now. Back in my day we just called it a go-fer."

"… Gopher?"

"Go-fer this, go-fer that. It ain't hard to work it out."

"Oh, right," Claire said through a smile that was becoming increasingly difficult to maintain. "I really think one or both of us have been misled. I'm coming off a very successful six-year run as an investment banker. I need something a bit more substantial—"

"The job pays $730,485 a year, plus tips."

Claire's mouth hung open for a moment.

"You're catching flies, honey," Ms. Thomas said.

She shut her mouth and straightened up.

"I thought that'd get your attention. It's always money with you young folks."

Ms. Thomas trudged deeper into the store. Claire quickly fell into step beside her.

"I have a résumé, if you'd like to—"

"No need to show me your pack of lies. It doesn't matter where you worked before or what your last boss thinks of you. The only way you'll learn to do this job is by working it for a few years. Now like I said, the job's go-fer. I get lots of private collectors through here. I try to keep things on hand to satisfy them, but it seems they always come up with some this or that, some doodad or some such that I don't have on my shelves. I can't be bothered traipsing around town or around the country anymore. So that's on you."

"There's travel involved in the position?"

"Whatever I decide is involved is involved. Why do you suppose I'm hiring a career-type like you instead of some fresh-out-of-high-school young lady eager to try out her new driver's license? Let me walk you through what you'll be doing. Someone comes in the front way, you handle it. Talk them up, find out what they want to buy, sell it to them. Get a good price. I can't be bothered with lookie-loos."

"You can't be bothered with people window-shopping in a *curio* shop?" Claire said. "I'm curious what your business model is, if not tourists looking for tchotchkes."

"Then if I hire you, you'll want to keep your eyes open, because I run a tight ship. Private collectors pay my bills and pay your salary. I handle them. The lookie-loos just fill in the cracks. You handle them and everyone else who comes in through the front way."

"Where *is* the front way?"

"You came *in* the front way."

"In the alley?"

"Yes."

Claire glanced about. Their plodding journey away from the doorway had taken them several layers deeper into the store. They'd gone past the eighties and nineties, and were now deep into the fifties. There were still at least three rooms ahead of them, and no sign of another entrance or exit.

"Then where is the back way?"

"That's none of your concern. I handle the folks from the back way, at least until I know you're not a ninny. You just answer their questions and get their goods. You'll get all the training you need on the job. And here's the first thing you need to know. Authenticity. I deal in the real thing. No reissues. No reproductions. If it's on a shelf, it's the same one that would have been on the shelf the year it was made. I'm even picky about restored originals. Replacement parts have to be authentic. New-old stock, that sort of thing."

Again, Claire glanced about. They were back to the turn of the century now. The turn of the *previous* century, more accurately. Clocks, furniture, and jewelry from the nineteen-hundreds and earlier were displayed on all sides, each looking pristine and new. If these *were* original, authentic artifacts from over a hundred years ago, and they were simply on-the-shelf stock, then Claire was beginning to see how an antique store could offer so significant a salary.

"Do we do much buying? I don't have much expertise in appraisal."

"You'll get it. And until you do, I do the buying. You do the selling. And again, just to the lookie-loos."

"How do I set prices?"

She came to a stop behind an anachronistic shop counter. It looked like something out of the sixties, which may as well have been the distant future when compared to the relics surrounding it. A semi-modern cash register, a tray of snacks, and a coffee maker were set up there.

"You don't set the prices. Not until I think you're ready. And I'll *tell* you when I think you're ready. So until then, you consult the binder."

Ms. Thomas leaned down behind the counter and tugged out an old-fashioned paper binder. She plopped it down and flipped it open. Every line was populated with carefully written hand-lettered entries cataloging the contents of each shelf in the store, the purchase price, a few short notes about its origin and quality, and the sale price.

"For you, the binder is law," Ms. Thomas said. "You don't sell for under the price here. If you sell for over it, fine. But you don't sell for under it. Do you want the job?"

"Do I… are you *offering* it? We've barely had an interview."

Ms. Thomas waved her hand. "An interview's the same pack of lies as a résumé. Anything you can't get out of a few sentences and a good hard look in the eye isn't worth knowing. Besides, you're Claire Daniels, right?"

"Right."

"Estelle's girl?"

"You know my mother?"

"Does restoration on garments. Eighteen-eighties straight through to the two-thousands. The woman knows how to match a stitch pattern like no one I've ever met. Anyone who could turn out a perfect match for a darner's stitch from the Victorian Era can raise up a daughter fit to work in this place."

She'd made the comment while gesturing to the contents of a chest of drawers. Sure enough, folded within were items of clothing just as authentic as the rest of the artifacts.

"So you want the job or not?" Ms. Thomas asked.

"Yes, please."

"Fine. You're hired. Wednesdays off. Most weekends off, too, but ask first. You start tomorrow Six a.m. on the dot. Dress sharp. Like you've got on now, only maybe less with the soggy shoes. Also, long sleeves. Some of my clients don't like seeing a lady's elbows. And bring a pad and paper. Training starts when you walk in the door, and I don't like repeating myself."

#

Despite stepping through the "front" door at 5:55 a.m. the next day, several minutes before the official start of business, she found Ms. Thomas already serving a customer. He was rather tall and thin, and was standing bolt upright as she reached up to fiddle with the collar of a well-starched shirt that looked as if it could have come out of a Sears catalog from the early fifties.

"Ah! You're early. Good, good. I like that. Get over here and tie this man's tie. The rheumatism is acting up," Ms. Thomas said.

She tossed Claire a strangely wide tie with a loud pattern. After a moment to kick her brain into the sort of "customer facing" mode she'd not had to affect since high school, she brightened her smile and got to work.

"Right away, Ms. Thomas," Claire said.

She had to reach up to drape the tie around the man's neck. He seemed strangely uneasy as he stared down at her, and he moved with the sort of rigidity of a tipsy person who had been pulled over for a sobriety check.

"So, what's your name, sir? And what brings you to Yesterday's

120

Tomorrow?" she said, chipper as ever.

"Don't answer her," Ms. Thomas called from the next room. "And Claire, no asking questions to folks who come in the back way unless they're on their way out the front way. Write that down. That's rule number one."

"Er… I'm sorry. One moment, sir," Claire said.

Normally, being scolded like that would have irritated her, but Ms. Thomas radiated a school-librarian level of authority that left her feeling more flustered than angry. Perhaps Mr. Nameless was suffering from the same problem. It would certainly explain the beads of sweat running down his temple despite the morning coolness still lingering in the freshly opened shop.

She pulled a small notebook from her pocket and jotted down the warning, then finished tying the tie. Ms. Thomas tottered back with a suit jacket to match the slacks the man was already wearing. It was mildly ill-fitting, the arms maybe an inch too short.

"There. That'll do you. We'll put this one on your tab, but next time, I want you a little closer to your appointment. I *hate* tardiness. Off with you now," Ms. Thomas said, handing him a matching fedora.

He nodded and hurried off to the back of the store. When he'd slipped through a door near the counter at the far end of the shop, Ms. Thomas turned to Claire.

"Read that first rule back to me," she said.

Claire fetched the pad. "No questions to people from the back way unless they are leaving via the front way."

"Good. That's fine. Rule two: no answering any questions unless they are leaving via the front way."

Claire jotted it down. "Why?"

"Rule three: don't ask me any questions about my motivation for my rules."

Claire raised her eyebrows and almost chuckled at the bluntness of it, but marked it down all the same. "And for rule two, does it matter of they came from the front way?"

"No. The only thing that matters is if they are coming from, or leaving through, the back way."

"Okay."

"Rule four: You see that door he left through?"

"Yes."

"That's the back way. I'm telling you *only* so you know not to open that door. I don't care if the building is burning and you hear a crying baby on the other side. The back-way door stays closed unless I'm the one opening it or a guest comes in from the other side."

"Got it," Claire said.

"Let's see… what else… Tips. You can take tips, but you've got to give them to me first. Tips go in the till, then I pay you out of the till. That's rule five."

"… Right…"

"Rule six: the store must *not* be left unattended at any time when there may be appointments. That could mean overtime."

"Paid?"

"You're getting \$2,000 a day, honey. Don't get greedy."

"And how will I know if there are appointments?"

"I'll tell you. I've got a ledger for them, but you don't get a look at that until I'm satisfied you're working out as an employee. Where was I?"

"Rule seven."

"Right, right. Rule seven. Let's see… you ought to understand this one, coming from banks and such like you do. You might hear me and my customers muttering about this and that…"

"I assume I should keep it a secret?"

"Don't get ahead of me. And yes. That goes without saying. But you shouldn't act on it either."

"Act on it?"

"Think insider trading, honey. You hear something? You keep it to yourself and you pretend you didn't hear it."

"What sort of customers do you have who might be talking about privileged—"

"Rule eight: don't ask who my customers are or where they come from."

The librarian effect was wearing off, as Claire's patience was running out already. She marked it down. "Anything else?"

"What next, what next… Ah, yes. This is very important. I—"

There was a knock at the back door. Ms. Thomas turned and glared at the door as it opened. The same man, dressed in a fuzzy white robe, stepped through the doorway.

"You've just *been* here, Mr. Barnaby," the old woman snapped.

He shuddered at the scolding, then glanced at the clock on the wall and sheepishly slipped back out of the store.

"Can't seem to keep to a schedule, that one," she muttered. "Where was I?"

"Something very important."

"Was it? … Damned if I can remember. We'll get back to it. What do you know about folding dress shirts?"

"Nothing, ma'am."

"Well, follow me. We've got to get stock back in order." She shuffled toward the nineteen-fifties-themed portion of the store. "That man has arms like an orangutan. Had to go through my whole stock to find a shirt that'd fit him… oh! I remember the important thing. Rule nine: ignore anything in the binder that doesn't pertain to the current transaction, and only mark down the date, time, and price of a sale or purchase. And while we're at it…"

She stopped abruptly and turned to a case of antique watches. "As I said, I run a tight ship. And one of the most important things is keeping to a schedule. I notice you don't wear a watch."

"I have a cell phone for that," Claire said.

Ms. Thomas pulled an elegant woman's watch from the case and handed it to Claire. "Now you've got a watch for it. When you're marking down times, this is the watch you work from. Every Thursday morning we synchronize all of these watches and clocks. And we do it to *my* time. That may not match the time on your phone, but phones are for phone calls, not telling time."

Claire admired the watch. "It's very nice, Ms. Thomas. Is this an employee benefit, or are you docking my pay for this?"

"It's on loan. So don't go hocking it. Right. Back to the shirts then."

#

For as confusing as the morning had been, the rest of the day went roughly the way Claire had imagined it would. In the absence of a customer to serve, she busied herself with menial tasks like sweeping the floor, sorting various little knickknacks, and doing other mindless jobs. It was actually refreshing. In the banking world, stress levels were seldom below a boil. It was one of the reasons she'd adopted her mandatory-positivity mindset and the only reason she'd eventually quit. Having time to think, and having no pressure, was a lovely change of pace. Even if the supposed salary was too good to be true, just having a few hours to let her mind wander was therapeutic.

Against all odds, two customers visited via the front door over the course of business hours. The first one left with nothing after looking through a folder of nineteen eighties comic books and failing to find something he liked. The other sold her a pocket watch that, while not running, was apparently authentic enough for Ms. Thomas to okay a sale for $350.

The only other *interesting* part of the day came when the back way opened again. This time it was a woman, and oddly enough, she was dressed in the same fuzzy white robe Mr. Barnaby had briefly appeared wearing. She and Ms. Thomas chatted quietly for a moment or two. Halfway through their conversation, Ms. Thomas handed her a stack of clothes, and she slipped behind a changing screen. When she stepped out again, she had donned an unremarkable T-shirt-and-jeans ensemble. Ms. Thomas flipped through her binder and ran her finger down it, then beckoned for Claire.

"How may I help you and our customer?" Claire said, once again calling upon her customer service insincerity.

"Claire, this young lady is Mrs. Crumb. She needs a... say it again, dear?"

The customer cleared her throat, then spoke with an accent Claire couldn't quite place. "A key fob for a 2008 Chrysler 300."

Claire jotted it down.

"Quality doesn't matter too much," Ms. Thomas said. "Anything on the good end of the spectrum. Functional is best, but whatever. And you know my taste. Original. No reproduction, no replacement."

"Um... Yes. And where would I find such a thing?" Claire asked.

"Don't know, don't care. The internet, I imagine. The point is, it's your job to find it. No deadline. Just let me know when it's here, and I'll mark it in the binder."

Mrs. Thomas selected a blank appointment card, glanced in her secretive appointment book, and jotted down a time and date. "There you go, Mrs. Crumb. Be punctual."

"Thank you, Ms. Thomas," Mrs. Crumb said.

She accepted the card, gave Claire a nervous smile, and slipped out through the back way. Despite her curiosity, Claire didn't bother even trying to catch a glimpse of what was on the other side of the door. You don't tempt fate on day one of a job.

"So, when I find this key fob, does that come out of a store account?"

"You buy it. I'll reimburse you. But only once I get a look at it. The internet has a nasty way of sending trash. May as well run along and get to it. Oh, and before you go." She tapped a button on the cash register and pulled a stack of bills from inside. After a quick count she handed them over. "There you go, $2,000. Payment for your first day."

"You're paying me in *cash*?"

"Why shouldn't I? Just keep good accounts. The IRS will be all over you if you don't."

Claire paused.

"Itching to uncover another rule, honey?"

She ran the situation through her head. Huge amounts of secrecy. Large quantities of money being dispensed in cash. The whole thing was beginning to seem a bit suspicious. But as concerned as that might make her, it wasn't as though she could just ask "Are you engaged in some sort of criminal activity?" If Ms. Thomas wasn't willing to show her what was behind the "back way," she certainly wasn't going to come clean about what, if any, scam she was running. Best to just keep her eyes and ears open and make sure that if there *were* some sort of shenanigans going on, she wouldn't be implicated.

"No, Ms. Thomas. I'll see you tomorrow."

"Six a.m. sharp."

#

Over the course of three months, Claire fell into a comfortable, if unusual, routine. She started to pick up some haggling skills through the odd walk-in through the front door. She even started to develop a rapport with people from the mysterious back way. Though there were new faces now and then, the same half-dozen people came through most of the time. They placed orders, picked them up, and acted generally tense along the way. Contrary to her experiences elsewhere, she found humor tended to put these people even *more* on edge. Claire tried not to let her imagination run wild wondering just what sort of business Ms. Thomas was doing with these people that could have them so nervy all the time. If there's one thing you learn talking to bankers, it's the value of ignorance when shenanigans are afoot.

The slowest progress in finding her place in this new job came with Ms. Thomas herself. Apparently, the old girl was allergic to small talk, and the proportion of the business she kept close to her chest meant that on the average day she was scribbling in books and making phone calls while Claire tried to keep busy. Ms. Thomas had revealed herself to be the sort of person who only talked to you if you were doing something wrong. The better Claire did her job, the less Ms. Thomas had to say. That's why it had been such a surprise when she'd arrived in the store that morning and was informed that she would be handling the store alone for most of the day while Ms. Thomas met with a private collector in the next town to discuss a major purchase.

Lest Claire feel *too* good about her progress, Ms. Thomas had made it clear that she was only being entrusted with the store because the two appointments were late in the day, and Ms. Thomas would be back in time to handle them herself. Just her luck, there were no walk-ins that day either. Within the first forty minutes of store hours, she'd run out of busy work. There was only so much time she could spend puttering around behind the counter. As interesting as it was looking at impeccably restored furniture from the nineteen-hundreds, she'd seen all there was to see long ago. More interesting to her were the rare bits of missed restoration. She turned to her left and eyed the door to a cabinet opposite the back way. An ancient ding in the door panel marred an otherwise exquisite piece of furniture. She wondered if that was why it was a display piece rather than having sold ages ago.

She heaved a sigh and paced over to the nineteen eighties section of the store. Ms. Thomas kept some genuinely nostalgic pieces of ephemera that were perfect for wiling away the hours.

She'd just finished the red side of an original Rubik's Cube when a knock nearly scared her out of her skin.

Claire turned to the door to the back way. There was a second knock, then the doorknob jiggled. She checked the clock. According to the schedule for the day, no one was supposed to arrive for another few hours.

"Just a moment," Claire called.

She hurried to the door and unlocked it. A man, wearing the ubiquitous white robe, stepped out and glanced around.

"Ms. Thomas?" he said.

This wasn't one of the regulars. She would have remembered a face like his. He had an odd look about him, as if he may be of some sort of ethnic extraction she'd yet to encounter. It was in the set of his jaw and in the spacing of his eyes. Something just felt *off* about him, but nothing she could put her finger on. He reached through the back door and fetched a brushed-aluminum briefcase.

"Ms. Thomas?" the man asked again, clearly uncomfortable with the thoughtful stare he was receiving rather than a reply.

Claire snapped out of her quandary. At this point, she was treading on the gray area between the various rules she'd been given, but if one thing had been made clear thus far, the people who came in the back way were Ms. Thomas's most valuable customers. It was probably better to tread lightly and deal with them directly than risk costing her boss a potentially massive pay day.

"I'm sorry. I'm afraid Ms. Thomas isn't in. Can I help you? My name is Claire; I am Ms. Thomas's personal assistant. She has stepped out for the day."

"That presents a significant bugaboo. I usually deal directly with Ms. Thomas," he said.

"I… see."

"If I am interpreting your tone correctly, you find my statement dubious."

"Ms. Thomas is probably fifty years older than I, among other glaring differences, so I'd imagine if you *usually* dealt with her, you would have known I'm not her."

"Yes. That is an exceedingly insightful assessment. And it is easily explained by the lack of face-to-face communication. As is quite common, you are well aware, my dealings have been primarily text based, both via small message service and electronic mail."

Claire raised an eyebrow. "That would certainly explain it. And while she prefers to deal with certain customers personally, unless you'd like to come back at another time, I am afraid I'm the only one here to help you."

He shut his eyes for a moment and muttered, head tilted back as though he were doing some complex calculations. "I am uncertain I have the resources to facilitate another visit in a timely manner."

"You're welcome to wait for her, but she might be a few hours."

"That would be un-ideal, but agreeable. Though I would imagine spending that time in a place of business while dressed in this robe would not be socially acceptable."

"If we get another customer, you'll get some strange looks, that's for sure." A nagging thought finally drifted to the surface. "*Oh!* Are you hoping to leave out the front way or the back way?"

"Today, I am leaving through the front way."

"Excellent. Then according to her arbitrary rules, I can actually offer some degree of help. What do you need, sir?"

"First and foremost, I need an outfit commensurate with nondescript pedestrian travel."

"Walking-around clothes. Gotcha. Anything in particular you have in mind?"

"Something modern. Fashionable. But not ostentatious. Something representative of the hoi polloi."

"Right, right. We *may* be able to help you." Claire hurried to the front of the store. If she was going to find something for him, it would be there. "We don't really deal in modern clothes much, sir. Normally, I'd ask why you came *here* for your fashion needs. But then, I suppose that's not allowed."

"Thoroughly prohibited. I would have foregone an answer had you asked. You are not the only one beholden to the fearsome Ms. Thomas and her criteria of interaction."

She tugged open the drawers of the dresser that held Ms. Thomas's less eye-catching inventory.

"You know, I find myself a little at a loss," Claire said. "Ms. Thomas's rules *really* cut down on the potential for small talk. Do you have any questions for me?"

He clicked open his case and consulted a pocket watch from within. Again, he closed his eyes and seemed to do some more math. "Not at present time. I think perhaps if I were to acquire and don my new outfit expediently, that would be ideal."

"Right. Let's see…" She found a pair of blue jeans and a plain black T-shirt. "These look about your size. There's a changing screen in the back there, next to the counter. And there is a pair of boxers in here too. Did you need those?"

"I believe those are still in fashion?"

"Uh, yeah. Boxers are pretty much evergreen."

"Then I will require them."

The Back Way

Claire hoped her expression didn't betray her bemusement at a man who was both willing to visit a store without boxers and was uncertain if they were still popular.

He took the clothes and stepped behind the screen. "This is your first week at this establishment, correct?"

"I'm newish, but it's been a few months."

"Ah. Right. That explains it."

"Explains what?"

"The nature of some difficulties I've been having. It's why Ms. Thomas wasn't here. I missed my appointment by not an *inconsiderable* amount of time."

He stepped out from behind the screen fully dressed. Without the robe, Claire was able to see the man's build. He was every bit of six and a half feet tall and rail thin. As tended to be the case when people were ready to complete their purchases when they came in via the back way, the fit wasn't *perfect*, but considering her current customer's build, it was impressive how close the clothes came to a proper fit.

"You really lucked out. When it comes to inventory, we're a mile wide and an inch deep."

The customer nodded. "Right, imperial units… What do I owe you for the clothes?"

"Let's check the binder." She leafed through the pages, trying to remember the key to deciphering the not entirely straightforward indexing system Ms. Thomas used.

"Might I inquire after your expertise in certain matters while we wait?"

"I'll do my best to help."

"I am not local to this locale, and this is not my native tongue. How would you critique my vernacular?"

"Um… Your *diction* is impeccable, but you're a touch more formal than is typical around here."

"Is it a glaring departure from the local norm?"

"Yes, if I'm honest."

"I shall reduce my vocabulary accordingly."

"Here. The outfit will cost you… let's call it a hundred dollars even."

"Ah. Excellent. I am appreciative of…" He shut his eyes. "Thanks for the help?"

"That's more like it."

He clicked the case open and counted off a stack of decrepit tens and twenties. "While I'm at it, what do you think of Richard Prentice?"

"I'm afraid I've never heard of him."

He nodded. "Good. I was hoping he hadn't caught on yet."

"Who is he?"

"Count yourself lucky if you never hear the name again. On another matter. I am going to be spending a while traveling locally. Aside from my vocabulary, does anything in my comportment stand out as out of place?"

She smirked.

"I take that I haven't quite calibrated my vocabulary appropriately?"

"I haven't heard the word 'comportment' since grade school."

"Noted. Please continue to indicate when I stray from modern slang. It is very important I not stand out."

"Will do."

Claire looked him over a bit more critically. Even standing still with his mouth shut, there *was* something off about him. It wasn't anything as obvious as some sort of poorly fitting disguise or botched plastic surgery. But there was something in the set of his jaw and the distance between his eyes. The whole proportion of his face was just a *bit* unusual, like he was the perfect specimen of a racial background she'd never encountered. Even the smaller things, like his posture and the way he curled his fingers, didn't seem quite natural.

"Untuck your shirt," she suggested.

He did so. It helped a bit, but he retained a vaguely distinctive quality that wouldn't blend nicely with the average crowd.

"You appear to be conflicted, Claire."

She held up a finger. "First, 'appear to be conflicted' is still a *little* highbrow for the 'hoi polloi.' So's 'hoi polloi,' by the way. But yeah, I'm conflicted."

"Why?"

"I want to help you, but I'm trying to think of a way to avoid sounding rude."

"By all means, be rude."

"Maybe it's just me, but…" She crossed her arms and sighed.

“You look weird.”

“Such was my concern. In what way, and how do we address it?”

“Let’s start with your hair. That’s a pretty ruthless part you’ve got there.”

“Fix it, please.”

She rummaged around for a hairbrush and gave him a more millennial degree of calculated disheveling. An old baseball cap and some sunglasses went a long way into rendering him nondescript.

“There. I think that’ll do the job,” she said. “I must say, I’m relieved you didn’t take that personally.”

“I’m terribly out of touch, ma’am. I need all the help I can get. Thanks again. It has been invaluable. I’m sure you understand how important it is to fit in when you’re visiting a new place.”

“Happy to be of service.”

He clicked open his case and looked over the contents. “Hmm… I’d not quite calculated the exchange rate correctly. I was hoping I’d have enough for a reasonable tip, but the hat and glasses cleaned me out.” He plucked a five-dollar bill from the case. “Five dollars is all I can spare.”

“Tips are entirely optional, sir.”

“No, no. You deserve more, particularly in light of your excellent service.” He pulled the pocket watch from his case and clicked it open. “Let’s see… If I…” He seemed conflicted for a moment, then tipped his head side to side. “Here,” he said, handing the five to her. “Next time you go to the local deli, grab a scratch-off.”

“Heh. Maybe I will.”

“I really suggest that you do.”

The phone rang, startling Claire. A lifetime of digital phones and cell phones had spared her the fire-alarm-level clang of Ms. Thomas’s precious princess phone. Even after several months, she’d still not gotten used to it.

“I’m sorry, I have to take this,” she said.

“Not a problem. My needs are met, so I will be on my way. Say hello to Ms. Thomas for me.”

“Goodbye, enjoy your day!”

She answered the phone as he walked confidently out the door. “Hello? Yesterday’s Tomorrow. … Oh, good. We’re expecting the buyer for those shoes in two days. We were getting nervous. … No, no. You know Ms. Thomas doesn't like delivery."

That, it turned out, was one of the key reasons her salary was so high. In the three months she'd been working here, she'd spent nearly as much time in the car as in the store. When she arrived, she frequently had to convince vendors and sellers to do business in cash and with as little paperwork as possible. She hadn't had to get on a plane yet, but that was just because Ms. Thomas's list of carefully curated artisans and collectors were all within a "short" three-hour drive.

If not for the fact that she *knew* she was picking up things like wallets, pocket calculators, and other period-perfect doodads, this would have been another check box on her drug dealer bingo card. As it was, the jury was still out on whether Ms. Thomas was a money launderer or not. Claire had banked the pay from her first few days to have a lawyer ready just in case this whole thing turned out to be as shady as it felt.

She checked her watch. "Okay, you're an hour away. How long are you going to be there? … That's cutting it close. Can you hold on a moment?"

Claire pinned the phone to her ear with her shoulder and stretched the cord to its limit to reach her purse and fetch her phone. She tapped Ms. Thomas's number.

"Ms. Thomas, the shoes are in, but I'd have to leave the store to pick them up right now if I want to get them by end of day. I've got the guy on the phone now. If I leave immediately, I can be back by seven."

"Dang it…" Ms. Thomas muttered. "I'm running late. I might miss the first appointment."

"Was it a tall, thin guy with kind of wonky eyes?"

"Did he come through already?"

"Yes. In through the back way. Bought some clothes and some stuff from the front of the store. Binder price, cash."

"I hate when they can't keep to a schedule," she muttered. "Fine then. Just this once, flip the sign to closed and head out. When you get back, open back up and be ready to stay until at least 10 p.m. This is taking forever and a day. There will be another customer through the back way sometime between 8 and 10. If anything else goes wrong, I'm bound to miss them. You'll have to handle it. Just follow the rules and you'll be fine."

"Will do." Claire ended the call and switched back to the landline.

"Yeah, hold on to the shoes. I'll be there in an hour."

She hung up and fiddled with her keys to get ready to lock up. Ms. Thomas had a high-school janitor-level key ring, but she'd created an abridged duplicate for Claire. Even with fewer than half the keys, it was a pain matching keys to locks. And it was incredibly important that she not miss a lock. Among the lengthy list of things Ms. Thomas didn't trust were security cameras and security systems, so the locks were the only thing standing between the store and several hundred thousand dollars of theft. It was a little hard to believe Ms. Thomas's claim that the place had only been robbed once.

When the place was secure, she hurried down the steps to see to her errand.

#

Just shy of two hours later, Claire was in her car with a pair of turn-of-the-century court shoes that cost more than her first car to repair. Her stomach was rumbling, and her eyelids were sagging. The early hours were beginning to get to her. If she was going to be staying on hand for another few hours, it was time for caffeine. Fortunately, she'd spent her lunch and coffee breaks for the first month tracking down the one and only place in the neighborhood that did a decent espresso. Oddly enough, it was a Greek deli that also made an excellent gyro.

"Order up, Claire," called the cashier.

She looked up from her phone. "Oh, that was quick," she said.

Another customer slipped in the door just as she stepped up to the register. The place was open nearly twenty-four hours, and they probably made *most* of their money on the usual early-morning staples, which included breakfast sandwiches, coffee, and lotto tickets. As she looked at the display of scratchers, something leaped back into her mind.

Despite getting paid in cash, she stuck to the credit card for purchases. In fact, she tended only to have cash on her for the ride from work to the late-night deposit box. Right now, there was a ratty five-dollar bill in her purse, her tip from the back-way customer. She'd been distracted by the phone call for the shoes and neglected to add it to the till.

She swiped her credit card. While she waited for it to go through, she eyed the price list for the scratch-offs. "Wow. It's been so long since I bought a scratch-off. They actually have five-dollar ones now."

"Yeah, sure," said the cashier. "You want one?"

"Uh… Yeah, why not?" she said. "Give me a number thirty-two."

He tugged a card from the reel inside the display. The motion took him all of two seconds, but in that time, a lifetime of goodie-two-shoes-level behavior and obedience reared its ugly head. She rode a roller coaster from "what harm could it do?" to "that whole tip rule is totally arbitrary" to "she'll never know," but ended inevitably on "it's the wrong thing to do," with the powerful postscript "and you'd be risking nearly a million dollars a year for a petty act of rebellion."

"Actually, on second thought, never mind," she said, taking her coffee and food.

"Don't put it away," said the man behind her. "I was going to get one of those and a coffee, light and sweet."

"Sure thing," said the cashier.

Claire stepped aside to organize her food into an arrangement that would survive the car ride. It was fortunate she was holding the bag and the coffee tightly, because when she was half through, the man at the counter crowed at the top of this lungs.

"I can't believe it! I won!" he cried, waving the ticket. "Three hundred dollars! Man, I've never won more than a few bucks on one of these!"

He turned to her. "I ought to buy you another coffee. This was *your* ticket," he said.

"What? Oh, uh, no, no. That's all yours, sir. Just the luck of the draw." She glanced down at the five-dollar bill, still visible in her purse. "Nothing but luck."

#

A few minutes later, Claire was back in Yesterday's Tomorrow. She stood at the counter with the five-dollar tip sitting in front of her.

"Buy a scratch-off at the local deli. That's exactly what he said. And that ticket would have been a winner," she muttered, staring at the money. "I mean… it's a coincidence, right? It *has* to be a coincidence. What else *could* it be?"

She fished her pad out of her pocket and flipped back to the first page. "Rule seven: do not act on anything that the customers say. Insider trading. But that was… how could that have been legitimate inside information?"

The Back Way

Claire glared at the pad and the money lying side by side as though they were conspiring against her. "Okay. Let's assume these rules *aren't* arbitrary. Just for a moment, let's assume she *knew* that if some guy came in the back way and told me something, I would be able to exploit that. And according to rule five, I should have given it to her to put in the till. I'm not supposed to have the *specific* bill." She picked it up. "What could possibly be wrong with having a specific bill?"

She turned the bill over in her hands. There wasn't really anything unique about it, as far as she could tell. It was extremely worn, but it was otherwise just a bit of currency. It wasn't until she pored over each individual bit of text on the bill that she realized it was a series 2018.

"What the hell did he do to beat up this dollar in just a few months? When do they even release the new bills? This doesn't make sense."

Her brain struggled with the clues, but all the answers she was coming up with were impossible. She turned to the list of rules again.

"Rule nine: ignore anything in the binder that doesn't pertain to the current transaction…"

Her burning curiosity and confusion had eroded her duty to Ms. Thomas enough that she didn't hesitate to pull out the binder. Her boss's indexing system was a bit obtuse. The order wasn't based upon anything as sane as categories like clothes and novelties. Even a simple date and time would be useful. Ms. Thomas had broken it into days of the week, first. That made entering in purchases simple enough, but entering in sales meant having to know *when* the purchase was made. The way around it involved a second binder to point her at the right date and time. It was already a recurring disagreement between her and Ms. Thomas that she should invest in a database system, which would have saved her several minutes a day of searching. It *also* would have made it trivial to browse through it and know what you were looking at. This method was awfully useful, and *only* useful if you were trying to hide information.

She flipped the book to the middle, placing her on a random Wednesday, her day off. Page after page of random purchases awaited her, with progressively newer pages having been added to the binder as the decades of sales history rolled on. Nothing seemed odd about them, except for the fact that some of them didn't use all available space, and thus there were far more pages than there should have been. She flipped forward until she reached the most recent Wednesday. But there were several more pages after it. She flipped to them and found them partially filled. There was a sheet of Sundays, two Mondays… Considering how precise Ms. Thomas was, it seemed unlikely she had placed them there in error.

Claire half expected to see some sort of contraband on these pages, but it was just more of the same. She supposed it could have been a code, but there was something else strange. The dates. She almost missed it, but most of the dates were incomplete. None of them had a time completely filled in, though some had at least the hour. Only a few had days filled in, a few more had months filled in, and most had years filled in. All of those dates were in the future, sometimes *years* in the future. It was one thing to know that a week from Sunday she would be buying a set of fine china. It was another thing entirely to know that in seven years she would be buying an engraved Rolex.

She shut the binder and checked the clock. It was only a little after seven. The ill-defined appointment wasn't likely to be for hours more, and Ms. Thomas seemed convinced she would be delayed at least that long, if not longer. If she were going to break what was clearly the cardinal rule of this place, it would be now.

The same voice that had quietly persuaded her not to buy the lotto ticket now spoke up again. Yes, this was all extremely suspicious. But Ms. Thomas was still the boss, and she was still paying *very* well for Claire's services.

This time the angel on her shoulder just wasn't convincing enough. She turned to the back way and, before she could lose her nerve, unlocked it.

The door creaked open to reveal… very little. A single naked light bulb dangled from the ceiling. The familiar fluffy white robe hung from a hook beside the door, and a thick black curtain closed off one corner of an otherwise empty storage closet. Beside the door, a folded newspaper article had been taped to the wall. She flipped it up.

It was a short snippet describing an unsolved assault and theft by an unknown assailant at a factory across town. There was no date on or in the article. Even the reporting was unremarkable. Just a matter-of-fact account of a group of thieves being apprehended, and a single set of unknown prints suggesting the identity of the assailant.

She scoured the article and searched it front and back. She was hoping for something to explain why it was there, but more than that, she was distracting herself from the elephant in the room.

Charlotte's stomach burned with anxiety as she abandoned the article and stepped up to the curtain. Just what could it be hiding that would explain everything she'd seen and experienced? Rather than give her mind any more time to run wild, she reached out and whisked the curtain aside. Waiting for her behind it was a sturdy assemblage of pipes and struts mounted to the floor, curling into something of a half-cage. They were highly polished brass with interspersed walnut panels. Plates spaced at regular intervals had lengthy and complex messages etched on to them in what might have been Greek. Some had small knobs mounted in sliders with out-of-sequence numbers labeling them. A silver platter of some sort had been mounted near the top of the lattice of struts, and a cluster of crystals hung from a silver chain a few inches in front of it. It had a curious Jules Verne feel to it, with a dash of cult-like altar thrown in.

Entirely absent was a second door. There was no other way into the room. She couldn't even see any seams that might betray a secret hatch. How did people get into this room? Did they just show up at night and stay inside until she let them out? Claire *knew* she couldn't have missed people sneaking into the room from inside the store. A childish, superstitious part of her mind suggested that the device was to blame. But she wasn't yet ready to accept that somehow people were entering the store via an antique array of plumbing and paneling. As the only thing of interest in the room she'd yet to investigate in full, she took in the finer details of the device.

It seemed to be entirely passive, no obvious power switch or power cables. There wasn't even a light switch in the room to turn off the bulb. Not that she would have been foolish enough to flip any switches if there *had* been any. She kept her distance and fumbled for her phone. She knew she would only be able to stay in here so long, so documenting this bizarre contraption would help her to work out what exactly made it worth concealing.

She snapped picture after picture, carefully zooming and steadying so that the resulting snapshot would be legible. The single light bulb wasn't nearly enough light for the little cell-phone camera to get a decent picture, so she had to rely upon its flash. She was taking a picture of the final panel when she realized the room was a good deal brighter than when she'd started. The light came from the bundle of crystals in front of the silver dish. Curious, she squinted at the glowing crystals.

As though it had been waiting for its chance to punish her, the crystals chose this moment to release a blinding flash and a wave of heat. She stumbled back and thumped into the far wall. The sharp sting of anxiety fell quickly away when she felt the coolness of the wall on her back. Her vision was awash with purple blotches, but she didn't need to be able to see to know why she was feeling such a draft.

Somehow, her clothes were gone.

She covered herself and backed into the corner, blinking her tearing eyes and trying to get her heart to settle. The room gradually sharpened into visibility around her. The first thing she could see clearly was the glow of the light bulb. The second was the growing smolder of the cluster of gems.

A fresh wave of panic washed over her. They were clearly the source of whatever had happened to her, and she did *not* want it to happen again. If there had been anything in the room with her, she would have smashed the gems. Lacking a weapon of any kind, she snatched at the gems and tore them free. The light within them vanished like a snuffed candle the moment they were out of position.

When only the light of the bulb remained, she shakily set the cluster of gems on the floor and backed away. The lack of an impending blast of an unknown nature allowed her mind to begin to function well enough to try to work out what was going on and why.

She looked to the hook beside the door. Rather than the familiar white robe, there was a classy red one. She snagged it and slipped it on. Being in a creepy room with a mysterious device was bad enough without being naked.

The robe's color wasn't the only difference in the room. The article on the wall was gone as well, and though she was certain she'd left it open, the door was now shut. She tried the knob.

Locked.

"No! Come on, come on!" she growled.

Claire rattled the handle and tugged the knob, but the lock was on the store side. There wasn't even a keyhole on her side. The room was virtually empty, but she looked around again just in case there might have been something she could use to pry it open. Nothing. The door was heavy, solid oak. There would be no breaking it down, and tempting as it might have been to tear off a chunk of the device that had done this to her in order to bash at the door, there were two problems with that plan. The first was that she'd probably just end up with a bent pipe and a dinged door. The second was that it would require her to get close to the device again, and that was *not* going to happen.

With no way out, and with her phone having vanished along with the rest of her clothes, she was left with nothing to do but think, fret, and curse her own curiosity.

#

After a few minutes of flexing her escape-room expertise and coming up dry, Claire heard voices at the front of the store. She took a deep breath, ready to call for help. Before she could, a male voice bellowed from the front of the store.

"I said where is the safe?"

Claire backed away from the door. The shop was being robbed. This couldn't be real. This was a nightmare.

She could hear a second voice, that of a woman. She was too quiet to understand, but she was young, and she was frightened. Claire inched away from the door as the voices approached.

"I don't want any trouble," the woman said fearfully.

"Then I want all the cash. And dump that jewelry in a bag. … Yeah. Look at all that cash. … What's in that room?"

Claire gasped.

"You can't open that door, Mister. Please. There's nothing there for you," the woman said.

The doorknob rattled. Claire immediately went from wishing the door was unlocked to praying it remained locked just a bit longer.

"Open it!" the man barked.

"Sir, please. It's a broom closet. Just—"

"Give me the damn keys!"

For a moment, there was silence. Then the scrape of a key in the lock. Claire's mind snapped into focus. A violent criminal was about to open the door and find her defenseless and barely dressed. There was no time for fear. She had to do something. She didn't even want to think about the alternative.

She took a deep breath and took another step back. The only thing in the room that might conceivably work as a weapon was the recently liberated cluster of gems. She snatched them up and held them

139

tight, never taking her eyes from the knob. It turned. She shifted her weight. Just as the door started to slide open, she took one full stride and thrust her heel into the door with as much of her weight behind it as she could muster.

The door flew open. It smashed into the robber. He stumbled back. Claire rushed out. She'd taken a single self-defense course, and it had been back in college, but that was enough for her to know exactly what sort of places to pummel during her adrenaline-soaked frenzy. She bashed his nose with the cluster of crystals. She drove her knee into his midsection. The main groaned and gasped for air. A second knee found a soft spot that didn't require any training to find. The robber's arm flailed. A pistol flew from his grip and thumped into the door of an antique cabinet. He spat profanities and finally heaved Claire off him. She tumbled against the base of the checkout counter. Red and white sparks raced through her vision from the blow to her head. Her hearing was lost in a low thrum. She lost her grip on the gems. The man climbed painfully to his feet and snatched at the bag of collectibles, shoveling cash and valuables into it and his pockets.

"Now it's your turn to start taking orders!" the young woman said.

Claire turned her throbbing head to see a young black woman in a blue dress shakily brandishing the revolver that had been knocked away. Judging from how she held it, the woman was familiar with such a weapon, but far from comfortable with it.

"Now calm down. Just—just don't get excited now," he said, holding still and clutching the bag of valuables tightly.

"On your feet!" she snapped.

He slowly stood. She kept the weapon trained on him.

"Here's what you're going to do. You're going to drop that bag and go out that door. You're going to run down the street, and you're never, *never* going to come back. Because in ten minutes the cops'll be here, and if you're close enough for them to catch your trail, you better believe I'll make sure the only way your momma ever sees you again is through bars."

The robber took the warning to heart and rushed for the front of the store. Claire leaned heavily on the counter and hoisted herself to her feet. The room was spinning. Getting herself upright and stable was a multi-minute ordeal. Before she was through, she heard the rev of an engine and the squeal of tires as the robber beat a hasty retreat.

"I owe you a drink, honey!" said the young woman, now by Claire's side.

The startling voice nearly sent her pitching over again, but the woman caught her and kept her upright.

"Whoa, easy there," she said. "I tell you what, I didn't have any appointments on the ledger for today, but it's a damn good thing you showed up."

"Who are you?" Claire asked, rubbing her head.

"Name's Elenore Thomas," she said.

"Elenore Thomas…"

Claire gave the young woman a good look for the first time. It was difficult to figure out how old she was, but she couldn't have been much older than her mid-twenties. There was *certainly* a familiarity to her youthful face. The curve of her cheek. The set of her jaw. And more than anything, the look in her eye.

"I work for your… *mother*?" Claire said.

Her tone was hopeful, almost pleading, because the alternative was unthinkable.

Elenore smiled knowingly. "Ah ha! No, no, honey. Unless you're mopping floors for a living, it's not my mother you work for."

Claire gazed around the shop. The layout was different than the one she'd left behind. The turn-of-the-century goods were still clustered here by the counter, but the section extended nearly two times farther toward the front entrance than it should have. The nineteen twenties and nineteen thirties sections were larger than they should have been as well. And nothing past the nineteen sixties was present at all.

She shut her eyes. "I can't believe I'm asking this but… what year is it?"

Elenore crossed her arms. "Sounds like somebody was checking out a room she shouldn't't've been. A good thing, too. Because if you hadn't been in there, the *best* way this night would have turned out would've been with me losing a couple thousand dollars. Worst case could've been me dead and the cat out of the bag about the back way. What's your name, honey?"

"Claire."

"Claire, you're visiting the year nineteen seventy. And judging from the way you're talking, you're not from around here."

"I'm from—"

She raised her hand. "I don't want to know. Better I don't. Just answer me these questions. You come here looking to buy something?"

"No."

"Looking to sell?"

"No."

"Didn't have a plan for what to do?"

"No."

"Then let's send you back where you came from. The past is no place for tourists. Sit tight, I'll get it ready."

Claire's head was clearing, but she wasn't sure that was going to do her any good. What good was there in being able to apply logic to an illogical situation?

"Did you break this machine?" Elenore called warily.

"It just stripped me naked, apparently sent me through time, and was going to flash again. So I pulled off the crystals. What would *you* have done?"

"Can't say I'd've done different, but that doesn't help much."

"Is this going to be a problem?"

Elenore marched from the room. "That depends on where you put the crystals."

"I bashed the robber in the face with them. Then I dropped them when he threw me off. They should be somewhere on the floor."

"If you don't think you'll keel over, I think you'd best get down on the floor and help me find them, because if we don't, you're taking the long way home."

"Seriously? I'd have to just… *live* the intervening years?"

"No. It was a joke."

Claire breathed a sigh of relief.

"Someone would probably come along and kill you."

"What?!"

"Like I said, the past is no place for a tourist. You could do serious damage."

"But it was an accident! I didn't know I'd get here, and I didn't—"

"Don't talk to *me* about it. I just run the prop shop. Talk to whoever they send after you. Or better yet, just help find the gems so we can send you back where you came from."

Claire blinked a few more times until she was sure the blurriness was gone from her vision, then carefully lowered herself to the floor.

"Are there no spare parts for that device?"

"There are. For everything except the crystals. You picked the perfect thing to tear off if you wanted to keep the thing from working."

"I've always been pretty good at breaking things."

"The thing is, half that device is there just to make sure the crystals don't flash without a destination set. You'd have been fine."

"It would have been nice if someone had included that on her long list of rules…"

"Was one of the rules not to mess with the back way?"

"… Yes."

"If you weren't going to listen to *that* one, why would you have listened to anything else?"

Claire didn't defend herself. Partially, it was because the blow to her head and the impossibility of her situation had conspired to make critical thinking difficult. Mostly it was because Elenore wasn't wrong. Instead, she stuck to running the whole disastrous few minutes over in her head as she reached under furniture and scanned across the floor in search of the crystals. Eventually, her brain replayed something she'd half seen that caused her to freeze. She climbed to her feet, eyes distant and expression stricken.

"I don't like the look of that face," Elenore said.

"The robber was stuffing things in his pockets when he was getting up."

"Are you saying he took the gems?" Elenore said gravely.

"What does it mean if he did?"

Elenore shut her eyes. "Nothing good."

"Is there a chance the police can get them back?"

"Ain't no police coming. Them sticking their noses in the back way would be worse than the robber. Besides, cops couldn't care less about what happens to a hole-in-the-wall shop run by someone like me." She shook her head. "Come on. Let's get some clothes on you. And I think we *both* need a drink."

#

A few minutes later, Claire was learning firsthand how much less comfortable and more complicated women's clothing had been in the late sixties. Elenore provided her with a bright floral dress to wear

143

and a shot of bourbon to drink.

"Okay, Miss Claire," Elenore said after knocking back a shot of her own, "since you're from the future—"

"Did I say I was from the future?"

"With ladies it's pretty easy to tell. As I was saying, since you're from the future, and since you apparently work for *me*, I suppose I can come clean about a few things. Information's allowed to flow downstream and all. And you need to know just how badly you fouled things up. Settle in. Oh, and keep your mouth shut. The less *you* say to *me* the better, because information should *not* flow upstream. Plus, I don't need you flapping you lip after the trouble you've caused."

She poured another shot. "Here's what you need to know. Time travel is real, plainly. Folks can show up at devices like that one there. Don't ask how many there are. I don't know. More than one, but not many. Whoever made them—and I don't know who—made them to send *just* people through time. When you leave from your own time and come here, it's supposed to be you and just you. At some point, someone figured out how to send more than that through the device, but it must be very hard, because for whatever reason most folks don't bring much at all through with them even when it's clear they're from a time that knows how. Short version, folks show up in their birthday suits. And that's why when people show up, they come through the back way in a prop shop like this. We give them whatever outfits they need, whatever props they need. Period perfect. That way they can spend their resources on bringing through other stuff that'll help them go off and do whatever they came here to do. Lots of times people come through and ask for stuff from farther back. Beats me why. Maybe it's easier to make a pit stop than do the whole trip in one go."

"What are—"

"What'd I say? No questions. If I don't tell you something, it's something you don't need to know. The time travel happens when that cluster of crystals flashes. The crystals flash when they absorb enough light. Like I said, the device exists half to keep time travel from happening by mistake, and the other half to make sure you get to pick where you want to go. Without the device, just as soon as those crystals charge up, everyone nearby them is going *somewhere*. No telling where. No telling which way. No telling who. And another few minutes of charge later, it'll happen again. And again, over and over. If they all go forward, that's bad enough. If *any* of them go backward, and they don't know the rules…"

She tipped back the shot and winced. "Problems. The good news is, it probably won't happen until the sun comes up. Without that reflector, most man-made light doesn't have enough juice to fill them up. That gives us until sunup to do something about it—without the cops, because they work slower than molasses. And knowing the boys in blue around here, they'll take the crystals for evidence."

Claire looked aside for a moment.

"A little much to take in, isn't it?"

"No, no… I just… you said I shouldn't tell you anything about the future, right?"

"That's right."

"What happens if I *do* tell you something?"

"I don't know. So far no one's broken the rules as bad as you before."

"Okay. What if what I have to say might help us find the gems?"

Elenore drummed her fingers on the table.

"I think this is a lesser-of-two-evils situation. And one bit of information out of order beats who knows how many people going back and forth all willy-nilly. But considering you got here by mistake, what makes you think you might be able to help?"

"In the back room I left from, there was an article from a newspaper."

"Seems like whenever you come from, people don't care much about following rules. Only four items are allowed in that room. The robe, the light, the curtain, and the device. What'd the article say?"

"It was about an assault in a warehouse on the other side of town. It was… oh, come on… Fishkill Boulevard. Five-oh-one Fishkill Boulevard."

Elenore huffed. "That's a shady neighborhood, honey. Stands to reason anything that gets stolen in this town would show up there. You're sure about that address?"

"Pretty sure."

"What else do you remember about the article?"

"Not much. It was about a break-in, and there was an unknown assailant. Police found lots of stolen goods."

"Unknown assailant."

"Yes. I remember that distinctly."

"Okay, then. You're going to go get the crystals."

"What? *Me?* If I'm not supposed to even *tell* you something, surely I'm not supposed to be running around and playing vigilante."

"Normally, no. But you read the article. Which means it already happened where you came from. Which is where I'm going. So not only *can* you go and do it, you *have* to go do it. Because you already *did* it."

"But I don't—"

Elenore raised her hand. "Dealing with time travel is more of an art than a science. Just try to remember: time travel exists, which means some stuff that already happened hasn't happened yet. If something's already been done, you absolutely have to do it."

"But that doesn't—"

"Try not to think about it too much. The more you think about it, the worse your nerves will start working on you. Let's figure how you're going to get in there and get the gems."

Elenore stood and marched through the store, browsing through the items on the shelves.

"Why do *I* have to do it? Why can't *you* do it?"

"Have you ever broken and entered? Ever assaulted someone?"

"No!"

"Neither have I. That's why you're doing it."

"That doesn't explain anything!"

"Whichever of us tries this, we're going to leave plenty of evidence because we're going to be lousy at it. Which means you're the one who did it, because so long as you succeed in getting out, and you don't lead the cops here, and you head home, no amount of evidence is going to lead to you."

"That's a lot of 'ands,' Elenore."

"Lucky for you, you've got causality on your side. You already did it. You just have to *do* it."

#

Claire rode in the passenger seat of Elenore's car, staring out the window as they drove through town. Elenore's inventory hadn't been assembled with infiltration and espionage in mind, so the pickings were pretty slim for equipment and outfits that might lend a hand. She'd topped Claire's dress with a long black trench coat. Since the rule about keeping proper went back at least this far, she'd loaned her a wristwatch too. Topping it all off was something she called a "sap." It was little more than a leather sack full of lead shot. The thought of using it was harrowing, but fortunately Claire was far too busy grappling with an existential crisis to dwell on it.

"Something wrong, honey?" Elenore said.

"Absolutely everything is wrong, Elenore." She pointed out the window. "That's not what this city looks like. There is fifty years' worth of urban development missing."

"You weren't supposed to tell me how far in the future you were from."

"I'm not supposed to be in the past."

"All right, all right. Calm down. It'll be over soon. And again. This *is* your fault."

"That's not making it any easier to take." She tightened her grip around the sap. "I could fool myself into believing it wasn't *real* back when I was in the store. A younger version of my boss? That could be a different woman. Rearranging the store? It's not *impossible*. But the whole city is different."

"Would it help you to know you're handling it better than some of the folks who've come through before you?"

"Not really."

"Well, you are. About half the time, people come through and they're talking in this over-the-top slang. Sweating bullets about how they're going to fit in. There's lots of handholding and coaching."

"I've seen Ms. Thomas… I've seen *you* deal with some people who seemed like fish out of water. I just got through with one myself."

"Me…" Elenore said. "Hah. I just realized. You coming through from where you came from means I'm guaranteed to live another fifty years. Not a lot of people get to say *that* with any certainty."

"How did you end up getting mixed up in running Yesterday's Tomorrow?"

"What's that matter to you?"

"I was thrust from a customer service job into a covert mission with dire consequences for the history of the world. I could use a distraction."

"Fair enough. This place used to belong to my uncle. The family's been looking after the device and the crystals at least since colonial times."

"Colonial times? Uh… Does that mean… I mean, *slavery* and all…"

"I'm a quarter Kichai Indian on my father's side. My family was here before any of you folks came over. Family legend has it we've been keeping those crystals in the dark for centuries. Every so often, someone would pop into the cave we kept them in from who knows where."

"People can show up at the crystals even if there's no device and even if it's in the dark?"

"Sure. It's *leaving* that's tricky. Anyway, eventually one of them must have shown up by mistake or maybe just realized they'd need something a little more useful than a place to show up. That's when the device was built. One thing led to another, and some ancestor realized the whole thing would be easier to manage if we had it wrapped up in an antique shop. Opened up Yesterday's Tomorrow back in 1810."

"It must have been difficult hanging on to it. History hasn't been terribly kind to minorities. Particularly not in this area."

"It turns out having access to a time machine that generations past and present are going to need for whatever they're going to need it for has a way of keeping the owners one step ahead of any would-be tragedies. It also keeps the coffers nice and full. We're never short on cash."

"Isn't it breaking the rules for people to help you?"

"The rules govern the usage of the device. There wouldn't be much use in *having* the rules if they led to the device being destroyed. I guarantee that's why you're here. Just making sure the device stays useful."

"Who made the rules?"

"Beats me. But if we bend them too much, a nice lady or fella in a silver jumpsuit tends to show up and chew us out. Ain't had to talk to one of them but once."

"What happened?"

She clicked off her headlights and made a turn. "I'll tell you when you get back with the crystal. We're here."

Claire turned and saw the street sign for Fishkill Boulevard creep past. In 2018, this whole neighborhood was fairly gentrified. High-end shops, loft apartments, etcetera. That had evidently occurred in the last half-century, because right now the place was terrifying. It was an industrial district, or had been until recently. Now it was neglected and forgotten. Warehouses lined the whole street. Number 501 was nestled between two of the larger ones. All the surrounding streetlights were broken or missing, leaving it shrouded in shadow.

Elenore pulled the car over and parked in the darkness a short distance past the warehouse.

"Now's your time to shine, honey."

Claire took a shaky breath. "How am I going to do this?"

"I don't know, but try not to worry about it. Back where you come from, you already did this. That article confirms it."

"There was nothing *explicit* in that article that guarantees this is what it was talking about. It didn't even have a date."

"It was in that room for a reason. This is the reason it was there."

"But can't it change? Can't it just change to some other story if I don't do it right?"

"This isn't *Back to the Future*, honey."

"I know but…" She narrowed her eyes. "This is nineteen seventy. That hasn't come out yet."

"Uh-huh. And when it shows up, it gives everyone such backward ideas about time travel that someone saw fit to prepare us for it. So don't worry about it. Get in there and do what comes naturally. You can't fail."

"If I can't fail, then what's the big deal with random people going back in time?"

"It's complicated. Let's just say, if it already happened, it is supposed to happen. If it didn't already happen, no one knows what'll happen if it does."

"But doesn't 'it already happened' depend on your frame of reference? What if—"

"Get in there and get it done, honey. Maybe someday someone will find out for sure what happens if you create an open time loop, but I'll be darned if it's going to happen on my watch."

"*Fine,*" Claire hissed. "But be ready to go as *soon* as I show up."

She held her breath and slipped from the car as quietly as possible.

#

Claire's heart hammered in her ears as she crept down the alleyway between warehouse 501 and its neighbor. She'd yet to pass a door, and all the windows were well out of reach over her head. She hefted the sap in her hand and shook her head.

"I knew that salary was too good to be true…" she muttered.

The first accessible door loomed out of the darkness. It was, of course, locked. There was a fire escape just overhead. Like everything else around, it was in a terrible state of disrepair. The staircase was sagging just barely out of reach. She slid a milk crate beneath it as silently as possible, stood atop it, and snagged the lowest stair.

An ear-splitting—and, in retrospect, completely predictable—screech rang out as the stairs hinged downward. She heard startled voices from inside. Thumping footsteps charged toward the door. Claire dashed for a nearby row of trash cans and slid behind them. Some manner of mangy critter with claws and wild eyes launched from one of the trash cans and streaked down the alleyway. The lock clicked, the door opened, and a rough-looking thug glanced about.

Claire huddled behind the trash cans and prayed to avoid being discovered. The thug, who was a good deal heavier and older than the one she'd grappled with at the store, gave the alley a once-over.

"What was it?" called a voice from within.

The thug eyed the fire escape.

"It's just the stairs. They finally came down," he called back.

"Then get back in here. I want to get this stuff divided up so I can get this nose checked out. I think I need stitches."

"Yeah, yeah…" the thug muttered.

He wandered back inside. The door shut behind him. Claire let a full minute pass before she persuaded her shaky limbs to drag her out of her hiding place. As terrifying as the near discovery had been, there was one minor detail that didn't escape her notice. She'd heard him unlock the door. She *hadn't* heard him lock it again.

With sap firmly in hand, she approached the door and pressed her ear to it. There were voices, but they were distant and muffled. She tested the knob again. It turned. The chances of such an oversight happening just when she needed it, and just *how* she needed it, must have been vanishingly small. Maybe there was something to this time-is-on-your-side nonsense.

She slipped through the door, and immediately her faith in her temporal guardian angel vanished. It was, indeed, a *warehouse*. There were no walls, no hallways. Just row after row of largely empty shelves that offered little in the way of cover. She was fortunate, at least, in that the warehouse was as dark as the alley. If there had been a light outside, there would have been no way the opening door would have escaped their notice. A spirited argument between what turned out to be a trio of thieves proved loud enough to cover the sound of the shutting door.

Once she was inside, she crept low to the ground. Realistically, doing so probably didn't help her chances of being undiscovered, but it just felt like the sort of thing one should do in a situation such as this.

All three thieves were clustered around a card table set up toward the north end of the warehouse. It was situated beneath one of only three overhead lights that was actually intact. The heavyset man who had checked the door leaned on a support column beside the table. A younger man of *maybe* seventeen years old counted out piles of cash. And finally, with a blood-soaked rag held to his face, there was the robber she'd attacked when she'd first arrived.

A night of ill-gotten gains mounded the table between them. Three stacks of bills made up the bulk of the night's take, but there were watches, pieces of jewelry, some hefty nineteen seventies electronics, and of course, the cluster of crystals.

Just what am I supposed to do? she wondered. Does Elenore expect me to overpower three thugs?

She gave the thieves a wide berth, working her way around the perimeter of the warehouse and watching through the shelves. Along the way, she encountered three more doors and unlocked them. If nothing else, she'd be able to make a quick getaway. She'd almost completely circled the warehouse before she found some shelves with enough empty boxes to give her a way to move closer to the crew.

"I don't see why I've got to give this guy a cut of my take," the youngest thief griped. "What'd he get? Sixty skins? He's getting more from my share of the haul than he got all by himself."

"We do it this way because most nights he brings twice as much as either of us," the big thug said. "Nights like this, it evens out."

"Who cares if it's even? If I cared about being fair, I wouldn't be mugging people."

"Just shut your mouth and count it out. You saw the pile of jewels I got. After I hit my fence, I'll triple what all of you got."

"You've been talking up that antique store for *weeks*. You should have come away with ten times what you got here, for all you were bragging about it."

"I told you! There were three big guys in there. Banged me up bad."

"You had a gun. You ask me, it takes a real turkey to head into an antique store with a gun and come out with such a pitiful haul. Don't act like you're going to bring back everything the fence gives you, either. You always skim off the top."

The bloodied thief stood, knocking his flimsy chair behind him.

"Listen, punk. I've had it up to here with your mouth. You've been an anchor around my neck for six months. If it wasn't for your dad, I'd've knocked your teeth down your throat weeks ago."

The youngster stood and puffed his chest out. "Don't let that stop you."

The altercation became more intense. The heftiest member of the group tried to separate the other two, and all three of them moved away from the table. Claire wasn't sure if this was posturing or the prelude to a legitimate fight, but she was certain it was her last, best chance to get her hands on the stolen gems without having to somehow incapacitate three thugs to do it.

She moved as swiftly and silently as she could toward the table. It wasn't as simple as she would have liked. The darkness and clutter that had kept her hidden thus far were now a major problem. It seemed like every other step threatened to dislodge this box or that pile of random debris. The thieves were spewing insults, but they'd yet to come to blows. Worse, the largest among them was on the verge of cooling the disagreement. It was now or never.

Claire rushed toward the table. She got all of three steps before her foot found its way into a half-empty cardboard box hidden in the darkness. She skidded and fell, tumbling into the light and knocking the table over. Money and valuables rained down around her. In the blink of an eye, the three thieves were upon her. The largest of them caught the wrist of her sap-bearing hand and hauled her to her feet. His grip was punishing, threatening to snap her wrist.

"It's *this* bitch," growled the bloodied thief.

"You know her?" said the youngest.

"She was in the antique shop too!"

"Jeez. Her, the owner, and three big guys. That place must have been crowded."

"Shut up!" the bloodied thief snapped. "How'd you find me?"

Claire couldn't have answered if she'd wanted to. Fear and panic had seized her. She was hyperventilating, and her heart was pounding so hard she could feel her chest burning. Her eyes swept over the grimacing faces and scanned her surroundings, desperate for some means of escape. The crystals were at her feet, mere inches away, for all the good they did her now. Thoughts of just what these men were capable of doing to her started to force any useful thoughts from her mind. Her eyes fell upon the watch on her wrist: 11:42:12.

An idea formed. It made no sense. It shouldn't even have been possible. But when you are out of options, the impossible starts to look pretty attractive.

"Did anyone follow you? Does anyone know you're here?" the biggest thief barked.

"It doesn't matter," the bloody thief seethed. "I've got *plans* for this bitch."

He took a step forward. Claire glanced one last time at her watch, then shut her eyes tight.

A flash of light and a wave of heat rushed through the room. All three thieves cried out in confusion, then one by one their shouts turned to yelps of pain. Claire opened her eyes just in time to see a punishing kick to the groin delivered to the oaf gripping her wrist. He released her, and both of them tumbled to the ground. A hand reached down and pulled her to her feet again.

"Ms. Thomas is going to kill us," remarked her savior. "Mind if I borrow that trench coat?"

Standing before her, nude and still high on the rush of foiling three potentially violent criminals, was Claire herself.

"So *Back to the Future* is bogus, but *Bill and Ted's Excellent Adventure* isn't?" Claire said, slipping off her coat and helping her duplicate into it.

"I don't even want to think about it. I'll grab the crystals. You tie these guys up. Then we'll call the cops and get out of here."

The original Claire nodded. Her creeping and sneaking had taken her past a few boxes of industrial cable. She fetched some and managed to get the hands and ankles of each of their would-be assailants bound before they were able to recover from the combined effects of a blow to the groin and the blinding flash of time travel. Her duplicate stuffed the crystals into one of the spacious pockets of the trench. She then gave the bloody-nosed thief an extra kick before heading for the door. There was a rotary phone beside it, another discovery she'd made trying to sneak to the table, so it was a simple matter of dialing 9-1-1 and giving the address.

The pair left the thieves squirming and cursing as they slipped back into the darkened alley and found their way to Elenore's car. The trench-clad duplicate slipped into the back seat while Claire took the front. Elenore looked back and forth between them.

"You got the crystals?" she asked.

Claire's copy held out the bundle.

"Give it here," Elenore said. "You really are a troublemaker, you know that? It'll be a miracle if I don't get an earful about this…"

#

A few minutes later, Claire sat across the table from herself. They were each drinking a cup of coffee while Elenore tweaked the length of the freshly repaired chain on the device.

"So… you think you'll keep working for Ms. Thomas, now that you know what's what?" Claire asked herself.

"I've been asking myself that same question," she replied.

"You still are," Elenore called from the other room.

"It helps me think!" both Claires declared.

"Well, while you're thinking about if you want to keep the job, remember that you broke all sorts of rules to end up here. That's on the one hand. On the other hand, you showing up kept this place from being robbed and maybe even me from being killed. Back on the first hand, you broke the machine and almost caused a catastrophe. Back on the second hand, you helped solve it. Back on the first hand yet again, now you're going to make *me* break my own rules to help you save the day." She stepped out of the back way, wiping off her hands. "Plenty of reasons to fire you if the notion strikes."

"And I'd deserve it," said one Claire.

"But Elenore has a good point," said the other.

"She's got a lot of good points."

"No, I mean the one she's about to make."

Elenore glared at both Claires. The duplicate smirked.

The Back Way

"I was *going* to say that being able to think quick and work out how closed time loops can work for you are rare things to have in an employee. But don't push it. Which one of you is the one who came back?"

The trench-clad Claire raised her hand.

"I assume I already taught you how to set the machine?"

"Yes."

"Then get in there and go home. Other one, get yourself ready to learn how to take yourself back to the warehouse."

"Why are you teaching me to do it? Why not just set it for me?"

"Because she already taught *me* to do it," Trench Claire said. "So she *has* to teach you to do it."

"Just get in there. I swear, I liked you better when you were bewildered and incredulous."

Trench-clad Claire stood and shook her own hand. "A pleasure working with you."

Dress-clad Claire nodded. "I'll see me in a minute, I guess."

The door shut. A moment later, the soft clap of the device activating signaled her departure. Elenore opened the door and glanced inside, then gathered up the trench coat that had been left behind and placed it back on its hanger.

"Get in there. Let's go over it," Elenore said.

"Why *are* you teaching me to use the machine?" Claire said, stepping into the back way.

"It'd be nice to say it's because I trust you to take care of yourself. Seeing as how I just sent another one of you through time, I know you pick it up well enough. But mostly it's because, even though I'm not aware of a device *ever* failing to send someone where they want to go, when set properly, it's still smart to make sure anyone who uses the device knows how to use the device, so if something goes wrong, they can just reset and try again."

"That's good thinking. But if that had been the case this time, I never would have been able to stop the robbery."

"How about that," Elenore said, as though it was all there was to say on the subject. "Now let's go through this, it'll take a while to learn."

#

Claire opened her eyes in a darkened room. For her it was a few hours later, or forty-eight years later, depending on how one measured. The method for inputting the date and time settings was coded a bit. It wasn't a complex code, but when the consequences of getting a final digit wrong were showing up in the wrong decade, it was usually worth taking the time to get it right the first time.

As she'd learned when she'd made her appearance in the warehouse, showing up with her eyes closed spared her the dizzying blindness of the crystal flash. For the third time, she found herself nude in an unfamiliar place, but this time there was a pile of familiar clothes against the wall that confirmed she'd arrived at the right place. Or rather, the right time.

Before getting dressed, she shut the curtain and watched as the smoldering glow of the gems dwindled away. Sure enough, even if the device *hadn't* been designed to prevent sending her somewhere prematurely, this was all it would have taken to deactivate it. Knowing that beforehand would have made for a much less exciting trip to the past.

She glanced to the door. It was shut. While that meant she could get dressed in privacy, it wasn't the *best* news. She'd left it open. On Elenore's instruction, she'd set the arrival time to an hour after her departure. Assuming she'd shown up *precisely* when she'd intended, that meant that someone had shut the door in the interim. Thus, it was quite likely her boss was waiting on the other side of the door.

Claire got dressed and tried the knob. Locked, of course. She sighed and knocked on the door.

Before she could knock a second time, the lock clicked and the door opened. Ms. Thomas glared at her from the dimly lit store, a tea in one hand and the key in the other.

"Well, well, well. Tonight was the night. I had a feeling you were tonight's appointment, but you can never be sure," Ms. Thomas said. "Well, don't just stand there, honey. I imagine you've got questions."

"Am I allowed to ask questions?" Claire stepped out of the back way. "There are rules against that, aren't there?"

"Sure there are, but since when do you follow rules?"

Ms. Thomas had already set up two folding chairs beside a flimsy folding table she usually used for temporary displays near the front of the store. There were a teapot and two cups. When they'd each taken a seat, Ms. Thomas looked at her expectantly. Having interacted with the same woman several decades younger, Claire thought it was remarkable how much of the same spark and fire were still present in her eyes.

"We'll get right to it. How did you know I'd use the machine tonight?"

"I didn't. I just knew when you arrived back then. So from the day I hired you I've been setting the device to that time."

"Clever. And you left the article taped to the wall because I'd told you I'd seen it."

She nodded. "Pain in the behind having to read through the paper until I came across it."

"And who was that man who started this whole sequence of events?"

"Come again?"

"The man who came through. He gave me a tip and told me to buy a lotto ticket. I didn't, but the ticket I would have bought was a winner. That's what made me start digging."

"A tip. That's the money on the counter here?"

"Yes."

Ms. Thomas shook her head. "Lousy meddling troublemakers. Remind me, did I tell you there are folks who come through and make sure things that get done get done?"

"I think so."

"Well, you just met one. Or someone he or she sent. But it didn't start with him. There's no beginning or end to it. It's all just one big thing that we catch glimpses of from different angles. Apparently, things would have gotten out of hand if what you went back and did didn't get done."

"Wait… So someone from the future sent someone else from the future back to the present to trick me into going to the past?"

"Monkeying around with time is like building a ship in a bottle. Can't do anything direct. It's always finding the right domino to knock down. Best not to worry about it. If you keep working here, you're bound to find yourself tangled up in a few dozen more threads. Lord knows I have."

"You mean I'm not fired? I broke nearly *all* of your rules."

"You also saved my life. You've been through time. There aren't more than a handful of people who can say the same. Tends to help you serve our customers a little better. Besides, you just learned my recordkeeping system."

"And I'll still keep my old salary?"

"You think I'd be paying you nearly a million dollars a year to help tourists pick out hats if that's all the job was? That little jaunt you just went through? That's the job. And you just passed your *real* interview. So it's yours if you want it. If not, give me two weeks' notice. Either way…" She plopped a full ring of keys on the table. "Lock up when you leave. And set out what we'll need for tomorrow's appointments. Small brass key, top left drawer. I'm too old to be running around all day."

Ms. Thomas finished her tea, pulled on her coat, and marched out the door. Claire sipped her tea and paced back through the store, marching back through the eras. When she got to the door to the back way, she swept her eyes over the ancient furniture. A few of the pieces were still precisely where they'd been all those years ago. She knelt and ran her fingers over the door of one of the cabinets until she found a divot. The same divot left by the gun she herself had knocked from the robber's hand. She could still feel the bumps and bruises she got from the struggle, but here the damage had been softened by decades.

She smirked. "Funny how you're a stickler for repair and restoration, but you left *this* here…"

She shut the door to the back way. There were about a dozen keys on Ms. Thomas's key ring. True to her fastidious nature, each was clearly labeled with punched lettering. She found *Back Way* and locked the door, then selected the small brass *Sched* key and opened the top drawer of a filing cabinet behind the counter.

A thick stack of appointment books was arranged neatly inside. Ranges of years marked the spine of each book, one per decade. They started at 1880 and continued up to 2120. Tempting as it might have been to look at just how many appointments were booked for the twenty-second century, she decided against it. The current was already 2010–2019. A year or so of the future was plenty for now.

She pulled the current book and leafed through until she reached tomorrow's date. It was mostly empty, just two appointments requiring period clothes for the nineteen tens and nineteen forties respectively. More interesting, though, was the handwritten note.

Stop pretending like you're not going to take the job. Trust me, you're going to love it.

Yours Truly,
Claire

Part-Time Heroes

Joseph R. Lallo

Part-Time Heroes

This story is a follow-up to one of my oddball stories, *The Other Eight*. It's a story about superheroes with lousy powers. And this is a story of what happened to them after finally forming their own super team. It is one of the only other canon entries in the setting, though there's a yet to be written outline in my "maybe" folder called *The Other Eight Against The Icon*, just in case you're in the mood to write me an email to tell me to actually continue the series.

Cover art by Chandra Free.

Asunny young soldier tapped away at heavy duty aluminum laptop in a rather crowded office. She had her own desk, but its positioning was less than ideal. She was directly beside the door to the office, and in order to actually sit *in front* of her computer, she needed to block the door. As footsteps approached from the outside, she rolled her chair aside with choreographed grace. She caught it as it swung open and held her hand out expectantly. The man edging his way into the room had one arm loaded down with printed reports. The other held a to-go tray from the local coffee shop with three iced coffees.

"Sorry, Jordan," said the man, handing her the tray of caffeine.

"Not a problem, Dr. Aiken. How are things going up there?"

"Not great. Not great," he said.

She set the coffees down and tugged one free for the doctor. He edged around his desk and took a seat. The reports flopped down and he set about opening.

"I can't help but appreciate the poetic coincidence that they seal these stupid things with red tape," Dr. Aiken muttered.

"That's not a coincidence, doctor. That's the literal red tape that the figurative red tape is based upon."

"… Really?"

"I was always told that when Americans talk about red tape, they're talking about the binding for Civil War bond coupons. It could be apocryphal. The last I looked it up it referred to something more general about the binding of legal documents in Europe, but I choose to believe it is just another part of our military heritage," she said with a bright smile. "You say things aren't great up there?"

"Not so much, no. I'm going to have to make some phone calls. Time to get the crew in here. They're not going to like this."

He opened his laptop and began the veritable ritual necessary to actually access it. A password, a PIN, and a thumbprint later, he was finally scrolling through a list of contacts.

"Do you think you can get us a conference room for this afternoon? I'd hate to have to do this eight separate times…"

#

Three hours later, a musty, forgotten room buried in the bowels of DARPA HQ was slowly filling with a colorful cast of characters.

"Hey! Getting the team back together!" crowed a somewhat

diminutive man of Mexican extraction.

He jumped to his feet as a taller, more laid-back fellow with a vivid green complexion arrived.

"Hey, Gracias," the man said, lacking the same level of enthusiasm.

"Team Green, buddy!" Gracias said.

He raised his hand for a high five. The newcomer half-heartedly obliged. A round of murmured hellos came from the rest of the assembly.

"Something wrong, Chloroplast?" asked Gracias.

"Well, yeah, probably," said Chloroplast.

"What makes you say that?"

He gave Gracias a pointed look.

"Are you serious? Look around you. Who have we got? Bomb Sniffer, Phosphor, The Number…"

One by one, the teammates he named perked up. An older, burly fellow with an old messenger bag. A young woman still in her teens. A lean, fit young man.

"Add in you and me, and you've got all of the members of the team no one cares about."

Gracias squinted his eyes and did a bit of mental arithmetic.

"Hang on. You saying Nonsensica and Non Sequitur are the only ones anyone cares about?" he said.

"Have you seen the cover of the Guardian Project press materials?"

"… No," Gracias said.

"I've got the pamphlet right here," Phosphor said. "I like to show it around."

He pulled a thin booklet from his bag. An unassuming man in army fatigues and a diminutive but dynamic young woman in goggles and a shiny red and white suit stood back to back. The pamphlet labeled them "The Beginning of a New Era of the Armed Forces."

"So they're on the cover. Big deal," Gracias said. "I'm sure we're in there somewhere."

He snatched up the pamphlet and flipped it open.

"Yeah, see?" Gracias pointed at the print of the third page. "Right there. We're the first few names in the roster."

"Yeah, and I'm sure the guy who played the sitar on *Sgt. Pepper's*

Lonely Hearts Club Band is in the liner notes, but no one cares who he is. What matters is who's on the cover."

"I think it was George Harrison who played the sitar on that album," Phosphor said.

"Yeah. He learned it especially for it," the Number agreed.

"Okay fine, but…" Chloroplast said.

"And wasn't pretty much everyone in the world on the cover of that one?" Gracias said.

"There must have been fifty people on the cover," Phosphor said. "*Sgt. Pepper* had a really memorable cover."

"Who is Sgt. Pepper?" Bomb Sniffer interjected.

"Stop being so young!" Gracias demanded. "You're making everyone feel old."

"Okay! Fine!" Chloroplast growled. "Bad example. But the point is, you know what it means when they bring in the low performers on the roster and leave out the darlings? It means people are about to be cut."

The door swung open and in walked Non Sequitur. He wasn't even wearing the fatigues he'd had on in the cover photo. Instead, he had a regular old T-shirt and jeans, as the rest of the group. The woman whom he held the door for, on the other hand, may as well have stepped right out of the photoshoot. Nonsensica's stretchy latex superhero uniform creaked embarrassingly as she walked in and took a seat, but the look of penetrating pride on her face completely offset any perceived lack of dignity. She radiated superheroism from the tips of her black pigtails to the soles of her hefty boots.

"What's up, crew?" she said.

All eyes turned to her, then to Chloroplast. He shrugged.

"Okay, fine, so we're *all* getting fired."

"No one's getting fired," Dr. Aiken announced as he stepped in behind them.

He and Pvt. Summers were carrying trays with glasses and pitchers of ice water. They set them on the table and took their place at the head.

"Then why are you calling us in?" Phosphor asked. "The performance review isn't for another three weeks."

"This isn't about performance. You've all been making great progress in the basic training. I'm pleased to say all of you are on track to pass the admission requirements for the US Army, which, as you know, was one of the things delaying your active duty."

"About time," Nonsensica said, somewhat clumsily pouring herself a glass of water thanks to her MMA gloves. "This team has been showing a pronounced lack of hustle."

She guzzled the water and quickly refilled the glass. Thanks to her chosen uniform, she tended to be suffering from some level of dehydration or another.

"Before we get started, is everybody here?" Aiken asked.

There was a general agreement that the whole crew was present. Pvt. Summers took a tally.

"I count seven," she said. "We're one person short."

Everyone looked around.

"You sure?" Chloroplast said.

Aiken flipped through his notes and found a yellow note pinned to the staff roster. He glanced at it. "Oh! Right. Afterthought. Did anyone invite him?"

"It is possible we did not…" Summers said."

"Right, right. Not your fault. He *is* Afterthought, after all. We'll catch him up later." He scratched his head. "Although I *swear* there was some reason we didn't attach him to the main invite. Eh. It'll come to me."

"The issue is two-fold," Aiken said. "Public image and funding."

"Sounds like a round of layoffs to me," Chloroplast said.

"It isn't a round of layoffs." Aiken cleared his throat and amended. "That is, it isn't *necessarily* a round of layoffs. Summers? Care to elaborate?"

She leaned forward to the center of the table and tugged up a flap that revealed a set of ports. A bit of fiddling and wire-connection caused a projector screen to lower and the screen of her laptop to flicker onto it.

"As you might imagine, after the recruitment portion of the Guardian Project leaked and became the internet spectacle it was, a considerable amount of media attention was directed our way. Not *all* of it was positive," Summers said.

"That'll happen when one of the advisers turns out to be a super villain," Gracias said.

"There's been a little bit a budget dust-up, and our continued funding is contingent upon our group not being a public relations liability. We need some good press."

"You know what'll get us good press? A theme song," Gracias said.

"That'd be killer!" Nonsensica said. "Who did the music for the Incredibles? You think we could get him?"

"No, no. That's not what we were thinking," Aiken said quickly.

"Gotta think outside the box to catch the public's attention," Nonsensica said.

"I play a little keyboard," Phosphor offered.

"We could totally do a song like the Wonder Woman theme!" Gracias said.

"I think I could manage that," Phosphor said. "I'm surprised you all remember that one."

"Of course we do," Nonsensica said. "We didn't *always* have monthly infusions of superheroism in theaters. Us aspiring do-gooders had to take it where we could get it."

"Does anyone else remember that there was actually a line about her wearing satin tights?" The Number said. "That always struck me as odd."

"Should've been latex," Nonsensica said, flexing her arm to produce a satisfying creak. "Real heroes wear latex."

Bomb sniffer raised her hand. "Are we talking about the movie, or…"

"Can we please focus?" Aiken said. "Go ahead, Jordan."

Pvt. Summers continued. "The higher-ups had a lot of ideas on how to make sure we show our best colors, but we've narrowed them down to one: Public Outreach."

She showed a slide labeled "Key Values."

"We want the Guardian Project, and The Other Eight, to be associated with some wholesome, family friendly ideals. Normally there'd be a whole team put together for this, but we don't have the budget for that. So we'd like to put together some teams."

Gracias's hand shot up. "Team Green! Team Green!"

"We'll assemble the teams later. What's more important is that we lay out some ground rules. You'll all have the opportunity to propose your own material for the outreach programs, but we'll be focusing on schools, maybe with some townhall-type meetings thrown in. We're open to other potential venues for public appearances. As you can see, we've got some core ideals we'd like you to focus on. Do we have the notebooks?"

Aiken dug around in his pile of materials and turn up a handful of memo books and pens. Summers handed them out.

"We're going to brainstorm some ideas. Remember. The future of the Guardian Project depends upon our success on this one."

"And by extension, the future of truth, justice, and the American way," Nonsensica said.

"Not to mention the future of me having a government job," Bomb Sniffer said. "Have you priced health insurance lately? It's crazy out there."

"Are we the only eight people working on this?" The Number asked. "I just want to know if we can maybe come up with ways to include some of the other members of the project."

"He just wants to find a way to 'team up' with Primadonna again," Bomb Sniffer said.

"Who *wouldn't?*" Gracias muttered.

"We're going to start with you eight," Aiken said. "You're the best operational unit."

"Darn right we are," Nonsensica said.

Summers pointed to the screen. "We're working on the themes of Physical Fitness, Community Service, and Commitment to Democracy. Let's break into groups and see what we come up with."

#

Two weeks later, Dr. Aiken was once again navigating the halls of the DARPA HQ with Pvt. Summers by her side, this time on the way to his direct superior's office. Despite having settled comfortably into his role of the overseer/babysitter/therapist of the unlikely superhero group, meetings with his boss still made him nervous. This was due in no small part to his personal aid, Sgt. Roberts.

"What time is it?" Dr. Aiken said.

Pvt. Summers glanced at her watch. "15:44:25."

"Did you synch your watch with the Cosmic Clock?"

"Atomic Clock. And yes."

"Give me the count down, then."

"You do realize you don't have to be *exactly* on time," Summers said.

"I don't need Robo-Roberts lecturing me on the schedule again. We're going to get this right," Aiken said.

She watched her watch.

"Three. Two. One…"

He turned the knob, entering the office. Inside, a man with a ruthless adherence to uniform code had leaned forward in his chair to tap the intercom on his desk. As far as Aiken could tell, Roberts's finger had touched the button at the precise moment Aiken had opened the door.

"Dr. Aiken is here for you, General," he said.

"Send him in," came the gruff reply.

Roberts nodded to Aiken and opened the general's door. That he didn't mention the time was as near to a full-throated praise of Dr. Aiken's punctuality as he was ever likely to deliver.

Aiken and Summers entered the general's office. They each took a seat.

The general had always looked like he'd been chiseled out of a particularly angry piece of granite, but since the formation of The Other Eight, his attitude had found a way to become even more grizzled. He stood and shook hands.

"Dr. Aiken. Pvt. Summers. Let's get this over with," he said.

The three of them sat. Pvt. Summers logged into her laptop.

"I think you'll be happy with the results," Dr. Aiken said.

"What, in the time we've been working together, has given you the indication that *anything* about this project will make me happy?" he said. "This is a secret project that has managed to become *entirely* about publicity."

"But now that it is *about* publicity, it, uh… It's been quite a success."

"Like I said, Dr. Aiken. Get it over with."

Aiken cleared his throat. "We'll start with The Number."

She nodded and brought up a video.

"The Number's focus was on physical fitness," Aiken said. "And he came up with the idea to illustrate that *anyone* can adopt a healthier physical lifestyle."

Summers clicked play and turned the screen to the General.

\#

Several Days Earlier

The Number marched out into the main floor of a gym and surveyed the people who had volunteered to attend the event he'd dreamed up. This particular gym was focused on 'plus sized' individuals. As a result, his audience was mostly on the portly side. He set down his sound system, an old school boom box that he'd adapted for just this occasion.

He clapped his hands together and smiled.

"Hello, everyone! For those of you who don't know me, I'm The Number. I'm a founding member in The Other Eight, and I am an honest to goodness, government sanctioned superhero," he said in his best motivational speaker voice. "Now, you're all here because you're trying to get healthy. And that's a great choice! Working out is good for your mind, your body, and your heart. And that is because it is a *challenge* for the mind, the body, and the heart. I know as well as anyone that sometimes it's hard to motivate yourself to really push the limits, get yourself moving, and burn some calories. But that's why I'm here."

The Number pressed play. A drumbeat started to play.

"Now, I see some eyes rolling in the crowd. I know motivational speakers are a dime a dozen. You've probably had fifty of them in here before. But you've never had a superhero…"

He started walking in place to the beat. Slowly, all in attendance started to march along with him.

\#

The general watched as the video progressed into a full, choreographed, compulsory dance routine.

"Can someone explain to me the value of a member of the armed forces making a room full of fat people dance?" the general said.

"Officially, it highlights the value of physical fitness. Unofficially, it has fifty million views and has reminded people that DARPA is doing something interesting and fun," Dr. Aiken said.

"Interesting and fun are not our *aim*."

"I realize that, sir. But it beats the pre-Guardian Project public view of the DARPA, which was complete ignorance."

"I can live with that. But I suppose the people writing the checks can't. What else have we got?"

"The Number's appearance was the most *viewed*. But Non

Sequitur and Nonsensica have gotten the best press coverage for a Q and A they did at a public school."

#

Several Days Earlier

Non Sequitur and Nonsensica stood in the hallway of a school, listening to the muffled voice of the teacher introducing them.

Nonsensica rubbed her hands together.

"I am *psyched!*" she said. "I would have lost my *mind* if real-deal superheroes ever came to my school. There's *never* a superhero booth on career day or anything like that. It's like they don't *want* kids to grow up to be costumed crime-fighters."

She looked to her partner. His eyes were distant, and his hands were in tight fists at his side.

"You're looking a little tense there, soldier."

"I'm not really looking forward to this," he said.

"Oh, come on! Little kids love supers." She elbowed him in the ribs. "They're going to bust your chops for not having a uniform, though. I'm telling you. A nice red and white ensemble. Even if you wuss out and go for leather."

He took a shaky breath. She furrowed her brow.

"You really *are* on edge."

"My dad did this at my school once."

"So?"

"So until this very moment, I hadn't felt like I was… I don't know… *competing* with my dad before."

"You're not competing. You're following in his footsteps! He'd be proud."

"You sure about that? Remember what happened to him at the end of those footsteps."

"He saved a bunch lives doing what he was born to do. And you're going to talk to some kids." She slapped him on the back. "It's just a quick don't do drugs, take your vitamins, clean your room speech. It's part of the job."

The door opened and they were led into a large classroom packed with kids. Rather than setting it up in a lunchroom or auditorium, they'd gone for the more hands-on choice of packing two or three classes of kids into a single large classroom. The ages ran from kindergarten to fifth grade. The kids cheered.

"Hey, kids!" Nonsensica said, brimming with enthusiasm. "I'm Nonsensica, and this is my sidekick Non Sequitur—"

"We're more of a Cloak and Dagger-style team," Non Sequitur clarified.

"And we're here to answer *your* questions about what it is to be a hero and how *you* can be a hero in your own way," she said. "But no questions about our secret identities!"

Hands shot up. The teacher picked a little boy.

"Can I play with your numchucks?" he said.

"Oh, these?" she pulled a pair of weapons from her belt. "Technically, they're called *nunchuks.* Or more accurately, nunchaku. Even *more* accurately, these are the one, the only, the *non*chucks. And I can't let you play with them. They're *very* highly skilled weaponry. You need to be *very* careful. But I'd be happy to show off a few tricks while Non Sequitur asks a question."

She twirled and flourished the weapons. The teacher picked an older boy.

"Can you fly?" he asked.

"Uh, no. None of us can fly," Non Sequitur said.

"Super strength?" interjected another.

"Just regular strength."

The questions came in rapid succession for a few moments.

"Can you see through walls?"

"I can see through *windows.*"

"Super speed?"

"Regular speed."

"Do you have adamantium claws?"

"I don't even have regular claws."

The teacher stepped up. "Now kids, one at a time. Allison, how about you?"

"What *are* your powers?" the girl asked.

"Uh. Well, I can swap cause and effect, so long as they're less than about thirty seconds apart."

"What does that mean?"

"Well, there's a ton of criteria, but…" Non Sequitur looked to Nonsensica, who had just finished up her little demonstration. "Which one do you think I should do?"

"It's a bunch of little kids. Do the catch," she said.

"Yeah, that's a good one. Watch closely, everyone."

Nonsensica holstered one of the nonchuks and took a few steps back. She hefted the other a few times, then hurled it at Non Sequitur. A fraction of a moment before it would have stuck his face, the weapon just *stopped.* It hung in the air in front of him. He let them linger for the count of five, then grabbed them and handed them back to Nonsensica.

The kids practically erupted with enthusiasm. The teacher quelled the uprising, which was primarily focused on getting him to do it again. At least one of the kids took it upon himself to throw something of his own, but Non Sequitur side stepped it rather than stopping it.

"Okay, okay. Calm down. We'll do more later. Who's next?"

A little girl raised her hand.

"What can the lady do?"

Nonsensica holstered the other nonchuk, then placed her fists on her hips.

"Aside from assorted Jeet-Kun-Do-based a—*butt*-kickery, I can also short-circuit people's minds with only the power of my voice."

"Whoa… What does *that* mean?"

"Slingshot millipede."

The little girl flinched.

"What was that?"

"Who wants to try? Raise your hand," Nonsensica said.

A bunch of the kids raised their hands. One by one, she pointed to each and said a pair of nonsensical words, producing the same odd little flinch.

"There was a murmur of excitement. Nothing compared to Non Sequitur's trick, but genuine. At least, for the most part. A young boy raised his hand.

"Why are your powers so stupid?"

Nonsensica narrowed her eyes behind her goggles. "What kind of powers do *you* have, kid…"

"We don't get to pick our powers," Non Sequitur filled in. "Some of us are born with them, and some of us aren't. But the thing that makes us super isn't the powers we have. It's how we choose to use them."

"That's right!" Nonsensica said, rallying. "Who saw us win that contest? Anyone?"

A few hands raised.

"There were some pretty good powers on the other side, weren't there? Spitting seeds at lethal velocities. Getting a do-over when something goes wrong." She narrowed her eyes again. "Just frickin' being in the right place at the right time… But who won? We did. Because being super is about doing everything you can as best you can. Who's next?"

"How do you know where the bad things are?"

"We've got *really* smart bosses who make sure we're right where we need to be, so long as we can get there and so long as it's *really* a job for The Other Eight," Nonsensica said.

"What happens if something happens and there's no superheroes around?" asked a boy. "There aren't enough superheroes to stop *every* bad thing, right?"

Nonsensica hesitated. "You want to take this one, Non Sequitur?"

"Uh… Right." He cleared his throat. "*We* can't always be there to save the day. But believe me. There's no shortage of superheroes out there. And I'm not just talking about The Other Eight and the rest of the team we work with. Superheroes are everywhere. This room is filled with superheroes."

"But we don't have powers," said a girl.

"Oh, don't you? How much do you think all of you can lift? Fifty pounds? No, you're a strong-looking group. I'll bet it's a hundred, easy. And there's fifty of you here. That's *five-thousand pounds*! That's superhero strength right there, if you work together."

"Yeah!" Nonsensica said. "And I'll be some of you know more stuff about science, and some of you know more stuff about history. But take the whole room, and we've got a super genius. And when you grow up? It gets even better. The president doesn't get to be the president unless *you* let her. That's pretty super. The key is that you're all great on your own, but you're all better together. There's a lot of bad guys out there, and they *know* that. They know that they can't possibly do their evil deeds with all of these superheroes walking around teaming up and saving the day. So they'll try to *stop* you from working together. They'll try to break you into little groups. Into *us* and *them.* But here's the big secret. There's no them. There's only us."

"That's right," Non Sequitur said. "When we talk about working together, we're not just talking about working together with people who look like us. If you split the class into, I don't know, left-handed people and right-handed people, there'll be more righties, and if you do the same superhero math, the righties will be stronger. But they won't be as strong as the righties *and* the lefties. We're always stronger when we work together."

"And the same goes for people who agree with us," Nonsensica said. "My buddy here doesn't think it is important for superheroes to wear uniforms—"

"Costumes," he amended.

"*Uniforms.* And I think it *is* important. Now, just because he's *obviously* wrong, that hasn't stopped us from teaming up. Same goes for all of you. Maybe this guy here likes chocolate. Maybe that girl there likes peanut butter. Doesn't make a different so long as you both like truth and justice."

And older girl raised her hand. "But there *are* bad guys, right? There *are* evil people. So they're a 'them.'"

"Ah," Non Sequitur said. "And that's where things get tricky. Nonsensica and I? We've got it easy. Our villains wear masks and give great big speeches about their evil plans. For you folks, things aren't going to be so black and white. Sometimes it's hard to know who's really bad, and who's really good."

Nonsensica nodded. "But if you keep your eyes and ears open, you can figure it out. It comes down to love and hate. And not always the way you think. If someone decides their whole life should be about hate? That's probably a baddie. If someone's whole life is about love? Probably a goodie. But sometimes the really bad ones can get tricky. They can tell you that they love you, but they're the only ones who ever can, and ever will. And those people are wrong. Because there's more love than hate. Always."

"You've got to be careful where you draw lines. We don't all have to think the same way. Otherwise we don't get that cool super genius thing from all of us being different. But sometimes you *do* have to draw a line. And again, it all comes down to love and hate. If you help the people who are kind and don't help the people who are cruel, you can't go too far wrong."

"And if things get too far out of hand? That's where us superheroes come in," Nonsensica said. "Next question!"

"Your goggles look silly," said a little boy.

"That's not a question," she said through clenched teeth.

"How come your goggles are so silly looking?"

"Because when I am fighting the forces of evil to make life safe for people like you, I need to protect my eyes."

"How come your suit looks so silly?"

"How about we all just throw more stuff at Non Sequitur, huh?" she offered.

#

"It seems like their message was really well received," Dr. Aiken said.

"Some of the biggest opponents of the Guardian Project is that it glorifies violence, right?" Pvt. Summers said.

"That's right. And having a couple of our top operatives preaching kindness was a huge breath of fresh air."

"Did you guys coach them up on that stuff?" the General said.

"You hired me to oversee this project based upon my psychological expertise. To a large degree, we selected applicants who had a proper mindset."

"I see. Much as I'd prefer to have them doing good in a military context, at least they are putting a happy face on the organization. I assume this has been sent to the PR wing?"

"They sent it to *us,*" Pvt. Summers said.

He rumbled with anger.

"I hate when the press wing gets information before I do… Is that about all?"

"I have reports on Gracias and Phosphor's convention appearance and a roundtable featuring Bomb Sniffer and Phosphor. There is some video as well."

"Leave them. And email links. I've got what I need for now. I'll go through the rest later. I imagine our funding is secure for the time being."

They stood and all shook hands.

"Keep up the good work."

Dr. Aiken and Pvt. Summers took their leave. The General sat and picked up his pen to start taking notes on the findings. He'd barely begun when Sgt. Roberts buzzed him on the intercom.

"Your appointment for 1600 has arrived."

He looked up.

"I was unaware I had a meeting for 1600."

"I have it down as Afterthought, sir."

"Who the hell is after thought?"

"He is a member of the Other Eight, sir."

"Fine. Send him in."

The door opened and in walked a somewhat dumpy fellow in a plain gray sweat suit. He had a nondescript face, an average build, and in all other ways was utterly unforgettable. He offered a lackluster salute.

"Roberts tells me you are… Er…"

"Afterthought, sir."

"Right. And why are you here?"

"I completed the mission you assigned me, sir."

"I assigned you a mission."

"Yes, sir. In North Korea."

"I sent *you* to North Korea."

"Yes, sir."

General Siegel pushed the intercom.

"Do we have a file on this man and his mission, Sgt. Roberts?"

"Yes sir," Roberts replied.

"Bring them to me, please."

"Yes, sir."

The general looked to Afterthought.

"I apologize."

"It's okay, sir. I'm used to it. I'm the Afterthought. No one remembers the Afterthought."

"Right. If you'll just wait a moment, we'll get through with your debriefing."

The general sat patiently for a moment or two, then picked up his pen and started taking notes. The door opened shortly after and Sgt. Roberts the door, toting a thick envelope.

"Your files, sir," Roberts said.

The General looked up.

"Did I ask for files?"

"Yes. Regarding Afterthought."

"Who is Afterthought?"

"This man here is Afterthought, sir," Roberts said.

Afterthought glanced up. "You remember who I am?"

"Of course. It is my job."

"That usually doesn't matter."

"I pride myself on my job. Let me know if you need anything else, General."

"Yes, Roberts. Thank you."

Roberts left them alone. Siegel picked up the sealed folders and flipped through the contents.

"Let's see… Ah. Right, right. The power to be overlooked. Audio recordings and automated reminders recommended." The General tapped through a few commands on the computer, then turned the small microphone toward the Afterthought before picking up the report again. "We received intelligence that the North Koreans have been working on a counterpart to the Guardian Project. You were dispatched to investigate and acquire information in that regard."

"That's right, sir."

"Well? Let's hear it."

#

Several Weeks Earlier

The art of espionage is the sort of thing that consumes a life. People are recruited young. They are trained in everything from physical fitness to social engineering. A well-trained spy can vanish into a crowd, with an encyclopedic knowledge of a dozen different cultures. The highest-level spies speak every dialect of the languages in their field of operation.

But most spies are not Afterthought.

He paced along a hallway in a dank, oppressive military facility. He wasn't making any special effort not to be seen. His outfit was identical to what he was wearing in the General's office. Most of his attention was focused on a smartphone, which he was holding up to each sign he encountered, snapping pictures to translate their content.

A soldier marched around the corner and, upon spotting Afterthought, raised a weapon. He shouted in a rapid-fire string of warnings that went completely uncomprehended by Afterthought. The US operative, having just been spotted in top secret facility, casually raised his hands. The soldier shouted a few more commands, but Afterthought simply waited. The shouting became less insistent, less frequent, and eventually the soldier lowered his weapon and continued his patrol as though nothing had happened.

Afterthought continued his slow, thorough search. Eventually his phone's translation of a sign revealed a door's label as "System Administration." He pushed at the door, but it was predictably locked. This was always the most irritating part. Waiting.

Three hours passed before he hit pay dirt, including one particularly troublesome search for and visit to the bathroom. A skittish-looking tech appeared, passed through the same sequence of alarm and amnesia before he scanned into the room and Afterthought followed him in. From there, it was comparatively little waiting for the opportunity to plug a drive into the system and let an NSA-level data scraper do its job. Normally it wouldn't be possible for an untrained agent to completely copy the data on a heavily encrypted system, but normally the system wouldn't be logged in and active. After a few minutes, he had everything he was likely to get and simply had to wander off the base as quickly and easily as he had wandered on.

#

"I got back a few days ago and handed the data over to the NSA. They sent this over to you," he said, presenting a thumb drive.

The General glanced up from his pad and squinted at him.

"Who are you, and how did you get in my office?" the General said.

"Afterthought, sir. And I was just leaving. Please check out the information on that drive, sir."

Afterthought stood and left the office. General Siegel eyed the thumb drive suspiciously. He eventually plugged it in and entered his credentials.

"North Korean Government File Analysis. Operation Icon."

He scanned the contents of the file. With each line, his expression became more grim. When he'd reached the end, he locked his computer and marched out of the office to address his assistant directly.

#

A physically imposing young man with a vacant expression stood in front of Sgt. Roberts's desk.

"No, Mr. On The Spot, I am afraid Dr. Aiken is responsible for the evaluations. His assessment will determine if you get a raise," Roberts explained.

"Sgt. Roberts, get me some time on the NSA and CIA calendars. We need to start talking contingencies. Roll in any other staff that will need to be involved. There's going to be a hell of a lot of bureaucracy on this one, and I want to get ahead of it. I don't like what I'm seeing here." He looked to the muscular gentleman. "Are you the one who secured this intelligence?"

"Yeah, sure. Why not?" said Johnny On The Spot.

"Roberts, put this man in for a commendation. If this information turns out to be what I think it is, you may have saved untold lives today."

"Right on," said Johnny.

"I'll contact the CIA and NSA heads, sir," Roberts said.

"Good man."

The General returned to his office. Sgt. Roberts began composing an email. After a few seconds he glanced up to Johnny, who was still lingering.

"Mr. On The Spot, you are aware that *I* am aware that you are not responsible for the operation that the general was referencing, correct?"

"Yeah."

"And you are thus aware that I will not be submitting you for a commendation. That honor goes to Afterthought."

"Who?"

"The individual responsible."

"Uh. Yeah. That makes sense."

"Then I think we are done here."

"Yeah. That's cool. I've got a tanning appointment anyway."

Johnny On The Spot paced out the door. Sgt. Roberts typed up the email.

Subject: Operation Icon-Discussion and Contingency Planning

Body: General Siegel has recently been briefed on materials associated with an NK information retrieval mission. He requests a face to face meeting to discuss the potential impact and begin planning contingencies pending the worst-case outcome of the NK programs uncovered in said operation.

He paused for a moment.

It may also be advisable to expand the security clearance of Pvt. Jordan Summers and Dr. Adam Aiken to include associated information. Contingencies are likely to require his expertise, and that of The Other Eight and other members of the Guardian Project.

Joseph R. Lallo

A Big Day for Blodgette

A Big Day for Blodgette

Pizza Dragon is the unofficial name for this series. I'd never really expected much to come of it. In truth, it started as a gift for an artist I follow, ProjectENDO. He is the creator of the Structophis species, and at first I didn't expect to write a full book. It would just be a chapter or two to give him. Then it grew to an entire book, but I still wasn't sure I'd release it. Then I decided to release it, and to help drum up interest, I wrote a prequel. Now I've written a follow-up! For a series that has basically become a running gag for being hard to market, it certainly has found its audience.

This cover is based on artwork by Merri Monster, used with permission.

184

A Big Day for Blodgette

A phone buzzed from its perch on a bedside table. After two more buzzes, a hand thrust out from beneath a mound of blankets and felt around for the bothersome device. Markus Spiros lifted his head and blinked his eyes blearily at the device. It took him another buzz before he realized that this was a phone call, not an alarm.

He answered. "Eee-yaugh…"

It was as near to a word as he could manage on such short notice.

"Hey, I'm at the gate and I forgot my pass. Buzz me in," said a frustratingly chipper voice on the other side of the line.

"Gale?" he muttered, sleep gradually clearing from his brain.

"Yeah! Hurry up. I'm carrying a bunch of stuff."

She didn't wait for confirmation, she just hung up. Markus released a few more sounds that probably would have been rude if he'd been able to wrangle the diction to form them properly. He climbed out of bed and hastily got dressed.

This wasn't his old apartment. It looked more like a dorm room or a particularly luxurious jail cell. He had a bed and nightstand, a desk with a computer, and a dresser with a TV perched atop it. There wasn't really room for anything else. He grabbed a comb from the nightstand and slipped his sandals on before heading out the door. Before it shut, he ducked back in and grabbed a lanyard with a photo ID hanging from it.

A florescent-lit hallway awaited him on the other side of this door. It still had the weird odors of recently completed construction. He pushed opened a door across the hall to reveal another suitably dorm-like bathroom and shower facility. With Gale waiting at the gate there was no time for a proper morning routine, but he dragged the comb across his head and washed his face so that he would look a little less zombie-like for the trek across the facility.

Markus trudged through the visitor's center. It was brightly colored and scattered with freshly printed posters containing the schedule for future events. Stuffed dragons of various descriptions lined shelves in the gift kiosk to one side. He nodded to an employee in an apron and paper hat that made her look like a chef from a 1960s greasy spoon.

"Morning, Mr. Spiros," the young woman said brightly. "Today's the big day, huh?"

"Yeah," he said, fighting off a yawn. "Today's the big day."

He continued walking as the statement bounced off a brain not yet functional enough to process it. He swiped his badge and wandered through two more hallways before he came to the employee entrance and buzzed it open. It had barely slid open a crack when a boot jabbed into the opening and swung it fully open.

"Up and at 'em, sleepy head!" crowed the young woman who had been waiting.

His friend and collaborator Gale Dekker perpetually had the sort of exuberant, amped up attitude that could only result from a steady diet of caffeine. She had a shirt with a manatee on it, khaki cargo shorts, and her arms were heavily loaded with goodies.

"Coffee and donuts," she said, holding out the to-go tray she'd gotten from the local breakfast joint.

He took the tray and held the door as she sidled in. The rest of her cargo was a seemingly random assortment. She had a planter with a flowering stalk wrapped about a wire frame. Some smaller plants were in their own plastic pots tucked in around it. The crook of her arm had a plastic bag with various cured meats emerging from it.

"It's the big day!" she said, handing over enough of her goods to make navigating the hallway a less precarious enterprise.

"Big day," he repeated mechanically.

He sniffed the non-iced coffee in the tray and managed to take a sip from it without removing it.

"Big day," he said again, this time actually trying to attach meaning to the words.

"Yeah! Final inspection. Don't tell me you forgot."

He blinked as the realization came tumbling out of his brain.

"Oh, right. Yeah. Yeah, big day."

"I'm *amazed* at how quick your uncle got this place together. Built in three months, almost ready to *run* in six."

"He's got experience getting things put together in a hurry. Since most of his enterprises don't last more than a year, the less of that year you spend under construction the better."

"I think this one's going to last. The Spiros Center for Observation, Parenting, and Education; Head Researcher: Gale Dekker."

"Uh-huh. You know, the rules of nepotism normally require that the boss's nephew get the head position."

"You *do* have the head position. Head caretaker. That's the more important job anyway. This place is *all* about Blodgette. How's she doing this morning?"

"Sleeping. Like I was supposed to be for another 45 minutes."

"The earlier the start, the better! Let's go see her."

They took a different route through the building, eventually coming to a room with a large glass window facing what appeared to be something between a large animal paddock, a community garden, and an outdoor bistro. It was open air, with chain link fences separating it from a ten-foot grass walkway and then a tall cement wall. The fences were thick with hanging planters and climbing vines. Each held a different flowering plant: marigolds, lavender, chamomile. Designated sections of the ground had raised beds with tomato plants, rose bushes, and sunflowers.

An artificial pond took up about half of the rear of the enclosure, and led under a tall awning that shaded the entryway to a high-roofed shelter with large sliding doors. Markus waved his badge over a reader and bumped open an employee-only door, then paced his way to a gate in the chain link fence.

"Blodgette!" he called. "Time to get started!"

The ground trembled and, somewhere deep inside the shelter, a resounding metallic rattle and clunk rang out. Then came an excited, burbling trill. The heavy door to the shelter rumbled open. From the darkness within, two smoldering eyes peered out.

What came waddling out probably would have been terrifying if not for how genuinely delighted it appeared to be. Blodgette had grown in the last six months. Not much, at least by dragon standards, probably a few hundred pounds and six inches or so. Her former home and current armor—the remains of a pair of steel pizza ovens—was almost unrecognizable now. Her unique physiology had taken it several steps further from its appliance origins and a good deal closer to the samurai-esque armor plating it had only weakly resembled in the earliest days. A gleaming stainless-steel mask somehow failed to conceal the broad grin on her muzzle. She thumped toward Markus with her arms wide.

He hastily put down the things he'd been holding. A few months of seeing Blodgette every morning had taught him there was no stopping the morning hug. She scooped him up in her pudgy arms and rocked back and forth. Gale dropped her things as well, eager to grab the camera that was perpetually around her neck so that she could snap some pictures.

"It's only been six hours, Blodgette. This isn't a grand reunion," he said.

Blodgette dropped Markus and waddled back, hands held out in front of her. When Markus took a step toward her, she trilled once and motioned with her hands again.

"Fine, fine. I'll wait here," he said.

The dragon rubbed her stubby hands together, then took a breath. She tapped the fingers of one hand against her chin, waved it once toward her, then turned the palm forward and jabbed her thumb twice against her chin. Markus smirked.

"That means 'Good morning, Mom.' Are you *sure* you wanted to say that?"

Blodgette nodded eagerly. Markus sighed. Since their earliest experiments in communication, Blodgette had gotten the thought lodged in her head that the right word for Markus was "mom." They'd taken great pains to try to make the meaning of the word clear to her, and to suggest alternatives, but Blodgette was firm in her insistence that despite all of that, Markus was Mom.

The dragon turned to Gale. She had switched from photos to shooting video. Blodgette repeated the same wave, but this time concluded it by swirling both hands about in the air. Gale nearly dropped the camera.

"Oh my gosh, oh my gosh, oh my gosh!" Gale squealed. "She said good morning to me! And I think I know that sign."

She grabbed her phone and navigated to an American Sign Language dictionary.

"Wind! She said, 'Good morning, Wind'! Did you teach her that?" Gale asked.

"It was her idea. We were working on spelling your name out and she was frustrated. One thing led to another and we ended up looking up the word that came closest."

"A *Structophis Gastrignae* gave me a nickname!" she said, hopping up and down.

Blodgette raised her hand expectantly.

"Yes, you get a high five for that, bring it down here!" Gale said, raising her own hand.

They clapped hands and Blodgette chirped proudly, then looked at the assortment of new things the two caretakers had brought.

"Oh, yes. These are for you," Gale said.

Blodgette delicately removed all of the smaller planters and lined them up, then picked up the largest one to sniff at the odd-shaped yellow bloom.

She set the planter down and signed.

Flower.

"That's right," Markus said. "Flower."

"It's a squash flower," Gale added. "Squash. Like this."

Gale worked her way laboriously through the letters of the word. American Sign Language was just as new to her as to Markus and Blodgette, but she'd made it a point to become fluent in at least the letters. The dragon blinked at her as she went through the motions, then repeated the only important part back at her.

Flower.

Every *Structophis Gastrignae*, or Pizza Dragon, as most people called them, eventually picked something to horde. They tended heavily toward edible or culinary items. As the decor of her pen suggested, Blodgette had quickly decided that flowers were worth collecting. Through some not-yet-fully understood instinct or mechanism, she'd illustrated a strong preference toward edible flowers. Not edible to *her* necessarily, but a part of human cuisine in some way. She loved all flowers, but given the choice between something that would look good in a bouquet and something that would look good in a salad, she always chose the entree.

She worked her way through the others. Gale gave the full name of each plant. Blodgette dubbed it *flower* and found a place for it in the raised beds and hanging pots. Then she came to the tray of donuts and correctly surmised they were for Markus. She handed the tray to him and patiently waited.

"Yes, Blodgette. Thank you," he said.

He knew what she wanted, but sometimes it was fun to make her work for it. She poked the tray, then pinched all of her fingers together and tapped her mouth with them.

Eat.

She planted her fists on her chubby hips and waited again. When Markus had taken a bite of a donut, she nodded once, then waddled toward the pond to wade in. When she entirely submerged, water hissed against the antler-like metal horns jutting off the top of her mask. She remained submerged until the hissing stopped, then popped to the surface again and shook the water from her head.

Gale took some notes

"Do you always eat breakfast in here?" she asked.

"No. But if I ever bring food in here that she knows isn't for her, everything stops until she sees that I've eaten some. It's not until recently that she stopped trying to get me to eat the oak logs and chunks ore we keep in here for her."

"Such powerful nurturing behavior at such a young age…" She scribbled some more notes.

She sniffed, then glanced at him. "You haven't showered at all."

"No, I haven't. Because someone woke me up before my alarm to answer the door. You know there are people in the lobby, right? They could have let you in."

"But they don't have access to Blodgette. Look, it doesn't matter, go get yourself ready. The official from the preservation society is going to be here in two hours and you need to be at your best. I'll keep Blodgette busy and then we'll start getting her ready."

"You hear that, Blodgette?" he called. "Ol' Wind here is going to keep you company. I'll be back in two shakes."

Blodgette bobbed in the water, splashing as she raised a hand to sign.

Goodbye, Mom.

He paced to the gate, then through the facility. For six months, he'd been living with Blodgette. First in a tent on the land that would become this facility, then in the skeleton of the facility as it was built around them. During that time, his Great-Uncle Dimitrios had been busy leaping through legal hoops. Blodgette was an extremely rare creature. Her presence in the country was the result of an illegal action, and her upbringing had been less than ideal. In the beginning, charges of everything from grand theft to child endangerment could have been heaped upon them. Her uncle and his questionably scrupulous lawyer had untied most of those knots. Markus didn't know or care just how that was achieved. Having something more important to focus on has a way of making even potentially life-ruining criminal proceedings seem pointless by comparison. Today was the last hurdle, as he stood alone in the shower, the full weight of it was coming down upon his shoulders.

A Big Day for Blodgette

A representative from the international governing body for all things *Structophis* was on her way. Markus had spoken to her on the phone at least three times already. Each time it felt like he was having a job interview with someone who'd decided before he walked in the door that he 'wasn't right for this company.' A lot hinged upon how things went today. If he was found to be an unfit caregiver, if Blodgette's health wasn't up to snuff, if her development was too slow, and even if the enclosure wasn't up to their requirements, they could decide that she should be taken away. That had financial consequences for Uncle Spiros—who had sunk much of his recently acquired wealth into the construction of this science center/tourist trap with Blodgette as its only attraction. It had legal consequences for Gale and Markus, each of whom were avoiding fines and jail time in part for their role in taking care of Blodgette.

Oddly, the only things that Markus found himself worrying about were the consequences for Blodgette herself. There was a reason Markus had agreed to *live* at the science center. For the first few months, Blodgette was timid and anxious around anyone else, with the possible exception of Dimitrios. Gale had eventually earned her trust, but even she couldn't calm the beast down if she got worked up. Blodgette had bonded with Markus and that gave him a solid and irreplaceable role in her life for at least the next two years. By then, Blodgette's mind and body would have worked their way toward something approaching adulthood, and she would become more fully self-reliant. But to lose Markus before then would be like tearing a child from its parents.

He finished his shower, brushed his teeth, and put on a fresh uniform. When he returned to the enclosure, he found Gale illustrating why Blodgette's patience for her was so limited.

The two were playing with clay. More accurately, Blodgette was trying to play with clay and Gale was narrating the copious valuable scientific observations of the act while Blodgette glared at her for not participating.

"As you can see, we've got easels set up with pictures of other *Structophis Gastrignae*. Today we are trying to get Blodgette to sculpt one."

Play, Blodgette signed, her expression flat and irritated.

"Communal activities are extremely important for *Structophis Gastrignae* at this stage of intellectual development. Blodgette's

191

intelligence at this stage is somewhere between that of a five-year-old and an eight-year-old, so she is more than capable of engaging in this activity alone now that she has been shown how, but she is happier and more engaged when others involve themselves as well."

Play, Blodgette signed again, waggling her pinkies a bit more emphatically.

Markus walked over and plopped down beside Blodgette and grabbed a handful of the modeling clay.

"Make sure you take notes on the North American Large Animal Zoologist, one of the most intelligent species in the animal kingdom who for some reason still can't take a hint and just sit down to sculpt a kitty cat," he said.

"Someone's got to do the research, Markus."

"Fine. You do that, I'll be Mom."

He looked up at the easel.

"What do you say we try to make that guy, Blodgette? That's Easy. Sort of the unofficial ambassador of Pizza Dragons. Poster boy for the species."

The creature he'd indicated was indeed quite famous, as Pizza Dragons went. If you knew anything about the species, and not very many people did, you at least knew about Easy. Looking at the creature, you could see why someone might be concerned for Blodgette's health. The two had at least a similar body shape, but for lack of a better term, Blodgette just looked a bit *wrong.* Easy's oven-like components were the proper ones, a little metal in the mask region, but the rest were brick and clay. He had a long straight neck rather than the stubbier, more kinked neck Blodgette had. His tail was a little thinner and a bit longer than hers, and again, lacked the worrisome kinks. The other big difference was the color of his skin. He had a soft, doughy appearance to his natural hide. Blodgette's skin had improved overall, but was still much darker and a bit more craggy. She looked worlds better than she'd looked on her emergence day, but a long way from being the ideal for her species.

Blodgette wadded and squished clay into a chubby snake shape, holding it up to the image frequently to compare. Markus started working on limbs for her creation.

Gale cleared her throat to get his attention, then pointedly glanced at Blodgette. Markus nodded and sighed.

"So, Blodgette. How do you feel lately?" he asked.

With both of her hands busy, she chirped pleasantly in response.

"There's a lady coming today to check you out."

Blodgette gave a less enthusiastic chirp.

"She's going to do a lot of the Gale stuff. Checking your temperature, weighing you. That sort of thing. Lots of pictures."

The dragon huffed.

"I know, I know. No fun. But she's a lady who knows more about pizza dragons than pretty much anyone. She's going to make sure you're okay."

Blodgette nodded.

"You know we all want to make sure you grow up to be the best you can, right?"

She felt around her for a stick and used it to poke some eyes and draw some lines on the surface of the clay.

"She's using tools again!" Gale quietly enthused.

"So if she decides you'd be better off, say, with other Pizza Dragons, you might be taking a trip."

Blodgette snapped her gaze toward him. She set down her clay on the clean tray they'd given her and began to sign.

Bus?

"No. We all know you don't like buses and vans."

She thought for a moment.

Flat bus?

"Probably."

We go?

"Probably you'd go and meet new people and dragons."

We go. This time the "we" part was fairly emphatic. It wasn't a question anymore.

"That's not really up to me. I mean. Let's be clear. It might not happen. I hope it doesn't. But if it *does* happen. Do what they say. It's for the best."

Blodgette shook her head. It wasn't an angry motion, just a simple statement that she would not, in fact, be cooperating.

He tried to come up with a more palatable way to introduce the concept to her, but before he could, the intercom system beeped.

"Dr. Morella has arrived."

Gale checked her watch. "She's early."

"I think that's a child services thing. Show up a little early so people have less time to prepare."

"You ready?"

"Ready as I'll ever be."

Gale trotted over to the gate, and stepped through to access the PA. There *had* been a PA panel in the enclosure, but Blodgette had found it and serenaded the entire facility with her chirping and trilling until they locked it out.

"Send her in."

"The lady is here now, Blodgette. Be nice, okay."

Play?

"She *might* play."

The woman appeared a moment later. She gave the immediate impression, both in her expression and her wardrobe, of a woman dispatched from the library to reprimand you for your overdue books. Markus looked at her.

"I don't think she'll be playing," he said quietly.

He climbed to his feet and wiped off his hands.

"Dr. Morella?" he said.

"Yes. And you are Mr. Spiros, correct?" she said, with a mild Italian accent.

They shook hands.

"That's right. Markus Spiros. You can call me Markus. And what should I call you?"

"Dr. Morella."

"Right…"

She turned to Gale. "And you are Ms. Dekker?"

"Gale Dekker. Hoping to be Dr. Gale Dekker if I can complete my research."

"I have read your papers. They were quite thorough."

"Thank you!"

"And this is Blodgette. I am not overly pleased with the name. It is more appropriate for a pet than a creature of her caliber."

"I hadn't really been thinking about the long term when I came up with it."

"I would be very surprised to discover you did much thinking of the long term at all, Mr. Spiros."

A Big Day for Blodgette

The dragon looked uncertainly at Dr. Morella. She climbed to her feet but didn't offer up the hug or anticipate the high five that she did for Markus and Gale. The doctor pulled a tablet from her bag and raised it to snap some pictures of Blodgette. The dragon huffed and grabbed Markus, gently lifting him and placing him between her and the newcomer before huddling down as though she could hide behind the much smaller human.

"She is inadequately socialized," Dr. Morella said.

"She's a little skittish around newcomers. Particularly strangers with cameras," Markus explained.

"That is a problem, is it not? As you are hoping to soon have many hundreds of people per day who fit that precise description."

"She's gotten very comfortable *in her enclosure*," Gale clarified. "It's just that you're in here with her."

"*Structophis Gastrignae* are extremely social creatures. She should be *very* comfortable with outsiders."

"As you know, she's had sort of a rough few years."

"I am quite aware. I believe I will begin by assessing the enclosure. Ms. Dekker, if you'll help me?"

Blodgette watched, strafing around Markus to keep her on the far side.

"Come on, Blodgette," Markus said. "Let's go inside and play with your blocks."

"I shall be checking in there next," Dr. Morella said.

"Let's just stand here and wait for the nice lady, Blodgette," he amended.

Gale and the doctor paced around. They stretched a tape measure from every conceivable position to every other position. She measured the PH and temperature of the water, recorded the species of every plant, and even took samples of the grass.

Blodgette tapped his shoulder. He turned to her.

Play?

"Let's wait until the nice lady is done, shall we?"

Blodgette chirped unhappily and turned to the bags Gale had brought. She found the meats. Though the pepperonis and salamis were full size deli-meats, in her hands they looked like the sort of meat snack you'd find beside the cash register in a gas station. She took a bite of one, then after a moment, paced over to the doctor and offered an entire salami to her.

She raised her eyebrows at the offer, but she was after all a professional when it came to these creatures. Rather than turn down the offer, she pulled a small knife from her bag, cut off a piece of the meat, and ate it.

"Thank you very much, Blodgette," she said, with all the cordiality of a person being introduced to royalty. "I think we know enough about the enclosure. Let's have a look at you."

Dr. Morella took a few pictures from a few different angles.

"To the scale, please."

"Let's go, Blodgette," Markus said.

They paced over and the dragon obediently stood on the scale. More measurements were taken. Dr. Morella tried to swab her skin at one point, but that crossed a line of personal space that convinced Blodgette to grab Markus again, clutching him like a teddy bear and waddling back a few steps every time Dr. Morella tried to close the gap and try again.

"If you would, Mr. Spiros."

"Come on, Blodgette. The sooner it's over, the sooner we can do story time."

Blodgette huffed a breath with the edge of a grumble beneath it. She relented and let Markus go. He performed that test, as well as the internal temperature check and a few simple imitation exercises to check flexibility.

"The last thing I'd like to assess is mental acuity," Dr. Morella said. "She seems to have a firm understanding of the English language."

"She understands everything we say if we speak simply," Markus said.

"Very well. Blodgette, I am going to show you some cards and ask you some questions. Answer by pointing to the proper card."

Blodgette glared at Dr. Morella and signed a few words.

"What's this?" she asked.

"Blodgette asked you to go," Gale said. "I think she's getting a little impatient."

"It will be only a few more minutes," the doctor assured.

You go. Blodgette repeated.

"I take she is still unreceptive?"

You go, please.

A Big Day for Blodgette

"She's being very polite about it," Gale said.

Markus turned to her.

"Blodgette, if you do this one last thing, I'll give you two whole cans of tomato paste, then I'll read you a story, and we'll both go swimming, okay?"

Blodgette's eyes literally flashed with the promise. She turned and prompted Dr. Morella to begin.

The questions were simple. Which card has more dots? Which of these is an animal? Which of these is a plant? She did quite well on most, though she only about half of the math questions. After each question, Dr. Morella took some notes.

"I think that will do."

"Okay," Markus said.

Blodgette tugged at his arm, trying to lead him inside to make good on his offer.

"Just a moment," he said. "When will we know the results?"

"Oh, immediately," she said, flipping back through her notes. "The enclosure is sufficient. I would recommend a better filtration system for the pond, but it is within acceptable levels. She is ahead of the curve on intelligence. I'm intrigued by this sign language experiment. She seems to have taken to it. She's behind in height and weight, though the weight may be in part to the thinness of the metal. Were she to have matured in a proper oven she would have a higher proportion of masonry. Her skin troubles me, as does the seemingly permanent deformation of both her tail and her neck. If you've kept proper notes, and it seems Ms. Dekker has done an exceptional job of it, then she has made improvements in all areas since she came under your care. Overall, she is on a good trajectory, and you have the facilities to raise her properly. If she were to be socialized properly, which simply requires careful introduction with a few more individuals over time, then I see no reason why SCOPE would not be an adequate home for Blodgette for the next two to four years, after which she will be more capable of making her own decisions regarding permanent residency."

Markus smiled.

"Then she can stay?"

Dr. Santino cleared her throat. "If you would be good enough to remove the *Structophis Gastrignae* from the area."

"Why?" Markus said flatly.

"I think you know why."

The statement came like a punch to the gut. It showed on their faces. Blodgette glanced back and forth between them.

Why sad?

"We, uh… We should go inside now, Blodgette," Markus said, taking her by the hand.

She shook it off.

Why sad?

"Don't worry about it. I'll tell you later. Gale just has to—"

Blodgette stomped her foot.

I go?

Markus paused for a moment.

"Yeah," he said, finally. "You're going."

"Mr. Spiros, I'd asked you to take her aside for a *reason*," Dr. Morella said. "I was hoping to spare the creature any anxiety in the short term."

"She figured it out on her own," he snapped. "I'm not going to *lie* to her for you. So you may as well come out and say why you made that decision, because based upon all you've said, I can't figure out why. And she deserves to know."

"There was never any chance of her staying here," Dr. Morella said coldly. "Regardless of what the courts have decided, it is not lost upon *me* that your acquisition of Blodgette was the result of a criminal act. Whether it was the work of Dimitrios Spiros or the antique store from which he purchased the egg, Blodgette's presence here is illegitimate. And the amount of neglect evident in her emergence, one of the most crucial moments in a *Structophis Gastrignae*'s development, is inexcusable. Permanent damage has been done, even if it appears to be superficial for the most part. To continue to leave her in the care of the individual at fault would be irresponsible."

No. Blodgette said with a stomp of her foot.

"Dr. Morella, my uncle is an idiot, I'll grant you that. But this whole place is only *bankrolled* by him. Every bit of care that's been given has been given by Gale and I. And you've said it yourself, she's done nothing but improve."

You go. Blodgette signed, stomping her foot again. *I stay.*

"She wants to stay," Markus added.

"And a child, if given the choice, would eat only candy.

Sometimes we must impose our will upon a creature for its own good.”

“Is there any chance I can go with her?” he asked.

The doctor scoffed. “The entire purpose of the move would be to keep her *away* from the individuals responsible for endangering her.”

Safe here. Mom good. Wind good. You bad. You go. I stay.

“This would all be so much simpler to resolve of you could understand American Sign Language,” Gale said. “She is telling you off, but good.”

“If you’ll take Blodgette inside, I’ll discuss what needs to be done with Ms. Dekker.”

Markus crossed his arms.“No.”

“This isn’t up to you, Mr. Spiros.”

“Dr. Morella, if you came here and told me Blodgette was terribly sick and needed to be taken away, then I’d have rushed her out the door with you. If you found that this place wouldn’t be healthy for her, then I’d have downright demanded she be moved somewhere more appropriate. If she was getting worse then, again, take her away. But she’s doing great.”

“That doesn’t change anything. I cannot allow such a precious creature remain with people who would engage in such unscrupulous activities.”

“My great-uncle did something he shouldn’t have. That’s not my fault, and that’s not Blodgette’s fault. We both know she’s at a point in life where she needs someone to trust to help her grow. Do you have any doubt in your mind that she trusts me?”

“You can be replaced with time and care.”

“And what happens between then and now? How much damage are you willing to do just to punish my uncle for what he did?”

Dr. Morella was briefly taken aback.

“You can’t answer, can you? Because if you don’t want to hurt her, then you know that you can’t separate us. And if you *still* want to separate us, then you can’t claim that you have her best interests at heart.”

You bad, Blodgette signed.

She crossed her arms and huffed. Markus continued.

“When I first met Blodgette, I did a lot more thinking about me than I did about her. But that’s changed. Blodgette’s my responsibility. I take it very seriously. So if you want to take her away from me, you’re going to need handcuffs, and you're going to have to watch what it does to her."

Dr. Morella was silent for a long time.

"Well," she said. "I certainly do not doubt your dedication to Blodgette. I shall—provisionally—grant my permission for Blodgette to remain here, under your stewardship."

I stay? Blodgette asked.

"Yes," Gale said with a sigh of relief.

Blodgette chirped triumphantly and swept first Markus, then Gale into a hug.

"We will be watching you closely. And in the coming months you'll have to prepare her for a trip to meet another *Structophis*. It is not uncommon for *Structophis* to acclimate to a human society without much contact with others of their kind. For species preservation purposes, it is best to acclimate them to one another at an early age."

"Right. Fine," Markus groaned from in her grip.

"I'll show myself out."

Dr. Morella paced out of the enclosure.

"Blodgette. You can let go," Markus said.

The dragon reluctantly did so, letting them drop to the ground. Gale was permitted to climb to her feet on her own and dust herself off. Markus, instead, was hauled off the ground by his hand and led into the shelter. It was rather spartan, with little more than a platform for her to sleep on and some additional flowers and plants. The one exception was the bookshelf against one corner. It was well stocked with storybooks, and a chair sat beside it along with a reading light.

She sat him down and pulled a well-worn book from the top shelf. After handing it to him, she thumped down on the ground to eagerly await what would probably be the twentieth read-through of the story.

Markus clicked on the light and thumbed the book open to the first page. It wasn't until he tried to read it, though, that he realized just how misty his vision had become.

"I guess I was a little worked up back there," he said, rubbing his eyes.

He blinked away the last of his tears and looked to Blodgette. She gave him a grin.

Thanks, Mom.

SOMETHING PRECIOUS

JOSEPH R. LALLO

Something Precious

This story started as a Book of Deacon tale, but as I wrote it, I felt it didn't fit the characters I had in mind. A story you'll be getting later (The Story of Roka) is my second attempt at a Book of Deacon dragon story, and this one was converted to a standalone fiction world. That there is a female dragon named Thorne is a residual effect of that. Myn is stated to, at some point in the future, have a son named Thorn. I was going to change the name along with the other Book of Deacon references in the story, but I had already created a character named Miss Rose. Having a Rose and a Thorne was just too good to change.

By this time, Fable's scheduled had tightened up enough to make monthly covers a bit more than she could handle, so I started taking on new artists. This cover is by Ashe.

Lianne folded her hands and waited as the adults paced among the children. She was wearing her prettiest dress. She only had two, but this one had a bow, that made it the prettiest. Every few weeks, a day like this would come. The adults of the surrounding villages would arrive. They would look over the children, and perhaps if it suited them, they would select one.

The nearest village, Frush, was a tiny place. It existed simply because of a crossroads at the corner of town. Those who lived here did so simply to offer food, drink, and stables for travelers. A cluster of mining villages to the east, a large trading hub to the northwest, and the farming communities to the south made for a town with few locals but many, many regular visitors. This made it an ideal location for Lady Bristol's Home for Unfortunate Girls. Tucked at the edge of town, the sprawling manor-turned-orphanage served every sort of parent.

Poor farmers were the most common. They were more interested in the extra hands than another child, but a good strong girl could get a good home with a farm family. The same went for the miners. It may have been back-breaking labor most often left to the men, but the tunnels were low and narrow, and someone small and nimble was always worth having. Even for girls, a strong back and an able body was sure to lead to a good home.

A good home. That was the key. That it needed to be a good home was what, in many ways, made things more difficult for the girls. Were the goal to simply assign each girl to a family, Bristol's Home would scarcely be necessary. Miss Rose, mistress of the house, had far stricter rules. Would-be caregivers had to prove themselves worthy of one of her girls.

Lianne smoothed her dress over her leg. Miss Rose would have reprimanded her for the way she was sitting. It wasn't ladylike to sit with one's legs folded as she did. It wasn't proper to speak to adults unless spoken to, to smile in anything but the most demure of ways. But Lianne preferred to sit this way; she preferred to speak and to smile. If she charmed them with her words, perhaps they wouldn't notice the crutches leaned against the wall behind her. If she folded her leg and let the skirt hang over it, perhaps might not notice that there was only one leg hidden beneath.

She knew that wouldn't be enough for the famers and the miners. These were people who bought horses and pigs. They knew better than to trust what they saw on the surface. But perhaps the people from the north would be fooled? These were people with more money than they knew what to do with. They had homes with empty rooms that needed filling. They had businesses that called for reading and the like. One hardly needed two legs for that.

"Hello!" she crowed as a couple approached.

The woman had the pale skin of someone who had lived a life indoors. The man had soft hands that had never seen a day's hard toil.

"My name is Lianne," she said, adjusting her bow to be sure they both saw it. "What are your names?"

The couple looked upon her with bemusement, as though a puppy had learned the trick of giving a chipper greeting. The man opened his mouth to say something, but his wife touched his arm and whispered something in his ear. His eyebrows raised. He glanced over Lianne's shoulder.

Lianne leaned aside to better block the view of her crutches. "I can count to twenty, and I can spell my name."

The man gave her what he'd likely intended to be a reassuring smile and nod. They fell short of the target and landed squarely in the vicinity of pity and condescension. The couple moved on. There were no others to follow. She turned back to them.

"Wait!" She reached back and grabbed her crutches. "I fashioned them myself! I'm good with my hands. Half the rest of these girls can't say that! And I can walk just fine, too."

She demonstrated by hopping down and hoisting herself to her feet. She thumped around in a circle.

"See? And I can climb stairs, too!"

The couple continued.

"I only need one shoe!" she cried after them.

Unswayed, the couple stepped from the room.

"Lousy northerners, always wanting things perfect," Lianne muttered, flopping down and stowing her crutches. "If you want a perfect little girl so bad, why not make your own instead of coming and getting someone's hopes up?"

#

In a few hours the light had gone, and it had taken the prospective caregivers with it. It had been a wonderful day for the home. Seven little girls had found homes. That left Lianne and only three others. It wouldn't stay that way for long. Every month, new girls from all over the kingdom were brought here. But it would be a few days before their open beds would be filled, and that made for a lonely time for those who had waved goodbye to their friends. It was a lesson Lianne had learned far too many times to count. Seven years she had been here, which was longer than she could remember. It may as well have been forever.

Experience had taught her that on nights like this, kind as it would have been to be company to the other girls, she was better off spending the evening with the head mistress. Little girls who had been passed over once were inconsolable, and trying to talk them through it meant fighting through a torrent of tears. One might call it selfish, and with good reason, but she was through being a shoulder to cry on. She'd done enough of that for a lifetime.

"What about this one?" she asked, pulling out a thick sheaf of pages.

The better way to spend the night after being passed over was to help the headmistress go through what few messages showed up. Most were donations of this sort or that, clothes or money sent by people hoping to do their share, or sometimes to ease their guilt for having too much. But sometimes, very rarely, someone seeking a child couldn't afford to make the trip and come home empty-handed. They would write letters, learn which girls might need homes. Lianne was clever enough to know it was a lot harder to notice a girl might not be perfect if you only had a description to go by.

Her criteria for picking the letter she wanted the mistress to go over was very basic. Anything fancy was probably from the north. Those were her kind of people. And anyone who wrote long letters was someone who liked to talk, and those were her people, too. This message was everything she could hope for. Thick as her thumb, six pages at least with something stuffed between them. They were written on a rough parchment that smelled old and musty. The pages were folded in thirds and fastened with a big, gloppy blob of red wax pressed with a seal larger than any signet ring.

"My," said Miss Rose as she took the message from Lianne. "This *is* a large one."

"Open it!" Lianne offered up a blunt knife from the table. "And read it!"

The mistress cracked through the wax seal and unfurled the message. Though there were indeed many pages, the message itself was very short. It was written in a very large, careful hand. The first page had all of three sentences on it.

"To the Friendly People at the Lady's Home. I understand you have a fine selection of little girls without caregivers. I have a great deal of care to give, and would be very interested in procuring one of these girls. I have few requirements. Any girl who can eat solid food is adequate to my needs. If you have a young woman to spare, deliver her to the cabin at the crossroads of Dire Dwarf Road and Sharp Road. Enclosed, please find evidence of my capacity to render care and support for this girl."

She flipped to the last page. A single gold coin was to it with the same wax as the seal.

"Heavens…" Miss Rose said. "A whole gold coin. And an old one at that."

"How do we write back that we found them a girl?" Lianne said excitedly.

Miss Rose smiled at Lianne with a far more successful attempt at reassurance. "Lianne, you don't want to go home with someone who would write a message like this."

'Why not? I eat solid food, don't I?"

"Listen to the words. A fine selection? Interested in procuring? Deliver her? This is a person negotiating the purchase of property."

"That's fine. Seems like half the people who come through here are doing that, too. Trina's arms are sore from folks pinching her to see if she'd be any good with a pick. At least this one's got money."

"Lianne, I am charged with ensuring your safety. These are not the words of one with whom I would trust a little girl."

"How do you know you can trust all the other folks who came and took girls today?"

Miss Rose pulled the coin from the page and tossed it in the coffer.

"There is a great deal one can learn by one's bearing, by one's tone, and by one's gaze that simply cannot be learned from a few oddly worded sentences. And I turned away twice as many as I accepted.

Whoever wrote this didn't even include his or her *name*. It is a decidedly shady way to conduct a very serious business."

"So if this person came in and looked you in the eye, then maybe you'd let them have me?" she said.

"There is no sense in--"

Lianne tapped the page. "Write and let them know! Let them know you need to give them a good look and good talking to and then you'd be happy to send them home with a girl."

Miss Rose looked at Lianne with tight lips and narrow eyes. If she was endeavoring to cow the girl into setting aside the notion without further argument, she was in for a fight. Lianne beamed back with unwavering resolve.

"Very well," Miss Rose said. "Fetch me the ink and quill."

She brushed the wax from the otherwise blank sheet that had held the gold coin.

"Watch closely now," she said. "Dearest sir or madam, The girls in my charge are my responsibility. I would be remiss if I did not do my due diligence in assuring that any would-be caretaker was of a high enough quality or caliber to provide them with a better home and life than they would have in my care. I request that you or a trusted representative personally meet with me for a frank discussion of your suitability, and to meet with our girls."

"Don't mention my leg," Lianne said.

"I shan't. But please, Lianne, try not to get your hopes up." She tapped the pages littered with the large, coarse script. "This is not a message sent by someone with the intension or notion to visit a place such as this for a girl--"

"Such as me?" Lianne finished.

"For a girl of any sort," Miss Rose said, offering no indication of whether or not those were the words she'd initially intended to say.

"But they sent a coin! A gold coin. Most people who send coins send copper. Even the wealthy ones send silver."

"Generosity is a fine trait, but the wealth to be *this* generous doesn't often come to a kind person with proper intentions." Miss Rose held out her hand. "The wax."

Lianne held out a stick of black wax, then pushed the candle over to the Mistress. Miss Rose folded the page again, melted some wax, and slid a ring from her finger to seal it with Lady Bristol's insignia.

"We will send it up Sharp Road. But please don't get your hopes up. I suspect this is the last we will see from this person."

#

A terrible rapping at the front door managed to shake the whole of the manor. The sound woke Lianne. In the five weeks since the strange message had come, fifteen new girls had come and six of them had gone. For the other girls who shared Lianne's room, the knocking wasn't enough to stir them, but Lianne was a light sleeper. What's more, Lianne knew for a knock to be heard this far from the front door, the person knocking would have to be *very* motivated.

She slid from bed and tried as hard as she could to make her way to the window without the thumping of her crutches waking the other girls. The cold of the north meant that a window was more of an ornament than anything else. To keep the room from becoming too chilly, the window was perpetually blocked by heavy drapes and sturdy shutters. Lianne pulled the drapes aside and squinted through the shutters. The coach house was just outside the window. If there was someone visiting from out of town, she would be able to see their carriage.

No amount of twisting or shifting her vision through the cracks in the shutters revealed anything against the gray ground and lingering white snow. Could it be someone from the town?

More knocking rattled through the manor, then the distant click of a door opening. Lianne lost the battle with her curiosity and made her way into the hallway. She'd paced these halls for so many years that she knew just where the creaky floorboards were and precisely where the treacherous, curled up planks were. She could navigate the hall with her eyes shut.

Not until she reached the stairs did she run the risk discovery. The steps were rather steep, and whether she decided to hop from step to step or use her crutches to ease herself down, there was a better than average chance that she would be heard.

Or, at least, that would *usually* be the case. Right now, Lianne suspected she could fall down the stairs and still have no fear of drawing the attention of the very weary and very perturbed Miss Rose. The late-night visitor was more than distracting enough to cover her descent.

"This is your message, yes? Delivered up the hill, for me to read?" proclaimed the woman at the door.

She wasn't shouting. Shouting implied effort. This woman's

209

words were at a downright punishing volume with no effort at all. Her proclamations tumbled out of her mouth with the force and intensity of a church bell without so much as a deep breath before.

"Yes, ma'am. In response to your request to… What were your words?"

"I want a little girl! Do you have a selection to procure?" she said.

Lianne's heart jumped. Despite the repeated advice from Miss Rose, she'd held onto the hope that the strange letter might bear fruit. There wasn't much hope to be had in her world, and this was a rare gem. But even *she* had begun to doubt anything would come of it. She simply had to see the face of this woman.

"You do not *procure* children, Miss… Miss…"

"Thorne. You may call me Thorne."

The little girl reached the landing and scurried behind a hallway table. The moonlight was just enough to illuminate a sight as curious as the shouted exchange. The woman in the doorway was, in most meanings of the word, terribly severe. Her features were sharp. Chiseled, even. Cheekbones like they were carved from marble. A nose and chin that each came to a soft point. And her clothes? They were elegant-- but more than that, they were extravagant. Everything she wore was a brilliant shade of violet, and her outfit was many-layered. From purple-stained leather boots with an impressive heel to a sculpted felt hat with a fluttering indigo feather. And yet, despite the fashion on display, the most striking shade of was that of her eyes, the darkest and most vivid of blue-browns, almost a match for the violet scarf about her neck. They flashed with an intensity to match her voice, wide and enthusiastic as she engaged the weary headmistress.

"Miss Thorne," Miss Rose said. "You cannot--"

"Just Thorne, please."

"Thorne, you cannot simply appear at midnight. There is a proper way of things. In the morning--"

"Not in the morning. I do not do business in the mornings. I do business when I do business, and that time is now. You are awake, I am awake. We are both here. Name your price. I have more gold if you wish."

Thorne plunged her fingers into a satchel hanging at one elbow and revealed a palmful of coins.

This, it seemed, was sufficient to inspire a somewhat gentler tone of voice from Miss Rose.

"Children, you understand, are not for sale. However, if you were to pledge a degree of support to the home, I can assure you that we would welcome you whenever our doors open. I will personally assess your desires and see what, if any, of our girls will suit your--"

"Your door is open now, and any girl will suit me."

"The girls are all asleep, Thorne. If you require lodging, I can provide it."

Thorne's thin nostrils flared and her dazzling eyes darted. They fixed upon Lianne as precisely as if she'd known where the girl was hiding. The little girl felt a bolt of anxiety, huddling lower behind the table. As much as she wished to see what this woman was about, Miss Rose was very strict about her schedule. Business time was business time. Bedtime was bedtime. If a handful of gold coins couldn't get her to bend the rules, Lianne had no chance of dodging the punishment for leaving her room.

The wild-eyed woman looked back to Miss Rose. But the arch of her eyebrow and the twist of her head made Lianne suspect that the next words were actually meant for her.

"I can give a good home to one of your girls. She will want for nothing. If you will not introduce your girls to me, let them know that if they choose, they can introduce themselves to me. They need only find their way up Sharp Road."

"For a modest donation, I am certain I can see my way clear to sending a few of our girls with a chaperone, if you are more comfortable conducting business in your own home."

"A chaperone. Would this chaperone be you?"

"Likely not. I am charged with overseeing the matters of--"

"Good. You do not seem interested in providing me with a girl. Perhaps another chaperone would." Thorne dropped two coins in Miss Rose's hand. "At midnight. Tomorrow, or the next day. Any day, but certainly at midnight."

"Oh. It is simply not appropriate for little girls to be traveling so late at night. Early in the morning, perhaps--"

"I will have food for them. Fresh food. Heaps of it. And it will be warm. But midnight. Certainly midnight." Thorne glanced skyward. "I will go now. Send someone at midnight with one of your surplus girls.

Any of your surplus girls, and any midnight."

"If you believe that your generous contribution is obligating us to provide you with a girl I simply--"

"I am off! I eagerly await whatever young lady you provide."

With that, the mysterious and majestic woman turned on her heel. The motion caused a flare of her many layers of violet and sent up a scattering of snow. Lianne desperately wanted to watch her go. There was something about this woman that was enchanting in a way she couldn't quite grasp. But she knew that Miss Rose's sleepy, dazzled mind would soon clear. A pair of gold coins was a worthy distraction, but it wouldn't last forever. If she was going to avoid being caught, Lianne would have to make her move.

She scurried across to the stairs and performed the tricky but well-practiced maneuver of stowing her crutches under her arm and teasing enough mobility out of her remaining limbs to climb the stairs. Lianne was fast with her crutch, though not as fast as one of the more able-bodied girls. But crawling with three and a half limbs was nearly as fast as crawling with four. She made it well clear of the dim light by the time the frazzled and sleepy Miss Rose pulled her eyes from the strange young woman and turned to head to bed again.

#

The following morning, Lianne was rattling with excitement as she gratefully accepted her bowl of porridge. It did not go unnoticed.

"You certainly seem chipper this morning," Miss Rose said as Lianne joined her at the table.

"I heard a noise last night. I wondered if something new happened. It's not so often that something new happens," Lianne said.

She was trying to be subtle. It wouldn't do for Miss Rose to suspect she knew what had happened. Subtlety wasn't her greatest strength, but she managed a near enough approximation to allay immediate suspicion.

"Mmm," Miss Rose said, sipping her tea. "A rather informal visit from the eccentric letter-writer."

"What did she say?" Lianne asked with a bounce.

"Nothing to diminish my concerns in the slightest. Quite the opposite in fact. I should say… Did I mention that it was a woman?"

Lianne's eyes widened briefly.

"Yes! Yes, you did. That's how I knew. How else would I know?"

Lianne urged the conversation forward, rather than let it linger on this rough patch. "What did she say, though?"

"She wished for a girl to be brought to her at midnight."

"Who will it be?" Lianne asked.

"Heavens, no one," Miss Rose said. "The words that woman used. Bizarre. I get the sense she is hiding something. It is exceptionally important that caregivers be *entirely* honest and forthcoming with me, and I do not believe I had that in this woman. And then there was the insistence of a midnight hour. It gave the overall impression of someone touched in the head at best. A witch at worst. No, no. Much as it could be put to good use, from this point forward I shall accept no further contributions from her, and should she persist in her inappropriate requests I will personally see to it that she is forbidden access to the house."

Lianne gripped her spoon tight and felt a flutter of anxiety in her chest.

"You are sure? Just from her words? Maybe she is just odd. It isn't wrong to be odd, is it? I'm odd, and I'm not wrong, am I?"

"One can be unique, certainly, but she demonstrated nothing to suggest she would be a proper caregiver."

"What *would* suggest she would be a proper caregiver?"

"What does it matter?"

"If she comes back and she shows the things you'd hoped to see in this visit, then she could still get a little girl, couldn't she?"

Miss Rose sighed. "Put it out of your mind. I pride myself on getting *all* that I need from a first impression."

Lianne clanked her spoon on the table and gathered herself into as dignified a bearing as she could.

"The girls of Lady Bristol's Home for Unfortunate Girls should always endeavor to learn and improve, the better to find a home or to prepare themselves for the world. You say that all the time, don't you?"

"I do."

"So teach me what you look for. After you and Miss Maya, I've been here the longest. If I'm here much longer, one of these days I'll be helping you find homes for the other girls."

Miss Rose gave her a stern look. It was a dirty trick, using her own words against her, but when you've got only one leg, you quickly learn that sometimes you can't hope to win a game without a bit of creativity with regard to the rules.

"If we are speaking of the *ideal* caregiver, we must first and foremost have evidence that he or she actually *cares*. Even a family hoping to find a girl to help with tasks normally reserved for stronger backs and coarser hands must demonstrate an interest in keeping a girl as healthy and happy as they are able. And that is another matter. No one comes to this place without a reason in mind for finding a girl. They must be honest and direct with that reason. No intention that must be hidden is likely to be acceptable."

Lianne nodded. "Honest, caring. Is there anything else?"

"Beyond the demonstration of proper means and intent, there are the subtler things, which were absolutely absent from the curious woman who visited. Decorum. Respect. Manners. Modesty. Things proper for a lady. If this… Thorne, I believe was her name. If this Thorne woman had paid her visit at a proper hour, if she had comported herself with grace, there would have been no concern. She should at *least* demonstrate the etiquette I've endeavored to teach each of you in your time here."

Lianne swallowed a mouthful of her breakfast.

"I see a lot of girls walk out of here with people still dirty behind the ears from mines. That's not the same etiquette you teach us."

"Yes, well… As I've said, I am speaking of the ideal. Things will not always be as we prefer. In the case of Thorne, she would have to illustrate herself to be *perfectly* ideal in order to undo the terrible impression she's made thus far."

Lianne nodded and shoveled more of her meal into her mouth. The wheels were already turning in her mind. This particular game was going to take a good deal more creativity, but that had never stopped her before.

#

That night, after the rest of the girls and the caretakers had fallen asleep, Lianne slid silently from bed. She'd spent most of the day hatching her devious plot. The night was far too cold for her to head out without being properly bundled. The warm coats for the girls were all kept in the cloak room, which was far too close to Miss Maya's room for her to be confident she could sneak through without waking her. Fortunately, she'd been here long enough to get to know the groundskeeper quite well. He kept a spare coat and trousers in the shed. She couldn't slip out through the main door. It was too heavy and too creaky. But she *could* slip down into the root cellar. There was a hatch that led from there to the outside. Few people knew about it because it was usually snowed and iced over, but during her daily chores she'd made certain it was clear.

Her plan unfolded flawlessly. It couldn't have been much past eleven by the time she was hobbling along Sharp Road in ill-fitting clothes, leaning heavily on her crutches and hoping the mysterious woman's cabin wasn't *too* far up the mountain.

#

Three hours later, Lianne discovered that no amount of hope and enthusiasm could make up for the difficulties of a missing leg and a harsh mountain road. She shivered and huffed, exhausted from the climb and chilled to the bone. If she'd been less exhausted, she might have had her doubts about the cottage ahead. It was large, but terribly rundown. Bits of the roof had slumped under the weight of the snow. Shutters hung askew from the windows. Rough, cracked planks had been hammered in place to keep the elements out.

She didn't care. This was a triumph. She'd made it this far by herself, without any of the people at Lady Bristol's home noticing. And now that mysterious woman who had been so interested in a little girl was just a door away.

Lianne trudged to the heavy door and thumped with a crutch. At first there was only silence. Her smile didn't falter. She simply wouldn't allow herself to believe that this would go any way but how she'd imagined. The plan had gone perfectly until now. She hadn't made any mistakes. Fate owed her the prize she was after.

The door shuddered on its hinges and eased laboriously open to reveal complete darkness within. For the first time, a flicker of doubt wormed its way into her mind.

"Ah! Little girl. Yes…" echoed the powerful, delighted voice she'd eavesdropped on.

An odd breath of wind rushed from within the cabin, then the elegantly dressed woman emerged. Her smile was bright, her outfit impeccable.

"You are terribly tardy. But then, I *am* aware this is not how you typically do business, so we can call this a compromise, I imagine. Come in! Come in, please."

"Thank you, ma'am," Lianne said, as sweetly as she could manage.

She stepped inside. The giddy joy of having her plan unfold as she'd intended was starting to falter. The inside of the cabin was in the same state of disrepair as the outside. Whoever this woman was, she'd apparently spent the night waiting in pitch darkness. The front door led to little more than a mudroom blocked off from the rest of the cabin by a second crooked door. There was no furniture, no candles. Even the coat hooks beside the door had been torn away.

"You… live here?" Lianne said.

"No, no. Certainly not. But my home is rather far." She lowered her voice. "And frankly I am not terribly keen on having visitors. That tends to end poorly for all involved. This seemed a worthwhile place to do business."

She paced to the door and placed a hand on her hip.

"This blasted thing always sags on its hinges. I swear these old buildings aren't built to last."

Thorne grasped the knob of the door and one of the cross pieces. With surprisingly little effort, she started to shift it about, lining up the crooked hinges with their pins.

"You were the little girl hiding behind the table, correct?" she said.

"Yes. That was… I wasn't… Thank you for not telling Miss Rose."

"Oh, I'm quite familiar with how frustrating it is to have someone shout out your hiding place. What is your name, dear?"

"Lianne."

"No last name?"

"I don't have a family, so I don't have a family name."

"Ah. There is a logic to that I suppose. And we have that in common. I have but one name, Thorne. Tell me, Lianne, why are you here alone? As I recall, your keeper required a chaperone."

"Um… This visit isn't for that. Not yet, anyway."

"I see, so this is the sort of transaction that requires multiple meetings," Thorne said, wedging the door into the proper place.

"Yes, ma'am."

"Wonderful! Acquiring valuable things *should* require a degree of negotiation and discussion. Down to business."

She crouched in front of Lianne, eye to dazzling eye. Lianne was enchanted by the liveliness in this woman's face. That sort of zest and zeal was utterly absent back in the home. It wasn't really a place for happiness and enthusiasm. The caretakers were devoted but weary, the girls were anxious and unsure. This woman was nothing but delight and excitement.

"As I believe you heard, I am interested in acquiring a young girl. Are you the one the Lady Bristol has selected for me?"

"No, I'm sorry. I would like to be, but that's not how it works."

"Oh. That is unfortunate. You have come to assess me, I suppose. I believe that was Miss Rose's intent."

"Um… Yes."

"Good! How clever, sending a little girl to assess the needs of a little girl. Let's begin with food, then, shall we?"

She turned back to the freshly re-hung door and tugged it open. Lianne's eyes widened and sparkled as golden light poured from within.

The room waiting for them beyond the rickety door had no place being a part of this dilapidated cabin. This one room must have taken up the remainder of the space in the cabin. Gleaming silver candelabras lit the room brighter than day. Most of the center of the room was strangely bare, though it did bear a plush, glorious rug from wall to wall. A table stretched the length of the far wall. It was heaped with all manner of sumptuous delights. Pastries glazed with sugar and bursting with cream. Fresh fruits Lianne didn't even know the names of. It was magnificent, the sort of meal that would be set out by a noble to impress his peers during an annual festival.

"I will take your coat. I believe that is proper for a hostess."

Lianne shakily slid her borrowed coat off without daring to take her eyes from the food, lest it somehow vanish.

"May I?" Lianne said hopefully.

"I should say so. I certainly don't intend to keep it for myself."

Children tend to be raised on fairy tales. Stories of mythic creatures and their machinations fill their minds. Most of these stories are meant for fun, to instill a sense of magic. But they also have far more important purposes. They exist in part to make it clear at a very young age that there are forces well beyond their control. The wide world was filled with wonder, but also danger and should be treated with care.

Lianne and the other girls of the home were *not* raised on such stories. If they had been, she might have had second thoughts about indulging in an unexplained, unlikely feast. Instead, Lianne abandoned any illusions of dignity as she scurried to the table. She heaped a plate with an assortment of decadent items. Navigating with two crutches and a heavily loaded plate in her hand was difficult, but she managed to thump to a table without spilling a crumb.

Her hostess stepped lightly to the table and set a porcelain cup down. She filled it from a teapot and swept her skirt gracefully to sit opposite Lianne.

"I trust this is sufficient illustration of my means to *feed* a hungry girl, yes?" Thorne said.

"Yaugh!" Lianne eagerly affirmed, somewhat more messily than Miss Rose's etiquette training would allow.

"Excellent. When can I expect my girl to be delivered, then?" Thorne asked sweetly.

Lianne looked up. For the first time, she allowed herself to be struck by the disconcerting phrasing. She wiped her mouth and washed down her current mouthful of pastry.

"It isn't a matter of delivery. Miss Rose takes this sort of thing very seriously. And you didn't make a very good first impression."

"I can't imagine why that would be."

"You… you talk about little girls like they are property."

"I see. And that is not the proper way to speak of them."

"We aren't property."

Thorne smiled and nodded, less in agreement and more in the manner of one taking a mental note.

"Why do you want a little girl, Miss Thorne?"

"Because I don't have one."

"You probably don't have a *lot* of things."

"Oh, I assure you, I have cultivated *quite* a collection. I don't intend for it to be comprehensive, but the list of things that I feel could add to my worth is quite short."

"What sort of a girl do you want?" Lianne said, gently pushing the plate away.

"I am not concerned with specifics. Ultimately, I would like a princess. They seem to have the greatest value." She tipped her head. "It is rather curious, because princesses aren't at the peak of the hierarchy, and I was given to believe that value increases with status. But my peers are *endlessly* seeking princesses, and going to great lengths to acquire them, so I must assume they exceed even queens and kings in value."

Lianne eyed the door. The question that surged to the front of her mind was what sort of peers she had that were 'seeking princesses.' Her instinct for gently manipulating adults had served her quite well in her time at Lady Bristol's. She decided more tact was in order.

"You do know you won't find any princesses at Lady Bristol's Home…"

"Naturally. But I have done some reading, and by my determination, there are many ways to become a princess. I am confident if I were to procure a little girl, I could grant the distinction myself."

Lianne's eyes locked back onto her hostess. Her mind shifted intently to the implication. Again, she'd not been raised on the sugary diet of fairy tales, but rare was the little girl who didn't have an innate sense of just how wonderful it might be to be plucked from tatters and made into a princess. For the moment, she let her suspicions slide to the back of her mind and helped herself to another mouthful of dessert.

"Are you a lady?" Lianne asked.

"I would hope I am quite visibly so."

"No, I mean do you have your own land?"

"More than sufficient to satisfy the requirements of a little girl, I would say."

Lianne nodded. "And you want a princess because they are *valuable.*"

"I do."

"So you wouldn't… err… You wouldn't want a girl like me then?"

"Why wouldn't I?"

"Well… because I'm… I only have one leg."

Thorne glanced down at her swinging leg, then back to her face.

"I am not familiar with how finely the value of a girl is divided among the anatomy. Are the legs a great deal more valuable than the rest?"

"The people who have come through the home seem to think so. They don't want someone who isn't whole."

Again, Thorne seemed to make a note of this information without her interest or enthusiasm softening in the slightest.

"I will admit that my assessment skills are not well-practiced in this particular area, but I pride myself in my eye for value. I will make my own determinations of worth. And, again, I mean to make my own significant contributions to that worth once I work out how properly to bestow the title of princess."

She leaned forward and raised an eyebrow.

"You would be surprised just how many of the most treasured portions of my collection were created rather than acquired."

Lianne wiped her mouth. "Then we've got to make sure you can convince Miss Rose to let you take care of me. Or someone like me. I wouldn't think to, um… presume."

"I would prefer to simply keep you, now that you have expressed the interest and capacity to come here, but if that is not how it is done, then I will bow to procedure."

"Yes. Yes. You have to do this right. People would come after me if I went missing."

"Ah. Well, we certainly don't want that." She leaned in again. "That sort of thing is terribly messy, and seems to be the primary difficulty my peers have in their own attempts to acquire a princess."

Lianne willfully forced the disquieting statement from her mind.

"The first problem is, um… Well, Miss Rose doesn't like you."

"I can't imagine why."

"She needs people to be *perfectly* honest and *never* hide *anything.*"

Thorne drummed her fingers on her leg. This, for the first time, seemed to give her pause.

"*Perfectly* honest?"

"That's right."

"Never hide *anything at all?*"

"Never."

She drummed her fingers some more, weighing the condition carefully.

"*Are* you hiding something?" Lianne asked.

"I am. Naturally. It seemed appropriate for the sort of business I wished to conduct. To be perfectly frank, if complete transparency is required to acquire a little girl, it may be simpler to pursue it through more traditional means. Thank you for your council. I will have to think this over."

Lianne's eyes shot open and she leapt to her foot, teetering a bit before she got her crutches in place.

"Wait! I know Miss Rose *very* well. Don't be so hasty. Why don't you tell *me* what you are hiding, and I can tell you if it would help or hurt to reveal it to her."

"If it would be troubling to her, surely it would be troubling to you as well."

Lianne gathered herself and stood up straighter.

"Don't worry about me. They taught me very well at the home."

Thorne looked Lianne up and down again. After a lifetime of being endlessly appraised by would be adopters, she was quite inured to the measuring gaze. Thorne must have been satisfied with what she'd seen, as she nodded once and took a step back.

"Lianne, what I will now reveal to you is something I have kept hidden for what I believed was a very good reason. I am trusting you to remain composed and to be as honest in your assessment of any potential problems it may cause me in my future dealings."

The little girl felt a strange, warm flutter in her chest. Something about someone of such elegance and grace uttering the words "I am trusting you" and truly meaning it… It felt like she'd just had a medal pinned to her dress.

"Of course," she said proudly.

"Wonderful," Thorne took another step back and rustled her skirt a bit. "It is rather late in the morning already. This will be something of a relief. I do my best work in the midnight hours."

Though she'd given the stiff cloth of her skirt only a brief swish, it continued to flutter and shift. Lianne wondered if perhaps there was a draft, but something deep inside her knew she wasn't lucky enough for the answer to be something so mundane.

The skirt started to shift and slip, layers sliding against themselves. Before they could reveal anything that might be hidden beneath, she leaned forward a bit and lowered her hands. While Lianne's eyes had been attempting to make sense of the fabric that appeared to have a mind of its own, she'd neglected to notice that Thorne's gloved hands had lengthened. Her fingers had tapered. The once-elegant woman continued to lean forward until it seemed she would topple over, but something swept and curled from behind her to maintain her balance.

Lianne watched in stricken awe as the change continued. Her mind had already worked out where this journey of transfiguration was headed, but she couldn't bring herself to close her eyes and miss even a moment of the spectacle. In seconds, the woman had smoothly shifted to a strikingly radiant violet dragon.

Thorne sighed luxuriously, with the relief of one tugging off one's boots after a long, hard day.

"There we are. Lovely." Thorne fluttered her eyes.

The dragon stared down at Lianne. For the tiniest moment, she felt the flare of fear that every field rabbit or squirrel feels when an eagle is bearing down on them. It passed more swiftly than she had imagined possible. In truth, despite everything, Thorne hadn't really changed much at all. She was larger, certainly. And more reptilian. There was *nothing* human of her face or body, yet every curve, every angle, every flourish of color was an echo of the woman who she had been. The pleats of her skirt had found their way into the fold of elegant wings. Claws and scales shined with the same glitter of her jewelry. This wasn't a dragon who had posed as a woman named Thorne. This was still very much the same creature. The bright look of interest and focus gleamed in her eyes. The same subtly encouraging expression graced her fearsome features.

"You are uncharacteristically silent, Lianne," she said sweetly.

Hearing her name shook her back from the racing thoughts that had consumed her. Her mind bounced back and forth between urging her to scream and run and demanding she ask a thousand questions. When words finally found their way to her mouth again, they were less than nuanced or complex.

"You… are a dragon," she said.

"Again, quite visibly so, I would hope."

"I… you're a *dragon.*"

"I am indeed. Do you suppose we could move on to a more fruitful avenue of discussion? I don't imagine you'll have all night to offer your assessment and there may be a great deal to cover."

She swallowed hard and shut her eyes. It didn't help much.

"What do you want to know?" Lianne said.

Thorne shook out her great wings a bit and settled down into a leonine sprawl, hind legs kicked out to one side and claws folded one atop the other.

"Foremost, were I to present myself as I am now to your current keeper, would that be suitably honest? Would I be permitted to collect you as my own?"

"No. No, you would not. I don't think Miss Rose would be willing to give me over to a monster."

Thorne shifted her head a bit, curiosity in her gaze. "And how would that apply in this situation?"

"You're… she would think you are a monster."

Thorne waved her paw dismissively. "Nonsense. Miss Rose seemed a perfectly reasonable woman. A monster is defined by her actions, and I have made every attempt to be proper and mannerly. To be frank, I would lose a great deal of respect for any woman who would willingly hand a little girl over to a monster. Not that she would need to. A monster would simply take her pick of the girls available. So if one need only avoid monstrousness, I am *quite* confident I could pass that criteria."

"Even so. Uh… You were right to disguise yourself. Being human will make it easier."

The dragon nodded. "It is gratifying to know my instinct was accurate in that regard. I suppose it would be proper to ask you, in light of this revelation, if you are still interested in coming under my care."

It should have been a simple question. A massive beast with teeth longer than her fingers was asking if she wished to *belong* to her. The answer *had* to be no. But at the same time, the taste of that sweet cream was still on her lips. Of all the doubts in Lianne's mind, that this exquisite creature was sincere in her kindness and interest was not among them. Miss Rose had rankled at the words that had made her seem like she was purchasing livestock. Now that Lianne had spoken with her, the creature treated her as more of an equal than even Miss Rose herself. No, more than an equal. An *expert*.

But she couldn't ignore the facts. There *were* important questions to ask.

"Would I have to live in a cave?"

"Naturally, but I assure you it is *far* lovelier than this little place."

"What would I eat?"

"Whatever you choose. Conjuring food was a simple trick to

learn, and I mastered it quite some time ago."

"What will *you* eat?"

"Whatever *I* choose. I prefer to hunt for my own meals, of course, but that is none of your concern."

"Wh-what sort of princessly duties will I have?"

"I don't know… For my purposes you need only be *regal* and *precious.*"

"But what does that *mean?* Will I be a prisoner in a… a… "

"A gilded cage?"

"Right."

"I should think not. If you insist upon attempting to escape, I suppose steps would have to be taken, but you seem reasonable. I am confident anything that might inspire you to wish to take your leave could be discussed."

"So I could come and go as I please?"

"So long as you return to me when you are through and don't run off to do something foolish that might cause either of us trouble, I don't imagine there would be any reason to keep you from exploring."

Lianne's heart was still racing, but the fear of facing down a terrible yet beautiful creature was beginning to crumble in the face of the life she was offering. A measure more freedom, even if it was the only offer, was compelling enough. But to become a princess? To indulge in sumptuous feasts? To share a home with someone who truly *wanted* her? It was impressive how such offers could so easily shift a set of scales with a dragon weighing down the other side.

"And… And you're sure you'd want *me?* "

"Any of the girls would do, if you aren't available, but you seem quite suitable."

Lianne's lips tightened. "I'll stay with you, and I'll help you convince Miss Rose to let you have me, but *only* if you give me your word right now that you will choose me and not one of the other girls."

Thorne raised her brow and leaned forward, inspecting Lianne closely enough to trigger some long-dormant prey instincts. She held her ground.

"You would demand the word of a dragon?"

Lianne crossed her arms.

"It's non… non…"

"Non-negotiable?"

"Right."

Thorne drummed her claws on the ground for a moment.

"Very well."

The dragon climbed to her feet. She spread her wings until they scraped the roof.

"I, Thorne, give you, Lianne, my solemn word as a dragon. In exchange for your aid in navigating the whims of your current keeper, I shall select you and you alone to be my princess." She lowered her head reverently. "This I swear to you."

Lianne's skin tingled, her heart fluttered. It took her a moment to realize that she was holding her breath. She'd never imagined that simple words could have such power, and that such power would ever be summoned on her behalf.

"Right. Yes." Lianne nodded vigorously. "Let's begin right now. You'll, err… Well, you'll need to look human again."

"Naturally," Thorne said, flopping down again.

"Shouldn't you change?"

"Unless it is your intention for us to attempt to negotiate your acquisition immediately, for the sake of comfort I would prefer to remain as I am. I note, however, that a glamour will be needed for further meetings with Miss Rose."

"Right… Right… We can… We can talk about it while you are a dragon."

"I am always a dragon."

"*Looking* like a dragon. We'll start with the… the glamour, though. You look too fancy."

"Should I not be glorious? Resplendent? It seems only proper."

"Miss Rose doesn't like when people show off. She likes people humble."

"Humble? But I am magnificent, and I am quite aware of it."

"You just have to pretend you aren't. Neat clothes, but plain. Simple. Black, or brown."

"I see… An achievable, if distasteful, adjustment. Anything else?"

"I don't suppose you can appear to be a different human. A different first impression would be better than trying to make her forget the other one."

"I cannot. I do not have a fluency in magic. The specific glamour

I know simply gives a glimpse into the woman I might have been if I'd been born human. Even changing the clothes will tax my capabilities."

"Oh… Oh, well. Do you have a family?"

"Not for some time, I am afraid."

"She won't like that. She likes a big family. The better to care for the child if something happens."

"I have lived for two thousand years. If I have not fallen to the whims of circumstance by now, I very much doubt I shall."

"You're *not* two thousand years old. You are…" Lianne tapped her chin. "You are thirty-one. You have a husband. He is wealthy. And you have two brothers and two sisters."

She raised a brow and leaned a bit closer to Lianne. "I am quite certain you'd indicated honesty was called for."

"Honesty is best. Except if it isn't what they want to hear. Then you just tell them what they want to hear. Now, she will have questions. We need to make sure you know *everything* about your new family…"

#

"…and I shall raise her with wisdom and care," Thorne repeated, chin held high and eyes closed.

"Good, good, and what if she disobeys?" Lianne asked in her best rendition of Miss Rose.

"I don't imagine I will deliver any orders *for* her to disobey. She shall do as she pleases."

"No!" Lianne corrected. "You will have a firm but fair hand. Punishments if they are earned. She likes dis… dis… uh…"

"Discipline?"

"Right."

Thorne grinned a bit. "This is rather enjoyable, in a way. I haven't had to learn so much so quickly in ages."

"And there is a lot more to learn, but I've got to go now. I need to get back before they notice I left."

"I see. Shall you return tomorrow?"

"I'll try. It's a long walk."

Lianne tugged on her borrowed clothes and made her way to the door. She paced through the entryway and hauled open the door to the icy road. A stiff breeze chilled her.

"Lianne?" Thorne called from behind.

She turned. The dragon, still in her natural form, gazed at her through a doorway far too large for her to slip through.

"Forgive me if I am mistaken, but is it proper and wise for a child to walk a mountainside so late at night in such harsh weather?"

"I'll be fine. It is downhill. It will be easier than coming here."

"I see. Well then, safe trip to you."

Lianne paused. She'd been prepared to argue the point. Miss Rose wouldn't even have let her outside on a night like this, let alone send her on a roadside hike. But Thorne trusted her. This mighty creature fully embraced the thought that Lianne would have no trouble at all with the mountainside. It was motivating in a way Lianne hadn't expected. She smiled and gave the dragon nod. Then made her way down the icy road.

A few paces along, Thorne's voice echoed across the mountainside again. Lianne turned to see her, now human again, hurry up with something draped across one arm.

"Forgive me, but if you are to be my princess, it seems wrong that you should walk the mountain in ill-fitting clothes."

She shook out the bit of cloth over her arm, revealing it to be a brilliant indigo over-cloak. The dim, cloud-shrouded moonlight danced across its surface, here turning it almost red, there a glorious blue. Thorne draped it around Lianne's shoulders and brushed away the wrinkles. Lianne shut her eyes and hummed. She could feel the warmth of the garment filter through the heavy coat with supernatural speed. It was like an embrace, warm and nurturing.

"You shan't need that shabby jacket any longer. Do hurry back tomorrow."

#

Six days later…

Lianne thumped down the stairs and plopped down at the table.

"Lianne. You've nearly missed breakfast," Miss Rose said. "That isn't like you."

"I am sorry, Miss Rose." She yawned. "I haven't been sleeping well."

It had been no small task. Constructing an entire human life for a creature who lacked one took work. Each night, she'd crept out after the others fell asleep and made her way to Thorne's cabin. They rehearsed the things a proper human woman would say--or at least, the things that Miss Rose would deem proper for a human woman to say. They planned for every question that might come up. It had to be perfect. Better than perfect, it had to be redeeming for the unfortunate first impression. When each night was through, she made her way back and slipped inside before the others awoke.

"Are you warm enough at night? I don't know why you insist upon the bed beside the window when we have so many others."

"I like the window."

"Ask Miss Maya for a second blanket, at least."

Lianne nodded and glanced to the stack of messages on the table. One was on very familiar paper.

"Is that from Thorne?" Lianne said brightly.

"I imagine so," Miss Rose said wearily. "I shall dispose of it."

"No! You have to at least read it."

"Lianne, she simply unsuitable to adopt a child."

"You barely know anything about her!" Lianne said. "Maybe you've got her wrong."

The caregiver plucked the envelope from the stack. "I have made it my business to work out who is and who isn't likely to care properly for one of my girls. I am *rarely* mistaken."

She cracked the seal and flipped the message open.

Distinguished Miss Rose,

I fear my behavior upon our last meeting may have cast me in an unfavorable light. I discussed the matter with my sisters around the dinner table. In looking back upon our prior interactions, my words could have been selected with greater care, and my intentions made clearer. I implore you to grant me a second meeting. Our grand house feels so terribly empty without a child to warm its halls with laughter, and I feel horrid knowing that we have a room going to waste while children within your care fall asleep longing for a place of their own. I would be pleased to meet with you at whatever time you would find most amenable to polite conversation.

I have again enclosed compensation for any trouble I may have caused.

Humbly,
Thorne

Miss Rose set the message down. "Well… That is certainly a tone I'd not anticipated."

"She sounds like a wonderful person," Lianne said.

"Mmm… Quite unlike the one I met."

"People can change!"

"So quickly? I have my doubts. One could easily have someone pen a letter on their behalf. I cannot ignore what I have seen and heard."

"Then invite her back! Look her in the eye and talk to her again. She was probably just having a bad day that day."

Miss Rose gazed at the page, running her fingers over the oddly large writing.

"It does seem to have been written by her. The penmanship is unmistakable. Very well. There is no harm in it."

"And if you decide she is suitable you'll let her adopt one of us!"

"*If* I decide she is suitable."

As before, Miss Rose plucked the gold coin free from the final page, dropped it into a coffer, and used the sheet to compose her response. Lianne's heart practically sang as she watched the dry, formal request for an interview fill the rough parchment.

Lianne could already see her grand new home stretching out before her.

#

Today was the day. It had been unbearable waiting for the message to be delivered and a reply to acknowledge it. She'd felt the same tingle of anxious anticipation before each of the endless string of disappointing days when families came to ultimately pass her over. And she would be lying to herself if she didn't acknowledge that nearly a week of consuming delectable desserts and fine tea each night had become a welcome routine as well. But more than any of that, she found herself longing for the discussions she and Thorne had each night. The lessons, and the little curious questions the dragon had for her, were so nice. Having more evenings like those to look forward to was almost the greatest prize she could hope to earn for all the hard work she'd put into training Thorne for today's performance.

There were three other girls currently in the home's care. They were all in one of the rooms downstairs, playing. Lianne had taken the time to tidy her bed and lay out her good dress.

"Are you certain you don't want to be with the other girls?" asked Miss Rose.

"No. I'm fine, Miss Rose. I want to be ready if Miss Thorne wants to see me."

"That is very mature of you, Lianne. But you shouldn't get your hopes up."

"I know, I know." Lianne tried to keep the giddy smile from her face. "But I have a good feeling about this one."

Her keeper knelt beside her and helped her tug out some of the wrinkles and folds of the dress.

"Maybe, if Miss Thorne doesn't choose you, we can make you a new dress. This one is fraying a bit, and… What is this?"

Lianne glanced aside. Her heart froze in her chest. Miss Rose had noticed a tuft of violet cloth tucked beneath Lianne's simple mattress. She tugged it free to reveal the luxurious purple cloak that she had been given.

"Lianne, where did you get this," she said, her voice stern.

"I… There was…"

Miss Rose rubbed the fabric with her fingers. "This is *very* fine. I am quite certain I would have noticed something like this in the home."

"It's just… I… There was…"

"Out with it, Lianne. Where did you get this?"

"It was a gift," she said quickly.

"A gift? From whom? We received no packages for you, and you aren't permitted to have visitors." Her expression hardened further. "Did you leave the home without permission?"

A heavy knock echoed through the building. Miss Rose turned aside.

"That's her! She's here."

"You stay here, Lianne."

"But she might want to meet--"

"You stay here," she said firmly. "We will discuss this later, but you've been up to something and I am very disappointed in you both for doing it and for hiding it."

Miss Rose marched from the room, cloak in hand.

"No, no, no…" Lianne muttered, tears in her eyes. "Not when I'm so close…"

#

Thorne stood before the door. Like so much else in her long

life, her knowledge of magic was merely an extension of the rest of her collection. The spells were tricks, not without their use, but hardly something she relied upon. That the glamour was never intended to be used in the broad light of day had never been a detriment until today. By night, she could maintain her human form effortlessly. For reasons that the spell book she'd read failed to elucidate, by day it was a tremendously taxing effect to maintain.

She looked herself over. On Lianne's instruction, she had rendered a rather drab black outfit. Despite her best efforts to maintain the funereal appearance, whenever her focus began to falter, it took on an iridescent sheen that she had to will away. Keeping her magnificence subdued was proving a greater challenge than she had anticipated.

Miss Rose answered the door.

"Ah, Miss Thorne. Come in," Miss Rose said.

"Thank you. And may I say, I greatly appreciate this opportunity."

The pair made their way to the sitting room.

"Forgive me for saying so, but there was very little in our initial interactions to give me confidence in your fitness to care for one of our girls. Your latest letter was persuasive, however."

"Thank you. Shall I take my pick of them now, then?"

Miss Rose narrowed her eyes. "It wasn't *that* persuasive. Now, there is little question that you have the means to care for our girls. Your generous gifts have been more than adequate to permit us to care for more than a dozen girls. Provided the coins you've given do not represent the entirety of your fortune--"

"They assuredly do not."

Thorne paused. Lianne had underscored the value of humility.

"I come from a family of modest but sufficient means."

"That is good to know. Tell me about this family."

The disguised dragon smiled, her teeth gleaming just a bit more than a human's might. This was a topic that had dominated her rehearsals.

"My husband is a landowner. Again, of modest but not inconsiderable means. We each have large, loving families, but he and I were lamentably unable to have a child of our own."

"I see. In most cases, both the mother and father attend when seeking one of our girls. Why has your husband not been involved thus far?”

"He is very busy with business elsewhere."

"Shouldn't you wait until he returns before seeking a child?"

"I am perfectly capable of selecting a daughter on my own."

"Surely your husband should have a say in such things."

"I fail to see how or why."

Miss Rose shifted in her chair. "Very well. We shall move on for now."

#

The conversation that followed was unbearably tiresome for Thorne. It was fortunate that Lianne had prepared her well. Less fortunate was the dull and seemingly pointless line of questions that left her fighting to maintain focus on the glamour. She may have slipped once or twice, a sparkle of jewels or a shock of purple showing here or there, but nothing sufficient to pull Miss Rose from her interminable string of questions. Finally, the interrogation neared its end.

"Well, Miss Thorne. It would appear I misjudged you. If you would like to return in a day or two, I can arrange for you to meet the girls," Miss Rose said.

"Why not now?"

"As it happens, one of the girls may have broken our rules. I need to get to the bottom of it and administer the proper discipline."

Thorne nodded. "Discipline is very important. But I am a busy woman. I would prefer to complete this transact… I would prefer to welcome my new daughter to her home as soon as possible."

"I suppose that is reasonable. I won't be a moment."

Miss Rose stepped away, leaving Thorne alone in the room. She took advantage of the brief solitude to permit herself a flash of color if only to clear her mind. After reveling in her own resplendence for a few moments, she restored her drab wardrobe. At the sound of approaching footsteps, she smiled. Soon enough she would have Lianne. Already that indescribable sense at the back of her mind that told her when she was in the presence of something truly precious was swelling and flaring like a flame kindled to life.

The woman entered with girls in tow. The smile faded from her face. While these girls were no doubt perfectly adequate, each was standing on her own two feet.

"Are these all of the girls you have?" Thorne asked, as politely as she could manage.

"All but the girl who has broken our rules."

"Present her as well."

"It would not be fair to the girls who can follow the rules to give a rule-breaker the same consideration."

"What possible rule could a little girl break that would deny her the chance at a proper home?"

"If you must know, I believe she stole something."

"Did you see her steal it?"

"No. But it is not possible for her to have acquired it without breaking our rules."

"Why is it not possible?"

"It wouldn't be appropriate to discuss it in front of the other girls."

Thorne looked down over the little girls. They each had an awed look on their faces, as though the glamour might not have held quite so firmly for their young eyes as it did for Miss Rose.

"I am sorry, children, but would you mind terribly if I discussed something with your keeper?"

They remained silent. One let her eyes drift to the door from whence they came. They all looked tensed for escape.

Miss Rose raised her voice. "Miss Maya, would you take the girls for a moment?"

The other caregiver arrived after a moment and led the other girls away. Thorne looked expectantly to Miss Rose.

"Lianne, a young girl who has been in our care for quite some time, seems to have acquired a rather expensive cloak. I've only just discovered it, and there remains the question of how she acquired it. And there is no legitimate means. She claims it was a gift."

"I see. So if we were to establish that she came by the cloak legitimately, then there would be no further issue."

"I suppose so, but--"

"It was a gift from me."

"It is kind of you to attempt to aid the girl, but naturally that isn't--"

"Was it an absolutely stunning and wonderfully warm cloak of vibrant purple?"

"It was."

"I provided it."

"When, Miss Thorne?"

"I fail to see how that is relevant."

"You have not come to visit her, as I would I have known. And she would *never* have been permitted to visit you."

"Well, she did."

"Then she has broken *that* rule. And frankly I am aghast that in all of our time discussing your fitness to be a caretaker you did not mention it."

"If I had, you simply would have made this same claim a bit earlier."

"Yes, and it would have saved us all a good deal of time." Miss Rose stood. "Miss Thorne, I pride myself on my judgment. I thought I had misjudged you, but it would appear I was quite correct in my initial assessment. I will not permit you to take one of my girls."

Thorne stood.

"And why not?"

"Because you have lied to me, which in and of itself is a sign of unfitness. And judging from your contact with Lianne and your insistence on seeing her, I imagine you came here expressly with the intent to adopt her specifically. I would certainly not permit you to be *her* caregiver."

"Explain yourself."

"I have explained quite enough. Good day, Miss Thorne."

Thorne's temper flared. "You have most certainly not. Why, of all of your girls, would you specifically deny me Lianne?"

Miss Rose sniffed and crossed her arms.

"She is willful. It would appear she is disobedient, though that is a recent discovery. And even if such was not the case… Well, you've met the girl."

"I have. Your point?"

"She is not a healthy girl. If you can be believed--and forgive me for impugning your honesty but you at the very least haven't been forthcoming--then this would be your first child. A first-time parent would be better served by a child who is more easily handled."

Thorn narrowed her eyes. "Miss Rose, how dare you? How dare you even *imply* that Lianne is somehow less desirable than one of these other girls. Willful? Is that a problem? What you call willfulness, I call *fire*. Drive. An asset by any measure. And disobedience? If presented with rules with no point or value I should hope she would disobey."

"The rules are meant to protect her."

"That girl needs no protection."

"She is a little girl, and she is missing a leg."

"That little girl has a sharper wit than half of the people I've met in my life. She slipped from this place without you realizing it—you, who are supposed to be so mindful of her needs. She found her way to me. She knew precisely the sort of woman you would require me to be in order for you to give me the chance to have a girl of my own. She taught me how to be that woman. And at no point did the presence or absence of a leg present itself as an impediment. If it is your opinion that lacking a leg impairs her, then her achievements reveal strength, not weakness."

Thorne stalked back and forth, hands clutching at the air as the intensity rushed through her.

"I cannot *conceive* of a right-thinking individual who would treat that girl as less-than. She is not less-than. Not less than any of those other little girls. Not less than you. Not less than *me*. And that, my dear, is saying something."

Miss Rose took a step back. "Miss Thorne."

"*You may speak when I am through,*" Thorne barked. "Now, I consider myself to be patient. I consider myself to be reasonable. I sought a girl here, through these means, because I thought it would be the most proper. I thought it would be the simplest, the easiest, and the least trouble for both me and the girl. You swiftly proved that otherwise, but it *did* bring me to that young lady. That has made it worthwhile. She is the jewel, Miss Rose. She is the standout. She is *precious*. And I mean to have her."

"Y-you need to leave this place."

Thorne glanced down. Her outfit had reverted to its proper radiance. From the unnerved look on Miss Rose's face, there was likely a draconic gleam to her eye as well.

"You need to understand something, Miss Rose. I gave that little girl my word. I swore to her that if I were to take *any* of these orphans, I would take her." She stepped closer, backing Miss Rose against the wall. "At this moment, you are standing between me and my promise."

"W-what are you going to do?"

"That is up to you. I've said there were other ways for me to acquire a little girl. Now you decide which of those methods I must choose."

Miss Rose shut her eyes tight.

"I-I will not give you that girl."

Thorne grinned.

"Good. In light of what you've seen, I would think far less of you if you handed her over now. But it doesn't change matters."

"Thorne, no," Lianne stated.

She looked up. The girl was in the doorway. The look in her eye was every bit as fierce as Thorne's own.

"Lianne. We were just discussing the circumstances of your adoption."

"You aren't going to hurt her."

"I am going to keep my word through whatever means are available to me. Miss Rose has unfortunately shut a great many doors in that regard."

"If it means hurting anyone, then I let you out of your promise."

"I've made no threat, Lianne. And I had no such plans."

"You're being scary, though."

Thorne's expression softened. "Am I scaring *you?*"

"No. But I know the real you and she doesn't. Not really."

"I was under the impression that if anyone were to know the real me, it would be unpersuasive at the very least."

"What you've done already will probably cause you trouble, right?"

"Not more than I can handle."

"But it *will* cause trouble."

"It will."

"Then give Miss Rose the benefit of the doubt. Let her know you."

Thorne looked to Miss Rose.

"Well, madam. You have a strong advocate. Let us resume the interview."

"Wh-what do you mean?"

"I have been dishonest in nearly every answer I have given. I now offer you honesty. Judge me as worthy or unworthy to be this girl's keeper."

"A-and if I find you unworthy?"

"Then I will take my leave. Though it saddens me, Lianne has dissolved our agreement. I still desire to have her as my own, but I will not take her if it is her will to stay."

"What… *are* you?"

"A dragon. I would show you my true self, but you haven't the room."

"How old?"

"Two thousand years, in broad terms. It would take a bit of thinking to be more precise."

"Where do you live?"

"In the mountains. I won't be more specific, as after this I suspect I would have visitors otherwise, and that could get messy."

"Is your home a proper place for a young girl?"

"I will make my home into whatever a young girl requires."

#

The second interview was a good deal more tense than the first. Miss Rose was, understandably, slow to alter her opinion. But she was a woman who had devoted her life to identifying the earmarks of a caregiver. In time, she allowed herself to entertain the possibility that Thorne, despite her true nature, might still be able to properly provide care.

"Naturally, if she chooses to pursue a husband, when she is of age, that will be her own decision. But rather think it would take quite a man to be worthy of her, and I would need to personally approve him," Thorne said.

Miss Rose's eyes drifted aside.

"You surprise me, Miss Thorne," Miss Rose said. "I… You certainly seem to be genuine in your intent. And I feel the truth in your words, far more than before. But you'll forgive me, this is unprecedented, a dragon seeking to adopt a child. I *need* to know that you will care for this child properly."

"What would it take to convince you?"

"Time. If I send this child home with you, you bring her back to me no less than once a month. If you do, and I deem her care proper, then in time she will be yours. If you don't… heaven help me, I will find a way to reclaim her."

237

Thorne tipped her head aside.

"That is acceptable."

Lianne perked up. "So… So, can I go?"

"I… " Miss Rose took a breath. "I believe so."

Thorne turned and approached Lianne. She knelt before the girl to look her eye to eye.

"What do you say, Lianne. Shall we see your new kingdom?"

Lianne threw her arms around Thorne. She wrapped the girl in a tight embrace of her own and lifted her from the ground.

"Come with me, princess."

Joseph R. Lallo

The Rills

The Rills

Between is a story that I enjoy so much more than I should. I really enjoyed writing a story with completely off-the-wall parameters. It contains some of my favorite characters. Even though it's never really made much money, I *had* to revisit it. As tends to be the case, the support characters in this ensemble cast are the most interesting to me, and Left-Rill, Rill, and Right-Rill were by far the most fun. As the final (and most substantial) story in this collection, enjoy their pseudo-sequel!

Artwork for this cover is provided by Nebulilac.

It was a lovely day on Upper Shard. Not a cloud in the sky. That time didn't pass in the Between, and thus there weren't any 'days' to speak of, didn't change that fact. Nor did the lack of weather, and thus permanent lack of clouds in the stark white sky. As far as Rill was concerned, it was a lovely day. And why was that? Because she was with Philo.

Rill's friend was a human, which was strange on two different levels. First, that they'd been able to befriend anyone at all. Even around here, the huge, three-headed hydra wasn't the sort to be welcomed with open arms. Second, that it was a *human* who had become their friend. Two-leggers in particular were not fond of anything big with sharp teeth that came from the sea.

"And I put a little thing on top! Did you see the little thing?" Right-Rill said, her iridescent black eyes sparking with pride.

"When we found it in the junkyard we knew this was the perfect little thing to make our home look just right," Rill said.

"I still think we should have found something shinier," Left-Rill muttered.

They were coiled around the outside of the mound of black slabs they called a home. All three of the lavender hydra's heads bobbed around an old television aerial they had roughly jabbed between the two blocks precariously tipped together to form the makeshift cave's roof.

"It's very nice, Rill," Philo said. "It gives the place character."

"We found it on the top of a house in the junkyard," Rill said.

"It looked like a *very* nice house," Right-Rill said.

"Nicer than Trixie's house," Left-Rill said.

"Do you know what it was supposed to be for?" Philo asked.

"For looking pretty," Right-Rill said confidently.

"It was for helping people get something called television in their homes. It was an antenna," Philo said. "A science-type thing."

"And *also* for looking pretty," Rill amended.

"It's very pretty," Left-Rill said. "Just not very shiny."

"I like how *this* part splits into three. And then on either side of each part *here*, there's two sets of three. And this part on top splits into three again. So that's two sets of three, and another two-sets of three, and another set of three little tines," Right-Rill said.

"Which is one set of three sets of three and two sets of three,"

Rill said. "Or…"

"Teen… Fifteen?" Left-Rill filled in uncertainty.

"That's right!" Philo said like a proud teacher.

All three Rills smiled happily and wobbled back and forth with glee.

"Thank you, Philo," they said in unison.

"And counting is *hard* for that part," Right-Rill said.

"The teen part is very silly. There's eleven and twelve at the beginning. Then all the teens come in with the bits on the front."

"The Between is supposed to automatically have you know what we're trying to say, so you *know* it's a very silly thing if it's hard to say. You should fix that about the way you think," Left-Rill advised.

"Is it straight? I think it should be straighter," Right-Rill said.

She reached around with their triple tail and tugged at one of the tines, straightening the antenna. It stood perfectly straight for a moment, then the blocks making up the roof of the house slid, ground against each other, and collapsed inside. They quickly coiled tight around the rest of the mound, bracing it with their long body in an attempt to steady it. They had limited success. By the time the blocks had stopped shifting and sliding, their home had almost entirely slumped in on itself.

"What'd you have to touch it for!" snapped Left-Rill.

"I wanted it to look nice! Our home should look nice!" Right-Rill countered.

"Does it look nice *now?*"

The pair of heads started snapping and looping at each other. The center head pulled back and looked wearily at the other two, then dove into the fray to try to separate them.

"Rill! Come on! It was a mistake," Philo said.

"Hey Champ," called a voice from above.

The Rills stopped their squabbling long enough to look up.

"Hi, Trixie," they said, less than enthusiastically.

The winged demon and fellow fetcher swooped down and clacked her hoofs on the most stable of the mound of dislodged stones. Philo climbed over one loop of Rill's coils and scaled the heap of former home to the aerial from the wreckage. It had gotten a little bent, but he deftly straightened it.

"Rill was just showing me her new ornament," Philo said. "What do you think? I think it suits them."

"Crooked, pointy, and more or less useless. Yeah, it's a good match. Looks like you went overboard on the redecorating though, worm," Trixie said.

"It's not *our* fault the stones don't stick together like the boards in *your* house," Right-Rill said.

"Yes. It is. It is entirely your fault, because you just pile things up and don't use any mortar."

The Rills blinked at her.

"Says you," Rill countered.

"Snappy comeback as always," Trixie said.

She wrapped an arm around Philo and flitted to the ground beside the pile.

"I see you're wearing the new uniform," Trixie said. "Looking good, Champ!"

"Oh, yeah," Right-Rill said.

"That *is* different," Rill said.

"Why didn't you notice?" Left-Rill said with a sharp butt to Right-Rill.

Philo smirked and straightened his outfit. His simple jumpsuit had been replaced by something tailored a little better to him. It was black and white, with the circle and spike that formed what, for lack of a better word, could be considered the flag of his new home emblazoned on the back. For her part, Trixie was very much out of uniform. She was dressed in her casual clothes, a snug T-shirt with some numbers on the front and a pair of jeans with flared bottoms to allow for her hooves. That she would leave her home without her full set of weapons and armor said a lot about how things had changed since what had been come to be known as "The Blinking of the Eye." Ever since the adventure that culminated in the near destruction of Heartcore, at the very least, relations between Heartcore and Shard had warmed considerably. If nothing else, it meant there was no threat of Heartcore sending a legion of its fetchers to poach the citizenry. Thus military readiness had fallen behind comfort in terms of wardrobe choices.

"I don't know. It feels a little 'henchman' to me."

"If the shoe fits," Trixie said.

"Oh, right!" Rill said.

She uncoiled and all three heads investigated Philo's left foot.

"Does the shoe fit?" Rill asked.

"That's not what I meant," Trixie said wearily.

"Those elves better have done a good job," Left-Rill said, ignoring the demon.

"I'm sorry we ate your other shoe," Right-Rill said sheepishly.

"Considering you were under the influence of a doomsday artifact at the time, I think we can let it slide. The new one fits great, though."

"Hey, what was she saying about mortar?" Rill asked.

All heads darted up to eye level and patiently awaited an answer.

"It's the stuff—" Trixie began.

"We *asked* Philo," Left-Rill snapped, glaring at Trixie.

"It's the stuff that sticks bricks together, like in the houses down on Lower Shard," Philo said.

"If we used that, this place wouldn't fall down?" Rill said.

"I'm pretty sure you could still manage to knock it down," Trixie said.

"Uh," Philo scratched his head. "You probably could. But you'd really have to work at it. It wouldn't be as easy as this."

"Where do we get mortar? Let's get mortar! Will you help us build a new home?" Right-Rill said.

"We'll lift all the bricks, you could just make sure we are doing it right," Rill said.

Philo glanced to Trixie. "Do we have any plans? Official or unofficial?"

"Nothing yet. Overseer's got his paws full schmoozing the Heartcore folks. I found that novel during our last junkyard trip that looked promising. So feel free to go for a wander with the worm. I'll meet you after. Just remember, next trip either of us takes to the Junkyard, we've got to find some… what did you call them?"

"Mechanical relays. Right," Philo said with a nod. "We're going to need a lot of them."

"Is this for the… thing?" Right-Rill said.

Rill whispered. "The 'for going home' thing?"

It was a closely kept secret that Philo, was slowly working his way toward what was easily the most sought-after piece of equipment in all of the Between: a functioning transporter. Though it was difficult to measure time here, for what felt like months he'd been painstakingly collecting parts and installing them. Getting the device working was still something of a long shot, but it was a far better shot than almost any other creature all of Between had. Hence the secrecy. If it was generally known, things would become horribly complicated.

"We can help you!" Left-Rill said. "Especially if you need to pull things apart to get them. But help us build the house first."

"Okay, Rill. Sounds good, let's go," Philo said.

Rill scooted her head between his legs and lifted him high. Once he was properly settled at the base of her neck, she sprang into the air and swam through the sky toward the little, oddly shaped planet below.

#

Lower Shard had changed quite a bit since The Blinking of the Eye as well. It was a good deal more sparsely populated. Many of those deployed to Heartcore had chosen to stay there. Conversely, a few of the more restless Heartcore folks who were curious about Shard had taken this (potentially brief) lapse in hostility between the two nations to stop by, see the sights, and meet the people. Even the Quartermaster, formerly either unwilling or unable to give full access to the riffraff of Lower Shard, had taken over one of the larger abandoned structures to distribute some of the lower cost items that might need to be distributed. All in all, things had flourished. Extra room, new blood, and greatly reduced threat of invasion had a way of revitalizing a place. It showed in the attitudes of the astonishingly diverse crowd milling about the largest of the little communities. They were pleasant, cheerful, and industrious.

At least, until Rill showed up.

From the moment those below had spotted her coiling through the sky toward the city, they'd spread out to keep their distance. Her rubbery body slapped down roughly onto the grassy field outside the city as she switched from "swimming" to slithering. Philo gracefully dismounted and paced beside her.

"Let's see… I guess the Quartermaster will probably have the mortar down here. If not, we'll probably be taking a trip to the junkyard."

"That's fine. I like the junkyard. Lots of stuff to see," Right-Rill said. "Right?"

She turned to the others. Rill nodded simply, more interested in guiding their shared body than joining in the conversation. Left-Rill

247

didn't reply. She had a distant look on her face as she swept her eyes across the people of Lower Shard.

"Philo…" Left-Rill said. "You're… You're our friend, right?"

"He's not just our friend, he's our *partner*," Rill said. "That's like having someone whose job is to be your friend."

"No! Because sometimes Trixie is sort of our partner, and she's not half the friend Philo is."

"Yeah! You're right!" Right-Rill said.

"Better than a partner," Rill said.

Philo raised his hands. "Okay, I'm all of those things. But certainly your friend."

"Why? What's wrong with you?" Left-Rill asked.

"I don't think there has to be something wrong with me to be your friend."

"No one else is," Right-Rill said.

"Trixie is your—"

All three of them shook their heads. "Nope."

"Not before you, anyway," Rill said.

"And only barely *after* you," Right-Rill said.

"Not at *all* after you," Left-Rill corrected. "But you? You're our fourth head. That's special."

"You've just got to give people some time to get to know you," Philo said.

"We've been here for a lot of eternities, Philo," Right-Rill said.

"And time doesn't pass here anyway," Rill said.

"You're not making any sense, Philo," Left-Rill said.

"I… Look. People got a bad impression of you because your job was to collect them and to keep them in line. The Overseer needed you to be scary, so you were scary. But now things are different."

"Really?" Rill said.

Right-Rill darted her head aside to come face to face with a skittering little fuzzy creature who hadn't given the hydra as much room as the rest.

"Do you want to be friends?" Right-Rill asked.

The creature screeched and bounded away, scrabbling onto a roof, then down a chimney to escape her.

"Things are sort of the same, Philo," Rill said.

"That's not how you make friends, though. You've got to be

more subtle," Philo said.

"But why?"

"It's just the way it is. May I ask, why the sudden interest in a social life?"

Left-Rill lowered her head and stared at the ground. "It's nice having a friend."

"We don't really get lonely," Right-Rill said.

"There's always three of us, which means there is always someone to talk to," Rill said.

"Except when two of us are asleep," Left-Rill said.

"Which isn't that often," Rill said.

"But we already know each other so well," Left-Rill said. "We can't really learn anything new from each other."

Rill nodded. "That's right. We learned all sorts of things once you became our friend. Like counting."

"And how good singing is," Left-Rill said.

"I *love* singing," Right-Rill said, wriggling with glee.

"And sometimes it's nice to have to *tell* someone what we're thinking," Rill said.

"You don't know all of our stories," Left-Rill said. "And you *care* about the stories we tell."

"Friends are nice," Rill said sagely.

"But we don't *really* need another friend, right?" Right-Rill said. "We've got Philo!"

"I just wonder why we could have *him* as a friend, but never anyone else," Left-Rill said.

"Rill, listen. Like you said, you learned counting and singing and such from me. If there's one thing I know how to do, it's break the ice, and—"

"We're very good at breaking ice!" Right-Rill proclaimed.

"You have to be careful, though. Sometimes there are *bears* on the other side," Rill said.

"You shouldn't break ice if you are a two-legger, anyway. Cold water kills two-leggers quick," Left-Rill said. "Be safe, Philo."

"No, that's not what I mean. I mean… uh-oh."

A raspy voice was chanting the same short phrase over and over as trotting little footsteps brought it nearer.

"New Guy, Trixie. New Guy, Trixie," repeated the voice.

The Messenger, adorable little ball of black and white fuzz that he was, slipped out from between two houses and marched up to them.

"New Guy?" the little creature said, peering up at him.

"Yeah, that's me. You can call me Philo, by the way. I've been here for a while."

"Message, New Guy!" the messenger trilled.

He tipped his head down to reveal a pair of scrolls sticking out of a little backpack. Philo selected the one intended for him.

Rill's tail coiled around and one of the three clawed ends lifted the Messenger in the air.

"What about us?" Right-Rill asked.

"Philo is our partner," Rill said.

"Not Rill. New Guy and Trixie," the Messenger said simply.

Despite staring down a massive, three-headed predator, the little creature was completely unafraid.

Philo opened the message.

"Oh… Yeah, there won't be one of these for you," Philo said. "It's from Wrunx. He wants Trixie and me to head down to Heartcore for sort of a diplomatic thing."

"I can do diplomatic things!" Right-Rill said.

"That's where you sit at a big table and eat small food and say nothing, but say it with as many words as you can, right?" Rill said.

"Uh… Yeah, that's about right," Philo said.

"I'm *good* at saying nothing. I say nothing all the time!" Right-Rill said.

"I'm sorry, but it just calls for me and Trixie. Hey, look at it this way! Without me, they're probably not going to send you on a fetching run, so you'll have some time to yourselves. You can practice making friends."

"You're supposed to show us *how*," Left-Rill said.

"We'll talk about it while we're building your house, I promise. Until then, give it a try around here. Just be nice." Philo reached up to grab Trixie's message from the messenger. "I'll deliver this. You're all done, little guy."

"Thanks, New Guy!" the Messenger said.

Philo trotted off toward the bridge at the edge of town that would take him back to Upper Shard. The Rills huffed.

"I'll bet Trixie did this," Left-Rill said.

"She *does* always like to be alone with Philo," Rill agreed.

"But they do boring things together. Like build clocks. And sleep," Right-Rill said.

"With the shades closed," Rill said.

"As if we would want to look at them while they were sleeping," Left-Rill said.

Right-Rill curled her head around to look the still dangling messenger in the eye.

"Hey, do you want to be our friend?" she asked.

"Okay!" the Messenger said instantly, swishing his big fluffy tail.

Right-Rill grinned at the others.

"Maybe this isn't as hard as we thought," Rill said.

Left-Rill darted in to talk to the messenger. "You know all the new people, right?"

"New Guys!" the Messenger said.

"Take us to meet some of them," Left-Rill said.

"That's good thinking," Rill said. "New people might not know us."

"That'll make it easier to not scare them, maybe."

"Okay!" Messenger repeated.

He wriggled free of Rill's grip and trotted happily along. The Rills slithered along behind him, taking their time to avoid overtaking the little beast.

#

Despite its promising start, their mission to find new friends didn't make much progress. It mostly followed the same pattern. The Messenger would sniff along the ground, following this scent or that, then raise his head and shout "New Guy" at someone who was already in the process of trying to find a way to avoid being engaged by the big lavender serpent trailing behind. The brief tour of the newer neighborhoods was educational nonetheless. If nothing else, they'd learned where the new people lived, or at least which houses they felt comfortable hiding inside.

"That's all!" the Messenger said, looking eagerly to the Rills once the centaur they spotted galloped away.

"Are you sure you found them all?" Right-Rill asked.

"Nope!" His ears flicked at a distant chiming sound. "New

messages! By Rill!"

He bounded away.

"Oh. He just ran out of time," Rill said.

"Everyone is getting things to do but *us,*" Left-Rill said.

"Maybe we should just sleep," Right-Rill said.

"After that trip to the junkyard where we found the pointy thing, I *am* a little tired," Left-Rill said.

"Too bad our house is busted right now," Rill said.

They swept their heads around.

"That one looks big enough," Right-Rill said.

They slithered toward a home that looked like the front half of a steel sea-going vessel of some kind. It was standing on end, with a door mounted in what had probably been a cargo hatch of some kind on the deck. Someone had, just moments ago, retreated inside and barred the entrance. The Rill leaned down and pressed their head against the door. It took very little effort to force it from its hinges and reveal the cargo hatch. It wasn't very large. If Philo or Trixie were with here they would have had to crouch to go through, but it was more than large enough for Rill's narrow body if she slithered low.

The same could not be said for the interior. As she crept in, she had to coil herself rather tightly to fit more of herself inside. This involved pushing some furniture around, but that was no trouble at all. By the time she'd tugged all but her tails inside, she had filled almost the entirety of this large central room of the makeshift house.

"This is nice," Rill said.

"I don't like the way the metal feels," Left-Rill said.

She shoved the wall a bit with one of her coils. It produced a worrying buckling noise.

"It feels so cold. Stone is better," Rill agreed.

"Do you feel something else?" Right-Rill asked.

The three of them kept quiet for a moment, then glanced around. Coils rippled and curled to shift aside. A muffled cry of anger rang out from somewhere. They pulled their tails entirely inside and rummaged around between their coils until they were able to retrieve a blue-suited creature of some kind whom they had unwittingly entangled in their when entering.

He wasn't a human, though he certainly satisfied the criteria of "two-legger," which meant he may as well have been one for all

Rill cared. The creature was some manner of goat man. He wore a blue blazer and heavily modified slacks, but had short curly hair on his head, along with two curling horns. His chin had a similar tuft of hair, and everything below the waist looked like it would have made more sense on a herd animal than a humanoid.

"How dare you invade my home like this! This never happened in Heartcore! You dunderheads! You ninnies!" the satyr barked.

"This is your home?" Right-Rill said.

"What does it *look* like?" he growled.

"A boat," Rill said.

"Only sideways," Left-Rill said.

He crossed his arms. "Yes, well. We take what we can get."

"You're from Heartcore?" Rill said.

"Is it not obvious?" he said.

"You do have the sort of 'I'm better than you even though I'm a weak little meanie who isn't actually better than you' thing that Heartcore people have sometimes," Left-Rill said.

"Wait! I have an idea," Right-Rill said.

The tail holding the satyr thrust him back down among her rubbery coils, where he struggled and complained again.

"Maybe we can make friends with this guy," Right-Rill whispered.

"I don't think he wants to be our friend. He seems very angry," Rill said.

"We just have to be *nice*, remember?" Right-Rill said.

"To *him?*" Left-Rill said doubtfully.

"That's what Philo said. He said we should be nice," Rill said.

"So let's try it," Right-Rill said. "Ready?"

The others agreed, in Left-Rill's case rather reluctantly. Right-Rill yanked their potential pal out from their writhing mound of body again and set him delicately down among the loops.

"Ahem," Rill said. "We would like to know if you would like to be our friend."

"What sort of a mindless pile of coils are you, that you think I would want to be your friend!?" he raved.

The Rills looked at one another, then whispered amongst themselves.

"Please?" Right-Rill offered.

"No! Get out of my home!"

"Your home is a very *nice* home," Rill said. "You should be proud of having a home this nice."

"And it was nice of you to come to Shard from Heartcore," Right-Rill said.

"*Get out!*" the satyr raved.

Right-Rill furrowed her brow, then snatched up the satyr and shoved him down among their coils again so they could talk privately.

"This isn't working," she whispered.

"We didn't *all* try to be nice, though," Rill said.

Right-Rill nodded and turned to Left-Rill. "That's right! You didn't say anything nice."

"It won't do any good," Left-Rill said.

"Philo said it would," the others said at once.

"Probably it's just that only two out of three parts of their visitor was being nice. Two-leggers only usually have one talking part," Rill reasoned. "Maybe they need *all* of the talking parts of the people they talk to to be nice for it to count."

"Stupid two-leggers and their stupid rules," Left-Rill said. "Fine."

She thrust her part of the triple tail into their heap of coils and retrieved the satyr. He was now dangling by one foot, but the other tails grabbed and righted him before setting him down. Despite the rough treatment, the angry satyr had apparently determined that his unwanted houseguests were a bit too formidable to be simply browbeaten into obedience. Left-Rill glared at him for a moment. Right-Rill nudged her with her snout.

"You are a very pretty and nice two-legger," Left-Rill said.

"Do you even know what I *am?*" he asked.

"You're a two-legger. I can tell, because you have two legs," Right-Rill said.

"That's what it takes to be one," Rill concurred.

"I am a satyr."

The heads blinked at him.

"We are a powerful mystic race," he said.

"Oh! Mostly the really mystical mystics used to hang out in Spearhead," Right-Rill said.

"That's the castle that used to be on Upper Shard," Rill said.

"It makes sense there'd be new mystics here now," Left-Rill said.

"Why did you come to stay here, Mr. Mystic Satyr?"

"My name is Strick," he said. "And I came here because…" He cleared his throat. "Because no one particularly needed my help in Heartcore."

"Do you do things that aren't helpful?" Right-Rill asked.

"Or are you just not very good at the things you do?" Left-Rill asked.

"I am *very* good at the things I do. But it just so happens that what I do isn't in very high demand."

"What do you do?" Rill asked.

"I facilitate empathic polymorphic treatments."

"So, change things to other things?" Rill said.

"I… yes, actually."

"I know things." Rill poked her head close and whispered. "I'm the smart one."

"Did you find people who need your help here?" Right-Rill asked.

"Some. But it is all very basic magic stuff. No one has needed my specialty."

"Why *would* someone want to change? You wouldn't be any good at being anything but what you already are," Left-Rill said.

"Do you take me for an amateur, madams? Any skills inherent to the form are inherited *with* the form," he said. "And there are infinite reasons one might wish to change one's form. Perhaps one is infirm or injured and wishes a brand-new form? Perhaps one wishes to pursue a new career that would be better served by another form. Perhaps one is an insufferable *oaf* who could benefit from some grace and beauty."

"How does it work? What do you do?" Rill asked with great interest.

"If you must know, I take hold of my scepter, which is buried somewhere beneath your bulk. And with it, I gather my strength and simply facilitate the change."

"And you can change *anyone* into *anything?*" Right-Rill said.

"Err… No. I am an *empathic* polymorpher. The change is actually decided by the target. I merely, as I said, facilitate the change."

"That's good!" Rill said. "That means you can't be mean and

turn someone into something they don't *want* to be."

"Not necessarily. The change is based upon some aspect of your need or desire. It may not always be what you expect. Occasionally it is precisely the form you believe you desire. Sometimes it is a change into something that suits your personality. Sometimes it is a change that lurks in your heart but you never consciously realized. Sometimes it is your heart's desire. The only change I can *guarantee* is the restoration."

"That's very—" Rill began.

"Change us!" Left-Rill demanded.

The others looked at her. "What?"

"Think about it," Left-Rill said. "People are scared of us because they know what we've done, and what we look like. We could make friends easier if we could get a fresh start."

"Hmm…" Right-Rill scratched her chin with her claw. "It *might* be fun to be something new. For a while. We can always get turned back later!"

"Now, see here. I have not offered my services. You've broken down my door and invaded my home. What possible reason could I have to wish to serve you?"

"Because we're going to ask very nicely," Right-Rill said.

"Because we are the favorite fetchers of the Overseer and he'll be happy if you are helpful to us," Rill said.

"Because if you don't, I'll bite one end of you and pull the other end of you until you start helping or stop complaining," Left-Rill said.

Strick swallowed hard. "You make some persuasive arguments."

Right-Rill nudged Left-Rill. "I knew we'd be able to do diplomacy."

"If you'll allow me to fetch my scepter, we can begin."

"I think I can feel it poking me," Rill said.

The three tails wove back down into the twist of coils. All three of the heads glanced and rolled their eyes, focusing on the sensations. When all of them lit up at the same time, it was clear they'd found what they were looking for. The scepter rose up in their grip, emerging from the center of their coiled mound like something that would be presented to the fated king of a mystic land.

Strick unsteadily hopped along her body until he could snatch away the tool of his trade.

"This is a very precious and delicate artifact," he said. "Now. The procedure is a simple one. Shut your eyes and clear your mind. This works best if you are not cluttering your thoughts with pointless need and desire. The spell will cut to the truth of the matter on its own."

"I'm very good at not thinking," Right-Rill said.

"I imagine you are," Strick said. "Then we shall begin."

The Rills did as they were told. As the satyr stirred the air with the scepter, they could feel the prickly energy of magic begin to crawl across their thick, rubbery hide. The spell felt like it was sinking into them, wriggling under their skin and seeping into their noses and mouths. It was an assault of sensations. The most curious of which was the churning of their minds. Images flickered from their individual and collective memories. Things that frightened them, things that brought them joy, secret shames, boastful points of pride, and a thousand other things swept in and out of their heads.

The change came slowly. Coils shifted and twisted, drawing into themselves like a deflating balloon. They were getting smaller. Bits and pieces were coiling off their serpentine body. At the edge of hearing, the clop of hooves signaled the satyr hopping down to a section of floor no longer occupied by their bulk. Disorienting dizziness flooded their minds. It all ended with a soft bump.

"Ouch!" yelped Left-Rill.

"My work is done. Open your eyes," the Satyr said. "And have a look at the mess you've made of my home."

The Rills opened their eyes.

No longer was there a huge, three-headed hydra in the room. Now there were three separate, distinct creatures. One hung in the air on buzzing, filmy wings, she was a fairy with a tiny dash of the features that had once defined her. Her hair was the same lavender color, her bare skin sparkling with a few streaks of the same sheen of her former hide. Beside her, drifting in the air as though it were water, was a mermaid. The creature was not one of the typical merfolk of fairytale and storybook. She had a strong, sweeping fish tail, but the fishiness continued all along the more humanoid portion. Scales covered her sleek body from head to tail. Once again, they were the same color as her former form. Long, lustrous hair of a bluer shade than the rest of her billowed out around her like drops of ink spreading in still water.

The last of them was in some ways the least remarkable, but in other ways the most. She was a human woman, just as naked as the rest of them. Unlike the others, she bore no colors, no markings to suggest the form she'd left behind. She was substantial in stature, easily six feet tall with a thick, strong build. Her hair was long and black. She had a strangely vulnerable look on her faintly scarred face.

"Wow!" trilled the fairy. "I've got arms *and* legs! And everything's so *big*!"

She buzzed back and forth between the two of them. "Which one are you? Which one are you?"

"Well, I can tell *you're* still the *dumb* one," the human remarked.

The others looked to her.

"And you're the mean one," said the mer-creature.

"Which means you're the smart one!" said fairy who once was Right-Rill.

Both Right-Rill and Rill swirled around Left-Rill.

"You're just a *human*," Rill said.

"I am," Left-Rill said quietly, looking down over herself.

"You didn't pick something that could fly or swim? That's going to be annoying," Right-Rill said.

"You're a fairy," Rill said. "And you look like a young one. What am I?"

"You're… I don't know. Like a mermaid. Except the half-not-fish part is… I don't know… still half fish? You're half fish and half-half-fish-half-human."

"There is a mirror in the corner," Strick said, adding under his breath, "Miraculously unbroken by your blundering."

The three crowded together to admire themselves while Strick gathered up the remnants of some of his furniture.

"Wow…" Fairy-Rill said. "Where should we go? What should we do?"

"May I suggest you first go get some clothes?" Strick said.

"Oh… Right. Once you have arms, people expect shirts," Mer-Rill said. "We should definitely get some tokens from our pile of home. That'll take some digging."

"Whatever you do, do it somewhere else," Strick said. "Service has been rendered. Explore your altered existence elsewhere."

"Yeah, let's go!" Fairy-Rill proclaimed, buzzing out the door.

Mer-Rill swam after her. A moment later, she returned to scoop up her human sister.

#

A short time later, Human-Rill and Mer-Rill were standing at the edge of their still-toppled home. Unaccustomed as they were to the embarrassment typically associated with public nudity, they were simply standing without any effort to cover themselves as a soft buzzing issued forth from the mound of stones. Every few moments, Fairy-Rill darted out from between two stones and dropped another gray Quarter Master Token or two on the ground. For the little creature, they were each the size of a large platter, so carrying more than that would have been difficult.

"There are a lot more than I remember," Fairy-Rill said, dusting the dark soil of Shard from her hands and taking a moment to rest. "I think maybe we lost a bunch of them in the dirt and didn't notice."

"It was always so difficult to pick them out with our tails," Mer-Rill said.

Human-Rill gazed down at herself, then crossed her arms. "I'm taking my share now. It is going to take a lot more effort to get anywhere like this, so I'll need more time."

She crouched and gathered up a handful of them, then paced gingerly off as her tender new feet had to cope with the jagged stones scattered across the ground of the Fetcher's Den.

"Where are you going?" Mer-Rill asked.

"First I'm going to go get clothes. Then I'm going to see what the world is like for me now," she said.

"You can't go without *us*," Fairy-Rill said.

"Yes, I can. We can go wherever we want now. We don't have to be together," Human-Rill said.

Mer-Rill blinked and scratched her head. "That's true, I guess."

Mer-Rill and Fairy-Rill looked at each other, uncertainty in their eyes. When they looked back to their sister, she had hurried off to the bridge that would take her wherever she chose.

"S-should *we* split up too?" Fairy-Rill asked.

Mer-Rill looked a bit conflicted, but straightened her posture and did her best to retain her "big sister" role.

"We'll stay together until we buy clothes. That way we can help each other pick."

"Should we catch her then? So we can help her too?" Fairy-Rill asked

Mer-Rill looked toward the bridge. Despite have had to stutter-step every few strides to brush away painful bits of gravel, she was already gone from sight.

"I guess she has somewhere she wants to be," Mer-Rill said. "We'll find her later. Let's go buy some clothes."

#

It took longer than they'd expected, but eventually Mer-Rill and Fairy-Rill found the Quartermaster's new warehouse and bought themselves some new outfits. They'd fully expected to find Human-Rill there already, picking out an outfit of her own, but she must have found a different place to do business, because she was nowhere to be found.

Mer-Rill swam along, tugging at the bodice she'd been fitted with. It was a shimmery blue fabric that draped loosely over her, cinched tight around her waist to keep it from shifting as she swam. A skirt of sorts hung down over the top bit of her tail. Buttoned pockets on either side of the skirt jangled with tokens.

"I don't like it," she muttered, adjusting the fabric. "I don't like that it's touching me. The pockets are useful, though. This mouth I've got isn't *nearly* large enough to carry things."

"I think clothes are pretty," Fairy-Rill said, buzzing around her.

The little creature was dressed rather strangely, at least for a fairy. Rather than the simple little dress so often favored by creatures of that size, she was dressed in a far more human manner. She wore somewhat ill-fitting trousers and a strange, open-backed blouse. Both were of bright, vivid colors.

"Can you believe they dress *dolls* in clothes like this?" she said. "Look how pretty my legs are! This is as pretty as my legs have ever been."

"Where do you think she went?" Mer-Rill asked, glancing about amongst the crowd.

"Who?"

"Rill."

"I'm Rill."

"I mean the one that isn't here."

"Oh... I don't know." Fairy-Rill buzzed forward to search.

Almost immediately bounced off the back of a centaur trotting along in front of her.

"Oh! I'm terribly sorry," said the deep-voiced stallion, turning to them. "Careful there."

"Ow…" Fairy-Rill said, rubbing her face.

"You flew right into him," Mer-Rill said.

"I've never had to worry about avoiding people before," she said.

The pair of them, for the first time, stopped to appreciate the gravity of the statement. They were among a crowd. Not in the center of a wide gap in the crowd, but actually a *part* of it. People weren't running. They weren't edging away or giving an anxious look.

"Is something wrong, ladies?" the centaur asked.

Mer-Rill shook herself from the moment of wonder. "I'm looking for my… uh… sister."

"What does she look like?" he asked.

"Just like us," they said simultaneously.

He tipped his head in confusion.

"Oh, wait…" Fairy-Rill said.

"She's a human," Mer-Rill said helpfully. "With… um…"

"Hair," Fairy-Rill added.

"And probably clothes by now," Mer-Rill said.

"You'll need to be more specific."

"Just a second," Fairy-Rill said.

She darted up to Mer-Rill's fin of an ear. "Humans all look the same, don't they?"

"They all look the same to *me*," Mer-Rill said.

"Um… Don't worry, Mr. Horse-Man," Fairy-Rill said. "We'll find her. Thank you."

"You two new around here? I don't recognize you," he said.

"Mostly new, yes," Mer-Rill said.

He held out a hand. "Well, if you need help, just call for Trush. That's me."

Mer-Rill awkwardly grabbed his right hand with her left in her first attempt at a handshake. Not to be left out, Fairy-Rill wrapped her arms and legs around his wrist like it was the trunk of a tree. He gave them another curious look after the shake ended.

"And you two are?"

"I'm a fairy!" Fairy-Rill said.

"And I'm… sort of a fishy two-legger without the legs," Mer-Rill said.

"Right, but I was talking about… Oh! You two are *very* new. Your memory is still failing you, correct."

"Yes!" Mer-Rill said eagerly. "That is what is happening. Not anything else."

"Right, right! We've *definitely* always been what we are," Fairy-Rill said.

"Well, things are a little mixed up since the Blinking of the Eye. I don't think we're set up for the preliminaries right now. Just try to make yourself comfortable. There's a pub just up the road here. You're probably not thirsty, but it's a nice place to get to know the locals. See you around."

He plodded off.

Fairy-Rill and Mer-Rill looked at each other. Excitement was gleaming in Fairy-Rill's eyes. Mer-Rill was a bit more reserved, but still clearly intrigued by the opportunities lying before them.

"People aren't afraid of us! And they don't know who we are! We get to see what we've been missing!" Fairy-Rill said. "Our sister will be *fine*. She's been part of us forever. *We'll* be fine, so *she'll* be fine. We can find her later. If she gets far enough away, we can just sort of *think* of finding her and fly off into the distance. We'll at least get *close*."

"… I suppose it couldn't hurt to do some exploring…" Mer-Rill said.

"Great! Let's go!"

#

The inside of the pub was bustling, though not in the way that pubs outside the Between would be. It was a tall structure, more of a hollow tower than a proper building. This was to facilitate the larger patrons—there was a giant and an ogre in the corner arm-wrestling—and also to give those less ground-bound visitors someplace to hang out.

Thanks to the quirks of this world, food and drink were more like medicine than sustenance. This meant the place was more about the activities than the refreshments. Spirited conversation filled the air. A few different types of smoke gave the air a strong, spicy scent. The walls and ceiling were covered with game boards, from the conventional like darts to incomprehensible games involving blobs of colored light shifting about of their own accord. Perhaps most importantly, an odd little collection of roosts had a dozen or so creatures of various descriptions harmonizing with one another.

"Singing!" Fairy-Rill squealed.

She darted up, leaving Mer-Rill behind. The little musical clique near the ceiling of the pub included six birds, the most majestic of them being a gold and red-colored phoenix. A hauntingly beautiful siren sat with two harpies on a hoop hanging from the ceiling. Each was lending its voice to a separate piece of a maddeningly complex melody.

Fairy-Rill buzzed up to the center of the group, clutched her hands in front of her, and watched with both mouth and eyes wide. She was transfixed by the melody. Despite the fact she'd never heard the song before, or anything like it, she found herself *almost* able to tell where the next note would be. The song reached its crescendo and climax, filling the whole of the tower with a single glorious, powerful chord. It dropped to silence with crispness and finality, followed by a round of applause and whistling that sounded cacophonous and crude by comparison.

The freshly-turned fairy rushed to the siren and hung in her face.

"Teach me! Teach me, teach me, teach me!" Fairy-Rill demanded.

#

Below, Mer-Rill gazed up at the conclusion of the musical performance and smiled at her sister eagerly seeking to join in the next. As she watched, though, her expression became somewhat puzzled.

"Something wrong, ma'am?"

She turned to find a handsome elf with a long, delicate pipe. The stranger smiled at her, which was still a novel experience for her.

"Oh, it's just… I really like music. A lot. It's one of my favorite things. But I think right now I like listening more than I like singing," she said.

"Nothing wrong with that," he said.

"I guess not…" She shrugged. "I guess *she* is the one who brought the love of singing into the mix. I didn't know that's how it worked."

"Come again?"

"Oh, nothing." She flashed a smile, revealing serrated teeth. "I am looking for new friends. Would you like to be one?"

"Ha! Who isn't looking for a new friend? I was just heading over yonder to play a bit of pro'zhat. Do you play?"

"Nope!"

"It's a bit like corshretti."

"Never heard of it."

"Poker?"

"Poke who?"

He smiled a bit wider at her. "I have you got any Quartermaster tokens?"

She jangled her pockets. "A bunch! I haven't been getting hurt much lately so I barely have to spend them on anything anymore, and I'm the only one with big pockets, so I'm carrying them for me and my sister."

He put an arm across her shoulders. "We're going to have *lots* of fun. Let me show you my other friends."

#

New Allimiss was a thriving city. While Lower Shard was nothing to sneeze it, it couldn't compare in size, grandeur, and variety. The capital of Heartcore, New Allimiss was the precise city that one conjured to mind when picturing a fairy tale kingdom. One could travel to a thousand different eras in a thousand different worlds and never find a place as vibrant and varied as this. Anything could happen here. Anyone could call it home. It was thus a genuine achievement that a simple human had managed to stick out like a sore thumb.

Human-Rill marched along the cobblestone main street in a radiant purple and pink ball gown. It was the sort of thing a princess would wear, and had been stitched together in a matter of moments by Kinnea, a multi-talented spider back in Lower Shard. If there was one place that the gown might not seem out of place, it was New Allimiss. Alas, the outfit required an elegance and poise that Human-Rill simply lacked.

She chose to believe the fault for this lay in part with Strick. He may have provided the instincts necessary to make proper use of these brand-new legs of hers, but the satyr had been quite stingy with the degree of expertise he'd offered. Walking across a cobblestone street in high-heeled boots was difficult enough for someone who had had a lifetime to become accustomed to the limbs involved. For someone who had been walking for mere hours, it was a clumsy, clompy mess.

The picture-perfect dress juxtaposed with the stumbling and lumbering attracted quite a bit of attention. But Human-Rill was nothing if not determined. She kept her eyes on the palace ahead and didn't stop until she was nearly to its gates.

"Hey!" she called, flagging down a brightly dressed dwarf guard.

"Yes, ma'am?" said the guard, doffing his cap.

She grabbed two wads of dress and hiked the skirt high enough to be able to thump over to him without fear of tripping over it.

"Is Philo in there?" he said.

"Who, ma'am?"

"Philo! He's a really smart human. He came here to do some diplomacy."

"Ah, yes. The delegation from Shard. Yes, I believe they are still present."

"Good," she said.

She stepped over the threshold of the palace entryway and marched onward.

"Oh! Uh, ma'am, I'm afraid the palace is presently by invitation only. I'm going to have to ask—*oof!*"

It turned out a beautiful ball gown didn't just set expectations of what a woman *would* do, it set expectations of what a woman *wouldn't* do. The dwarf probably didn't expect the delicate, knee-high boots to be used to deliver a punishing blow to his gut, for instance. The casual attack bowled the guard over and left him wheezing.

Now with a nice smooth carpet to walk on, Human-Rill paced up easily up the entryway with much less difficulty.

"Stupid feet," she muttered. "Stupid dress. Stupid underwear. Why do humans put so much stupid stuff on their stupid bodies?"

Behind her, Human-Rill could hear a bit of commotion as the toppled guard got his wind back and summoned others, but that was hardly her concern. Human ears seemed to be a little more sensitive than her own, as she was able to hear other voices echoing down the hall to her left. She followed the sound and soon discovered a gathering in the hallway. A meeting must have just ended, as collections of two and three creatures—mostly humans and the sorts of creatures that may as well *be* humans—were pacing out of some manner of conference room quietly discussing the finer points of this and that.

Human-Rill's face lit up as she saw a familiar face.

"Philo!" she called.

She rushed over to him, nearly knocking over some of the other diplomats along the way. He looked to her curiously as she approached. Before he could react, she threw her arms tight around him and pressed her cheek to his.

"Whoa! Back off, princess," snapped an unwelcome voice.

A firm hand on Human-Rill's shoulder pulled her away from Philo and spun her to face Trixie, who had look of challenge in her black and red eyes.

"Do I know you?" Philo asked with a bemused smile.

"I'm curious about that myself," Trixie said.

Human-Rill pulled herself from Trixie's grip and slapped her hand away.

"I, uh… You don't know me," she said. "But I know you. You're the one who worked with Trixie and Rill to defeat the queen."

"Heh. That's a more accurate version of the story than most of the locals have, Princess."

Human-Rill ignored her. "I just wanted to meet you and maybe talk to you a bit."

"Me?" Philo said. "Really?"

"You were very brave and smart and I want to talk to you, please. For a while."

"We're really not in the mood for groupies," Trixie said.

"*You* don't have to stay and talk. I just want to talk to him."

"There she is! Get her!" shouted some guards down the hall.

Philo glanced in their direction. "What's going on?"

"Oh. I had to kick a guard to get in here. This place has really lousy guards."

The dwarf, along with a pair of his associates, charged up and grabbed Human-Rill by the arms. They were more substantial races, in this case a stout stone golem and a minotaur. Human-Rill struggled against them and, for a moment, was genuinely confused why she couldn't hurl them aside effortlessly. The transformation had given her the instincts necessary to be a human, but hadn't done anything about the expectation and habit associated with being a mighty sea serpent.

"Let go! I'm here to talk to Philo! Leave me alone!" Human-Rill growled.

"You are trespassing in the palace and you have assaulted a guard," the golem uttered in a voice like grinding stone.

"It's not trespassing if you're able to defeat the person trying to keep you out!" countered Human-Rill.

"Uh, yes. Yes, it really is," Philo said.

"Well that's dumb. How am I supposed to go someplace people don't *want* me to go?"

"You aren't supposed to go those places," Philo said.

"But I won the fight!"

Trixie rolled her eyes. "Oh, this one's a peach."

"What is the meaning of this?" called a commanding voice from down the hall.

The voice belonged to Medea, a mermaid as beautiful as she was respected among the palace staff.

"Just what we need," Trixie muttered.

Medea swam up and surveyed the situation.

"This woman assaulted a guard to gain entrance to the palace and accost this diplomat," the minotaur said with a huff.

"I'm not *really* a diplomat. And I wouldn't call that accosting me," Philo said.

Medea glanced down and, for the first time, noticed Philo was present.

"Oh! Philo, and Trixie as well. How lovely to have you in Heartcore. Had I known you would be visiting I would have arranged to welcome and escort you myself."

"Shall we take the intruder away?" the golem asked.

"You do and I'll start biting and I won't *stop* biting," Human-Rill warned.

Medea crossed her arms. "Marius, were you the one who was assaulted?"

"Yes, Medea."

"You seem uninjured."

"Not *badly*," he said, rubbing his gut.

The mermaid placed her hands on her hips. "It has been a good long while since we've had to lock anyone up here in New Allimiss. I would prefer not to spoil that now. I shall take you into my personal custody until I am convinced that either your intentions were pure or you are deserving of corrective action. What is your name?"

Human-Rill blinked. "… Princess."

"You are a princess?" Medea said.

"No. I'm just Princess. Like Trixie said."

"Very well then. Princess, do you agree to behave yourself and follow the rules?"

"As long as the rules don't stop me from doing what I want to do, sure."

Trixie laughed. "I like this one. Just the right combination of malignant and stupid."

"Guards, release Princess," Medea said.

The guards did as ordered. Human-Rill straightened her puffy sleeves. She felt the overpowering urge to pummel both of them, but without a powerful set of jaws and a mighty tail she was at a loss as to how to do the job properly. After a few hard looks, the three guards departed. Most of the rest of those who had attended the meeting that had just concluded had already wandered off, leaving just Medea, Philo, Trixie, and Human-Rill in the ornate hallway.

Medea dug through a satchel at her side and retrieved a small amulet.

"Princess, if you would please put this on," she said, holding it out.

"Why…" Human-Rill said warily.

"Because you are now my responsibility. It will allow me to keep track of you should you decide to misbehave."

Human-Rill reached out and took the piece of jewelry.

"… Okay. I'll wear it," she said, slipping it over her head. "But only because it's shiny."

The business at hand done, Medea smiled at Philo.

"So you are a diplomat now?"

"No, no. I'm really not. I just know good junk when I see it. Same with Trixie."

"I'm willing to let them call me a diplomat," Trixie said. "It pays more than Fetcher."

"Now that The Overseer is spending so much time here, there's talk about combining our Junkyard with your… What did they call it, Trixie?"

"Trove. Because it's just *so* important that everything sound like a treasure around here," Trixie jabbed.

"Right. It'd just be easier for everyone if there was one spot to drop off resources that we don't really need," Philo said.

"Oh, I agree!" Medea said. "Tell me, have you seen much of the city? I know that your prior visits have always ended in a bit of excitement. It would be a shame if you'd never gotten a chance to see the sights peacefully."

"Not really. I was just supposed to come here and do this. I've got a friend back home who is waiting for me so I can help her rebuild her home."

"Oh, did something happen to it?" Medea said.

"Her own muddle-headed attempts at masonry happened to it," Trixie said. "The pile of rocks she calls a home spends as much time collapsed as it spends standing."

Human-Rill glared at Trixie.

"Still. The idea is to help her solve that problem," Philo said.

"She'll figure out how to knock it down, properly built or no." Trixie slapped Philo on the back. "Come on! Prissy here's practically offering up a guided tour. I'm anxious to see what's become of this place since the Overseer started putting his two cents in."

"It would be lovely to show you my city. Our tour was cut short last time, as I recall. But I'm afraid that would require the prisoner to come along."

"So bring her! She seems like she'll be good for a laugh," Trixie said.

Philo shrugged. "Works for me. The more the merrier."

"Very well, then. Oh, this is delightful! You simply *must* see the view from the topiary garden…"

Medea led the way. Trixie and Philo followed. Behind them Human-Rill trudged along, eyes narrowed as she kept pace with a group far larger than she'd intended.

#

Fairy-Rill sang at the top of her lungs. She and the others in the musical clique had worked their way through three songs. Most of them were firmly in the realm of classical or orchestral choir performances. As much as she would have liked to muscle her way to the lead vocals as she so often did with her sisters, she was having a little more difficulty slipping perfectly into the beat than she was used to. It was strange. Even when they were a single being, the moment-to-moment mental link she shared with her sisters was practically nonexistent. They only *really* combined their thoughts and memories when they slept. But apparently that little rhythm that filtered through their minds was a crutch she relied upon to stay in sync. Her voice was still as pristine and clear as it was when she was her old self, but it was a genuine effort to keep her place in the song and select her pitch to match with her fellow singers.

"That was lovely," trilled the phoenix beside her. "Your voice is so much more powerful than any fairy *I've* ever heard. And I've heard quite a few fairies, mind you. Quite a few *indeed.*"

Of all of the members of the impromptu choir, the phoenix had been the most interested in the enthusiastic newcomer. The others called her Red. Like so many creatures in this place, her anatomy didn't seem like it would permit her human-level speech, but she nevertheless enjoyed perfect diction.

"Thanks! Quick, quick. What do we sing next? Can we sing the same song again?"

"I don't think the others would enjoy hearing the same song again so soon, little one. No, they wouldn't enjoy that very much at all. Variety is the spice of life! Isn't that right?"

"Um… Okay. But I don't really…"

Red poked her head down at Fairy-Rill, turning her face aside to get a closer look without spearing the little creature with her beak.

"Is that anxiety I see? Anxiety on a fairy's face? No, no. That's not normal at all. What is the problem, little one?"

"Oh, it's no problem. It's just that I don't normally only hear a song once. To really remember it, I usually have to hear it three times."

"Come here whenever you can. We sing all the time, oh, yes, we do. And though we have many songs, it never takes long to hear another one again. I think we've all learned all of each other's songs. Yes. Yes, we certainly have learned them all."

Fairy-Rill clapped. "Do you know 'Dancing Queen,' then?"

"We know many songs about queens that dance. Yes, yes." Red raised her head. "Everyone, let us sing Lady Rubina's Celestial—"

She zipped up in front of her again. "No. No I mean the song *called* 'Dancing Queen.'"

"No… No I don't think we know that one. No, that doesn't sound familiar. Do you know this song, little one?"

"*Do I?*" Fairy-Rill buzzed into the middle of the group.

"Everyone, listen! A wonderful group of people called ABBA wrote this song, and we're all going to learn how to sing it right now! Here we go!"

#

Mer-Rill "sat" in a chair at a large round table in a back room of the pub. Sitting, it turned out, was something a mer-creature could do just fine despite the lack of proper legs. Technically, Mer-Rill also had all of the anatomy required to play a game of pro'zhat. Ostensibly it was just a matter of holding a stack of disks with assorted designs on them. There were things like placing bets and claiming disks from other players hands, too. But no matter how she tried, Mer-Rill couldn't understand what part of this "game" was supposed to be fun.

The others at the table seemed much more confident in their ability to win. There were five other players. One was a diminutive creature wrapped in rags. It was difficult to tell what sort of a creature was underneath all of that, but she was surly, quiet, and won as many rounds as she lost. Two large ogre-type creatures sat on either side of her. They weren't very good at the game, but they had no difficulty beating Mer-Rill. Her elf friend had a she-elf with him. The two of them were *very* good at the game.

"Well? What is your call?" said her new friend.

"Um…" Mer-Rill looked at the disks in her hand. "This is the part where I put one of these down, right?"

"That's right. *After* you put down the tokens you bet on the hand."

"I don't want to put any tokens down. You take my tokens every time I put them down."

"That's simply because you haven't won a round yet. Here, put one down and I'll help you."

Mer-Rill grumbled and fished out a quartermaster token to drop on the table.

"Just one?" he said.

"One's enough. I have lost half of them and I haven't had any fun yet."

"That's fine. That's fine. Now, remember. The goal for *this* round is to pick another player, and put down a disk that you don't think they have in their stack, right?"

"Right."

"So what do you think that is?"

"I don't know, because none of you have shown me which ones you have."

"That's what's fun! You look at what you have and you try to guess. Like here. Here you've got a red triple circle."

The other players shuffled through their disks.

"That's a very rare disk," the elf continued. "There are only four of those in the whole pile."

"A set of three and an extra," Mer-Rill corrected.

"Er… Right. So there are six people at the table."

"Two sets of three."

"And only three… a *set* of three of them could have the disk. So it might be a good choice."

"Right."

"This double blue curve. That's a common one. And this yellow quad-loop, that's pretty common too."

He worked his way through each disk in her stack, critiquing them one at a time. Each new disk seemed to cause the other players at the table to rearrange their stacks.

"So, knowing all of that. Who are you going to pick, and what are you going to pick?" the elf asked.

She glanced up at the others, then back at her stack. "I'm going to pick that ogre there…"

The player she'd indicated tossed down a token to match hers.

"And I'm going to pick… The red circles."

Mer-Rill placed down the disk. The ogre twisted his face up into a grin and dropped a matching disk.

"Oh, too bad," the elf said as the ogre took his winnings.

"You people are very lucky," Mer-Rill grumbled.

"It's all skill," the elf said. "You'll get it."

The two played disks were removed from the table and the other elf threw down a token and quietly worked through who and what to choose.

"You know who was really lucky?" Mer-Rill said. "Mr. Stubbs. He played games like this, I think. Him and an old fetcher named Fronde. They played games all the time. And he won all the time, too."

The runt of a player opposite her paused for a moment.

"Did you guys ever meet him?" Mer-Rill asked.

"We don't hang around with fetchers," the elf said.

"I think I'm out," said the rag-covered player, sweeping her winnings together.

"Fine, fine. See you later," Rill's elf friend said.

The little creature trotted out of the room, leaving her disks on the table. Mer-Rill gazed at them, then furrowed her brow.

"I think I'm going to—" the next player began.

Mer-Rill raised her hand. "Wait. We've played two sets of three and an extra rounds."

"And?" said the ogre.

"I only have two sets of three and two extra disks left. That pile has one set of three sets of three and two extras."

"You count quick," said the other ogre.

"And you have a set of three sets of three and an extra…" She narrowed her eyes. "And *you* were helping me by saying all of my disks out loud. So *they* all know what my disks are!"

"You said she was an idiot," snapped the other elf under his breath.

"I want my tokens back now, please," Mer-Rill said firmly.

"Look, friend, you lost fair and square," her 'friend' said.

"No. I lost *unfair* and… round," she said. "My tokens, now! Two sets of three and an extra."

"Why don't we all just calm down and—"

Mer-Rill darted up from her chair and tackled the ogre who had just won the previous round. When he was bowled over backwards, she turned and snatched his pile of tokens from the table. The other players dove upon her and a brawl began in earnest. Mer-Rill put her tail and teeth to work, pummeling and gnawing at her foes, but things weren't going as smoothly as she was used to. Those she hit didn't stay down. Fists and previously concealed weapons thumped into her tough hide. The fought back, but even the reduced strength and the unfamiliarity of fighting in her new form didn't explain all of her problems. It wasn't just that she lacked the strength to hit as hard as she used to, it was that she lacked the *will* to hit as hard as she could. She wasn't even giving as good as she got. She was losing.

"Hey! What are you doing to my friend!" shouted a small voice from the door.

It was Fairy-Rill, a look of vengeance in her little eyes.

"Stay out of this, pip-squeak," the ogre said. "This is between us and the—*argh!*"

She darted in and clamped her tiny teeth down on the ogre's ear. He swatted at her like she was a wasp. Mer-Rill took full advantage of the distraction. A mighty shove of her tail hurled the ogres off her. She swept up a pile of tokens, enough to make up for what had been stolen from her and then some, and bolted for the door. Fairy-Rill followed. The pair bolted up and away, leaving the ground-bound cheaters far below.

"What happened?" Fairy-Rill asked.

"I thought I made a friend, but they turned out to be a bunch of cheaters and they were trying to take our tokens."

"Did you get them back?"

She rummaged through her pockets and took a quick tally.

"Three sets of three sets of three, and two sets of three sets of three, and a set of three and an extra," Mer-Rill said. "That's a set of three and two extras more than we had before."

"So you won the game!" Fairy-Rill said.

"Yeah… I *guess* I did…" Mer-Rill said.

"Is something wrong?"

"I don't know… I'm the smart one, right?"

Fairy-Rill nodded. "You're smarter than the mean one, that's for sure. And smarter than me, too."

"I didn't feel smart down there," she said. "They cheated for a while before I saw they were cheating. I feel like I was smarter before. And I don't feel quite the same about singing as I did either."

"I feel the same about singing, but I'm not quite as *good* at it as I was."

"Even the fight felt wrong. I used to… I don't know. I used to *like* it more. And I could feel the viciousness more."

"I guess none of us are quite the same since we changed."

"Yeah. Being a we is a lot different than being a you, me, and her." Mer-Rill rubbed her side. "I've got broken bits that weren't even bits before. I think I need a snack."

"Do you want me to come with you? Because I was just getting to 'Take a Chance On Me' with the singers in there."

"No, no. This is about making friends. I'll be fine. I'll just get a snack from the quartermaster."

"Oh!" Fairy-Rill said. "Why don't you try Tenta? Now that we're not *us*, it's Tenta-type food that people will expect us to eat."

Mer-Rill grinned. "Yeah. Yeah, that might be fun."

"Enjoy! And tell me if it is any good. If I get hurt, I want to try some sort of fairy-type food. I'll meet you there if I finish first. You meet me at the pub if you finish first."

Fairy-Rill darted off. Mer-Rill watched her go. It *was* intriguing, the possibility of trying some new food, but something in Mer-Rill's heart just didn't seem in it.

#

Strick clopped around his home, broom in hand. He'd been working for quite a bit, and he was fairly certain he'd finally gotten the worst of the mess cleaned up.

"Ugh. And to think I was excited about offering my services to these people," the Satyr said, setting his broom down. "Now I've got to get almost all new furniture. Perhaps I can have a word with this Overseer character. The fetchers are his employees, after all. He should be responsible for their behavior."

"Hah! Good luck getting a token out of *that* little critter," echoed a voice from his fireplace.

He turned to see a small form step, soot-covered, out onto the hearth.

"Who are you, what are you doing here, and *why are you tracking soot all over my clean floor!*" Strick snapped.

The blackened figure unwrapped a raggedy bit of headgear to reveal a blue-green head with ears the size of cabbage leaves.

"Name's Mrs. Stubbs. I'm here because I went asking around town if anybody'd heard tell of where Rill got off to."

"Ugh. If I never hear—"

"Shut yer trap and listen!" Mrs. Stubbs screeched.

She shook her head.

"It don't matter what kind of race ya are, men don't got the wits to listen past a sentence. I was over in the pub, playing a nice game. Haven't been back in Shard in too long—the Mister made a bit of a mess of things and the two of us had to leave the bloody place. But he got himself all busied up with a new project and he said it'd be a good idea for me to come back and see what's what. And what's what, you ask? What's what is there's some fishy trollop fumbling through a game, and

275

she starts telling stories about my man. And these stories, these're are the kind of stories only another fetcher'd know to tell. There weren't too many fetchers working then that're working now, and only one that was half as dumb as this fishy miss seemed to be. Only *that* fetcher wasn't a fishy trollop, she was a snaky trollop with two too many heads. And that selfsame trollop is one of the ones Mr. Stubbs supposes we should keep an eye on."

"Are you through?"

"Not nearly as through as you're likely to be if you don't explain how she came to be a fish instead of a snake."

"Rill came in and requested a polymorph. I obliged."

"And made her a fish lady?"

"As a matter of fact, I made her into three different forms of her own subconscious design."

Mrs. Stubbs gritted her pointed teeth. "That'll complicate matters. What else did she end up as?"

"A human and a fairy."

"Well isn't that just lovely. If there isn't too much of one of those, there's too much of the other. It's going to take an awful lot more asking around to nail down all three of them."

"Why would you want to find them anyway? She seems to be an intensely unpleasant creature."

"Never you mind, Mr. Goat. Never you mind…"

#

Human-Rill crossed her arms and endured a lengthy description of the botanical garden atop one of the many roofs of the palace. It was a pretty place, certainly. But Medea's pride in the assorted flowers had led to an interminable amount of talking about things Human-Rill couldn't care less about.

"And of course, this may interest you, Philo," Medea said. "Time does not pass in the Between. And plants cannot grow without time. But we have learned the memories are, in essence, crystallized time, and we extract memories and use them to mimic the passage of time. That means that each of these magnificent specimens are thanks in part to the memories donated by the sleepers."

"Really…"

"Isn't it wonderful? A thousand dreary, bland moments harnessed to bring about such beauty!"

276

"Makes me wonder what sort of flowers *good* memories would make," Human-Rill said.

Medea smiled and shook her head. "It doesn't work that way, Princess. Memories are time, and time is change. It's a simple as that."

"Do we know that? Is that proved?" Philo asked.

"Heh, I don't think it *has* been tested. That's not the sort of thing people around here do," Trixie said. "That's science."

"And science doesn't work here," Medea said.

"It does if you know how it works, though. Right?" Human-Rill said. "And Philo knows all about it, I bet."

"See, that's the thing. I realize a lot of stuff that relies upon science doesn't seem to work here, but when you get right down to it, science isn't about *making* things work. It's about figuring out *how* things work. Where I come from, and I've got to imagine where a lot of you come from, plants are influenced by their environment. Coffee, grapes, tobacco. There are all sorts of plants that pass the uniqueness of their nutrients and impurities through to the final product. If time really is as much of a resource as soil and water, then maybe it *does* influence the growth and development of the plants."

Human-Rill stood tall and smiled proudly. "See."

"Do you come from a particularly scientific place?" Medea asked. "You don't seem to be terribly magical."

"Yeah, what's your story?" Trixie said.

"Me?" Human-Rill said. "No. Where I come from is mostly water and things."

"Water? I come from a place with lots of water. And there were humans there like you. Did you come from *my* world?" Medea said. "We called it Moordrew."

"No. Or… maybe yes? I don't know. I didn't really worry about words and things where I came from."

"Didn't worry about words and things…" Trixie said slowly.

She slapped Philo on the back.

"You've got a real knack for making friends with nitwits, Champ."

Human-Rill scowled. "Maybe that's why he likes *you* so much."

"Quite the clever zinger, Princess. Couldn't see that one coming a mile away," Trixie said.

"Hey, come on," Philo said. "No need to fight. We're all friends here."

Human-Rill smiled faintly.

"I think it would be fascinating to do some experiments," Philo said. "Grow some plants with neutral memories, some with sad ones, etc."

"To what end?" Medea said.

"To know. It's to know, right? Because the more you know, the more you know," Human-Rill said.

"That's right. You never know what knowing something new will lead to."

She bobbed up and down and clapped her hands, then clutched Philo's arm. "We're so much the same, aren't we, Philo?"

"We certainly think along the same lines. Nice to know Trixie's not the only one with a mind for science."

Medea tapped the side of her face thoughtfully. "This *is* rather interesting. I think we could see our way clear to letting you have some seeds. They're this way."

The mermaid led the way to a well-fortified room at one corner of the garden. Trixie tugged his arm, holding him back a step or two. Human-Rill lingered to eavesdrop.

"This is pretty major, Champ. The 'benevolent' Queen Kintalla jealously guarded anything associated with the palace. There's a pretty good chance these plants don't exist anywhere else in the Between."

"If I take some seeds, I'm not taking them for the value," Philo said.

"Of course you aren't, but it *is* a big deal. See that one, over there?" Trixie pointed. "The Rose of Nocturne. If you're going to run an experiment, I recommend that one."

"That wouldn't be because it would look absolutely glorious in your front garden, would it?"

She gave his shoulder a shove. "You know it. Come on. Let's see what we can get while the getting is good. When you've been in the Between as long as I have, you'll learn to take advantage of good fortune while you can, because it never lasts long."

#

Mer-Rill drifted into the dimly lit interior of the eatery that had come to replace the palace on the blunt edge of Upper Shard. The place still had a temporary feel to it. Considering the palace's departure was rather sudden, there was every possibility that the overseer would decide to return it whether the land had been put to better use or not. Even so, rickety walls and lightweight tables were an enormous improvement over Tenta's old place, which was little more than a kiosk.

The proprietor of the establishment sat in the back of the dining room. The was a kindly fellow who had quite gracefully made the transition to Between's bizarre way of life. In his home world he was a short order cook. Here in the Between, food was only consumed in any quantity when someone was injured. Thus, he was in essence a paramedic. He treated the job with the same enthusiasm and eye for customer satisfaction that he had in his pre-Between years.

"Hello there," he said, rising to his feet. "You look like… Mmm… Cheating at cards?"

"Disks. And I wasn't cheating, *they* were," Mer-Rill said. "How'd you know?"

"You start to get an eye for bumps and bruises when you cook in a place like Shard. I'm not sure I've seen your face around here."

"It's new."

He raised an eyebrow, then shrugged. "Have you got any tokens?"

She pulled out a handful. Now both eyebrows raised.

"That's a lot of tokens for someone who *wasn't* cheating. But who am I to judge? A customer's a customer. What can I get you?"

"I don't know," she said. "Mostly I just eat crunchy, crabby, raw things."

"The sort the Quartermaster provides?"

"Yep!"

"Those'll get you by, I suppose. I've got some in the back. You want one?"

"No. I want to try something new. But I really don't know what to get."

"Chef's choice then. Been a while since I've had the opportunity. You're the only customer. I've got some chairs in the back if you'd like to chat while I'm cooking. That is, if you're not too sore."

She gave him a cautious look. "Are you being friendly to try to steal my tokens? That's what the last 'friends' did."

"Wounds like yours will cost about two tokens to heal up. If you're fine with that, I couldn't care less what you do with the rest."

"Good! Not caring less is probably a good way to start a friendship."

She swam after him as he stepped through the door to the makeshift kitchen and pantry. Mer-Rill's eyes widened. It was a bit of a wonderland, the kitchen and pantry Tenta had built for himself. Food was everywhere. Ingredients stuffed baskets, hung from the ceiling, sat in careful arrangements on racks. Aquariums along one wall held live sea creatures, cages here and there kept other tasty animals on hand. Mer-Rill knew that she had more willpower than her sisters, and it was good that she did. If they were present, it was very likely the three of them would have launched into one of the shelves and devoured as much as they could eat before being kicked out by Tenta.

"So much food..." Mer-Rill said, gazing longingly at the aquarium.

"Yeah. With things cooled down between Shard and Heartcore, we've got plenty of stock and better than average selection. So you picked a good time to take some lumps. You look aquatic. Do you want to dine in that realm or are you feeling adventurous?"

"You choose," she said. "I don't feel like I'd make a very good choice right now."

"I'll start you with something small so we can spread it out over a few courses. You've only got so many wounds to heal, and that'll help you find something you like for next time."

With one hand he grabbed a bowl. With another he dipped a ladle into a steaming pot. With a third he grabbed what looked like a small bird's nest made from noodles, and with his fourth he grabbed a wooden lid. The noodles and broth went into the bowl, which he topped with the wood lid. He paced to another station and put a pan over a flame while prepping some meat.

"You seem a little down," he said.

"I do?"

"You just got beat on, so that's liable to wipe the smile off the average person's face, but even so, that head's hanging a little low. Something wrong?"

"I suppose..." She huffed. "I have two sisters who I don't normally get any time alone from."

"Missing them?"

"Yes. Very much, actually. But that's not why I'm sad. I'm sad because I don't think I'm as good of a sister as I thought."

"What did you do?"

"Not much, I think."

"You didn't do much?" He thought for a moment. "Ah. You mean you don't feel useful to them."

"Yes. We usually do everything together. And we don't really talk about it, because we don't really need to, but I we all sort of know which of us is better at this or that. Which of us is useful for something, you know?"

"Sure."

"Except all the things I thought I was good at, I'm not very good at. And all of the things I thought we were *all* good at, it turns out it was one of them. I'm supposed to be the smart one, but I got fooled. I can't feel the raw joy of singing without my sister. I can't feel the savage glee of a fight without my sister…"

"I can see how that would get you down."

Tenta pulled the lid off, releasing a lovely meaty scent, then dropped a slice of fried meat into the broth with the noodles and chopped some greenery to sprinkle on top.

"There. Ramen. A very popular dish. I learned about it as a special order for a group from Earth. Comfort food. It's really started to catch on with others. You can eat it with a spoon or—"

Mer-Rill thrust her face into the bowl, slurping at the broth until she was able to snag some of the noodles. She worked at the noodle for a moment, briefly looking like a baby bird not quite able to wrangle its first worm, but eventually she worked out that she could use her hands to gather it up and shove it into her mouth.

"I like it. It burns my face a little, though."

"Most people use eating utensils," Tenta explained simply.

Mer-Rill plucked the meat from the bowl and threw it in her mouth.

"This is nice though. Being hot makes it better. This brown part from where it got fried is different. And I've never had something that was so wet and still so *food*. The meat is softer. I miss the crunchiness though. And it could use some leg squeezings."

"A little contrast in the texture is nice. I could fry up some more of the meat and get it nice and crispy if you'd like. What's this about leg squeezings?"

"The crunchy crab things. The legs aren't as juicy as the rest, but they've got this… stuff that tastes like it would be good if it was in this too."

"I usually save the legs up and just use them for feed for other critters, whenever I can acquire enough time to grow my own."

Tenta paced over to a tray full of cut-offs and retrieved some of the legs from the crab creature that until this meal had been among the only things Rill would eat with any regularity. He used the flat of a blade to crush the leg and dabbed a finger into the oily juice that leaked out.

"It's… potent. But it's not without its charm."

He garnished her bowl with a few of the legs. She eagerly snatched one and crunched it up in her mouth, then slurped up a generous helping of what was left in the bowl.

"You used to be Rill, didn't you?" Tenta said.

She paused and looked at him uncertainly. "How did you know?"

"Talk of sisters. A taste for raw seafood. It shows."

"Is that going to hurt us maybe being friends? This whole thing is supposed to be about maybe getting new friends."

"As long as you don't try to wreck the place and you pay your bill, a customer's a customer."

"Good. I am not good at pretending to be something I'm not. Even when I *am* something that I'm not. I guess that's just another thing I'm not very good at."

She continued her meal. Tenta took a small cup and filled it with the broth, then topped it with a few drops of the oil and sampled the combination.

"You may be onto something here," he said. "That's a good palate you've got."

"Thanks. It's new," she said between handfuls of noodles.

"I don't suppose you've ever tried your hand at cooking?"

"The hands are new too. But sometimes we would put things we catch over where the hot water plumes up. Is that cooking?" She finished the meal and leaned back to feel her tender spots. "That was very tasty. But it still hurts here, and here. And a little here."

"I had expected you'd need a second helping. Tell you what. I've got something I was working on, and I couldn't quite get the balance right. Come over here and help me make it and I'll just charge you the one token."

"Is it hard to do?"

"In the beginning. But it gets a little easier each time. Besides, it'll get you out of your head. Good to keep those new hands of yours busy when you're in a bad mood."

She shrugged. "Okay. If it means more food, I'll try."

#

The door to a heavily cluttered house shuddered and shifted. When it heaved open, it slid aside a mound of hoarded knickknacks and doodads that must have collapsed the last time the door shut. Mrs. Stubbs squeezed through the half-open door and slammed it behind her.

"Ah…" she said with a sigh of genuine contentment. "Good to be home again."

She waded through and scampered over the tangle of goods.

"Shows just how thick those idiots are. Didn't even bust in and steal our stuff while we were gone."

Mrs. Stubbs burrowed into one of the piles and emerged a moment later with a tarnished brass medallion. She clutched it tight in her little hand and muttered an arcane phrase. It gleamed, then faded with little other effect.

"Lousy stupid worthless junk," she muttered.

She spat on the medallion and shined it up with one of her rags, then tried again. This time the dingy surface offered a half-seen reflection not of herself but of what may as well have been a male duplicate.

"Stimpson!" she barked.

The hobgoblin in the reflection winked at her. "It's been ages, dumpling. Been busy?"

"Busy running errands for *you*. And boy, things've gone sideways while we were gone."

"Give me the short version."

"The Overseer's spending all his time with those goody-goods in Heartcore, so that trollop and the pickled brain in a jar are calling the shots, more or less."

"Any motion on Philo's little project?"

"Not that I could see. Her being a demon, and demons being what they are, she's probably helping him keep it hid. But there's a better than average chance we can cross off one of our concerns."

283

"Oh?"

"That three-headed idiot went and made herself into three one-headed idiots."

"Did she now?"

"Yeah. Lots of new wizards about. One of 'em split her up into a mermaid sort of thing and a fairy and a human. Don't know about the other two, but the mermaid isn't half as tough as Rill was."

"Oh… That's what I like to hear, dumpling. If we can get the purple bruiser out of the way, we'll be able to have our way with the other two. You think you can kill her as she is?"

"I don't even know where the other two thirds of her are. And she might've taken a beating at the hands of some pro'zhat players, but she survived it, and that's more of a beating than I could hand out. When are you coming back?"

"You know I'm not coming back until I find who I'm looking for. But the good news is, I've got a lead. So I can probably send Hooks back to help you out. It'll take him some time to make it on his own, though."

"Well a fat lot of good that'll do us if the Rills decide to get back together before then."

Mr. Stubbs scratched his chin. "True… tell me, has Trixie redone her landscaping?"

"What difference does that make?"

"Just answer me. Has she got all the same ornaments out?"

"Yeah, I suppose."

"Then here's what you'll do. Get yerself a hammer, and head on out…"

#

"That was such a lovely bit of novelty, little one!" said Red as she fluttered out of the pub. "So many new songs, and with such interesting new forms. I have never heard a fairy sing songs like this, never once!"

Fairy-Rill buzzed after the larger creature, struggling to keep up.

"I'm glad you liked it. You sing so fancy!"

"But where, little one, where did you hear these songs? Are they the songs of your home? Somehow it seems that they are not."

"No, I heard them on a machine. My friend is a science-type."

"Do not play tricks. Science-types can't build machines that sing so beautifully.”

“My friend can. He’s busy but you should meet him. And my sisters too!”

“Your one sister was the one in the fight, yes?”

“Yeah, that’s her. If you’re my friend, would you be her friend?”

“Does she sing? If she sings half as nice as you and she knows songs like yours than she will be *welcome* to sing with us.”

“Are you sure? Even though she looks different?”

“It doesn’t matter how she *looks*. It only matters how she *sings*. Yes, indeed. Singing is the language of the soul. That is a truth we all know. All of us who sing.”

“You’re sure? You’re *sure* you’re sure? No matter *what* we look like or *who* we are?”

Red laughed. “Yes! Yes, my nervous little one. Very much so. No doubt at all. But I shall have to meet them later. I have to work to do. I am a new spotter for the Overseer and I must spend some time spotting.”

“Have fun! Next time we’ll sing some Queen. The three of us like to sing it, but I think it takes at least four people to sing it right.”

“Lovely. That sounds like a truly delightful time, and I will look forward to it.”

“How will I find you, once I get them and once you’re done?”

“Oh, little one, I am a spotter! You needn’t find *me*. No, not at all. I will keep an eye on *you*. I will glance in your direction every now and then, and if the time seems right, we shall have another sing-along.”

The phoenix flew off to a roost somewhere in the stretch of shard that now held those who had once lived in the palace. Fairy-Rill hugged herself and giggled with glee.

“This is great! Oh, I hope that’s true what she said, about singing being singing no matter what. Because once I get back together with the others, I would *love* to keep them as friends.”

She flitted up toward Upper Shard. The trip had never seemed like a very long one while she was in her old form, but as a fairy her little wings had to work hard to reach the sliver of black stone hanging in the sky of the ice cream scoop-shaped little world. When she finally reached Upper Shard, she was nearly as fatigued as when she would return from one of their fetching runs.

Out of habit, she returned to Fetcher's Den, expecting to find her only other friends waiting for her there. What she found instead was her currently crumbed home and no one home at Trixie's house.

"Oh, that's right. I was supposed to meet her at Tenta's. I wonder where the mean one got off to, though. And what's taking Philo and Trixie so long? Diplomacy can't be *that* hard. How long can you *talk*?"

She buzzed up to Trixie's front window to gaze inside, wondering if perhaps the pair had come home and simply gone to bed early as they always seemed to do. It didn't appear to be the case, but before she left to find her sister, Fairy-Rill gave the porch a once over.

"Something feels off about this place," she said. "What's changed?"

Fairy-Rill looked around. A chain hang from the awning had nothing attached to it. A trail of broken glass lay beneath it. She scratched her head.

"Something used to be here… Trixie would flick it every morning. What was it?"

The answer struck her, quite literally, a few moments later. A set of grasping claws closed around her tiny body as a black and purple blur ripped through the air. She struggled and tugged at the grip. Her dizzied gaze peered up to find a red-eyed bat had gotten her. At her present size it seemed absolutely enormous, but even if she were her normal self it would be clear it was no ordinary bat. She knew just who, or what, this was.

"Duke!" she cried, struggling against the claws.

"I know what you are," the bat hissed down to her. "Petulant, insignificant fraction of a former worm!"

Fairy-Rill struggled and shoved against the claws. Though they were clamped down upon her like a vice, the creature was not as strong as it appeared. Duke was not, as his size indicated, truly a bat. At least, he wasn't a *single* bat. There was a time when he was an imposing human-like creature. A vampire lord who could, at will, take the form of a legion of bats. Bad luck and worse judgment had led Duke to face off against the Overseer. This resulted in him being systematically captured and encapsulated in glass. Trixie, who had her own reasons to hate Duke even more than everyone else did, kept one of the bats as an ornament. Regardless of how he escaped, the creature who held her now was perhaps one thirtieth of his former self, and it showed.

The Rills

She wrenched herself from his grip. A more intelligent creature, or at least one more accustomed to being bite-size for the attacking creature, might have attempted to flee. But Fairy-Rill was a rare combination of things. She was foolish enough to be fearless. She was enthusiastic enough to be spoiling for a fight regardless of size. And most importantly, she was accustomed to being large and strong enough to be a match for Duke at his full size and strength. It all combined into a potent cocktail that made her a nightmare to do battle with.

Fairy-Rill buzzed and bashed against Duke. She flailed her little limbs, thumping him in the eyes and any other tender spot she could find. She chomped her little teeth down on anything she could fit in her mouth. When it was clear Duke wasn't agile enough catch her without sneaking up on her, she started pulling back farther and farther to dart in and thump against him with head butts and thrust kicks. Against all odds, Fairy-Rill started to gain the upper hand. She might even have pummeled him enough to convince him to flee if not for an encounter with one of the most ancient enemies of fairy kind. A butterfly net.

Sheer cloth snatched her out of the air. Before she could work out what happened, she was forced out of the net and clinked painfully against a smooth, cool surface. The soft squeak of a cork squeezing into place left her trapped inside what turned out to be a jar just a bit larger than she was.

"Hey!" she bellowed. "Let me out! Let me out right—"

Her tirade was cut short by a vigorous shaking of the jar. She rattled about, clinking off alternate sides of the glass until she was dazed and sore. When she blinked the blurriness out of her vision, she found she was staring through smudged glass at a familiar face.

"Mrs. Stubbs!" she said. "What are you doing back here?"

"Starting a little collection," she said with a grin. "You're the first part."

"Not for long," Fairy-Rill fumed.

"If I had my way, you'd be right. I bet that little head of yours would pop like a grape if I put these teeth to work, but the Mister seems to think you being just one third of the old Rill means doing you in would do about as much good as doing in that hunk of Duke that snatched you."

"I say kill the petulant former worm regardless," Duke said, swooping down and landing beside Mrs. Stubbs. "We can find and kill

287

the rest of her later."

"No, no," the hobgoblin said. "As much of a fool as Stimpson can be, he's fair at wrapping his head around a plan. We need this one as a bargaining chip to find the others. Once we gather them up, we use them to convince Philo and Trixie to play by our rules."

"My little flying fox will return to me in time. And what good does the pathetic man-thing do us?"

"The two of them are favorites of the Overseer. And apparently Philo's got some tricks up his sleeve that he's not letting on. Or so Stimpson says. The point is, we'll get a better deal with her alive than dead."

"I have no interest in negotiation. They have nothing to offer me."

"Oh no? Aren't you just a *wee* bit curious who has the rest of you and where it's gotten off to?"

He paused.

"There may be value in plying the others for information..."

"That's Stimpson's thinking. And lucky you, I asked around and I think I've got a line on where a couple more hunks of you are stored. Now let's go. I've got to find something to leave a note. With the poor show you put up, I don't like our chances unless we find a good hiding place, break a few more bits of you out their glass, and get some more help besides."

#

The storage shed of the palace garden contained a very carefully cataloged collection of seeds from an infinitude of worlds. Elegantly painted placards depicting a blooming flower or ripe fruit sat in little frames on the front of handcrafted drawers. Inside the drawers were paper envelopes stuffed with seeds.

"Oh, excellent..." Trixie said, looking over the assortment with glee. "You've got coiling funeral-flower! And blood blight. Why aren't these in the garden?"

Medea gazed at the painting. "They seem a little... macabre for an ornamental."

"You just think that because you haven't seen them used properly. The contrast of the thorns against the vines is like nothing else in creation. And the scent. By the depths, it is sublime..."

She snatched envelopes of each, as well as a dozen others.

"It seems like you classify these by color and such," Philo said.

"How else would you classify them?" Medea asked.

"Back home, we've got a whole branch of science called botany that deals with plants."

"Fascinating…" She drifted a bit closer and touched his arm. "The things people do when they don't have magic to properly interact with their world. Tell me more. I feel a fool for not taking the time to talk to the science-types in depth before."

Human-Rill narrowed her eyes and clutched Philo's other arm a little more possessively.

"I bet Philo knows more than anyone else about plants and stuff, right?" she said.

"Well, no. Not really. But I know that things get grouped into families and the like."

He looked at one of the rows of drawers, organized by color.

"For instance, even though a rose is red and a poppy might be red, a botanist wouldn't put them together. Color is a little superficial to be a proper way to study plants."

Medea tapped her chin thoughtfully.

"I see. So even science-types believe that certain things in nature belong together." She smiled. "Like fate."

"Uh… No, not quite like that."

"Yeah," Human-Rill said, physically tugging Philo away from Medea's touch. "Philo means that little things like how something looks don't mean they don't belong together."

"That's not really what I mean either. See, there's this stuff called DNA."

"Oh! And what is that?" Medea said.

"Yeah, I want to hear all about it," Human-Rill said.

Both the mermaid and the human leaned in, awaiting further explanation.

"It's actually super interesting. You see—"

Philo's explanation was cut short as Trixie stepped into view and firmly placed a hand on the shoulders of both Human-Rill and Medea. She separated them with a stiff push and took her place beside Philo.

"Hold that thought, Champ. It looks like a little marking of territory is in order." She glanced back and forth between the others. "Prissy? Princess? Maybe I didn't make it clear, but this one? Off limits."

"I think you misunderstand," Medea said.

"No, no. I think *he* misunderstands. See, I trust Philo. He's not the philandering type. Too much of an attention span for that. He locks in and devotes himself. And right now, he's devoted to me. So you can flutter your eyes and pretend like you're interested in his scientific blather. All it'll convince him is to keep talking. But I know what you're both doing. So I'm going to lay it out, plain and simple. This is my man. And I'm his lady."

She pointed at Medea.

"You should have known better. Princess here seems thick enough to have missed it. But now it's out there. You make a move on him, that's a slap to my face. And I slap back. Hard."

"Ms. Zalthea, I assure you. No harm was meant. Philo performed a valuable service for New Allimiss. He helped me to save our queen, sparing her life despite her cruelty to him and her questionable ethics. I wanted to reward him."

"Yeah, I'll *bet* you did."

Medea crossed her arms. "With kindness. And with generosity. Perhaps *your* sort is quick to turn affection into some sort of physical competition, but we are not."

"Great. So we see eye to eye then." Trixie hardened her voice. "Hands off the merchandise."

Human-Rill put her hands on her hips.

"Are you saying Philo can't have friends besides you?"

"Are you kidding?" Trixie said. "The guy's mister congeniality. Champ makes friends with everyone he meets. And that's fine. A great way to be. But there's friends and then there's *friends*. You make a move I don't like, I'm going to let you know."

"Trixie, come on," Philo said, stepping forward. "Don't you think you're over-reacting a little? Medea, *you* understand that Trixie and I are a couple and you and I are just friends, right?"

"Of course," the mermaid said simply.

"And Princess, *you* understand that Trixie and I are a couple and you and I are just friends, right?"

Human-Rill blinked. "Just friends. Right. Because you're friends with everybody. There wasn't... There isn't anything special about me."

"Princess, that's not quite… When you put it like that, it doesn't sound great, but…"

Human-Rill turned away. "Can I go? I'm supposed to be your prisoner, right? Can I just go somewhere else, please?"

"Princess, I didn't mean—"

"I'm going," she said firmly.

Human-Rill marched out of the storeroom.

"Oh dear," Medea said, darting after her.

Trixie nudged Philo's shoulder. "Did that face strike you as someone who was just interested in botany, Champ? Or does it look like someone who just got rejected? This is what I was talking about."

"We've got to follow her. I didn't mean to hurt her feelings."

"By all means," Trixie said. "But you'd better believe I'm going to watch over your shoulder to make sure you don't lead her right back into the same cockeyed way of thinking that'll just get her hurt again. Some people can't take hints."

\#

Some boiling water and a few scalded digits later, Mer-Rill dumped the contents of a large tin onto a dish. It wasn't a very attractive concoction. The whole mess wobbled and had an unpleasantly translucent color. The smell was just this side of perfection, though. It had a robust, spicy aroma with all the complexity and nuance of a fine perfume.

"What do we call this?" Mer-Rill said, eying the food.

"It was supposed to be a quiche. I don't think those eggs we used quite firmed up like I'd expected," Tenta said.

One of the chef's arms reached into a pocket to fetch a clean spoon and portioned off a morsel to taste.

"Is it good?" Mer-Rill said. "Did we do it right?"

"We're a good two steps closer than I've ever gotten." He spat the unneeded nutrition into a bucket. "But see for yourself. You're the one with some healing left to do."

She reached down to grab two handfuls of the stuff.

"Uh, uh, uh!" Tenta held out a spoon.

"Right, right. Tools because other people might eat the stuff we make," she said with a nod. "And also because it will hurt less when the food is hot."

She took the spoon and, after trying to use the wrong side twice, finally scooped up some of the food.

"It has a lot of flavors. I like how they go together," she said.

"I never would have thought of adding the goat cheese with those oysters," he mused as she shoveled more of it into her mouth.

"They smelled bad in the right way," she said, munching happily. "The way things smell usually tells you the way things taste."

"You've got a pretty good nose on you."

"It's even better when I'm not a fish-person," she explained.

"I don't doubt it." Tenta stretched with two of his arms and crossed the other two. "So. You want a job?"

"I'm a fetcher already."

"Do you think the Overseer would see his way clear to giving you permission to help out when there's no fetching to do?"

"The Overseer barely knows I exist when there's no fetching to do. But why do you need my help? Can't you just put a big bucket of food out when there's a lot of people who need healing?"

"Given the time and the resources, I like to do a good job. Customer satisfaction. There's more to food than just getting something in your belly so you can heal up. There's enjoyment. There's artistry."

"And you can't find someone better than me?"

"You've got a unique point of view. And also no one else has shown the least bit of proficiency or interest."

"I'm not always going to be a fish thing, you know." She twiddled her fingers. "I'm not going to have these forever. And also I'll be huge again."

"There's room. But if you don't want to do it, I won't twist your tail about it."

She chewed slowly and considered his words.

"Do I get to taste the food?" she asked.

"How else do you know if it's worth serving? But if you don't need to heal, you'll be spitting it in the bucket."

Mer-Rill smiled. "I'll *do* it! But not right now. I've got to meet with my sister. She should have been here by now."

"That's fine. When you're ready for it, come see me."

Mer-Rill smacked her tongue happily as she swam out the door.

"Flavor," she said. "I never thought of trying to mix flavors to make them better instead of just trying to find a better thing to eat. ... Or just eating whatever you find."

She glanced around, expecting to find her temporarily tiny sister buzzing about outside, but she was nowhere to be seen.

"She must still be singing," Mer-Rill said with a shrug.

Strong thrusts of her fishy tail made short work of the distance between Upper Shard and lower. In no time at all, she was inside the pub again. Another creature might have thought twice about barging into the pub so soon after causing a rumble. The notion never occurred to Mer-Rill. She simply swam in, spotted one of the singers, and darted up to her. It was the siren, who until Mer-Rill's sudden arrival was chatting pleasantly with one of the harpies.

"Hello," she said. "You were singing with a new fairy earlier, weren't you?"

She looked to Mer-Rill. "We were. Interesting new songs. A bit simple."

"What was simple, the songs or the fairy?" Mer-Rill asked.

"Both. But nice."

"Both were nice too?"

"Yes."

Mer-Rill smiled. The siren recoiled a bit from her predatory teeth.

"Do you know where she went? She was supposed to meet me and she didn't."

"She left with Red. The phoenix."

"Do you know where they—"

"Hey!" a voice shouted thickly from the floor. "You stole my tokens!"

A stone glanced off Mer-Rill's shoulder. She sighed.

"I have to go thump that ogre's head again. Would you excuse me?"

"Of course."

The siren watched without any particular interest as Mer-Rill launched herself downward and barreled into the gut of the ogre. Such battles were evidently a common occurrence here. The pair hurtled back into the room where Mer-Rill had not so long ago been taken advantage of in her first game of pro'zhat. She rattled about in the room with him for a bit. The others had left to lick their wounds, so the fight wasn't nearly so one sided. When the ogre had learned his lesson—or at least when Mer-Rill grew weary of teaching it—she returned to the siren with a few deep purple and bumps and bruises.

"I am sorry," she puffed. "I didn't expect it to take so long. My heart just isn't in it like it usually is. The fairy, and Red?"

"Red is a spotter. Over that way. But I do believe the fairy intended to go home."

"Home! Right. I was just near there. Thank you!"

She worked her tail again and retraced the path back to the orbiting spike of stone that she called home. In the Fetcher's Den, she came upon the mound of stones that, with a bit of work, would eventually make for a nice cozy place to sleep again. Fairy-Rill had probably slipped in amongst the gaps in the stones to wait for her larger sisters. Mer-Rill was about to call for her, but then her eyes fell upon a bit of parchment pinned down with a tacky souvenir paperweight on top of her crumbled home. It was scrawled with the broad, crooked script of someone who knew care had to be taken to render their handwriting even remotely legible.

Mer-Rill's eyes flicked over the writing.

"No… No, no, no." She turned to Trixie's house and saw the mound of broken glass.

"No, no, no, no, no…" she fretted. "I need help. I… I… *I've got to pull myself together!*"

Mer-Rill thrust her tail once again and dove toward the mottled green ball spinning below. She pumped and swam just as fast as she could manage, curving up and covering her head with her arms as she approached the half-ship-turned-abode that held the person responsible for her current state. She struck a door that was still much the worse for wear from her last visit. The full force of her speed knocked it from its hinges again and both she and the door tumbled into the wizard's home.

"Egad!" squawked the mystic, clutching his chest as the tumbling collection of wood and mermaid narrowly missed him.

"Strick! Strick the wizard!" Mer-Rill said, shaking away the dizziness of the blow. "Fix us! We need to be the old me again!"

She urgently held out the note, which Strick shakily took and read.

"If you had enemies that could have taken advantage of your change, you shouldn't have changed," Strick said simply, handing it back.

"I did, and they did, and now I need to be back like I was. So do it! Do it or I'll go find the mean one and she'll think of something really awful to do to you if you don't do it!"

"This may come as a surprise to you, but I've never before been asked to change a single being into three individuals before. I don't know for certain what will happen when I try to revert the change."

"Then do it and then we'll know."

"It could be catastrophic."

She waved the note again. "It already *is* that!"

He looked at the sorry state of his home. Barely cleaned up from the last assault, it now had a fresh mound of debris thanks to her swift entry and the various things that were in the path of it.

"Fine. It would be good riddance if you *did* come to a bad end because of this. But outside. Please. My home can't take another thrashing."

She nodded desperately and swam outside. He clopped outside after her and shut his eyes. Assorted mystic words slid from his mouth with an unnatural cadence. His scepter traced a few shapes in the air. She felt herself tingle as some manner of spell took hold, but when the ritual was over, she was still the peculiar Mer-Rill she'd been when she started.

"I'm the wrong me! You didn't do it right! I need to be the big scary me with my sisters!"

"I should have supposed as much," he said. "You can't change back until all three of you are able to touch each other."

"You mean I have to find them and bring them back so you can change me back so I'm strong enough to find them and bring them back?" Mer-Rill raved.

"By the gods, don't you dare bring them back. The spell is cast. All that remains is making contact. Find them and… oh, I don't know… *join hands* I suppose. That will let the magic do its work and you shall revert."

"But I need to be the old me to do that!" She waved the note yet again. "These are bad people who fight better than I do like this."

"Then you are liable to have a hard time of it!" Strick said. "Forgive me if I'm not sympathetic to your cause, as thanks to you I've got to *completely* redecorate."

He clopped back into his home and, in lieu of a door, barricaded his entrance with what was left of his dining room table. Mer-Rill clutched the note tight in her hand and took a breath.

"Philo. Philo will know what to do," she said.

She worked her tail and darted into the air.

#

Human-Rill must have moved with remarkable speed, as by the time Trixie and Philo exited the garden to search for her, both she and Medea were nowhere to be seen. New Allimiss was an awfully large and busy place to have to try to find someone, but there were only a few places she was likely to be. Their first stop was the palace's holding cells to see if Medea had decided to lock her up for the deferred assault charge. No such luck. Fortunately, at their second guess, they struck pay dirt.

A long rut ran the length of the impossibly long pillar of stone that made up Heartcore. In New Allimiss, dams had been built at either end of the portion of the rut that ran through the city. They'd flooded it, and aside from giving the fairytale city a pleasant water feature, it served as a place where the more aquatic creatures could make themselves feel at home. A bit of asking around directed them to the humble little cottage beneath the surface that Medea called home.

Philo and Trixie gazed through the rippling surface into the window of the little cottage. There, the mermaid could just barely be seen consoling the elegantly dressed woman.

"I can't believe it. I knew Medea was a goody two shoes, but a woman puts the boots to a guard and not only does she take her on a tour of gardens, but she brings her to her own home when she starts to get huffy. Call me hard-nosed if you want, but I don't think this is going to serve as much of a deterrent."

Philo waved to get the mermaid's attention. "I get the feeling Medea's positions as both a fetcher and a member of the city guard were more out of duty to the queen than a desire to put her weapons to use."

"You'd think in a place like this where there are actually alternatives, she would have found a better way to work to her strengths."

Medea noticed her visitors and swam to the surface. When she rose out of the water, it sheeted off her as though she'd never been wet.

"I'm never going to get used to that," Philo said.

"Philo, do you know that woman? Before you met today, I mean?" Medea said, her face the picture of compassion and empathy.

"I don't think so. I certainly don't remember it. Though since I got here I've learned one can't always trust one's memory." Philo gave Trixie a pointed look.

"Hey. I apologized about that," she said.

"The way she's acting. I don't know. I think she may not be who she said she is."

"Can I talk to her?"

"I think you should. But be gentle."

"I'm coming too," Trixie said.

Both Philo and Medea looked at her sternly

"I won't say anything nasty." She considered for a moment. "Not unless it's called for, anyway. But your emotional intelligence has got some gaping holes, Champ. Consider me a tutor."

"Very well." Medea held out her arms. "Take my hands, and don't hold your breath."

They each held tight and were swiftly pulled beneath the surface. A wave of magic swept through them a second or two after the bracing coolness of the water surrounded them. Trixie was the first to embrace the effects of the spell. She opened her mouth and took a deep, hearty breath of water. Philo was more resistant, but reluctantly he followed suit. A bit of hacking and gasping later, he discovered that his lungs had developed a taste for water.

"That's… unsettling," he said, grappling with the new sensations of weight and inertia that came with replacing air with water. "This is going to make my lungs tired in a hurry."

"Eh," Trixie said. "I'm just glad I don't have the long hair anymore. This would wreak havoc on it."

Philo smirked and glanced in her direction. "You used to have long hair."

"Easy, Champ," she said. "Don't hold your breath on that coming back. It's a liability for a fetcher. Besides, we're down here for a reason."

"Right, right."

The trio approached the door of the cottage. It was a simple abode. Little more than one large room for entertaining and a doorway at the back of it leading to what was presumably her bedroom. Human-Rill was in the den. She looked tiny and lost at the center of her dress, which had billowed out enormously around her. At the same time, she seemed perfectly comfortable beneath the waves. Whereas Philo found himself constantly adjusting and scrabbling to try to keep himself more or less on the ground, Human-Rill was content to let the water orient her as it chose.

She noticed the newcomers and turned away a bit, flaring her dress like a wild animal attempting to make itself larger to intimidate opponents.

"Princess, I think Philo wants to talk to you."

"He wants to talk to everyone," she said sulkily.

"Can you give us some space?" Philo said quietly.

Medea nodded. She and Trixie lingered near the door while Philo treaded water through the doorway.

"Princess?" he said, swimming around to face her.

"That's not my name," she said.

"Yeah… Medea says she thinks we knew each other. Or at least that you knew me."

"It doesn't matter," Human-Rill said.

"Look at me. Maybe I can remember," he offered.

She turned her eyes to him and he scrutinized her.

"I don't know…" he said slowly. "There's something… It's in your eyes, a little. And your expression. Not now, really. But before. And… Wait a minute."

Philo cleared his throat and spoke with rhythm.

"If you see a faded sign by the side of the road that says fifteen miles to the—"

"Love *shack,*" Human-Rill said with a blush.

"Rill?" he said, astonished.

"No way…" Trixie said from the doorway.

Medea hushed her.

"I'm not the whole Rill," Human-Rill explained. "I'm—"

"No, wait. Let me guess. You're the… I was going to say the side you're on, but you're all in the middle according to you, so you're… Uh…" He seemed to be grasping for a descriptor that wouldn't be an insult. "The one with the scars."

She nodded. "How'd you know?"

"Well, the *scars,*" he said, gesturing at her face. "But you're all pretty distinctive, and of the three of you, I think the one most likely to use a freshly acquired pair of legs to kick a guy in the gut would be you.”

“That’s true,” she said with a nod.

“So what happened? Why are you like this?”

“There’s a… he had a fancy word for it. The smart one knew it. But he is a person-changer.”

“Strick,” Trixie said from behind him.

“That’s him,” Human-Rill said. “And he talked about why people might want to change, and I just thought about how even after we were here for so long, you were the first person to be our friend. I liked it. I like having you as a friend. I like it more than just about anything. It’s important to me. The others thought about changing and how maybe it would mean finding *more* friends. But just wanted to be sure of the one I had. That’s all.”

“You weren’t sure we were friends?”

“We, me and the other Rills I mean, were still this big strong thing. When we met you, you *needed* a big strong thing to be useful. And even if you weren’t just using us—and I don’t really think you were—there are the other heads.”

She huffed a breath, causing a whorl of water to swish her billowing dress.

“The other heads are nicer than I am. Even when someone is afraid of all of us, they’re more afraid of me. I’m not supposed to think of me as a me. I’m supposed to be part of an us. But it felt nice to imagine that you liked *me*. It felt nice to be liked. And I just felt like… If I was something else. If it wasn’t just the big strong creature who could help you when you needed it. If I wasn’t just grouped with a couple of nicer heads. If it was just *me*… I wanted to know that we’d still be friends.”

“You could have just asked.”

“You’d have said yes. You’re nice, Philo. I wanted to find out for myself. This was a way.”

“But why a human?”

“I don’t know. The wizard said it was a thing that just ‘happens’ based on what you need or what you want. The others aren’t humans. One’s a fairy. The other’s fish… mermaid… *thing*. I’m a human. Maybe I thought it was what you’d like best.” She gritted her teeth. “But it doesn’t matter. Because you’re friends with everyone. That you became my friend together or apart doesn’t mean anything because you would have been friends with *anyone*. It’s not that you liked me. It’s nothing to do with me. You're very special to me, but I'm not special at all to you."

"Rill," he said. "You *are* special to me. You're special to everyone who really knows you. For a while, and this was a crime, it was just *me* who really knew you. You and the other Rills saved my life, sure. But even if we were just working together, just digging through the junkyard and picking out parts, we'd still be friends."

"If the others were here, you'd say the same to them."

"Of course I would. But me being friends with them doesn't make what I said any less true about you. We're friends. Separate, together. Human, Hydra. Whatever it is. We're friends."

"Mind if I weigh in?" Trixie said.

Philo gave her a sharp look, but his expression softened when he saw hers. Trixie seldom showed anything but a tough, impenetrable exterior. It was subtle, but there was a tenderness to her eyes now. Philo drifted aside with a bit of difficulty. She swept in and took his place, using her wings just as effectively in the water as in the air.

"Rill, there are some things you need to realize. First, it doesn't do you any good to measure yourself by how others feel about you."

"That's easy for you to say. People like you."

She laughed. "What gave you that idea?"

"There was Duke, and before him a bunch of others. They bring you gifts and things. No one ever did things like that for me."

"None of those people liked me, Rill. For Duke, I was just a triumph. He coveted me and I let him believe he'd acquired me. At least until it became untenable. I really don't think there is a single person in the Between who ever treated me as someone who actually mattered until Philo, here." She gave him a shove. "My little silver medal. But I don't hang my self-worth on if he or anyone else likes me. If I did that, I'd have been hollow and shriveled up long ago. It feels good to be liked. To be needed. But plenty of things feel good that aren't good for you. It just so happens we were lucky enough to find one of the people who *is* good for us.

"And that's the other thing. I've scraped out a place for myself in this world, and most of that has come down to the fact that I was raised, like all of my kind, to understand emotion at the deepest of levels. We were meant to use that knowledge to manipulate and dominate others— and I've done my share of that—but the same education has taught us to see why people work together. And you, all three of you, are a team with Philo. You work together. You fit together like a puzzle piece. If you changed one little thing, that piece wouldn't fit. And you're *not* a little thing. You're a third of the equation. You're exactly who you need to be. And don't you forget it."

Trixie smirked.

"Just don't expect me to always admit it," she added.

"I hope that helps settle things," Philo said.

Human-Rill looked back and forth between Trixie and Philo. She blinked a few times with what might have been tears if they hadn't been underwater. Then, like a serpent striking, she worked her arms and legs and darted toward Philo. She threw her arms around him and hugged him tight, pressing her cheek against his.

"I should have known from the hug," Philo groaned. "No one hugs like Rill."

The grateful, emotional hydra-turned-human waved with her hand, beckoning for Trixie. She rolled her eyes and drifted close enough to be snagged into the hug as well. They all squeezed cheek to cheek as Human-Rill rocked back and forth.

"You're our fourth head, Philo," she said. "Always and forever. And Trixie, you're our friend. Not just or sort of friend and sometimes partner. Our friend."

"Aw…" Medea cooed from the doorway, hands clutched in delight. "I never would have dreamed the fetchers of Shard could be so loving to one another."

Human-Rill continued to hold them tight. In the distance, the muffled sound of a splash rolled through the cottage. Then, a familiar sound.

"Philo Philo Philo Philo Philo!"

Outside, Mer-Rill streaked by, eyes wide and searching.

"That's her! The smart one," Human-Rill said, releasing the others and pulling herself toward the door.

"Rill!" she called.

Her sister turned, then swam up to them.

"Philo, Trixie! I know you don't know me, but—"

"We heard. Shape-changing," Trixie said.

"Good! Then I don't have to explain. Listen, the other Rill didn't show up where we were supposed to meet, so I went to try to find her and I found *this!*"

She held out the note left behind. It was lucky that Mrs. Stubbs had gone with ink on parchment, because the note survived the dunk in the water largely intact.

"Rills and other worthless fetchers," Philo read. "I've got the fairy, and I've woken up the hunk of Duke that Trixie was keeping."

Trixie muttered to herself. "Just great. I knew I should have kept him locked up inside."

"We want the rest of Rill, we want the rest of Duke, and we want in on Philo's plans."

"Philo's plans?" Medea asked.

"It's a long story," Trixie said.

"You can find us in the Junkyard, next to the bell tower. And it's signed 'Mrs. Stimpson Stubbs'" Philo looked to Trixie, then the Rills. "Do we know the bell tower?"

"Sure do," Trixie said. "It was a major landmark when trying to navigate the place a while back. Not so much anymore."

"Good, then we're going," Philo said.

"Whoa there, Champ," Trixie said. "Hold your horses."

"We've got to go!" Mer-Rill said.

"She's got a part of us," Human-Rill said.

"I appreciate that, but it's a bad plan to go charging into a place you've been invited when it was your enemies that did the inviting."

"That's sort of what diplomacy is, though," Philo said.

"Do you really think Duke and one of the Stubbs is in the mood for diplomacy?" Trixie said. "Let's think this through. Is there any way you can get back to your old self, minus the missing head for now?"

"Ugh!" Human-Rill said, recoiling.

Mer-Rill shook her head. "I asked. We have to *all* be there to change back. I tried to get the wizard to turn me back on my own and it didn't work."

"You tried to turn back without us!" Human-Rill growled.

"I thought you'd just… come back!" Mer-Rill said. "But he says now that the spell's undone, once the three of us are together, we'll change back."

"What are we waiting for?" Philo turned to Trixie. "Lead the way."

"They want *you*, stupid," Trixie whispered to Philo. "This whole thing is about getting you. Stubbs knows that you're working on a way out. At the very least, stay behind."

"I'm not going to stand idly by while someone's got Rill kidnapped," Philo said.

"Not to sound heartless, Champ, but Rill's a hydra. Technically they've only got one of her heads. Severed heads grow back."

"They grow back on *hydras,*" Mer-Rill said. "We aren't a hydra right now. Who knows what will happen!"

Trixie fumed for a moment. "Fine. But we're stopping by my house to stock up."

Medea swept into the cottage and grabbed her sword and shield. "I'm coming too."

"Why in the Between would you want to do that?" Trixie said.

"'Princess' is still under my custody. And besides, what are friends for?" she said.

Mer-Rill perked up. "You made a new friend?"

Human-Rill glanced at Medea in confusion. "I guess I did."

"So did I. I'm friends with Tenta. We're good at making friends like this!" She snatched Philo by the hand. "But come on. We've got to go!"

#

The Junkyard was a mildly organized floating array of potentially useful items that had tumbled into the Between in the past. One way or another, each building, vehicle, or chunk of land in the assortment had been caught in an event that took it from its home world. Some of them were so innocuous one would be hard-pressed to imagine how something so calamitous could have occurred there. Such was not the case for the bell tower.

Built from white stone that sparkled eerily despite the lack of shifting light, tower stood tall and proud in the Junkyard. The belfry alone was as large as the pub back on Lower Shard, and the height of the tower spanned three of the layers of carefully arranged junk. It likely would have spanned four, except whatever ceremony had brought the tower here had perfectly sheared off the bottom of the bell tower, leaving a mirror-smooth finish on the affected stone.

A massive brass bell dominated the belfry. It was easily twenty feet high, dwarfing the already diminutive Mrs. Stubbs as she reclined near its peak. She was leaning back upon the man-size headstock that

303

affixed the bell to the pivot above. She held a meat tenderizer as her weapon of choice, though the original owner must have had to do battle with some terrifyingly large roasts to require one so large. Its head was as large as *her* head, and the textured face had red and brown remnants that may or may not have been of a culinary origin.

The Duke had become a bit more numerous in the intervening time. Six bats of assorted sizes hung upside down from the bell yoke. They twisted and flapped every few moments, clearly restless. Their discomfort and impatience weren't helped by the fact that a soft tinkling sound randomly rang from a bag at Mrs. Stubbs' side.

"Waiting here is foolish, unshaven she-fungus," the Duke's many bat-selves said in unison. "We should take them all head on. Show them our strength."

"If we had strength to show, that'd be the plan. Until then, we wait," Mrs. Stubbs said.

"I am the most powerful figure in the between."

"Right now you're the rodent-shaped residue of a boastful blowhard."

"A temporary status…"

"Yeah, and one that we're in."

Another rattling tinkle visibly shook her bag.

"For the love of…" she snapped.

Mrs. Stubbs reached into her bag and revealed the jar containing Fairy-Rill. The little creature must have been tougher than she looked, as tended to be the case for fairies. Her near-constant ramming into the sides of the jar had barely left a mark on her.

"Would you cut it out in there?" Mrs. Stubbs demanded. "If you finish scrambling what's left in your noggin before the others show up we'll be short one bargaining chip."

"Let me out! I don't like being in a jar!" Fairy-Rill shouted.

"That's the general idea."

"It's small and it's lonely," she said. "I don't like being alone!"

"Well that's good news, because as we speak the rest of your friends are on the way, and we're going to find out just how much they like you. The Mister seems to think your buddy Philo has a lot to give."

"Let me out so I can bite and kick and punch you!" Fairy-Rill demanded.

Some of Duke's ears twitched. He shifted several red-eyed gazes to the outside. A few points of darkness were shifting toward them among the scattering of buildings and resources.

"They come," he said.

"So they do." Mrs. Stubbs shoved Fairy-Rill's jar back into the bag and fetched a much-abused telescope. "Looks like we've got two mermaids. The Rill one and… I think that's a Heartcore fetcher. Some fancied-up dandy of a human's getting dragged between them."

"If you are to be believed, that will be the other Rill."

"And that trollop of a demon is on her way, dragging Philo with her."

She collapsed the telescope and stowed it.

"*You* are worthless in battle," Duke said. "It will take a great deal of effort before I finally kill them all."

"Nobody kills anybody until we get Philo. Then everybody else can die."

#

"Okay. Everyone listen up," Trixie said, dictating orders like a general. "As far as we know, there's only Mrs. Stubbs and some of the Duke, but I've got to believe they wouldn't have picked a fight unless they thought they could win. Eyes open for tricks."

She hefted her war hammer and gave her modified football helmet a light tap. The "fetcher rig" hadn't seen much use recently, but that just meant she'd had time to give it a little tender loving care. Fresh license plates layered the front, and she'd added in some spiked shoes to slide onto her hooves.

Philo, on the other hand, had done little to enhance his arsenal. If anything, he'd trimmed it down. Two types of electronic stun devices hung at his belt, one for up-close usage and the other of the barb-at-the-end-of-a-wire variety. A conspicuous silver cylinder hung at his belt precisely where a sword might.

Medea hadn't taken the time to fully don her armor, but the shield and sword still gave the gorgeous creature the look of an avenging angel. And then there were the Rills.

Pickings were a little slim with regard to quickly accessible weapons, but they'd made do with what they were able to snag from the Quartermaster. They'd selected matching dwarf picks. In essence, they were battle axes on one side and pickaxes on the other. Neither of the

Rills had seen fit to don any armor, though Human-Rill had torn away much of the frilly skirt and kicked off her shoes, the better to use her temporary legs without stumbling.

"You sure you know how to handle those weapons?" Philo called down.

"You hit people with the sharp part," Mer-Rill called back. "It's not hard."

"They're like teeth you can swing!" Human-Rill said with a worrying amount of zeal.

"The vampire has shown himself. The battle begins!" Medea said.

The handful of bats flitted out from the belfry

She swam forward, sword at the ready. The others swept low so that Philo and Human-Rill could touch down on the stone surface of the tower. Thanks to the Between's largely contextual laws of physics, "down" was a flexible concept. With no other surface available, the physics of the place were more than happy to consider the side of the bell tower to be the ground.

Trixie heaved her hammer left and right, knocking the attacking bats away with a viciousness that spoke volumes of just how pleasant their past relationship might have been. Since Mer-Rill and Medea were armed with edged weapons, Duke's many-winged selves gave them a bit more space, but they nonetheless harried and slashed at them. Worse, whenever two or more of them gathered together, they swept in a tight circle and unleashed a curling ball of dark energy to hurl at their foes.

It was chaos, but the chaos was centered in the air beside the tower, leaving Philo and Human-Rill to scale it more or less unmolested. That changed once they crested the tower and reached the belfry.

Both Philo and Human-Rill were moving at a full sprint when they ran out of wall. Without the surface that had been the previously agreed upon "down," the Between had to pick a new thing to fall toward. In Philo's case, it selected the floor of the belfry. He took an awkward arc through the air and sprawled out on the floorboards. Human-Rill continued far enough forward that the roof of the belfry became her new floor. She "fell" toward it and sprawled face-first, her ax embedding into the rafters beside her.

"Legs are hard…" she wheezed.

Philo climbed to his feet and grabbed the stun gun.

"Don't come any closer!" Mrs. Stubbs demanded, brandishing the meat tenderizer in one hand and Fairy-Rill's jar in the other. "One wrong move and the little ex-hydra gets it."

"Cut her head off, Rill!" shouted the little creature in the jar.

Human-Rill shook her head and wiped a now-bloody nose, then pulled the ax from the rafter. Below, Philo climbed onto the lip of the bell and started scaling it. The mass of the bell was so tremendous that Philo's weight barely shifted it.

"I'm serious!" Mrs. Stubbs hopped from the bell to the top of the yolk. She set the jar down and held the hammer high. "You want to see what happens if one third of you gets pummeled to paste, come a step closer."

Philo stopped climbing. Human-Rill stopped getting any closer too, but for a different reason. Her unique entry to the belfry had left her upside down from the point of view of Mrs. Stubbs, so she was busy trying to work out how to flip her frame of reference. It had gotten as far as dangling off one of the rafters and trying to cling to the bottom.

"You don't really think you're going to win this, do you?" Philo asked. "Duke is tough, but we've got three trained fetchers out there."

"Two and a third!" Mrs. Stubbs defended.

"Right, fine. The point is, it's only a matter of time before one of them gets in here to snatch that jar. And if you smash it, you're not going to have any collateral. This was over before it began. You didn't bring enough muscle."

Mrs. Stubbs waggled the tenderizer over her head, eyes wild, then tipped her head and grinned.

"That's where you're wrong," she said with a wicked smile.

"Scatter!" Trixie called from outside.

A massive gray blur launched past the belfry. Medea and Trixie cried out. Mer-Rill swam into view just in time for a huge beak to snap shut around her waist.

Another swift motion and flap of wings brought the huge form back and fully into view. It was a huge vulture. Specifically, it was Hooks, the steed of Mr. Stubbs. While his hobgoblin rider was nowhere to be seen, it hardly mattered. Hooks had all three of the members of their team who were capable of flight grappled, and none of them were strong enough to break the grip.

Streaks of black darted in and, in the blink of an eye, both Philo and Human-Rill found themselves restrained by the powerful grip of ghastly bat claws.

Mrs. Stubbs hopped down and slid along the bell. She gracefully thumped to the ground just beside it. Duke maneuvered the two captives in front of her.

"What's that you were saying about not having enough muscle?" she asked.

"Let them go!" Philo demanded.

"Oh, certainly. Just what I had in mind. Just as soon as you agree to come with me and let ol' Duke and us Stubbs in on whatever it is the Mister thinks you've been working at."

"We don't even know if it will *work*! And if it *does* work, we'll make sure it works for *everyone!*" Philo said.

"Listen to me, man-thing," Duke said. "I know you are utterly useless, regardless of what this unshaven she-fungus thinks. But heed my words. I will flay the skin from your friends' bones if you do not oblige."

Mrs. Stubbs leaned on the tenderizer like a cane and tossed the jar with Fairy-Rill in it up and down.

"The longer you stall, the longer all your friends suffer." She tossed it. "And I haven't..." She caught it. "Got all day. So you're coming..." She tossed it. "With me."

Her hand held out, waiting for the drop. Instead, a whistling rush of motion blasted through the belfry, followed by a sharp clink. Whatever it was, it left Mrs. Stubbs empty-handed.

All eyes turned in the direction of the motion. A magnificent red and gold phoenix hung in the air, the jar clutched in her claws. The mythic bird peered down at the jar.

"I told you I would keep an eye on you. Oh, yes, I keep an eye on all my friends. That's what spotters *do.*"

"Get her! Get the bird!" Mrs. Stubbs raved.

One of the dukes peeled off from each of their prisoners to streak after the phoenix and fairy. Red soared away, the jar still in her grip.

"Lend a hand," shouted Duke, as Philo started to struggle. "I cannot hold him."

Mrs. Stubbs dove at Philo, tenderizer held high. He wrenched himself from the grip of the bats and ran at her as well. The hobgoblin may have been a frenzied attacker, but she was still less than half Philo's size, so when the two met, Philo came out the winner.

The pair of them launched toward the bell. A muted, reverberating tone rang out as the pair thumped into it, and after a brief roll, they both made it to their feet. The fickle nature of what passed for gravity in this place left them standing on the side of the bell as though it were level ground. Mrs. Stubbs was crawling over Philo like a wild animal. Philo got a grip on her weapon, lest he be tenderized. She scratched, bit, and clawed at him. Finally he wrenched the weapon from her grip and planted a boot against her to heave her away.

Her light frame thunked dully against the bell twice before she rolled to her feet empty-handed.

"Hah! Who's got the upper hand *now!*" Philo said, brandishing the weapon.

"It's still us," Mrs. Stubbs taunted. "You're still out-numbered and out-muscled. You can't take all of us out. Just give up now."

Philo looked about. Despite her best efforts, Human-Rill was unable to escape. The others were struggling with Hooks to no avail. Red and Fairy-Rill were staying ahead the bats that were after them, but just barely. Things were hardly to his advantage. If they were going to come out on top, he was going to have to even the odds.

After a glance down, he grinned.

Mrs. Stubbs realized what he had in mind just a moment too late. Philo raised the tenderizer high and brought it smashing down on the bell. Unlike their fleshy impacts, the heavy metal of the tenderizer produced a punishing peal. The sound was well short of deafening for Philo and *most* of the others. But for Duke, who had a dozen large and highly sensitive ears and no fingers to plug them with, it was a different story entirely.

Duke's many voices cried out as one and his selves thumped to the ground to tremble in audio-induced agony. The moment she was no longer pursued, Red darted toward the now-freed Human-Rill and tossed her the jar. Human-Rill caught it and tugged the cork free as she sprinted for the edge of the belfry. Hooks tried to swoop back and away, but what a creature of his scale gains in strength, he loses in agility. Human-Rill slammed into his belly and held tight to the feathers there.

The freed Fairy-Rill flew up and assaulted the big bird's eyes. The attacks did virtually no damage, but they *did* convince it to screech angrily, which was just enough of an opportunity for Mer-Rill to pull free. She looped up and grabbed Fairy-Rill, then rushed down and snagged Human-Rill. Brilliant light and wafting mist suddenly filled the area outside the belfry. When it cleared, a very large serpent with three very angry heads was staring down the vulture.

The massive bird decided it wanted no part of the battle, but to his dismay, he found he had no choice in the matter. Rill coiled around him and put her long absent jaws to work. Medea and Trixie easily slipped free from the claws of the now hapless bird and charged into the Belfry.

"Where is she?" Trixie said.

"What?" Philo replied.

"Where did the hobgoblin go, Philo?" Medea asked a bit louder.

"*What*?" Philo replied.

Standing on the bell during his inspired bit of sound-based assault had left him a bit worse for wear, it would seem. Red flitted into the Belfry.

"She vanished. The hobgoblin vanished right before my eyes. And I am *trained* to see things, even when they are too far to see!"

"Of course," Trixie grumbled. "Mr. Stubbs always kept a pile of charms to keep from being spotted. Stands to reason his wife would have a mess of them as well. Forget about her. We're never going to find her now. Let's get Duke trussed up before he recovers though."

"Should we help Rill?" Medea said.

The hydra was laughing with demented glee as she grappled with the vulture.

"Nah. Let her have her fun," Trixie said, pulling some rope from her belt. "Hey, did anyone make the bats in the belfry joke yet?"

"What?" Philo yelled.

"Good," Trixie said. "Let's not and say we did. Come on, prissy. These bats aren't going to tie themselves up."

#

Later, the shard fetchers and their new friends gathered outside Tenta's restaurant to lick their wounds. With the exception of Red, everyone had taken their lumps, so a nice meal was definitely in order. As tended to be the case when Rill got something into her heads, she had been very persuasive in getting Tenta to oblige something she wanted to try. It had been a bit of a production, but he was able to cart out his old kiosk and its mobile cookery to allow the now fully restored Rill to try her claws at preparing a meal for the others.

"No, no, no. We don't put the shells in," Rill explained. "The shells go here. In this bowl. And that gets cut into pieces."

"But then people don't get to rip and tear!" Right-Rill said, flopping the knife clutched in her tail.

"Rip and tear is for the *roast*, right?" Left-Rill said.

Rill nodded. "Yes. And for the ribs. Ribs are good for rip and tear."

"And *crunch*. Because of the bones," Right-Rill said dreamily.

Philo, Trixie, and Medea were seated at a round table set up outside the eatery. The demon watched as Rill's coiled body looped and snared bits of meat to butcher and assorted plants and other ingredients. Tenta shouted advice and recommendations from the side. It looked like some terrifying combination of a wrestling match, a circus act, and a Teppanyaki performance. That Rill hadn't managed to skewer herself was an achievement in and of itself.

"She's not going to poison us, is she?" Trixie said, an eyebrow raised.

"Look how happy she is," Medea said. "It warms my heart to see someone so enthusiastic."

"Yeah, she looked pretty enthusiastic when she was trying to twist the head off Hooks too. Happy does not equal safe," Trixie said.

Philo eyed one of the hunks of meat she'd carved a slice off.

"Does anyone know what happened to Hooks?" he said warily.

"Relax. The big dumb buzzard got away," Trixie said "He's not on the menu. And neither is the various Duke pieces. That *would* have poisoned us. Vampire meat is bad news."

"What *did* happen to Duke?" Medea asked.

"Never you mind," Trixie said darkly.

"Soup!" the Rills declared.

The hydra performed the complex sequence of overlapping and side-slipping coils necessary to sidle up to the table while hauling a pot of thick stew. She managed to get it to the table without spilling much. Tenta quickly set the table with large white bowls and stout spoons, then helpfully ladled out the food she had prepared.

It was about as haphazard, multi-faceted, and complex as Rill herself. Floating in a rich blond gravy were irregularly hacked bits of vegetable, slices of assorted beasts, and unidentifiable things that had been pounded flat. The one overarching design conceit of the dish was that everything at least fit on a spoon.

"Oh, and an egg! Make sure everyone gets at least one egg," Rill said.

"Eggs are very good," Left-Rill said.

"They *aren't* crunchy without the shell though," Right-Rill warned.

Tenta topped each bowl with a somewhat battered poached egg, and pinched a dash of seasoning over the rest.

"Take a bunch, everyone," Rill said.

"Take more," Left-Rill said rather pointedly to Philo.

"Make sure you heal up good," Right-Rill said.

The three friends picked up their spoons, somewhat hesitantly, and sampled the meal. It was different, to say the very least. No one in their right mind would have paired the things she paired, but somehow, as a whole, it worked. It was a masterpiece by no means, but it was that first doodle in the margin that suggested there was an artist waiting to be discovered.

Trixie was the first to voice her assessment.

"Rill." She pointed with her spoon. "Impossibly, this doesn't suck."

"There is a balance to it," Medea said.

"Yeah. It's balanced in the same way that a seesaw with an elephant on one side and twenty-five hundred chihuahuas on the other side is balanced, but it's balanced."

"Yay!" the Rills proclaimed.

"Did everyone get enough?" Rill asked.

"Make sure you have all you need," Left-Rill said.

"Take more if you want," Right-Rill said.

"I didn't take too many hits," Philo said, "And it seems like the hearing is more or less back."

The others agreed. When the Rills were satisfied their guests were fed, they gleefully plunged their own heads directly into the pot, ravenously gulping at the contents.

"She… er… She certainly is indulgent, isn't she?" Medea said, moving back a bit to stay out of the splash zone of the feeding frenzy.

The group chatted happily as they finished the hearty meal. Right-Rill was the first to pull her head out and sigh contentedly. After industriously licking her face clean, she poked toward Philo.

"We're going to fix up the house next, right?" she said.

"I don't think we've got anything else to do today."

"Do you think we can get more stones? Make it a little bigger? Can we build it strong enough for that?"

"I'm sure we can. There's more than enough room in the Fetcher's Den for an expansion. Why?"

"My friend Red the phoenix said she'd come over and help us learn some new songs if there was room. And I want room there for you too."

Rill pulled her head out of the pot. "Things are better when you can share them."

"We'll make it nice and big for you," Philo said.

"So, let's hear it, Worm. What'd you think of getting some time to yourselves?"

"It was okay," Right-Rill said. "People not knowing who they were talking to was nice. It helped get past the stuff we did and get to the things we could do."

"But being alone was bad," Rill said.

"Especially alone in a jar. If someone offers to stuff you in a jar alone, say no," Right-Rill advised. "Stuffed in jar with friends only."

Left-Rill finished her share of the meal and pulled her head free.

"We're better as a we, though," she said.

"I think that's a fine lesson," Medea said. "We are *all* better as a we."

She flitted up and away from the table. "It was lovely paying a visit to your home without weapon in hand. I hope this is the first of many such visits. But I'm afraid I must be going."

The mermaid said her farewells and took her leave. While he was waving to her, Right-Rill grabbed Philo by the neck of his jumpsuit and tugged him to a standing position. Rill slipped her head between his legs until he slid down into his typical riding position.

"What do you say, Trixie? Want to come along to fetch some goods?" Philo asked.

"You go have fun, Champ." She rubbed her hands together. "I've got some redecorating to do."

"See you later!" Right-Rill said.

With that, the serpent and rider sprung into the sky and off toward the junkyard, her minds alive with the possibilities of her new friendships.

Afterword

Thanks for reading this first of what I hope will be many collections of Patreon stories. If you enjoyed them, please consider picking up some of the books that inspired them, like *The Other Eight* or *Between*, both of which are available wherever paperbacks or ebooks are sold. And if you enjoyed the shorter, standalone stuff, you can get more of the same *as they are written* by supporting my Patreon. And if you'd like to keep tabs on future releases, consider signing up for my newsletter.

I'd like to take a moment to give special thanks to some of the people who made this collection possible:

ProjectENDO: Inspiration for Blodgette and creator of the Pizza Dragon species. A talented artist and animator.

Fable Siegel: Artist of the majority of the covers for the original Patreon stories, as well as a bunch of other artwork associated with my stories.

Chandra Free: Artist of the front cover, as well as the story covers for *Part-Time Heroes, Bella's Journey,* and *The Back Way.*

Ashe: Artist of the cover illustration for *Something Precious.*

Nebulilac: Artist of the cover illustration for *The Rills.*

Merri Monster: Artist of the cover illustration for *A Big Day for Blodgette.*

ViiStar: Artist of the cover illustration for *Blot's Arrival.*

Tammy Salyer and **Anna Genoese**: Editors who cleaned up the vast majority of these stories (as well as my novels).